just be her

INTERNATIONAL BESTSELLING AUTHOR

KAYDENCE SNOW

JUST BE HER

Copyright © 2019 by Katarina Smythe

All rights reserved.

This is a work of fiction. The events described are fictitious;
any similarities to actual events and persons are coincidental.

Cover design by Sonder Publishing Pty Ltd
Photography by Lindee Robinson Photography
Book design by Inkstain Design Studio
Edited by Kirstin Andrews

www.KaydenceSnow.com

just be

her

Chapter 1

TONI

hree spoonfuls of sugar went into my black coffee before I pulled the wedgie out of my ass and tiptoed out of the kitchenette. I kicked clothes and shoes out of my way as I passed my bed and headed to the balcony doors, trying to be quiet.

Every step of my bare feet on the timber floor sent a jolt of pain through my skull—and threatened to wake whomever it was I'd brought home with me last night.

As I turned the handle, the guy in my bed stirred. I cringed, waiting for him to settle before completing my escape. I couldn't remember his name, but I did remember opening a condom packet, so at least that was one less thing to worry about.

I settled onto the balcony's little chair, dropped my coffee onto the round table next to it, and lit a cigarette.

Between the caffeine and the nicotine, I slowly started to feel more like myself. The familiar sounds of cars and people going about their day drifted up to me—the soundtrack of New Orleans coming to life.

Judging by how close the sun was to infringing on the edge of my balcony, it had to be approaching midday already. I was just trying to remember what day it was, if Andre would be expecting me, when I heard shuffling behind the open balcony doors.

"Morning," a deep male voice croaked. He sounded worse than I felt. "How about some breakfast?"

I lit another cigarette and finished the dregs of my coffee before turning to face him. He was leaning in the doorway, wearing nothing but faded jeans, the open fly exposing his pubic hair. His dirty-blond hair looked like he hadn't even run his hands through it yet.

"I don't have any food here." I gave him a thin smile, hoping he'd get the hint.

"That's OK, beautiful." He flashed me a grin, but that just made the dark circles under his eyes more pronounced. What the fuck had I been thinking last night? "We can go out, get some Cajun eggs at this place nearby."

I took another puff of my cigarette and rolled my eyes as I blew the smoke out. "Listen, dude." I wasn't even trying to remember his name. "We don't need to play this game."

"What game?" He chuckled nervously and did up his fly, subconsciously defending his junk from my attitude.

"You know." I took another puff. "We go to breakfast, try to pretend this wasn't just a hookup, exchange numbers, you never call, blah, blah, blah. It's all good. We fucked. You fell asleep and didn't bail before I woke up. Shit happens. Seriously, just go."

"Uh . . ." He rubbed the mess on top of his head, frowning. "Can I at least get a cup of coffee before—"

"No." I stared him down.

Finally, he scowled. I could practically hear him calling me a bitch in his head. He turned and shuffled around in my studio, then the door slammed shut.

I breathed a sigh of relief and leaned my head back against the brick. Lifting my feet onto the edge of the chair to evade the encroaching sun, I finished my smoke as the sounds of the vibrant city below invaded my balcony's little slice of solitude.

My phone went off, making me drag my hungover ass inside. I dug it out of a pile of clothes by the door, the battery nearly dead, and read the message from Andre.

ANDRE: It's Thursday. Get your ass downstairs or get another job.

I groaned. It was later than I thought. My shift was starting, but I needed a shower. Andre was all bark and no bite; I could spare ten minutes.

I showered, threw my hair up into a bun, and dressed in my favorite ripped jeans and a Jack Daniel's tank I'd won in a pool game, which showed my electric-blue bra through the extra-wide armholes.

The rickety stairs at the back of the building led to a narrow corridor. One door went to the back alleyway, one to a stock room, another to the bathrooms, and a fourth to the Cottonmouth Inn.

The dingy bar was on the ground level and had two studio apartments above it. The rent was cheap, and it was also really damn convenient, as I did most of my drinking and partying at the Cottonmouth. I also worked there . . . some number of nights per week. Whenever Andre reminded me. He was the owner of that fine establishment *and* the building, so he was also my landlord. And my neighbor, as he happened to live in the studio across the hall.

If he minded me getting wasted at his bar every other night, he certainly didn't say anything about it. When one of his staff bailed on a shift, he'd call up the stairs and I'd step in to help out. It worked for us.

"You look like shit." Andre didn't even look up as I walked behind the bar. His full focus was on counting the previous night's takings, the cash stacked neatly in front of him.

He was in blue jeans, his tall frame hunched over the bar, a sky-blue T-shirt stretched across his broad shoulders. The bright fabric popped against his dark brown skin. Andre had a deep, gruff voice and could look like a mean motherfucker when he wanted to, but he was a softie for the most part. I'd seen him break up more fights than I'd even started.

I flipped him off and grunted, moving straight to the servery at the other end.

"There ya go, sugar." Loretta slid a plate over to me before I even had to beg. She'd made my favorite hangover cure—a bacon and egg sandwich with double cheese, mustard, and ketchup.

My mouth watered even as my stomach heaved. "I love you, woman." I groaned, taking the plate and settling onto one of the bar stools.

"I know." She waved me off and went back to her food prep, only pausing to hack out half a lung on yet another coughing fit. Loretta was somewhere between forty and sixty years old and all elbows and collarbones under her jeans and T-shirts—the kind of skinny that made you wonder if she was slowly dying from some disease. She perpetually had two inches of gray roots showing beneath her otherwise red hair, as if she specifically asked them to leave a strip when she went to the salon, and wore makeup two shades too dark for her pale complexion.

But she always showed up on time, and she made a mean cheeseburger. She'd worked at the Cottonmouth longer than Andre. I wasn't sure exactly how that worked, seeing as he owned the place, but I wasn't going to pry if he didn't want to share.

That's why Andre and I worked—we weren't in each other's pockets. We helped each other out when needed and left each other the fuck alone the rest of the time.

I was halfway through my meal when Andre finished counting the money, leaving enough change in the till and tucking the rest into a pouch ready to deposit in his safe upstairs. He leaned his big hands on the bar and gave me an expectant stare.

"Wha?" I spoke around a mouthful.

"Your shift started an hour ago."

"Yeah, but if I try to lug those cases of beer out on an empty stomach, I might hurt myself." I bugged my eyes out, then grinned before taking another bite.

He shook his head, but I saw the little amused twitch in his lip. "I gotta go run some errands. I want this place spotless and ready in time for opening." He picked up the pouch and walked out the back without sparing us another glance.

"Yes, boss," Loretta and I both yelled after him. Then she hacked up the other half of that lung.

Ten minutes later, Dennis arrived for his shift. Dennis attended one of the local universities—I couldn't remember which one—and bussed at the Cottonmouth a few nights per week.

We put music on and set to getting the place in order. It was ridiculous to demand we make the place *spotless*. It probably hadn't been spotless in a good twenty years. The building was old, complete with wrought-iron railings and window coverings, and the interior looked like it hadn't been touched in decades. A little carved black sign—with the bar's name and a snake below it—hung off an iron post above the front door; we had to take it down whenever there was a hurricane warning so it wouldn't fly off.

We restocked the bar fridges, wiped down the counters, swept and mopped, straightened the furniture.

With fifteen minutes left until opening, Andre still hadn't returned. I gathered the trash and carried the black bag out to the dumpster, then settled onto the back stairs and pulled out my cigarettes. I lit one and sighed, leaning against the brick building.

The sun was setting, casting the alley in shadow. The humid heat made the dumpster smell perpetually putrid, but the smoke from my cigarette masked the worst of it as I watched people walk past on the street.

We didn't get a lot of tourists at the Cottonmouth. It was on a busy street, but it wasn't in the French Quarter. Tourists were more likely to stumble across it than seek it out on purpose. We catered more to the locals—good burgers and bar food, great beer and bourbon. We had our regulars, our career alcoholics, and the college crowd.

The squeal of tires, followed by a door slamming, had me narrowing my eyes. The front of a shiny black car was just visible at the end of the alley.

"Stay there, George." The feminine voice was loud and confident but sounded shaky around the edges. "I just need a minute."

A woman walked around the corner, her heels clicking rapidly on the concrete. Halfway up the alley, she leaned on the wall with one arm, the other clutching her chest as she doubled over as if to vomit.

I rolled my eyes and took another puff of my cigarette. It was way too early in the night to be dealing with assholes vomiting in the alley. I had half a mind to turn the hose on her—we kept it behind the dumpster specifically so we could hose away the vomit and piss. Occasionally some jerk would even take a dump in the corner. People were disgusting.

But something about her made me pause. She didn't look like she was vomiting. She looked like she couldn't breathe.

The hand she was using to lean against the wall clenched and relaxed even as it shook. Her other hand pulled at the neck of her linen dress, clawing at her chest as though to rip open a hole for the air to get in. Her shoulders shook, and a sob tore from her throat, the sound one of pure helplessness.

I knew a panic attack when I saw one.

Not my problem.

I took one last drag of my cigarette and put it out on the step. Flicking the butt into the trash, I got to my feet and turned for the door.

Another pathetic sob made my hand freeze on the knob. That desperate sound pulled on the last few redeemable strings of my black heart.

"Dammit." I sighed and rolled my eyes.

I jogged back down the few stairs and grabbed an empty crate on my way past the dumpster, approaching the woman slowly.

Her dress was a pale blue, her feet tucked into white pumps. The pristine shoes had clearly never seen the dirty back alley of a building. Her perfectly straight black hair was slicked back in a low ponytail. This chick even had a string of pearls around her neck. Definitely not from around this neighborhood.

I crouched down, lowering the crate to the ground and holding my other hand out in a calming gesture. "Excuse me." I made my voice gentle but loud enough for her to hear me over the sound of her own despair.

She reeled back, her shoulder hitting the wall as she glanced at me with wide eyes. The settling dusk made it more difficult to see her properly, but there was something kind of familiar about her.

"Please . . . just . . . leave me alone." She spoke between trying to breathe and control the sobbing.

"I just want to help." I took another tentative step forward, and she turned away and sobbed into the bricks. "Look, I've been there, OK? I've had panic attacks. I know exactly how you're feeling."

"How could . . . you . . . possibly?" Even through hysterical anxiety, she managed to enunciate perfectly.

I resisted the urge to walk away and leave this bitch to deal with her own shit. "Just have a seat. It'll help."

My patience with her was wearing thin, so I took a chance. I reached out and placed my hand on her delicate shoulder. The linen dress was ridiculously soft. She let me wrap my arm around her shoulders and guide her to sit down on the crate.

"Put your head between your knees." I rubbed the top of her back gently.

She took her heels off, pressed the fabric of her dress down between her legs, and leaned over, rocking back and forth on the spot. After a few moments, her breathing started to even out.

I crouched in front of her, my arms resting on my knees, and waited.

Eventually she stopped rocking and raised herself back up a little, staring into her lap. She had really long lashes. They kept brushing her cheeks as she blinked. I couldn't shake the feeling that I knew her somehow, and I wished she'd look up so I could see her face properly.

"What's your name?" She didn't lift her head, but her voice sounded much more even.

"Toni. What's yours?"

"Alexandria. Pleased to make your acquaintance."

I snorted. *Who the fuck speaks like that?* "Yeah, nice to meet you too. You all right? You in some kind of trouble, Alex?"

The words were out before I could stop them. I tried to avoid getting involved in other people's shit as a general rule, but there was something about this chick . . . Maybe the fact that I couldn't figure out why she was so familiar had me more curious. Regardless of my rules, if she was having trouble with some asshole boyfriend, I had no qualms about running inside to grab the baseball bat Andre kept behind the bar.

"It's *Alexandria.* And no, I'm not in any trouble. Just in an impossible situation, partly of my own making, to which there is no alternative."

"Oh, come on. People say shit like that all the time. 'I have to.' 'I have no choice.' 'There's no other way.'" I shrugged. "But that's a load of crap. It may be a choice between something shitty and something even shittier, but we always have a choice."

She finally looked up, her back straightening; somehow she managed to look like she was perched on a throne, not sitting barefoot on a crate in a dirty alleyway. The only light came from the streetlamps around the corner, but it was enough to see her tear-streaked face, enough to make out her features.

I frowned. My spine stiffened, and the hair on the back of my neck stood up, despite the sticky Louisiana evening.

A cat hissed and jumped down from the dumpster, activating the motion sensor. The bright lights at the back of the door lit the alleyway up.

Finally, I got a good look at her.

My eyes widened and I gasped. Losing balance, I fell back onto my ass. I was so shocked I just stayed there, sitting in the gutter and staring at her.

She had the same wide-eyed, bewildered expression on her face, her chest heaving, as if the panic was about to come roaring back.

Sitting on the crate, staring back at me, was the same person that stared back at me every damn day in the mirror.

She had my black hair, although hers was neatly tied back and mine was in a messy, unbrushed bun. She had my olive complexion, the same full breasts and hips, the same thin nose and chocolate eyes, the same heart-shaped face with a slightly pointy chin. My arms were more toned from carrying all that beer every day, and her stomach looked flatter than mine, but other than that—and the fact that her dress probably cost what I made in a month—we looked *identical*.

"Oh my," she breathed, taking me in, her manicured fingers playing with the perfectly round pearls at her neck.

"Holy shit." I threaded my dirty hands into my hair, making the bun even messier.

How the hell was this possible? Vague notions of adoptions, distant relatives, and evil doppelgangers flashed through my mind, but I was so shocked I couldn't think straight.

The automatic lights flicked off, plunging us back into near darkness and breaking the spell.

I scrambled to my feet and took a step away, my heart hammering against my rib cage. She stood too, smoothing her dress and sliding her feet back into her heels.

"Alexandria?" a deep male voice called from the mouth of the alley. The backlight turned him into an almost perfectly black silhouette, the wide shoulders and firm stance menacing.

I took another step back.

Alexandria looked over her shoulder, then back at me. "I'm all right, George." She wiped her face with her hands and smoothed her dress once more.

"Your phone keeps ringing," he replied. I couldn't see his face, but I felt him watching me.

"I just need a moment." She took a step toward me, and I took another one back. George folded his hands in front of himself and angled his body toward the street, but he was still keeping an eye on the alleyway.

I wished the light would come back on. It would be safer to run for the door if the light was on.

"What the fuck is this?" Feeling like I had no escape, I went on the attack.

"I haven't the slightest clue, I assure you." Her voice was now even. "But I intend to get to the bottom of it . . . discreetly." She frowned and looked down. The faint light glinted off her matching pearl earring.

"This is weird, right? I mean, this is . . . what *is* this? Who *are* you people? I'm not . . . I need to . . ." I backed farther away.

"Toni." She held her hand out in a calming gesture. "I don't know any more than you—"

The back door screeched on its hinges, interrupting her

midsentence. Andre leaned out, and the lights came on. "Toni? What the fuck? I need you in here."

I rushed up the stairs and turned back to look.

She was walking away, her heels clicking on the concrete, her shoulders back—a complete contrast to the blubbering, struggling-to-breathe mess I'd encountered at first.

"I'll be in touch," she called over her shoulder as she rounded the corner. George turned to follow.

"What? No!" I called after her. "You hear me? Don't get in touch. Just fuck off!"

"What's going on?" Andre took a step farther out the door, but I spun around and shuffled him back inside, closing the door firmly behind us.

"Toni, you in some kinda trouble?" he persisted.

"Nah, it's all good. Let's get in there. They need us behind the bar." I tried to weave around him, but the corridor was narrow, and he was a big guy.

He crossed his arms over his chest and narrowed his eyes at me. "Toni." His voice was half warning, half demand.

I huffed and propped my hands on my hips, looking up at him. "I'm fine, Andre. I promise. It was just a misunderstanding."

He stared me down for a long moment. I held his gaze, waiting for him to drop it.

"OK." He finally lowered his arms. "But you know if you need any kind of help . . ."

I patted him on the shoulder as I finally managed to squeeze past him. "Yeah, yeah. But really, I'm good."

I didn't wait for his response, rushing straight to the bar and letting the increasing noise in the Cottonmouth envelop me.

Evenings usually started with food orders, burgers and beer at the counter. As the night progressed, the patrons moved on to harder drinks as the available space slowly and surely filled up.

Tonight's band arrived to set up before it got too crowded.

I handed three beers over to a college guy and turned to the other end of the bar, half tidying the area as I spoke. "What can I get ya?"

"Yeah, can I get a . . . ah, fuck." The man rolled his eyes as we both looked up and saw who we were speaking to.

Ren was the guitarist and lead singer of the Thousand Lies. They played at the Cottonmouth regularly. I had mixed feelings about it. Ren was a total and complete douchebag. The tattoos, piercings, and bad attitude perfectly complemented the giant chip on his shoulder. On the other hand, the man's music was like a drug—I didn't want to like it, because I didn't like him, but I couldn't help myself, couldn't get enough. Not that I'd ever admit it.

"Ugh. *You.*" I looked him up and down without even trying to hide my disdain.

"Hello, you raging bitch." He smiled at me sweetly.

"Hi, asshole." I leaned on the bar and waited. He'd either make a rude comment or place his order. I could handle either.

Andre's big hand landed on my shoulder. "There's a bunch of chicks wanting to order slippery nipples or some shit at the other end. Why don't you go deal with that?"

"Why don't you?" I whined.

"Don't wanna." He shrugged. "And I have staff I can pay to do the shit I don't wanna."

He shooed me away, and I reluctantly moved off toward the lesser of two evils. Andre and Ren slapped their hands together and hugged over the bar, then started chatting like old friends as Andre served Ren his Old Forester 1920 bourbon. Maybe they were old friends. I'd never bothered to ask.

I spent the rest of the night working hard. The Thousand Lies always drew a big crowd.

It was a good distraction, and by the end of the night, the bizarre situation in the alley almost seemed like a disturbing dream. Maybe I'd imagined the whole thing. Maybe I'd done more than just get drunk the night before. I didn't *remember* taking any hallucinogens, but I supposed it was possible there were still some in my system. That was a pretty fucking specific and vivid trip though . . . But what was the alternative? I had no idea how to explain why there was a rich chick walking around with my face, and I had no interest in trying to figure it out. That was just asking for trouble. It was easier, and frankly made more sense, to assume I'd just imagined the whole thing.

Chapter 2

ALEX

When I got back into the car after meeting my body double, I had nearly a dozen missed calls. I didn't even bother calling my mom back, just waited for it to start ringing again.

When I picked up, she sounded frantic. "Alexandria? What's happening? Why didn't you answer? Are you all right?"

"Hey, Mom. I'm just on the way to the hotel. Everything is fine. My phone was on silent. Nothing to worry about."

"You sound off. Are you upset?"

"No. I'm just tired. Traveling takes it out of me." I smiled, hoping it would make me sound more relaxed.

It took a full ten minutes to get her to calm down. She'd been overprotective and overbearing my whole life, and she didn't handle bad news well. I loved her for it most of the time, but sometimes it drove me nuts.

Once she was convinced I was OK, there was a pause on the other end. "You don't have to do this, you know. We can still call it off. We'll figure it out. Maybe we could sell some of the land."

"We've been over this." I sighed. We'd been over every conceivable option to get the winery out of debt. This was the only way.

"I know." Her sigh was almost identical to mine. "I just wish . . ."

"I miss him too, Mom." My father would've known what to do. He would never have let it get to this stage in the first place. "We're about to pull up at the hotel. I'll speak to you tomorrow?"

"OK, sweetheart. I love you."

"Love you too."

I was spending a few nights in a suite—courtesy of rewards points, because I was in so much debt. I'd told my mother I wanted to get beauty treatments and prepare for meeting my future in-laws, but really I just wanted a few days to myself before I signed my life away.

One of the hotel staff opened my car door as a bellboy started removing luggage from the trunk, but I left the man waiting and scooted forward in my seat.

"Did you get a good look at the woman in the alley?"

"I did." George nodded. After a beat of silence, he said over his shoulder, "I'll get the wheels in motion. You get some rest."

"Thank you, George." I gave his shoulder a squeeze, grateful to have someone I could truly rely on, before getting out of the car.

Despite the luxurious suite, I hardly slept. I tossed and turned, unable to get the images of my face on someone else out of my mind.

After reassuring my mother I hadn't died in my sleep, I tried to spend the next day relaxing, as planned, but ended up working. It was the only way to keep my mind occupied.

George had dropped a manila folder on my table over breakfast. It had taken him only a few hours to find out Toni's full name—Antoinette Mathers—and to learn she was from Wisconsin, working at the Cottonmouth Inn, and living in an apartment above. But anything regarding why she looked like my carbon copy was going to take more time and effort than a simple background search. Especially considering I needed it done discreetly.

Not knowing was driving me almost as crazy as the ludicrous plan starting to form in my mind. Maybe I could get more than just a few days of freedom before I married a man I didn't love.

One thing was certain—I still needed to speak to this Antoinette properly.

Using the number in George's report, I tried to call and text her a few times, but she didn't answer. This was probably not a conversation to be had over the phone, but there were no etiquette rules for pursuing a dialogue with your body double. And I was running out of time.

Tomorrow, I was due to arrive at Hazelgreen Manor to spend the month with Oren Charles Winthrop the third—my soon-to-be husband.

I couldn't really call it an arranged marriage. Oren and I were going into it with our eyes wide open, our decisions our own. Yes, our parents had helped set it up, but I was not being forced into anything. I may have been forcing *myself* to marry a man I didn't love and had never met, but that was a different issue altogether.

The alternative was to either do nothing or implement one of the other options we'd discussed and go bankrupt in *twelve* months instead of *three*. I refused to do that. I refused to be the Zamorano under whose watch a generations-old business ceased to exist.

I deleted another email from a debt collector and sighed, slumping in my chair. Splashing and children's laugher drifted up from the hotel pool and through my open window. It was a hot afternoon, and I wanted to go for a dip myself, but how could I rest when everything was such a damn mess?

Zamorano Wines was one of the oldest vineyards in the country, established when my ancestors immigrated from Spain and settled in California. It had been passed on to me five years ago when my father died in a boating accident that nearly killed my mother and me.

At twenty-two years old, I'd had no idea how to run a business that employed more than one hundred people and had a reputation the world over. My father had been grooming me to take over, but I was nowhere near ready when he passed. My mother had shared the burden while I finished my business degree and we mourned my father.

I could point to a multitude of things that led to my family legacy teetering on the edge of destruction, but hindsight is twenty-twenty.

Mostly it was a series of bad investments, some of which were in place even before my father took over the company, some of which I chose to take a chance on. Any investment was a risk, but the timing couldn't have been worse. A bad crop, made even worse by a horrific storm that damaged half our vines, didn't help.

As we started to realize there was no way to save the company other than to take it public and sell the majority, my mother floated the idea of a marriage of convenience. It sounded insane at first—I mean, which century did she think we were in? But the more we discussed it, the more it became apparent it was the only way to save the business *and* keep it in the family.

It wasn't long before her brunches, benefits, tennis tournaments, and other high-society social engagements yielded a result.

I closed the latest depressing financial report and opened the Internet browser, entering the name of my betrothed into the search bar. It was something I found myself doing several times per day, trying in vain to find some emotional connection to a man I'd never met.

Oren was thirty years old, an eligible bachelor and poised to take over his family jewelry business. Just like us, they didn't want their generations-old business to end up outside the family, but their problem wasn't money. It was an archaic, ironclad clause in the company bylaws and family trust. The male heir had to be married before he could take over.

Mr. Winthrop senior was getting old. Oren was already running the business for all intents and purposes, but he needed a wife to make it official. We'd get married; he'd inherit his family business and bail mine out. We both benefitted equally from the arrangement.

It was the right thing to do. I was absolutely determined to get the business back on its feet. I couldn't stand the thought of telling all our staff they were out of a job, couldn't stand to see the sadness in my mother's eyes.

Realistically, I knew not all the blame sat on my shoulders, but I had contributed, and I felt responsible. I should've been able to avoid letting it get this far. If only I'd worked a little harder, was just a little smarter . . . I felt like I'd failed. I needed to prove to everyone, prove to *myself*, I was better than that.

I could fix this.

So why did it feel like I was marching to an open grave, ready to jump in and be suffocated by the tons of earth about to pile down on top of me?

I got up and started to pace in front of the balcony.

From the pictures I'd seen online, Oren was handsome in that classical way—auburn hair, square jaw, hazel eyes. He could have easily graced the cover of *Esquire*.

We'd spoken on the phone a handful of times. He was polite, gracious, professional. I didn't want to say *cold*; he wasn't unyielding or mean. I just didn't ever feel more than politeness between us.

I groaned and sank into the couch, my knee beginning to bounce immediately. *I guess a polite marriage is better than an abusive one. Oh lord! Is that the bar? As long as he's not abusive, this is fine? There's nothing* fine *about this!*

My heart threw itself against my ribcage as though trying to break free of my body, as desperate to get away as I was nervous to enter this arrangement. My breathing was getting shallower; my throat felt like someone had wrapped a gentle hand around it and begun to squeeze.

I knew it wouldn't let up.

It hadn't let up the night before, when I had to make George pull over so I could break down in a dirty alleyway.

The panic attacks had started after my father died. I'd learned how to manage them for the most part, but they were getting worse and more frequent as the wedding day approached.

There was no way out. I was stuck, tethered to the gravity of my own decisions.

It had been such a long time since I hadn't felt the overwhelming stress of a failing business, a family legacy, and so many livelihoods. I almost couldn't remember what it felt like to be carefree. This was the only way, but I just wanted a break from it.

Toni's face—my face—popped into my head once more, providing just the distraction I needed to pull me out of my anxiety spiral.

My Spanish heritage was responsible for my black hair, olive complexion, and curvaceous body. Where had Toni gotten her identical looks? As the myriad of possible explanations flew through my mind, I considered the possibility that my mother had another child. A difficult delivery meant she'd been unable to have any more children after I was born, but had she had one before? Although that didn't fit either. George's report showed that Toni and I had different dates of birth but definitely the same year.

I couldn't broach the subject with Mom—not until I had more information. She'd freak out and probably demand I come home. I didn't have time for that.

Instead, I let myself wonder what her life must be like— working at a bar, no one to answer to, no one else's life or legacy her responsibility. Of course she would have her own issues and stresses, just like everyone else, but they would be vastly different from mine. What did it say about me that I longed for someone else's problems?

I made myself take deep, measured breaths. I listened to the laughter of children below. I felt the fabric of the navy-blue couch under my hands.

The panic attack receded.

I leaned back and stared at the bright blue sky peeking in between the curtains.

I had one more night before it was time to go to Hazelgreen Manor—one of many properties owned by the Winthrop family— and spend a month making the engagement look real before we were married another month after that.

One more night of freedom.

One more month before I went home to prepare for a wedding.

For a moment, I allowed myself to imagine living Toni's life, just leaving it all behind.

What did it matter if I got to know Oren a little better? It wasn't as if it would change anything. He'd be spending most of his time working anyway, overseeing the opening of a new flagship store in New Orleans.

I chewed on my lip. The idea had sparked in the back of my mind as soon as I'd laid eyes on her, but I hadn't really considered it properly. Now it was all I could think about, even as every practical, logical part of me warned that it was insane, dangerous, and stupid.

George chose that moment to let himself into my suite.

"Anything?" I asked, getting to my feet.

"Not yet."

I sighed. I never pestered George for updates when I gave him a task. The man was more than competent; he'd tell me as soon as he had new information. "You saw it right? I'm not losing my mind?"

His professional mask softened. "Yeah, Alexandria, I saw it. It was uncanny."

George wouldn't lie to me. He'd more than proven he was willing to tell me the whole, awful truth no matter the situation. Even if it was hard to hear. Even if it meant he was bringing me news of a dead parent.

George had been with my family since he was a teenager. Before I even started school, he had a summer job on the vineyard doing manual labor. My father saw something in him, and over the years, George became his most trusted employee.

Now George was my right-hand man. Other than my own

mother, there was no one I trusted more.

After a beat of silence, I came to a decision. "Can you please pull the car around?"

"No problem. Where to?" he asked, already heading for the door.

"The Cottonmouth Inn." I nodded and took a deep breath. At the very least, I still needed to speak with her, and I couldn't sit around doing nothing any longer.

Chapter 3

TONI

That bitch had been calling and texting me all damn day. Was I curious about why we looked identical? Of course! But I wasn't willing to deal with the shitstorm that would come from digging into it. I just wanted to be left alone, but this woman was like a damn dog with a bone. It was like she was outraged that someone dared walk around with her face. I was half expecting her to show up with a bag of doorknobs to "fix" it for me.

I was so distracted the previous night I didn't even get a little drunk, didn't take any hot losers to bed, didn't even wake up feeling like shit. It was kind of a nice change, and I found myself with hours to kill before my shift.

I threw my hair up—I hadn't washed it in three days—and headed out. I got a po' boy for lunch and sat in the park. As I patted every dog that came past, I found myself wondering what my life would've been like had my parents not both died within a year of each other.

Mom died from cancer in my senior year of high school. I'd been looking at colleges, getting good grades . . . and then I wasn't. Then I was driving to appointments and counting pills and holding her hand as she died, and I cried and cried.

We were in so much debt from her medical bills I had to get a job, not that I would've been accepted to any college with the way my grades had tanked. Then Dad got in a car wreck and, a week later, got a really bad infection no amount of drugs could fight, leaving me a nineteen-year-old orphan.

I sold our home, and it was just enough to cover the mortgage and all the medical bills. With the little left over, I got as far away from all that pain as possible. I packed my shit, got on a bus to New Orleans, and never looked back. I stopped replying to my friends' messages, and they stopped calling.

I just wanted to start over, go somewhere no one knew me. I didn't want to stay in that town and be the local sob story for the rest of my life.

I was in my second week in New Orleans and running out of money when I stumbled on the Cottonmouth Inn. It was actually Ren's music that drew me in. He was doing a cover of "Dead Inside" by Muse, and my feet took me through the door without even thinking about it.

It turned out to be the last song of their set, and I was disproportionately upset I couldn't listen to more of their music—at the time, I didn't know he was a giant jerk. After weeks of not being able to get a job or a place to live, it was the straw that broke the camel's back. I sat down at the bar, ordered a beer, and started crying.

That was the first and last time I poured my heart out to Andre. He'd played the silent bartender role perfectly, wiping glasses and listening to every sad detail. I didn't know what the fuck about my homeless, penniless, blubbering self had screamed "stellar employee and tenant material," but he'd hired me and offered me the apartment on the spot.

Eight years later, I still worked for him.

A Dalmatian ran up and startled me out of my memories, his long snout demanding pats. I indulged him until his human whistled and the good boy rushed to his side.

Then I remembered why I didn't spend a lot of time taking it easy. I much preferred the partying, drinking, meaningless sex, getting up just in time to get to work, and keeping myself busy. It kept me from thinking about my dead parents and dead dreams. What was the point of making myself depressed when there was nothing I could do about it?

Frustrated with myself for letting the emotion make my throat tight, I pushed up and walked out of the park. It was stinking hot, the sun beating down and the humidity unbearable in the late afternoon, but I decided to walk back. It would be good to focus on my body for a while.

As I exited the park, I spotted a man leaning against a familiar expensive black car, eating chips and staring right at me. At first I hoped it was just a coincidence, but he didn't even remotely hide the fact he was watching me.

I glared at him as I got closer. Unless I wanted to walk all the way around the park, I had no choice but to walk past him. I hoped my "fuck off" look would be enough to make him fuck off.

As I approached, he finished his snack, licked his fingers, and scrunched up the empty bag. He rapped on the blacked-out window and folded his hands in front of himself, giving me an almost mocking smile.

I picked up my pace. If I made it past before she got out of the car . . .

"Toni." The door swung open and there she was, blocking my path, her silky hair falling over her shoulder, her linen shorts and sleeveless shirt impeccable.

"Why?" I looked to the sky and groaned, then narrowed my eyes at the man who was clearly the silhouette from the previous night—George, she'd called him. "How the fuck did you even find me?" For all they knew, I was just a patron at the Cottonmouth.

"Never lost you." He shrugged.

Son of a bitch. He must've had someone watching me this entire time. "That's stalking."

He grinned, not denying or confirming my accusation. *Crafty* son of a bitch.

"It really is not my intention to frighten you." Alexandria drew my attention back to her. She stood tall, her shoulders back, but her hand wringing gave her nerves away. "I'm just running out of time, and you weren't returning my calls."

"Generally, when someone ignores your calls, it means they don't want to speak to you. No means no, Alex. And I'm not scared." I folded my arms and scowled.

"Aren't you even a little curious about why we—" She cut herself off as a woman walked past with a stroller, waiting until she was out of earshot before leaning forward to finish her question. " . . . have the same face?"

"No," I declared.

She gave me a skeptical look. "Really?"

"Yes. No. Look, yes, it's weird, but I don't need any drama in my life. And this"—I gestured in her general direction—"reeks of drama."

She watched me for a moment. "OK, fine. You don't want drama. I get it. What about money?"

"Money? What *about* money?" Was she trying to pay me off? Make me go away? She was stupider than I thought. All I'd been trying to do was get the fuck away from her.

"I'd like to offer you a substantial amount. And all you have to do is dress nicer and cuss less for a few weeks. You never have to see me again after that."

"What the fuck is wrong with what I'm wearing?" I looked down at the ripped jean shorts and the T-shirt with a skeleton hand giving the middle finger.

"Can we please discuss this in the car?" She held her arms away from her body, as if she didn't like her own skin touching the pristine fabric. "It's unbearably hot."

"I don't know you." I took an exaggerated step back. "I'm not getting into a car with you."

"Toni. Please." The way she looked at me reminded me of the moment we first met. It was raw, desperate. She was breathing hard, not just from the heat but from another impending panic attack. Most of all she looked genuinely sad.

And because I'm a fucking idiot, I rolled my eyes, pushed past her, and got into the car. She rushed in after me, and we were on the move before I could say "leather interior."

I breathed a sigh of relief at the air-conditioned comfort before speaking. "OK. Tell me what you want so I can knock it back and we can be done with this."

I turned to her, then reeled back.

Her face was inches from mine, her eyes squinting. "Remarkable." She studied me as if she were looking in the mirror trying to find blackheads. "It's like looking in the mirror," she said, echoing my thoughts.

"Lady, you're creeping me the fuck out."

"Right." She coughed and backed away to a more respectable distance. "As I said, I have a proposition. I'd like you to take my place for one month, assume my identity. At the end of the month, I'll be married and come into quite a bit of money, and I'll pay you handsomely for your time. Also, I'll need a sample of your saliva."

"Jesus." I pressed my back against the door, getting as far away from her as possible. "Lube me up before you shove something that big up my—"

"Toni!" She actually clutched her pearls, her eyes going wide.

Despite the bizarre-as-fuck situation, I couldn't help the laugh that burst out of me. After a moment, she cracked a smile too, and then we were both having a good laugh in the back of the most expensive car I'd ever touched. Hers was a little more reserved than mine, but even our laughs were the same.

"This is insane." I tried to reason with her. "Why would you want to do this?"

All the humor left her face. "I have my reasons."

"You can't expect me to just jump into your life without knowing what I'm getting myself into."

"So you're considering it." Her eyes lit up again.

"No . . ."

She ignored me. "OK, yes, you're right. I'll tell you whatever you want to know. The main point is that I'm getting married soon, and I just want . . . a break. A month to just not be me for a while, to not feel the immense pressure I'm under."

I could relate to not wanting to think about heavy shit. "You want me to plan your wedding?"

"No." She waved her hand. "It's all organized. I just want you to spend the month with my fiancé and his family at their property just outside the city. You'll hardly see them. They're busy."

"What the fuck? Are you insane? Don't you think he'd notice? He'll take one look at me and know it's not you."

"No, he won't. We've never met."

"Who's never met?"

"My fiancé and I."

"You're marrying someone you've never met?"

"It's complicated." She sighed.

"Yeah! Exactly the kind of complicated I'm trying to avoid."

"Look, it's more of a business deal—a quid pro quo situation. He needs a wife to inherit his father's company. I need his money to pay off some debts. Like I said, he won't know you're not me, and he won't care that you're not spending much time with him. You can just take a month off. There's a pool and a chef on call and every luxury you could think of. And if you like activities, there's a tennis court and stables."

The mention of "stables" had me actually considering this. I loved horses. Bitch *had* to tell me about the horses. "You're telling me you're about to enter a marriage of convenience with a super-rich guy who has multiple horses on his giant property? What century are we in? Did I hit my head and fall into a fucking Regency romance novel?"

She laughed again. "It's more common than you might think."

"Rich people, man . . ." I muttered. "Even if I entertain this idea, I can't just disappear from my life for a month. I have a job, a . . . uh . . . rent to pay, and . . ." I was struggling to think of things I couldn't walk away from. "My point is, at the end of this, I need to be able to come back to work, and there's no way Andre will let me just take a month off."

"Oh, that's not going to be a problem." She smiled, as if she had everything figured out. "While you're pretending to be me, I'll pretend to be you. I'll do your job and . . . whatnot. The only snag may be that your friends will probably realize I'm not you. So maybe we should let them in on it."

I snorted. "Don't worry. No one will suspect a thing. We just need to put some makeup on you, get you comfortable with the word *cunt*, and you'll be fine. I'm not that close to Andre, and he's the only one who sees me every day."

She nodded, but her lips kept twitching up into a smile.

I narrowed my eyes. Then, as I realized I was helping her plan this insanity, I huffed. "What the fuck am I saying? No. I can't do this. It's too weird. Pull over."

For the first time, I looked out the window. We were in the French Quarter somewhere—the traffic was worse, and there were people everywhere. The sun was beginning to disappear behind the buildings.

"No!" She grabbed my arm. "George, keep driving." She spoke with so much urgency you would've thought we were in a high-speed car chase, not crawling along a traffic-clogged street. I could've probably opened the door and just stepped out.

I looked at her fingers wrapped around my arm, then arched my eyebrow at her.

"Please," she begged again. "I *need* this."

"Nah, man. It's not worth it." I removed her hands from my arm and turned toward the door.

"Fifty thousand dollars!" she yelled.

My eyes widened, and I slowly turned to face her again. "Fifty grand?"

"A hundred," she rushed out.

"Whoa." For a moment we just stared at each other. That was

tuition *and* rent money. I could go to college. Maybe my dreams weren't as dead as I thought . . .

I chewed on my lip. "Fuck. OK."

She threw her arms around my neck and started sobbing. "Thank you. You have no idea how much this means to me."

"A hundred grand, apparently." I patted her on the back awkwardly.

George pulled the car up outside a five-star hotel. There was a fucking fountain in the circular drive, along with half a dozen other ridiculously expensive cars.

A fancy hotel guy rushed over, and Alexandria pulled away and quickly wiped her face, smoothing down invisible wrinkles in her shirt.

"Stay in the car." Suddenly she was whispering. "It's better if you come up with George through the parking garage. In case someone sees."

I frowned, questioning my rash decision. She was paranoid. Paranoid could be dangerous. But before I could raise any concerns, she was out of the car, and George was pulling away.

"OK then. Guess I'll come through the servants' entrance." I rolled my eyes.

George chuckled. "She's not like that. But a certain level of discretion is necessary if you want this to work. You may want to call and let Andre know you won't be able to work tonight."

"What? Why?" I leaned forward. "Wait. How did you know I was working to—right, the stalking."

"The *thorough investigation*," he argued. "And it's going to take some time to make sure you're both ready to take on each other's roles. We only have until tomorrow morning."

"Whatever." I pulled my phone out and called Andre.

"What do you mean you ain't coming to work?" he growled, but he didn't even miss a beat before asking the next question. "Are you all right?"

"I'm fine. I promise. I just have to take care of something. It's really important. I just . . . can't talk about it." I cringed, my eyes meeting George's in the rearview. He shook his head as he pulled into a spot and killed the engine.

"Toni . . ." Andre's voice was both questioning and reprimanding. He didn't like this. I wasn't sure I liked it either. Maybe that's why I was struggling to lie to him.

"Come on. Just . . . do me a solid and let this one go. It's important, and it won't happen again. I'll be back tomorrow, I swear." I brought it home by doing something I never did—plead. "Please, Andre."

He sighed, and I knew I had him. "Fine."

I ended the call, and George and I headed up to Alexandria's room.

In the elevator, George turned to me. "For someone with so much attitude, you're a shitty liar. You're going to have to up your game."

In place of an answer, I just flipped him off.

Chapter 4

ALEX

Toni took three steps into the room and paused, her eyes going wide. The suite was luxurious, swathed in dark velvet and imported marble, the view of New Orleans spectacular. "Your hotel room is bigger than my apartment."

"That's as good a place to start as any," I said. "Please, sit. Tell me about where you live. What I can expect." I gestured to the couch, and she finally shook herself out of her shock and moved to join me. George settled into the chair at the desk.

"What do you wanna know?" Toni practically fell into the cushions, slumping against the back before yawning without covering her mouth.

I looked down at myself. I was sitting on the edge of the

cushion, my back straight, knees together. I looked over my shoulder at George. He was silently laughing.

"Tell me how to get inside, I guess? What does it look like? Where do I go? Where do you keep things?" As I spoke, I maneuvered myself until I was leaning back on the couch, my knees open, my shoulders hunched. It felt . . . unnatural.

She frowned. "What the fuck are you doing?"

"Trying to sit like you?" I didn't quite know what to do with my hands, moving them from the couch to my lap to over my head.

Toni burst out laughing. She sat up and faced me. "Stop trying to force it. We look *exactly* the same. A little black eyeliner and a little more relaxed and no one will even notice. You just need to . . . how are you reclined on the world's softest couch and you look *that* stiff?"

I frowned. I *felt* stiff. I was trying too hard. Taking a deep breath, I rolled my shoulders and let myself sink into the couch. I supposed I'd need to start using more colorful language too. Not that I was opposed to cursing, necessarily. I just found myself in situations where I had to speak politely and professionally most of the time; it wasn't part of my vernacular. But there was no time like the present. "This is a pretty fucking soft couch."

Toni beamed at me. George couldn't hold it in any longer and burst out laughing. That got me chuckling too.

We ordered room service for dinner. I didn't realize how hungry I was until the grilled salmon was placed in front of me. I hadn't eaten most of the day, too anxious and nervous to even feel hungry.

"Enjoy that while you can." Toni spoke around a giant mouthful of club sandwich. "That's the last five-star meal you're going to have for a month. *Damn*, this is a good sandwich." She moaned and took another bite. I watched her closely as I ate my meal, amused by how thoroughly she enjoyed hers and how much she let it show.

We spent the evening tutoring each other about our lives.

I hadn't been to Oren's property before, so there wasn't much I could tell her. That would work to our advantage—it wouldn't be strange when she couldn't find her way to the bathroom or had to ask someone where the pool was. But she told me the layout of the Cottonmouth Inn, the staircase leading to the two studios upstairs, and her apartment.

She also ran me through what she did at work. I'd never bartended. I hardly went out to bars, let alone knew what was behind one. I had a lot of questions. It sounded like hard work, but I was looking forward to even that!

She gave me brief background on the people I'd most likely interact with. Andre—tall black man, owner of the bar, her landlord and neighbor in the studio across the hall. Loretta—white woman of questionable age, the cook. Dennis—the college kid who worked a couple of nights at the bar.

There was also a handful of casual bar staff and bouncers. "The other staff tend to come and go. That's the nature of the business—high turnaround. Some realize they don't want to work the late hours. Others can't hack the pace." She shrugged.

We stayed up very late, sharing the minute details of each other's lives. But whenever we got close to a difficult topic, one of us would back away from it. I needed her to know as much as possible, but she was still essentially a stranger. I wasn't entirely sure I could trust her.

Which was insane considering I was about to let her step into my life. On more than one occasion, I questioned my decision, questioned my own sanity. Toni, on the other hand, after the strong push of resistance, was all in. It seemed she was not easy to convince, but once she made a decision, she didn't look back. I liked that about her. I could be the same at times—very sure and determined once I'd committed to something. Like this marriage . . .

There were other things we had in common. Little things, like we both despised pineapple on pizza, worked best with music pumping, could touch the tips of our noses with our tongues.

We tried to get a few hours' sleep, but neither one of us could, and we gave up. We ended up on the balcony. The hotel was quiet, but the sounds of Bourbon Street nearby carried on the warm summer breeze.

Toni lit her fifth cigarette of the evening and dropped the lighter on the table between us.

I cringed. "You're going to have to stop that. I can't have people thinking I smoke."

She glared at me and took a deliberate, long drag, blowing the smoke in my direction. I held her gaze, refusing to let the smoke get to me. Eventually she rolled her eyes and leaned back in her chair. "Fine. I've been meaning to quit anyway."

I nodded, satisfied, but she finished the cigarette.

"What do you think this is? Really?" She gestured between us, her eyes on the dark sky.

"Honestly? I'm trying not to think too much about it. It's a little overwhelming."

"Yeah. I feel that."

"If you're happy to provide that saliva sample, I'll have George order some DNA tests. Then at least we can rule some things out." *Or confirm them.* But I didn't want to say that. It was too intimidating to think about.

"Sure. I guess." She didn't sound sure, and I could understand that. The implications of the results could be just as life altering for her as they would be for me.

Vaguely alluding to family made me remember another question I needed to ask. "Are there any family members I need to be aware of? Anyone that might pop in to see you and immediately realize I'm an imposter?"

She remained silent for a long moment. "No. I don't have any family."

"Oh . . ."

"Both my parents died years ago. I came to New Orleans for a fresh start. I don't have any extended family, and I didn't keep in touch with any of my high school friends. The people I work with are decent, and we all keep to ourselves. They stay out of my business and vice versa. Trust me, no one will even notice I'm gone."

It was an interesting choice of words—that no one would

notice she was gone, not that no one would notice she'd been replaced. I had an urge to lean over and give her a hug but had a feeling it wouldn't be received well.

"I'm really sorry about your parents," I said instead. "I lost my father a few years ago too."

"That fucking sucks."

"Yeah, it does."

She sat up. "So your mom is still around then? Should I be worried about her?"

"No. She wasn't able to join me for this trip. She calls me every damn day, but you won't have to deal with that." We were keeping our own phones and making sure we had them on us—in case the other one needed to clarify something.

Eventually the sun started to brighten the sky, and we headed inside to get ready.

I put on her ripped shorts and middle-finger top and threw my hair up in a ponytail, resisting the urge to smooth it back with a brush. Toni took a shower, and I blow-dried her hair and picked out a peach day dress for her to wear.

"I fucking hate heels," she whined at the three-inch sandals I held up. I huffed. We were running out of time, so I gave in and handed her a pair of flats.

"Just remember to keep your back straight and your shoulders back and smile, but not ironically like you always do. Smile pleasantly—like you actually enjoy it," I said, giving her a last few tips before leaving. "And please, for the love of god, do not curse in front of Oren's parents, at least. And if you have any issues,

George will be there to help." I turned to George, my eyes wide. Was I making a massive mistake?

He placed his warm hands on my shoulders. "Alexandria, I'll take care of Toni. You just take care of you—for once in your life." He gave me a reproachful look, and I squeezed his wrist, willing myself not to get emotional. He was right. I needed a break. I deserved a break. I couldn't remember the last time I'd done something for myself or even purely for the fun of it. That was a pretty pathetic thought but one I couldn't dwell on, because the door was swinging toward my face.

George stepped out of the way just as Toni cleared her throat, one hand on the door handle. "Please leave immediately, or I shall have security remove you, you . . . unsavory person," she said in an exaggerated voice.

It made me laugh as I stepped through the door, then immediately turned back. "Oh, I almost forgot!" I removed the engagement ring from my finger and slipped it onto hers.

She held it up in front of her face and whistled, raising her eyebrows. "Maybe I should just run off and pawn this. I'd have enough to live off for the rest of my life."

"Don't you dare!" I wagged a finger at her. "That's a Winthrop family heirloom." Oren sent it to me—escorted by its own security guy—when we locked in the deal and announced the engagement, stating no one would believe it was legit unless I had that Victorian-era, six-carat rock on my finger. I'd almost gotten used to its weight on my hand.

"Relax. Go." Toni shooed me away.

With a final warning look, I walked away from my life.

I followed Toni's instructions and took public transport back to the Cottonmouth Inn, constantly reminding myself to lean back and trying to remember every detail of what she'd shared about her life. I had to walk for ten minutes for the last leg of my journey and was glad for the flat boots.

I turned down the alleyway where we first met and headed straight for the heavy door next to the dumpster. As instructed, I used the square key to let myself in, then went up the back staircase and down the corridor. There were only two doors and a narrow window at the end, providing only some hazy light despite the bright sunshine outside. The doors were old-fashioned timber with frosted glass, more like office doors than apartment doors.

I moved to the one on the right. The glass rattled a little in the frame even though I didn't slam the door closed.

Toni wasn't lying when she said her apartment was smaller than my suite at the hotel. She'd also neglected to mention the overwhelming stench of stale cigarette smoke that permeated every inch—but I guessed smokers didn't notice these things.

Directly to my left was the bathroom. On the opposite wall was a kitchen—one row of overhead cabinets with a counter underneath and a fridge wedged into the corner.

Between that was everything else.

I walked down the middle of the space, nearly tripping on a pile of clothing and then accidentally kicking an empty beer bottle. It went rolling toward the bed, making an obnoxiously loud sound on the timber floors.

The couch next to the kitchen was half-buried under clothes and other things I couldn't make out in the dim light. The bed was in the corner to my left, the only space free of debris.

When I finally made it to the other side of the room, I pulled the dark curtains back . . . and almost wished I hadn't. Now I could see the absolute mess I was supposed to live in for the next month.

I propped my hands on my hips and sighed, then nearly gagged on the smoke smell again.

She never said I couldn't clean up a little, and there was no way in hell I was sleeping in that bed until it had fresh sheets.

I threw the balcony door open. I hadn't done my own laundry since college, but I stripped the sheets and put in a load, then found a trash bag and started to gather up all the trash—empty beer bottles, pizza boxes, the few items of expired food in the fridge.

Halfway through the third load of washing, I found a portable speaker and put some music on through my phone. Having a clear task with a concrete goal felt good, and it was nice to do something physical. It provided a distraction for my usually overactive mind.

I was singing along to the Backstreet Boys when the door flew open, the glass rattling, and startled me half to death. I jumped and dropped the freshly dried pile of sheets at my feet.

Filling up almost the entire doorway stood tall, dark, and handsome in distressed jeans and a red muscle shirt. His big hands were in fists, his face set into a scowl. He was *very* tall, his head nearly reaching the top of the doorway. He was *very* dark, his closely cropped, thick hair black and his eyes shaded by his drawn brows. And he was *very* . . . damn, Toni did not mention how handsome he was.

"Toni?" His posture relaxed as soon as he locked eyes with me, the scowl disappearing. "Shit, girl, I thought someone broke in and put shitty nineties music on. Thought I was about to have to throw a junkie out or something." He walked halfway to me as he spoke, and I could finally see the color of his eyes—dark brown, almost black.

"Oh, hey, Andre." I was 90 percent sure that's who it was, but I was kicking myself for the music. Toni hadn't exactly told me not to blast nineties boy bands, but I had a feeling it wasn't her usual choice. "Uh, I don't know why that came on. So weird!" I lunged for my phone and turned it off, plunging us into silence.

"Wait." He was frowning again. "Are you cleaning?"

"Yes." I picked the sheets back up and dropped them on the bed. "I thought it was overdue?" It came out sounding like a question.

"I mean, it was overdue six months ago." He chuckled. "Whatever. Look, are you all right?"

"Fine! Why?" I put on my best pleasant smile. He narrowed his eyes, and I turned it down a notch.

"You bailed last night with no explanation. Add that to the couple you were shouting at in the alleyway the other night, and I'll ask again. You in some kind of trouble?"

I busied myself with the sheets. "No. I promise. Everything is completely fine. I just had something personal come up. It was important and . . . uh . . . personal. But it's all fine now. Thank you for your concern."

He was silent for a long time. Just as I was about to abandon the pillowcase, he spoke. "Your shift starts at four. Don't be late."

"You got it! No problem!" I turned just in time to see him stride out the door, his toned, round shoulders hunching to pass through the frame.

I released a massive breath, then smiled to myself. It was a rocky start, but he didn't suspect a thing. Even told me to come to work!

I finished cleaning around midday and took a shower. Too nervous to eat lunch, I started going through some of Toni's stuff instead. I knew it was intrusive, but I'd already gone through half of it while cleaning anyway, and it could give me more valuable information.

She didn't have a lot of personal items—no pictures on the walls or journals—but I did find a stack of books and a corkboard with concert tickets. The books were an eclectic mix—some fiction, a handful of biographies, and several books about birds and other animals. The tickets were all rock concerts.

I found one small stack of pictures in the bottom drawer of her dresser. A young Toni (it could've so easily been a young *me*) posed with girls her age and with an older couple who were clearly her parents. They looked nothing like her . . .

I put the pictures back and sat on the bed. The DNA test would take a few weeks. There was no point stressing about it yet.

I lay back and wondered how Toni was getting on. But the stress of considering all the things that could go wrong in that situation had my heart hammering, so I tried to put that out of my mind too.

Lying down made me realize I hadn't slept at all. With a wide yawn—and a conscious effort not to cover my mouth with my hand—I rolled over and took a nap.

The afternoon sun streaming across my face woke me up a few hours later. It was hot upstairs, and there wasn't even a fan to move the air around.

I groaned and rolled over to check the time, then sat bolt upright. I only had half an hour to get to work!

There were no uniforms I could find, and Toni didn't seem to have any more presentable clothes, so I put on black pants with ribbed fabric up the sides and a simple gray V-neck T-shirt, hoping it was appropriate. After braiding my hair and applying an obnoxious amount of eyeliner, like she showed me, I was ready to head down ten minutes early.

I rushed down the stairs and let myself into the empty bar.

The floor was sticky, and the walls were painted a dark blue above the four-foot-high wooden wainscoting. The long bar looked like a rough section of a tree cut down the middle. It was pretty cool, but the barstools in front of it had peeling faux-leather seats. A handful of rickety tables and chairs scattered along the edges of the space completed the tired look.

"Hello?" I called out. There was no one behind the bar.

A woman's head popped out of the servery. "It ain't ready yet, sugar." Her voice sounded like sandpaper. I caught a glimpse of gray regrowth and a skinny, wrinkled face before she disappeared.

Loretta. Had to be, based on Toni's description.

"That's no problem," I called back. I had no idea what wasn't ready. I glanced around again and figured I couldn't go wrong with cleaning something, but before I could even look for a cloth, the door to the back alley screeched, and Andre barreled into the bar.

He spotted me and ground to a halt, frowning in confusion. "What in the . . ."

I propped my hands on my hips, making sure to slouch a little. "Ready to work, boss."

"You're ready to . . ." He looked perplexed. "What the fuck are you doing here? Are you sure you're all right?"

Now it was my turn to frown. "You said I start at four. It's four."

"Yeah, but you never actually show up on time." He finally shook himself out of his stupor and went to the bar, pouring himself a soda.

I should've known. Of course Toni would be chronically late.

"I'm . . . turning over a new leaf." I did my best to sound confident without coming off too cheery.

"Coupled with the state of your apartment, I'm inclined to actually believe you," he grumbled, his attention on his drink. He chugged it down in one go, but he still wasn't giving me instructions, and I was suddenly blanking on what Toni said she did at work.

"So where do you want me to start, boss?"

He paused, straightened, and looked at me again. "The beer." He said it as if he were speaking to someone with a mental disability.

"Right . . ." I felt my eyes go wide. I mean, we were in a bar.

Of course beer would be involved—I just didn't know what he wanted me to do with the beer.

"Bring the cases up to restock the fridges." He was still using that slow voice.

"Right! Of course!" I slapped myself on the forehead and rushed past him, in the direction of where Toni had told me the storage room was. Her instructions were starting to come back to me. "On it, boss!"

"Stop calling me that! You're creeping me the fuck out!" he called after me.

"Sure! You got it . . . dude!" I called back and cringed as I ducked around the corner.

I hauled case after case of beer and lined them up in the fridges under the bar. Dennis arrived not long after I finished, and I let him take the lead in what else needed to be done. He gave me a few odd looks, but I told him I wasn't feeling the best, and he seemed to buy it.

Around five thirty, Loretta declared, "It's ready!" punctuating the yell with a coughing fit so severe I started to wonder if we should take her to the hospital. No one else seemed worried though, so I didn't say anything.

The "it" turned out to be burgers. It was the greasiest, unhealthiest thing I'd eaten in years, but Toni was right—they were damn good. And after the hard work I'd just put in, and the fact that I'd skipped lunch, I needed it. I wolfed it down without a second thought for manners.

The four of us sat at the bar and ate as Andre, Dennis, and

Loretta chatted.

"That was freaking delicious, Loretta. Thank you!" I told her honestly. The guys turned to look at me as if they'd forgotten I was there.

Loretta jumped off her stool and collected the baskets. "You're welcome, doll. Thanks for joining us. It was nice." She smiled at me, a genuine, wide smile that showed her crooked teeth.

"Yeah, you usually disappear to stuff your face and have a smoke before opening. What gives?" Dennis leaned on the bar.

"Oh . . ." How the hell was I supposed to keep this going when I was doing out-of-character things left and right? Was Toni having this much trouble? "I'm cutting down. Trying to quit."

"Hey, good for you!" Dennis grinned and got back to work.

Andre just watched me for a few moments, then nodded and got behind the bar. Dennis opened the front doors, Andre turned the sound system on, and the Cottonmouth Inn was officially open for business. My first night as a working-class girl was underway.

A: Hey. How are you doing with the clothes and stuff?

T: Fine? Why?

A: Oh ok. Good! It's nothing. Just making sure.

T: Spit it out, Alex.

A: It's just . . . maybe we should've at least taken our own underwear with us?

T: OMFG! Yes!

A: Oh thank god! It's not just me?

T: No! I mean, everything fits perfectly and it's all clean, but there's something just . . . off about wearing someone else's panties.

A: Yes! Exactly! It's weird.

T: So weird . . . Hey, while we're on the topic, you may wanna wash most of mine. Sometimes I run out and I just wear them inside out until I can get the laundry done.

A: Toni! That's disgusting!

T: Hey! Don't judge me! You didn't exactly give me time to prepare for this brilliant plan.

A: Whatever. I already washed everything you own.

T: Of course you did . . .

Chapter 5

TONI

I fidgeted with the dress, readjusting my position in the back seat. I couldn't remember the last time I was nervous. George throwing me glances in the rearview really wasn't helping.

"Stop looking at me, you creep!" I snapped at him.

Asshole just laughed. "I'm just making sure you don't bail out of the car while it's still moving."

"I'm not a fucking quitter," I shot back.

"Well, then get your shit together. Alexandria may not feel it all the time, but she always makes sure she goes into any situation *looking* confident."

I huffed. Then I took a deep breath and made myself roll my shoulders back. He was right—not that I'd ever say it to his face. Alex's confidence was quiet and steady; mine was cocky and came from a place of not giving a shit. Which was probably why this was getting to me. I actually did give a shit—one hundred thousand shits, to be precise.

"What're you in love with her?" I deflected, taking the focus off me.

He laughed again. "I'm fifteen years older. She's more like a younger sister. I may *work* for the family, but make no mistake, they are my family."

I knew a thinly veiled threat when I heard one. "Relax. I have every incentive to make sure this goes well."

"Good, because it's showtime."

I sat up straighter and paid more attention to what was outside the car. After more than half an hour of driving, we were slowing down, pulling up to massive iron gates.

George put his window down and pressed a button on an intercom. The speaker mumbled, George mumbled, and then the gates swung open and we were driving down the path to one of the Winthrops' many estates. The drive was lined with massive oak trees, the twisted branches creating a kind of tunnel. I could see manicured lawns and structures in the distance—so much land the edge of the property wasn't even visible.

As we emerged from the trees and drove around a *motherfucking fountain*, I took another deep breath. I shoved all the uncertainty and stress down and pictured Alex—her perfect posture, her gentle mannerisms, her proper way of speaking.

George pulled to a stop in front of a house that looked like it belonged in *Gone with the Wind*. It was multilevel and white, with a wraparound porch and columns and shutters all over the place.

"You can do this." George's little encouragement was spoken so low I almost missed it, and then he was out of the car and opening my door for me.

I swung my feet out and pulled myself out of the vehicle, doing my best not to let my eyes widen in awe as I looked at the grand house.

Several people came forward, but before I could so much as smile at them, they attacked the trunk, extracted all the luggage, and disappeared.

An older couple came down the stairs toward me. The man had auburn hair, speckled with gray at the temples, and the woman was short, curvy, and a bottle blonde, but the color was expertly highlighted and suited her.

"Miss Zamorano." The man smiled politely. "I'm Oren Charles Winthrop the second. It is a pleasure to meet you."

He extended his hand, and I shook it, smiling. "Likewise."

"Allow me to introduce my wife, Caroline Ann Winthrop."

I turned to the woman.

"Oh, we are so happy to have you here, Alexandria, *so* happy." She had a southern accent and a bright smile with perfectly straight teeth. Her eyes dropped to my left hand, and she gently lifted it. "It looks gorgeous on your elegant fingers. Perfect fit."

"Oh! Thank you." I kept my response brief. I couldn't say anyone had ever referred to any part of me as elegant.

Alex had said the parents were aware of the nature of the

engagement and helped set it up, but Caroline was acting as if she was meeting the love of her son's life. I'd been expecting polite professionalism, not actual warmth. Oren senior, on the other hand, was polite but looked like he'd rather be literally anywhere else.

After a few more pleasantries, I was shown to my room to "settle in and freshen up." But all the luggage was already in there, and I'd just showered and dressed an hour earlier, so there really wasn't anything to "freshen."

The maid closed the door behind me, and I took the room in. It was massive, bright and airy despite the large, heavy furniture. There was a white four-poster bed, a lounge area with couches but no TV, and a large desk. The space somehow blended the historical tones of the house with modern, light features. It felt expensive, and I stood near the door for a really long time, feeling like maybe I shouldn't touch anything.

But then I rolled my eyes; I was going to be living there for the next month. I took a quick glance at the en-suite bathroom—so much marble—and ran my hand over the softest sheets my peasant, yet apparently elegant, hand had ever touched as I went past the bed to the window.

This bedroom faced the back of the property. The view was incredible—rolling hills, manicured gardens closer to the house with wilder forest farther out. Several additional structures, like barns and sheds, were dotted about. Someone on a horse came out of what had to be the stables. The rider took it easy for a while before pushing the animal into a trot and disappearing over a hill.

First chance I got, I was going down there to check out the

horses. I may have agreed to this insanity mainly for the money, but there was no reason it couldn't be fun too.

A knock at the door dragged my attention away from the window and my thoughts. I rushed across the room and pulled it open.

On the other side stood the prettiest man I'd ever seen. Dressed in light gray pants and a blue polo shirt covering his broad shoulders, he was tall and lean. He had his father's auburn hair— cut short with enough length on the top to style back into neat waves—and his mother's hazel eyes, a perfectly straight nose, and full lips.

He was the exact opposite of the rough, tatted, ripped-jeans-and-piercings guys I usually went for. He even smelled expensive— like the perfume counter at a department store, only more manly and sharp.

I smiled politely and extended my hand. "Oren. It's a pleasure to meet you." I took a page out of his father's book and greeted him in almost the same words, hoping I sounded as polished and proper as Alex.

He took my hand in his, stuffing his other hand into his pocket. "Alexandria. Welcome to Hazelgreen Manor. My apologies for not greeting you at your arrival. I only just got in myself."

"Oh, no problem." I gently pulled my hand out of his grip, not entirely sure what to do or say next.

He cleared his throat. "Can I interest you in a walk? A tour of the house and grounds?"

"Yes, that would be lovely."

I closed the door and followed him. He spoke at a leisurely, calm pace but never left too long a silence as he pointed out different rooms and features of the house.

His bedroom was at the other end of the hall to mine, his parents' in the opposite wing of the house. There were about a thousand more bedrooms and a lounge room with a large television.

"It's the only television in the house." He cringed. "Sorry. This is my mother's childhood home, but we don't stay here often and it's usually for business, so the bedrooms were never modernized."

"Oh. It's no problem." I plastered a smile on my face. Inwardly I cursed seven ways from Sunday. I fell asleep to the sound of infomercials turned down low most nights I didn't pass out.

"Of course"—he stuffed both hands into his pockets—"you probably don't watch a lot of television. I'm sure you'll be as busy working as I will."

Thankfully, he didn't give me a chance to answer before moving off.

The house had three levels, several wings, staff quarters on the ground floor, a catering kitchen and a nicely decorated *second kitchen*, multiple formal and relaxed living and dining areas—even a parlor with a fucking piano—and fireplaces everywhere. I really was in a Regency romance novel.

Halfway through the tour, I gave up trying to remember where everything was. We ended up on the back porch, looking out over the same view I had from my room, as he told me there was a full staff on call twenty-four seven, including a chef and butler.

"I was going to suggest a stroll of the grounds, but it is getting hot." He leaned on the railing, his knuckles turning almost white from the tightness of his grip.

That was odd, considering how calm and relaxed he seemed.

"I really don't mind. I was actually hoping to see the horses . . . uh, the stables?" I wasn't sure what the correct word was. I really didn't mind the heat, and it was only midmorning, not even close to the oppressive heat of the afternoon.

His grip on the railing loosened, and he gave me the first genuine smile since we'd met. "All right. Follow me."

He set an easy pace, pointing things out along the way—the pool on one side of the house, the path to the tennis court, the various sheds and barns and their uses—but he wasn't filling every second of silence with his words. I settled into the pauses in between.

"I have to admit," he said halfway to the stables, "that your silence earlier made me . . . uncertain? Usually you're very talkative on our calls, so when you gave me next to nothing while I showed you the house, I started to feel like I'd unknowingly committed some faux pas."

"I couldn't get a word in." I chuckled. It wasn't entirely true, but I didn't know what else to say. "I guess I'm just a bit nervous, meeting you for the first time, face-to-face."

He nodded. "I can understand that. I suppose I was a bit nervous myself." He laughed unexpectedly, throwing his head back. "I was considering showing you every damn room in the house to make sure I had something to occupy the silence."

I laughed too but tried to put him at ease. "Look, this is an . . . unusual situation, but it doesn't have to be uncomfortable. We both know what we're here for. It's basically a business deal, right? So let's just try to relax and be friendly about it."

He nodded and smiled, but it didn't reach his eyes. "Yes. Very good point, as always. We'll keep things professional but friendly. Ah, here we are!"

He gestured to the stables like a salesman and rushed ahead inside.

I'd never been inside a stable, but even I could tell this one was impressive. It was huge and well-stocked with all kinds of things I didn't know the name for that were probably very expensive— saddles and reins and things. Tidy stalls lined one wall.

I'd always loved horses. When I was in elementary school, a friend who rode horses would take me with her from time to time. I so badly wanted lessons, but my parents couldn't even afford that, let alone an actual horse. My love of the animals never went away. I had a sneaking suspicion it was that brief interaction with the magnificent animals that started my love affair with all things furry, scaly, and feathered.

"The stables can house eight horses, but we currently have only four here. One is a racing horse, the others are leisure horses. This is one of the reasons why we keep this property open and staffed year-round, regardless of the fact that we rarely come here. Mother loves them." Oren walked over to the prettiest damn horse I'd ever seen. It was blonde and shiny and looked like it could sell shampoo better than any model. "This is Honeymustard." He stroked the horse's nose, and it nuzzled into his touch.

I came closer, completely failing to contain the smile threatening to split my face open. "May I?"

"Please." Oren smiled and took half a step back to give me room.

"Hey, Honeymustard. Hi, girl. Oh, aren't you beautiful?" Gently, I let her sniff my hand, then stroked her nose. She was so soft; I couldn't get enough of her. I kept one hand on her nose and patted her neck with the other. "She's magnificent. Is she the racing horse?"

"No," another voice said, and we both turned to face a man coming out of a door on the far side of the building. "That would be Benson." He gestured to a stall a little farther up. "And I'm Jack."

He stopped in front of us and extended his hand. He was a little shorter than Oren, in jeans and boots, and his messy black hair stuck to his sweaty brow. Straight teeth flashed behind a brilliant, slightly crooked grin. A sleeveless flannel hung off his shoulders, unbuttoned, and tattoos on his arms and chest peeked out of his shirt. He looked like trouble.

Which meant I was in trouble.

Do not fall for the sexy horse guy, I mentally told myself as I extended my hand and tried really hard to keep a polite expression on my face. "Pleased to meet you, Jack. I'm . . . Alex." I gave myself a mental high five for not giving him my real name.

Oren's parents, Alex's mother, and George were the only ones who knew the true nature of the marriage arrangement. As far as anyone else was concerned, it had to appear legitimate. It would therefore be really fucking bad if I went and slept with a sexy stable guy when I was pretending to be her. This was going to be more complicated than I thought.

"Jack is our stable master and Benson's trainer. He lives on the grounds, takes care of the horses, and runs the property in our absence." Oren made introductions as I shook Jack's warm, calloused hand, trying not to think about what it would feel like gripping my breasts. "Jack, this is Alexandria, my fiancée."

We shared a smile that I prayed was polite, but it lingered just a little too long.

"Do you ride, Alex?" Jack asked. Was I imagining the hint of teasing in his voice?

I cleared my throat. "No, I don't."

Oren frowned. "I thought you'd been riding horses since you were three?"

Shit! "I have. I just meant I don't anymore. I mean, I don't really have the time lately. I haven't ridden for many years." That wasn't a lie. "But I'd really like to get back into it, although I'm not sure I remember how." I laughed nervously and turned to give Honeymustard another pat.

"Well, hopefully you'll have plenty of opportunities while you're here," Oren said. "I'm sure Jack would be happy to assist you."

"It would be my pleasure, ma'am," Jack readily agreed. Was that a slight southern twang in his voice? He was practically a cowboy. A tattooed cowboy with a drawl . . . I was in *serious* fucking trouble.

"Thank you. That would be lovely." I nodded.

Oren introduced me to the other three horses—I cooed and patted them all—then followed Jack into the back office to go over something. I wandered around the stables for a while longer before walking outside.

The sun was hiding behind patchy clouds, coming and going.

I couldn't wait to ride one of the horses. The anticipation almost made me forget the fact that I hadn't had a cigarette since just before jumping in the shower that morning. It had been hours—most of that time spent in a state of anxiety. I couldn't remember when I'd needed a cigarette *more*.

I wondered when I'd be able to sneak one without anyone noticing. I fidgeted with a piece of straw, resisting the urge to bring it up to my lips between my fingers.

"Apologies for keeping you waiting." Oren walked out to join me and placed a hand at my back. "Should we continue our walk?"

"Actually, is it all right if we head back?" I stepped toward the house, out of his reach. "I'm suddenly f . . . famished." Much better than "fucking starving."

"Of course." He stuffed his hands into his pockets, and we started to walk back in silence.

After a few minutes he cleared his throat. "I'm sorry if I made you uncomfortable."

"Uncomfortable?" I gave him a questioning look.

"When I, uh, touched your back just then." He rubbed the back of his neck and avoided eye contact. I'd been groped, grabbed, smacked, picked up, and shoved while working at the

Cottonmouth, and this guy was apologizing for lightly touching the middle of my back?

"Oh! You didn't, I promise. It's just hot and I'm a little sweaty."

He didn't look like he believed me. "I understand this is going to be difficult—keeping up appearances." He kept his voice low, even though there was no one around as we walked across the grass. "Perhaps we can sit down and figure out some boundaries? Things that will help us appear to be a real couple but that won't make you uncomfortable."

He wanted to have a meeting about PDA? "If you think that will help." I smiled. "But really, I think it will get easier as we get to know each other. We only just met." To punctuate my point, I wrapped my arm around his loosely.

He stiffened for a moment, then relaxed and matched his steps to mine.

We had a casual lunch on the front porch—and by "casual" I mean a table was set up with linen and silverware and a waiter served us. Afterward, Oren had to get back to work, and I had the afternoon to myself. As much as I wanted to explore the house and grounds more, I ended up locking myself in my room for fear of bumping into someone else I could potentially say the wrong thing to and out myself.

When I was sure I wouldn't be spotted in the window, I lit a cigarette and took a nice long drag, my shoulders relaxing for the first time all day.

T: Hey, on a scale of 1–10 how bad would it be if I were to . . . say . . . fuck the stable master?

A: What??? Toni, do NOT sleep with any of the staff.

T: I don't think you understand how hot he is. Tattoos, Alex! And a southern twang. He called me ma'am and looked at me lasciviously. He has the word "master" in his title.

A: What is wrong with you?

T: So many things! Like SO. many. things.

A: Toni, please, for the love of god, do not sleep with any of the staff. In fact, don't sleep with anyone at all.

T: Even my fiancé?

A: MY fiancé! And I don't want to go back to a situation where he expects marital relations. This is supposed to be a business transaction, remember?

T: Relax. There's no way in hell I'm getting in bed with tall, rich, and uptight.

A: Oh no. Is he horrible in person? Does he have bad breath? Is he mean to his staff? Shit! What did I get myself into?

T: LOL! Would you relax? He's just not my type. Also, did you just curse? *gasp!

A: You must be rubbing off on me . . .

T: Excellent! Now, since I'm not allowed to get any, you need to get some for both of us. Also, people will notice you're not me if you don't get laid at least 3 times per week, so spread 'em!

A: Have you no shame?

T: Hahahaha! No.

A: Seriously, Toni, keep it in your pants.

T: I will if you don't!

Chapter 6

ALEX

Working at a bar was damn hard. Running a business had all kinds of stresses and frustrations, massive pressures and responsibilities, but bar work was physical, fast-paced, and exhausting.

Toni had given me a rundown of how the bar functioned, where things were, what the most commonly ordered drinks were, but I was positive I didn't do any of it anywhere near as proficiently as she did. I fumbled through, giving everyone the excuse I wasn't feeling well while still managing to get in everyone's way.

At the end of my first night, I collapsed into bed without brushing my teeth, barely managing to remove my clothes before crawling under the covers and passing out.

I woke up the next day sore all over. After a long shower and a stretch, I headed out for a walk, hoping movement would ease my aching muscles. I picked up some groceries and a box of green tea at a store a few blocks away. It was not the loose-leaf I was used to, but it would do. I needed my green tea in the morning.

As I climbed the stairs back up to Toni's place, I kicked myself for not checking her kitchen more thoroughly. I was starving and planning to make myself a grilled chicken salad but had no idea if she had a frying pan or even a cutting board.

When I reached the top of the stairs, Andre's door swung open. He froze on the spot once he spotted me.

"Hey, Andre." I gave him a smile and a friendly wave.

"Uh, hey, Toni. Have you not been to bed yet? You don't look strung out." He leaned down to look into my eyes.

"What?" I leaned away. "No, I woke up an hour ago. Just went to the store." I lifted the bag as proof and resisted the urge to lean in again. He must've just showered. He smelled amazing—like green apple and some woodsy, manly scent I couldn't place.

He crossed his big arms over his chest and frowned. He was in jeans, boots, and a tank, with a checked shirt left unbuttoned over the top. The sleeves were cut off, making his arms look bigger, the biceps bulging.

I mentally rolled my eyes at myself as I turned toward the door. *His biceps were bulging?* I'd never thought about someone like that *ever*. Toni's texts were getting to me. Maybe she was rubbing off more than I thought.

I let myself into the apartment, then screamed and jumped

back, colliding with the solid wall of muscle that was Andre. I'd left the balcony doors open overnight, hoping to coax a breeze in, and hadn't closed them before leaving. A giant black bird had let itself in while I was gone.

Andre wrapped his hands around my upper arms, twisted me out of the way, and stormed inside without hesitation.

I peeked in after him, but he turned to me, confused, his arms held out at his sides. "What the fuck, Toni?"

Slowly, I edged into the room and pointed at the harbinger of death standing in the middle of the apartment as if it owned the place. "You don't see the . . . the bird?"

"The raven?" He gestured at it. It looked between us, cocked its head, and squawked.

"Yes! He must've let himself in through the open balcony." I remained plastered to the wall by the door with my hand pressed to my chest, trying to breathe. I *hated* birds.

The raven squawked again and half opened its wings, shifting from foot to foot as if it was getting ready to charge.

"Yeah, I'd say he let himself in." Andre bugged his eyes out at me. "Since that's what you taught him to do."

Shit! Did Toni have a pet raven? Why would she not mention this? Why hadn't I seen it yet? Where was its cage?

"Right . . ." I nodded and swallowed, keeping the bird and the man in sight as I internally panicked. What the hell was I supposed to do?

"Toni, why are you scared of Ken?"

"Ken?" Why was he changing the topic?

"Kennedy." He pointed at the death-bird again.

"Oh! I'm not scared." I laughed, not even remotely managing to sound not scared. "I'm just . . . uh . . . this is a game we play."

Kennedy squawked again, flapping his wings. Traitor.

Andre watched me for a few silent moments. Then he thudded over to the door, closed it, and turned to face me, his giant arms once again crossed. "OK. Who the fuck are you?"

"What?" Another nervous laugh escaped. I was trying to peel myself away from the wall, go to the damn bird so I could prove I knew what this was about, but my feet just wouldn't move. "What do you mean? I'm . . . me."

He huffed and started ticking things off on his fingers. "You disappeared without explanation, you cleaned and got groceries, you were acting like it was your first damn day at work yesterday, you didn't get wasted or bring some loser up here to screw, you haven't had a cigarette or called anyone a 'cunt' for a solid twenty-four hours, so *who are you*? Because you sure as fuck are not Antoinette Mathers."

His voice boomed, laced with an angry, demanding tone. Suddenly I didn't know if I should be more scared of the raven or the man yelling at me.

I hated myself for it, but my breathing got even shallower as my throat tightened, my eyes stinging with unshed tears. I was either about to have a panic attack or break down crying. Neither option was ideal—they both left me vulnerable to attack from bird or man.

My eyes kept flicking between the raven, which was now

almost constantly squawking and flapping its black wings, and Andre, who was scowling and waiting for an answer I couldn't give. I was frozen, both physically and mentally—completely incapable of doing or saying anything as I suffocated under the stress.

A single, infuriating tear slid down my cheek.

Andre's features softened, and he sighed.

Abandoning his post by the door, he moved over to the raven and crouched down, speaking softly and holding out his wrist. After a few minutes, Kennedy stopped screeching and flapped up onto Andre's arm, his black claws digging into his skin. Andre walked the bird out to the balcony and set it down on the railing, then came back inside and closed the balcony doors.

Despite the oppressive heat, I felt like I could breathe easier. I closed my eyes and slid down the wall. One problem solved, the other walked back to my side.

His boots came to a stop inches from my feet.

I couldn't seem to raise my head to look at him. I could run an entire property, manage hundreds of people, have all the confidence in the world in a business meeting, but I had no idea what to say to this man who was not supposed to know Toni well enough to realize I wasn't her.

He crouched in front of me, his hands hanging loosely between his knees. "I just wanna know that my friend is OK," he pleaded in a much calmer tone, "and who the hell you are, because . . ."

I lifted my head to look at him. "It's uncanny, right?"

"Unbelievable." He shook his head as his eyes took in every

inch of my face.

"She said you didn't know her well enough to pick up on it."

"Of course she did." He chuckled. "Toni has a massive chip on her shoulder, and she doesn't like to get too close to anyone or admit she gives a shit about anything, but she's hardworking and smart and kind . . . when she wants to be. I've seen her nurse a damn feral street cat back to health after it got into a fight with another cat *and* kick a guy in the nuts for hassling a girl at the bar in the same day."

We both chuckled. I could see her doing that.

"My point is, she may like to keep her walls up, but I know she'd have my back if I needed her to. I'm just trying to have hers now." He shrugged.

I leaned my head back against the wall and took a deep breath. The panic was subsiding, even though it shouldn't have been. I was busted on my second day. I had no idea what Andre would do next, but there was something inherently calming about him. Maybe that was why Toni, a self-confessed antisocial loner, had stuck with him for so many years.

"Are you in love with her?" It seemed like the logical conclusion.

He laughed lightly, his eyes sparkling with genuine amusement, before dragging his hand down his face. "Nah. I care about her, but not like that."

I wasn't sure I believed him, but I had no doubt he was worried about her.

"Now, you gonna answer any of my questions," he pressed, "or just keep asking them?"

"Fine." I sighed and stretched my legs out in front of me. He sat down, one leg bent on the floor, the other propped up.

"My name is Alex." I'd insisted on the full Alexandria my whole life, and I had no idea why I was suddenly introducing myself with the nickname Toni had slapped me with.

"Nice to meet you, Alex." He gave me a genuine smile I couldn't help returning.

"You too. I don't really know where to start." I rubbed my palms down the front of my shorts.

"The beginning?"

I gave him a withering look and sighed. "Honestly, Toni and I only just met a couple of days ago. In the alleyway behind the bar."

"Oh, you're the mystery person she was yelling at."

"One and the same. Obviously we noticed our . . . similarities." I figured I had nothing to lose, so I told him the whole story. If he lost it and blew the plan up, we'd just switch back; Oren didn't need to know. It had been a fun day at least. Not quite the month I was hoping for but better than nothing.

He didn't interrupt except to ask a few clarifying questions. He just sat next to me and listened to the whole crazy tale. I kept it as short as possible, but I didn't hold anything back, not even my embarrassing panic attack.

"I can't believe she agreed to this." He shook his head in bewilderment.

"Honestly, neither can I. I think she mostly did it for the money."

"Are you sure that's the only reason?" He narrowed his eyes.

"You're not threatening her or . . . something?"

"No," I snapped. "I would never do that. I was always going to do my best to convince her, but I'm not a monster."

He held his hands up. "Hey, I don't know you. You may have my friend's face, but you could be a psychopath for all I know."

I shrugged. "Well, I don't know what I can say to convince you otherwise. What are you going to do?"

"What do you mean?"

"Are you going to tell? Ruin this for us?"

"For you, you mean?"

I crossed my arms. "Yes, it was my idea, and yes, I had to convince her, but make no mistake—Toni is going to benefit from this too. I think we both know she doesn't do anything she doesn't want to. So are you going to ruin this for us or not?"

He studied me, those dark eyes feeling like they were peeling back layer after layer, digging right down to my soul.

Finally, he pushed himself to his feet. "I don't know yet. I need to speak to Toni."

I got up too. "Fair enough. I'll get my phone."

I pulled it off the charger by the bed, but by the time I turned to face him, he already had his held up to his ear. I rolled my eyes and went to gather the groceries that had ended up on the floor in the hallway, then deposited the food in the fridge.

"No answer," he announced.

"Yeah, she's probably busy pretending to be me."

"Yeah, well, until I speak to her and confirm that, I can't promise anything."

"What's with the hostility?" I leaned back on the counter. He'd listened, been kind to me a moment ago. "I told you the whole sordid truth. It's not my fault she's not picking up."

"I just can't take your word for it. I'm sorry." His harsh tone softened again, but his expression remained determined. "I need to speak with her myself and make sure she's OK. And if I don't in the next few hours, I'm calling the police. In the meantime, don't go anywhere." He pointed one big finger at me, the rest still wrapped around his phone.

I huffed. "I'm not going anywhere. I have a shift in a few hours."

"No. Toni has a shift. And you better hope she backs your story up, because all you have otherwise is a date with the boys in blue."

He stormed out, the glass rattling dangerously in the door. I ran my hands through my hair and texted Toni.

There was nothing I could do other than show Andre I was trustworthy. That meant staying in that oven of an apartment and making sure Toni returned his call.

I went to the balcony doors but flinched back when I spotted Kennedy still perched on the railing, watching me with his beady eyes. With a sigh, I stripped down to my underwear and focused on making lunch, texting and trying to call Toni myself.

This was worse than waiting to hear if I'd gotten into Harvard Business School. Which I did, so I had to have faith this would work out in my favor too.

Toni finally replied as I finished eating lunch, but then I had to wait with bated breath for the result of her conversation with Andre. I hated being out of the loop.

They kept me waiting for another whole hour, but at least Kennedy flew off with a loud screech, and I was able to open the balcony doors and let in some air. I lay on the bed and fanned myself. Just as I was thinking I should put some clothes on for when the police came to drag me away, my phone went off. I groaned and sat up slowly, reaching for it, but then someone pounded on the door.

I walked halfway to the door and paused.

"Alex?" Andre's booming voice called from the other side. "I spoke to Toni."

His tone wasn't giving anything away. I moved closer to the door. "And?"

"And I don't like it, but it's her damn life, so who am I to tell her what to do with it?"

That wasn't exactly reassuring. He could still just throw me out of his bar and his apartment if he wanted to.

"What does that mean?" I pressed my hand against the glass.

"Means you can stay." His sigh was audible even through the door. "I'll keep your secret."

I gasped, grinning like an idiot, my heart soaring with excitement.

I wrenched the door open and launched myself at the man standing on the other side—the man agreeing to give me my month of freedom. Wrapping my arms around his neck, I practically shouted in his ear, "Thank you! Oh my god, thank you so much!"

His hands went to my back, pulling me closer as he chuckled. "You're welcome." His breath stirred the hair at the side of my face.

He pressed his cheek to mine, and I reflexively rubbed against his stubble, the prickles sending a warm tickling sensation down my neck and chest.

His right hand shifted lower—only a fraction of an inch, but enough for his fingers to brush the top of my panties, enough for me to realize I was hugging a stranger in my damn underwear! My heart thudded in my chest, and I pulled back, but then our eyes met, and I forgot what I was doing.

"But I have conditions," he finally said, his lips inches from mine.

"Conditions?"

His eyes flicked to my lips, then back up to my eyes, then back down, lower. When he looked up again, they widened. "You should probably get dressed first."

He cleared his throat and turned those mesmerizing, distracting eyes up to the ceiling, but his hands were still at my back, holding me against him.

"Oh my god!" Mortified, I stepped out of his arms and rushed back into the apartment, slamming the door.

"Uh, why don't you get dressed and come down to the bar. There's no one around. We can talk." He walked away without waiting for a response.

I stood with my back against the wall, listening to his heavy footfalls and trying to catch my breath. I was hot, but I was also *hot and bothered*. I couldn't stop thinking about how good he smelled, how hard his chest was against my breasts, how his touch made me feel both grounded and like I was seconds away from being taken to new heights. His hands were big and strong. What would it have felt like if he'd kept moving them down, over my ass, under my panties, his big fingers sliding inside . . . ?

I shook my head and locked the door, heading for the bathroom and a cold shower before I made my way downstairs.

Andre was very polite, not bringing up our moment in the hallway as he ran me through his chat with Toni.

His few conditions were perfectly reasonable. He wanted me not to slack off on Toni's shifts at the bar, as he couldn't afford to look for someone else on such short notice; he wanted Toni to check in with him every few days; and he wanted a promise from both of us that should either one decide she felt uncomfortable or unsafe, we'd shut it down.

I readily agreed. These were things Toni and I had already discussed.

We spent a bit of time chatting about inconsequential things, and before long it was time to get to work.

Loretta showed up and cracked a joke about me being out of bed before she'd fired up the grill. "Can't remember that ever happening!" She laughed and coughed as she disappeared into the kitchen.

Andre and I exchanged a look and a silent laugh. Having someone to share the secret with was really nice. It wasn't how I'd planned for this to play out, but I was supposed to be having a break from my planned, regimented, obligatory life, so I chose to embrace it.

My body was still sore, but Andre helped me restock the

fridges and quietly instructed me on a few other things anyone working behind a bar should already know. The other wait staff didn't take long to arrive—both casuals whose names I didn't know—and Andre managed the bar seamlessly, giving them the more complex tasks and getting me to do things that wouldn't make it so obvious I had no idea what I was doing.

The Cottonmouth filled up as night fell, and one of the casuals came behind the bar with a tray of empty glasses. "Band's here!" she announced and turned to take an order.

Andre smiled and rushed around the bar to greet them. I couldn't see much through the crowd, but he stayed with the band as they set up. I caught several glimpses of him speaking to a guy in ripped jeans and a black vest over a white T-shirt, tattoos covering his entire right arm. They joked and chatted with an ease that indicated closeness, even intimacy.

"You do something to piss him off?" the blonde casual asked.

"What? Who?" I turned my attention to her. She was pouring drinks while I unstacked glasses from the dishwasher tray.

"Andre. He's got you bussing tables, and you keep throwing him weird looks. What'd you do?"

"What? I'm not throwing anyone any weird looks. Everything's fine." I smiled, but my eyes once again drifted to Andre through the crowd.

"Fine. Keep your secrets." She gave me a pointed look and turned to take another order.

The bar was getting busier as the band started to check their instruments, and I had to take a few orders. Thankfully, they were mostly just beer and easy to handle.

I closed the till and looked up. The guy Andre had been speaking to stood in front of me on the other side of the bar.

He wasn't as bulky as Andre, but he wasn't skinny either. He was lean, the fabric of his T-shirt clinging in all the right places to show off the lines of his toned body. Several leather necklaces hung around his neck, which displayed another tattoo along the side. Where else did he have ink? I had the distinct urge to find out with a thorough examination.

My encounter with Andre must've still had me worked up. I forced a smile to hide the lust in my gaze.

His eyes met mine, the color indiscernible in the low light, and he scowled. With a tilt of his head, he leaned forward on the bar, challenge joining the disdain already present in his expression. He had brown hair—short at the sides and long and messy on top. Several stud earrings sparkled in his left ear, and a ring through the middle of his bottom lip caught the light as he moved.

The look he was giving me threw me off guard; it seemed like he wanted to throw a beer in my face.

"I got this." Andre appeared beside me. He gripped my hips loosely as he shuffled behind me to my other side, then they both proceeded to ignore me. Confused, I frowned and turned to take another order.

Things really picked up then, and there wasn't time to ask Andre what his friend's problem was. But when the band started playing, all thoughts of what an asshole he was left my brain.

They started with a cover of "Rescue Me," but it sounded

almost nothing like OneRepublic's hit. It was still up-tempo and full of energy, but the new rock arrangement gave a whole new, deeper meaning to the lyrics.

Tattooed asshole was lead singer and guitarist, and his voice was like sex. Every grunt into the microphone, every smooth note made heat shoot down my spine almost as intensely as Andre's hands had in the hallway.

All night I couldn't keep my eyes off him. I'm sure I looked like a lunatic, staring at the stage every chance I got. He kept meeting my gaze.

Every time our eyes met, his would narrow.

As the night started to wind down, the band packed up. On their way out, the lead singer paused by the bar. He reached over and did a sideways high five followed by a fist bump with Andre. Then with the same hand, he pointed at me. "Nice try with the crazy eyes." He flipped the hand to give me the middle finger, walking backward toward the door. "Didn't work."

He flashed a cruel grin—perfectly straight teeth and that piercing digging into his bottom lip. As he turned, he punctuated his perplexing words by calling me a bitch over his shoulder.

I propped my hands on my hips and ground my teeth. What the hell had Toni done to piss this guy off? I hoped to hell it had nothing to do with a romantic past. It would be too weird if we slept with the same guy.

I shook my head and stormed into the bathroom for a breather. Why was I even thinking about sleeping with someone who'd just called me a bitch?

A: We have a problem! I need you to call me ASAP!

A: Toni?

A: TONI!!!

A: This is serious! Call me NOW!

T: Fuck! What? I'm having brunch with your boo. I can't exactly talk right now.

A: We're busted!

T: WHAT?

T: How?

A: Andre! He clearly knows you way better than you think. He had me figured out in the first 24 hours. Now he's demanding to speak with you or he'll call the police.

T: Shit! OK, I'll call him as soon as I can get away.

T: How did this happen?

A: Oh, I don't know . . .

A: Maybe because you failed to mention that you have a GIANT FUCKING BIRD THAT LIKES TO LET ITSELF INTO YOUR APARTMENT???

T: LOL! What does Ken have to do with anything?

A: I have a fear of birds. He scared the absolute crap out of me. Andre saw the whole thing.

T: Hahahahahahahaha!

A: Not funny.

T: It's a little funny.

Chapter 7

TONI

Wearing one of Alex's white swimsuits, a wide-brimmed hat, and some sheer linen thing George had referred to as "resort wear," I made my way out to the pool. I'd given George shit for even knowing what "resort wear" was, but if I was being honest, he had saved my ass several times. It was as if he was constantly hovering just out of view, waiting to jump in and provide some bit of information I didn't have or pretend he needed to speak with me.

Since Alex's panicked message and a very long conversation with Andre, I'd come to realize I maybe had more people in my corner than I originally thought. It was nice to know but also a little scary.

Taking care of myself was so much easier. And it was even easier in the lap of luxury.

I picked a lounger in the shade and removed the sheer thing, settling into the chair. Even the towels at this place were thick and soft. I wondered if anyone would notice if I took a few when I went.

Other than the few times George had intervened and saved my ass, the past few days had been going great. The Winthrops were busy people, and I'd only seen Oren's parents a handful of times in passing. I, on the other hand, had nothing better to do than take full advantage of a life of luxury.

A servant delivered the Bloody Mary I'd asked for on a silver tray.

I smiled at the young man. "Thank you."

He nodded and disappeared.

In the past few days, I'd tried on every article of clothing Alex had packed—it was more than I owned—every piece of jewelry, even the multiple pairs of heels.

I'd tested out the devotion of the hired help by ordering the most pompous things I could think of at all hours of the day. Caviar, lobster, champagne, truffle pasta, and strawberries dipped in Swiss chocolate were all delivered with a smile and without any question or complaint.

I'd taken baths in the ridiculous tub, wandered around the house looking at artwork that probably cost a fortune. I'd gone into every room I didn't think I'd find another person in and confirmed the only television was in the tucked-away lounge Oren had pointed out.

I'd discovered the library—they had a *fucking library*—on the third day and decided to fill my time with reading.

I opened the thriller I was halfway through and sipped on the Bloody Mary while wishing for a cigarette. I'd been cutting down. A lot. Having fewer was easier when you were worried about someone busting you. I smoked almost only at night at my open window, but it was still damn hard.

I refocused on the book, trying to keep my mind off nicotine, and managed to get engrossed in it. Dropping the now empty glass on the side table, I turned the page, but the sound of the door opening made me look up.

Oren strode toward the pool area from a side door I knew led to the fully equipped gym. I was giving that particular area of the house a wide berth.

"Good morning." He smiled and waved from the other side of the pool.

"Morning." I waved back.

He was in shorts and a tank, his breathing a little labored, his hairline sweaty.

"I hope you don't mind the intrusion." He unfurled a jump rope. "I'm going to be cooped up in meetings all day—thought I might take advantage of the sunshine and finish my workout outside."

"Of course!" I gave him a wide smile and lifted my book before mumbling under my breath, "It's your giant house. Do whatever the fuck you want." I just wanted to be left alone, but what was I supposed to say?

He picked a spot on the paved area. The steady rhythm of the rope hitting the ground grated on my nerves, and I was glad he couldn't see me roll my eyes behind the dark sunglasses.

What the hell was he doing out here anyway? If there was one thing I'd learned about Oren Winthrop, it was that he was a creature of habit.

He got up at precisely six—I knew because, despite the property's grandeur, the old plumbing was loud and creaky—took a shower, went down to breakfast, worked for an hour. By this point I'd gotten up, unable to get back to sleep after being woken by the loud pipes, and had to walk past his office to get to the kitchen. Then he made his way down to the gym and exercised for one hour before getting dressed and either working in his office or leaving to do whatever the fuck it was he did.

Dude ran his life like clockwork; I was beyond shocked to see him breaking his routine.

It may have still been morning, but the heat was already rising, making me contemplate having a dip. And I was just reading in the shade. I couldn't imagine how hot he had to be jumping like that.

He must've had the same thought, because he stopped, dropped the rope, and took his shirt off. After depositing the sweaty garment on the ground, he picked the rope up again and got back to work.

I hadn't read a word of my book since he'd come out, but I kept it up in front of my face as I watched him.

I had to hand it to him—the guy was ripped. Every muscle in his body clenched and rolled as he jumped faster and faster.

His face was pure focus, his lips parted. The skin of his defined shoulders and abs fucking glistened with sweat in the morning sun. He even had that V so many men wished for, pointing to the promised land. Er . . . some other chick's promised land. Not mine. I wasn't into privileged guys with control issues and ridiculously ripped bodies.

Even his hair looked good, the auburn waves bouncing, a sweaty strand falling over his forehead. He clenched his teeth, punishing his body, and I wondered if he ever made that face during sex.

I slammed my book shut. That was quite enough of that. Clearly I needed to get laid. It had been well over a week since the blond who'd tried to take me out for Cajun eggs, and that didn't even count since I couldn't remember most of it.

The hat and sunglasses joined the book on the side table, and I waded into the pool. I ducked my head under, letting the cool water distract me from my lascivious thoughts. Thoughts that had nothing to do with Oren fucking Winthrop. Nope, I was just horny and projecting it onto the perfect specimen of male beauty jumping rope.

I emerged in the middle of the pool and took a big gulp of air.

From this vantage point, I could see his junk bouncing in his shorts. I averted my gaze immediately, swimming to the other side of the pool. The rhythmic *whoosh-thwack* of the jump rope suddenly stopped, and a splash had me turning back around.

He had dived in and was shooting through the water. When he emerged near me, he was breathing hard from the cardio. His hair looked darker wet, but the morning sun was also bringing out some of the natural red hues in it.

"Good workout?" I asked, looking for something to fill the silence.

"Yeah," he panted.

"You usually go that hard?"

"No. Sometimes. I had something to work through." His breathing was calming down quickly. He lazily swam over to my side, and we both propped our elbows on the edge.

"I hope it's nothing too serious." I didn't actually give a shit. What kind of problems could a guy with that much money have?

"Every problem has a solution." He smiled, his gaze on an ant making its way across the pavers, inches from our faces.

Cryptic much? I resisted the urge to roll my eyes.

After a beat of silence, he turned his gaze to me. "How are you enjoying your stay? I'm sorry I haven't had more time to spend with you."

"Oh, that's OK. I've been taking full advantage of this pool."

He nodded. "Honestly, I'm surprised you haven't been cooped up inside working more. I was under the impression . . . If I'd known, I wouldn't have packed my work schedule so tightly."

Shit! Of course Alex was a workaholic; there was no way she would've been having as much leisure time as me. "I'm doing what needs to be done." Great. Now I was being cryptic. "But I have very reliable people, and honestly, it's been nice to slow down a little."

"Good." He pushed off, floating backward through the cool

water. "In that case, I'd like to take you to dinner."

"Dinner?" *Shit fuck shit!*

"Yes. You know, tablecloths, silverware, food delivered to the table?" Rich boy had some sass.

I turned and cocked a brow. "We have that here. Daily."

He laughed "Yes, but I'd still like to take you out. Show you New Orleans a little. You've never been, right?"

I'd only lived here for eight years. "No. First time."

"It's settled then. The day after tomorrow?"

"Sure." I smiled, hoping it didn't look as tight as it felt. What else was I supposed to do? Alex would've gone, because it was what she needed to do. Maybe I could make an excuse, pretend to be sick or something.

"Perfect!" He swam to the steps leading out of the water and climbed out. The water dripped off him, droplets trickling over defined muscle. I may not have liked the guy, but I could appreciate a fine body when I saw one. His back was as toned as his front, his ass firm and round, and he had those little dimples just above the waistband of his shorts. "Have a great day, Alexandria."

I flicked my gaze up and just caught the knowing grin pulling at his lips before he turned and walked away. I was busted checking him out.

I dipped below the water and resisted the urge to scream. I had to get this shit under control or he'd get the wrong idea, and Alex would skin my ass.

There's nothing like realizing how long it's been since you've had sex to make you constantly think about sex. Oren's little performance in the pool the previous day hadn't helped. I was like a hormonal teenager, the ache between my legs almost constant, the knowledge that I couldn't have something only making me crave it more.

After breakfast, I decided if I couldn't ride a cock to satiate my desire, at least I could ride a horse and have some innocent fun while distracting myself.

As I let myself out the back door, George came around the corner.

"Going riding?" He fell into step with me.

"What gave it away? The riding pants?" I rolled my eyes. Apparently rich people couldn't ride horses in regular pants

He laughed. "Are you always this sarcastic?"

"Probably." I shrugged. "I think it just comes out more with you because I have to rein it in with everyone else here. Also, do you know how fucking hard it is to watch your language when you haven't had to since high school? Sometimes all I want to do is scream 'cunt,' just to get it out of my system."

We both laughed, and then he asked, "Your parents didn't mind you cussing?"

"They did. Before they died. I've been on my own over eight years now."

"Shit." His smile fell. "I knew that. I'm sorry for bringing it up."

"Fucking stalker." I gave him a reassuring smile. "It's fine. But maybe stop stalking me?"

"Too late." He didn't sound even remotely apologetic. "I already know everything a private investigator could've found out."

"Fucking rich people." I shook my head but kept my voice down. We'd nearly reached the stables.

"Toni." He halted me with a hand on my arm, his voice even lower than mine. "How are you handling this? It must be a lot of pressure. Alexandria really wants this, but she wouldn't hesitate to shut it down if you needed to."

And shut down my payday with it. "It's all good, big guy. I'm handling my shit. And Andre already gave me the 'you can back out at any time' spiel." I didn't know why everyone felt the need to tell me I could bail. I was *not* a quitter, and I needed that money.

Jack came out of the stables and waved, cutting off whatever George was about to say. George wiped the frown off his face and folded his hands behind his back.

"Thank you for the update, George," I said a little louder, letting Jack hear.

"Have a good day, miss." George nodded, turned on his heel, and walked back toward the house.

"Good morning." Jack stuffed his hands in his pockets and smiled, his full attention on me.

"Morning." I walked the last few steps to stand in front of him. "I hope I'm not disturbing you."

"Not at all. Ready for a ride?"

I chose not to read a double meaning into his question. "Yes,

I'd love to try if you're not too busy?"

"I'm all yours." His grin definitely had a hint of mischief in it that time, his eyes lingering on mine just a bit longer than what could be considered polite.

"Great." I cleared my throat and walked past him. But of course, he hardly moved, and my shoulder brushed against his chest. He smelled manly—like hard work and a hint of something sweet and musky.

I focused on putting one foot in front of the other, doing my damnedest to ignore the way my nipples hardened.

He overtook me and led the way inside to Honeymustard's stall. She was just as beautiful as the first day I saw her, and she seemed to remember me, nuzzling her head against my hand.

I smiled, cooing, "Should we go for a ride, girl? Would you like that?"

"I'd love that." Jack's voice was almost a whisper. He was standing behind me, one arm coming around to rest on the stall.

"Excuse me?" I paused my pats but didn't turn to look at him.

"I said, I think she'd love that. She loves to go past the exercise yard, and I can't take each one of them out every day." There was no hint of teasing in his voice, but I was positive I'd heard him right the first time. This asshole was looking for trouble. If only I wasn't so attracted to trouble . . .

"Let's get her saddled." He walked away and came back with riding gear in hand, the muscles in his arms straining from the weight. I did my best not to stare.

"You said you haven't ridden in a few years?" he asked as he let himself into the stall.

"Quite a few." I leaned on the wall. "In fact, just pretend I've never been on a horse. Treat me like a total newbie."

"I have a feeling you have more experience than you're letting on." When I didn't respond, he kept speaking. "I mean, riding horses can be like riding bikes—some things you don't forget. It'll come back to you once you get goin'."

"I hope so." I smiled, getting excited despite the struggle to contain the sexual tension between us. I had to keep telling myself to behave.

When Honeymustard was ready, he placed a block next to her, and I climbed up, swinging my leg over. He laid an unnecessary hand on my waist to steady me—I didn't waver. His hand lingered on my ankle as he adjusted the height of the stirrups, then came dangerously close to my ass as he fiddled with the saddle.

It took all I had to keep my poker face on, to not let it show that I wanted him to drag that hand up from my ankle, over my knee to my inner thigh.

I shook my head to clear it as Jack took the reins and led Honeymustard out of the stables. For the next fifteen minutes, the sexual tension eased, and his passion for his work shone through. He talked me through how to pull on the reins to get Honeymustard to go where I wanted her to, told me when to take more control and when to let her do what came naturally, warned me that she liked to stop and snack on every bush she could get close to, so I'd have to move her along firmly. He reminded me how to bounce up and down in the saddle in rhythm with her movements, then let me practice while he got her into a trot around the fenced yard.

A massive smile split my face when I got it. The few times I'd gone riding with my friend as a preteen were coming back to me, my body remembering how to move.

"See? You're a natural." Jack beamed at me from under his cowboy hat. I couldn't help smiling back.

"All right, let's go for a ride." His voice dropped a little and his eyes narrowed—the flirt was back. He ran back into the stables and came out moments later riding Benson.

I followed him out of the gate and rode out toward the back of the property, alternating between a leisurely pace and a trot—when Honeymustard didn't get distracted by delicious bush snacks.

"How big is this place?" I asked as the house disappeared behind us.

"Around ten thousand acres." Jack looked so natural on horseback, his body moving with the animal so seamlessly it was like poetry in motion. "Didn't your fiancé tell you about it?"

"He didn't mention it," I said, then kicked myself. Maybe he did—to the actual Alex. I quickly added, "Or I forgot. We've had a lot to discuss lately."

"Oh?" Jack kept his focus on the path ahead, but he was listening intently.

The motion of the horse under me, the sun poking through the trees, the birds flitting from one branch to another, the warm fresh air—it all put me at ease, and I nearly said something about negotiating the terms of our marriage as a business contract. But I caught myself and deflected. "What time is it? Should we head back? I'm sure you have work to do. It must be nearly lunch."

OK, so I rambled more than deflected, but it worked . . . kind of. He dropped that track of conversation but picked something much more dangerous to put my focus on.

"We've got plenty of time." He grabbed Honeymustard's reins and pulled her through a narrow gap in the trees. "I wanna show you somethin'."

I had to duck as we passed under a low branch and leaves brushed against my arms.

We emerged into a clearing that led down to a slow spot in a small river. Crystal clear water ran over rocks and glistened in the sun, and colorful wildflowers near the edge of the trees climbed twenty or so feet into the air, blocking the rest of the river from view as it curved around.

The scene was picturesque, untouched.

Jack got off Benson and came to stand next to me. "Beautiful, isn't it?" He patted Honeymustard's rump gently, his chest bumping my leg.

"It's stunning," I breathed. The sun was climbing higher in the sky, bringing more heat with it, and the water looked so inviting.

"Mr. Winthrop wouldn't even know it was here." Just a hint of a hard edge sharpened his tone. "We're at the very edge of the property. The other side of the river belongs to someone else. I don't think he's even been out of sight of the main house."

I cleared my throat, wishing I'd brought a bottle of water.

"Want some help getting down?" He smiled up at me, his eyes crinkling from the bright sun, his tone light and friendly.

"Uh, no thank you." I shifted in the saddle. He must've thought I was about to get down myself, because he backed away.

"*Hoowee*, it's hot! I'm goin' for a dip," he called over his shoulder as he whipped his T-shirt off over his head, heading for the river.

He had a massive backpiece—a horse rearing up, the artwork so beautifully done I could see the movement, the detail in the animal's body and mane, even from this distance.

Jack toed his shoes and pants off at the edge of the water and waded in in his underwear, diving under and emerging facing me. He flicked his hair, the water flying, and gave me a brilliant grin. "You comin' in?"

His eyes narrowed just slightly, flicked down to my chest for a split second. I was breathing hard, my mouth open.

I was thirsty. I wasn't entirely sure what I wanted more—to cool off in the river, have a long drink of it, or have Jack . . .

I cut that thought off and made myself square my shoulders.

"I have to head back," I called and turned Honeymustard just like he'd shown me.

I didn't wait for his reaction, didn't give myself a chance to give in to my desire. I set a quick pace down the same path we'd come, every bounce in the saddle reminding me of the ache between my legs.

T: Did you know that they have a chef on call 24/7 here??

A: Yes, I told you that, didn't I?

T: And there's a pool and the AC is always on!

A: OK?

T: Is this what it's like to stay in a fancy hotel with room service? Except you don't have to pay for the room service when you check out?

A: haha! I guess.

T: BTW all your clothes fit me perfectly.

A: Of course they do. We're identical.

A: Wait! Why were you trying on all my clothes?

T: *shrug I was bored.

T: Man, this place is amazing!

A: I'm glad you're having a good time :)

T: I bet their heat's never even gone out in winter.

A: ??? Why would their heat go out?

T: When we couldn't afford to pay the gas on time, they'd cut the gas. No gas, no heat. It's one of the reasons I moved south after my parents died. Winters aren't so harsh.

A: Shit, Toni. That's awful.

T: Happens more than you realize, princess. All over the country.

T: Hey, you get laid yet?

A: OMG! No.

T: WTF are you waiting for?!

Chapter 8

ALEX

After the dramatic start to my life as Toni Mathers—aloof bar chick with intimacy issues and a mysterious past—it was a relief to settle into a kind of routine.

The jerk who'd called me a bitch hadn't been back with his band, but Andre had a different live show on almost every night. With his help, I started to get the hang of this bartending thing and even learned how to make a few cocktails. On the rare occasion someone ordered wine, I was all over it.

The aches and pains from suddenly doing so much physical work were constant, but after a day off, they started to feel a bit better. I was too exhausted to be up before midday most days, but I made the most of it.

I checked in with my mother daily, feeding her the bare minimum of information, loosely based on Toni's text updates about what I was supposedly doing with the Winthrops. I also spent a few hours each day working—returning emails, making sure everything was OK at the winery, keeping the debt collectors at bay. But George helped with that too, and my property manager was fantastic, so I was mostly free to enjoy my taste of freedom.

I put on one of the few dresses I'd found in Toni's closet. It was emerald-green light cotton with lace skulls all over it, but it went OK with her sandals. Pulling my hair back into a ponytail, I reminded myself to get more green tea from the corner store on the way back from my walk. In my spare time, I was exploring the neighborhood—enjoying the little voodoo shop I'd discovered a couple of blocks over, the balconies with ferns hanging off that seemed to be a staple of half the buildings in the area, the market near the bus station that had the juiciest oranges I'd ever tasted.

A knock sounded on the glass door. I took another bite of my toast and opened it to find Andre on the other side, dressed casually in jeans and a T-shirt, his feet in high-tops. He was freshly shaven, had probably just gotten out of the shower—I could detect the fresh smell mingling with his cologne and resisted the urge to lean forward and take a deep breath.

I swallowed my bite of toast. "Hello, Andre. What can I do for you?"

He chuckled. "You're so fucking polite. I don't know how I didn't pick up on it immediately."

I frowned "Why is that bad?"

"It's not. It's actually kind of refreshing."

I just eyed him with suspicion and took the last bite of my toast.

"So I noticed you've been wandering around the neighborhood." He leaned in the doorway and crossed his arms over his chest, making the biceps pop out even more.

"That's not a crime, is it?"

"Not at all." He chuckled again. Why did he keep laughing at me? "I was actually wondering if maybe you wanted to see some of New Orleans past this neighborhood."

"Yes, I'd love that." I crossed the room and closed the balcony doors, suddenly feeling awkward about admitting why exactly I couldn't explore farther, but I'd promised Andre I'd be honest with him. "I can't exactly afford it. With my current financial situation, I'm stretched to my limits, and I don't feel right using any of Toni's money. So I'm just making the best of it." I finished straightening the sheets on the bed and turned to face him, putting a bright smile on my face.

He watched me for a beat. "I can understand that. Admire it even. You know what? You've been working damn hard these past few days. Harder than Toni does half the time." There was that deep, sexy chuckle again; this time I laughed with him. "How about I show you around? Would you like to see the French Quarter?"

"I would *love* to see the French Quarter. But I can't ask you to do that."

"You're not asking. I'm offering. The bar's closed tonight, so it's not like we have to rush back. I've got the afternoon free, and

I'm craving beignets anyway. Plus, I figure I should get to know you if you're hanging around for a while."

"Beignets?"

"Yeah. Those fluffy pastry things covered in sugar. Really bad for you, but really damn delicious. We could even get some coffee while we're at it."

"I don't drink coffee."

He rolled his eyes. "So get an iced tea. Are you coming or what?" He raised his eyebrows expectantly and gave me another tempting smile.

I chewed on my bottom lip, hesitating, but I really did want to see more of New Orleans, and his invitation seemed genuine. I grabbed my bag off the bed. "All right then, let's go."

The bright sun beamed down on us, though it wasn't as startlingly hot as it had been recently. It was a perfect afternoon for a walk, but we didn't walk far. Andre led the way to a bus station, waving and yelling hello at several people he knew along the way. He bought tickets for us both and pointed things out through the window as we took the twenty-minute trip into the French Quarter.

When we got off in a busy section, I couldn't keep the smile off my face. I loved to travel, and up until a year ago, when the extent of our financial issues became apparent, I'd done it as often as possible.

Something about the charm and atmosphere of New Orleans reminded me of certain European cities, but it still had a unique energy. Every once in a while, the sound of a big band would come drifting on the breeze, making me want to chase it until I found the parade.

"You hungry?" Andre asked as he took the lead down a narrow street.

I shrugged. "I could eat." As we navigated the busy streets, I realized I was actually ravenous and had only been distracted from it by the sights and sounds.

We emerged on a main street lined with stores and restaurants. Andre took a left, then opened the door to a little hole-in-the-wall restaurant. It was basic, with stiff chairs and linoleum floors, but packed, not a free table in sight.

"Andre Stevelo?" A short woman with dreadlocks down to her waist came out from behind the counter. She enveloped him in a hug, her stubby arms wrapping around his middle. He was nearly twice her height.

She released him and whacked him in the stomach. "You never come to see me. Where have you been? Sit down, I'll make you lunch," she said in a Creole accent, shuffling us into stools at the counter. As we settled in, she asked Andre a million questions, which he answered in rapid succession.

"And who's this?" She nodded in my direction. "She's pretty."

Andre laughed. "This is Alexandria. And yes, she is pretty."

I bugged my eyes out at him, ignoring the fact that he'd just called me pretty and focusing entirely on the fact that he'd used my real name.

"Relax," he leaned in to whisper. "No one here has met Toni."

I breathed a sigh. "It's nice to meet you." I smiled at the old lady, who was busy throwing food together behind the counter.

She deposited a plate in front of each of us and fixed me with a serious look. "I like you, but you're too skinny. Eat." She ended on a big grin and then turned back around, getting back to running her restaurant.

The plain white plate contained nothing but a white bread roll, overflowing with fillings. Andre was already devouring his in giant bites. "Best damn po' boys in the city," he said around a mouthful. "Eat."

"I'm not too skinny," I mumbled into my full breasts, Toni's dress showing more cleavage than I was used to.

Andre swallowed his massive bite, his shoulders shaking with laughter. "Don't mind Delphine. She's . . . eccentric."

"How do you know her?"

"She used to be friends with my mama."

"Used to?"

"My mama died when I was in high school, my daddy just after I turned twenty-one. I think that's why I was so hell-bent on helping Toni—I know how isolating it is to lose parents. Suddenly, the people you're supposed to be able to rely on are gone, and you have to make your own way in the world."

I didn't miss the fact that he said "supposed to" and not the people you *do* rely on, but I chose not to push it. I just gave him a glimpse of my own pain. "I lost my dad in my early twenties too. Very suddenly."

For a moment we just stared at each other, understanding exactly what the other person was feeling. Then Andre cleared his throat and got back to his meal.

I picked up my own sandwich, took a bite, and lost the next ten minutes of time, my full focus on the deliciousness assaulting my taste buds. The bread was crispy but feather soft on the inside, the roast beef tender, the pickles bursting with flavor.

We left with shouted goodbyes to Delphine and Andre's promises to come back soon and "bring the pretty girl" with him.

"All right." Andre clapped his hands together on the sidewalk outside. "I promised beignets."

I groaned. "I don't know if I have room."

"How about a walk first? There's a market nearby."

I nodded and he led the way. We wandered slowly through the covered market area. Food stalls lined one wall, and stalls selling everything from magnets to clothing to jewelry made from spoon handles spread out along the rest of the area. We stopped at several stalls, Andre chatting to the vendors as if he knew them, joking and goofing around while I admired the wares.

At the end of the market, Andre pointed down the street at what looked like a cafe with a massive outdoor seating area. "Beignets?" He practically bounced on his toes, his anticipation palpable.

I rolled my eyes. "Fine. Lead the way."

We ordered and found a spot in the shade of an umbrella. I was only planning to have a taste, just one little puffy sweet treat, but when I tasted the sugary goodness, I couldn't seem to stop. Before I knew it, the whole plate of beignets was gone.

I leaned back in my chair and rubbed my belly like a pregnant lady, breathing hard. Andre sipped his coffee, watching me with an amused expression.

"What?" I narrowed my eyes but couldn't hold back the smile.

"Nothing." He shrugged, a teasing grin on his face.

"They were really good, OK?"

He threw his hands up. "I didn't say anything." He took another sip of his coffee, trying to rein in his laughter.

"Thank you for bringing me here. I really appreciate it."

"You're welcome." He nodded. "Alex. Why are you doing this?"

"What do you mean?"

"The swap. Why pretend? Why not just take a vacation or say you won't marry the guy? You obviously don't want to."

I sighed and thought about how to answer such a complicated question. "Can't afford a vacation." I shrugged. "Yes, I come from an old, rich family, but the debts are at breaking point. The money I used to get here was the last we had, the hotel was booked using loyalty points, and my credit cards are starting to get canceled. And that's exactly why I can't not marry the guy."

"Because of money?" He tried to keep the disgust off his face, but it leaked in.

I resisted the urge to get defensive. "Yes, the arrangement comes with a substantial amount of money, but it's not about me wanting to maintain a luxury lifestyle. I'm trying to save my business, my family's legacy, generations of history, dozens of jobs and livelihoods. A lot of people are depending on me to sort this mess out. I can't let them down."

He frowned at the table. "I'm sorry. I didn't . . ."

"It's OK. I know how it looks. That's why no one outside our immediate families knows. The point of this trip was for Oren and me to meet each other, keep up appearances so the engagement looks genuine to anyone looking in. But at the end of the month, nothing will have changed, regardless of how well I know Oren or how much I like him—I still have to marry him. So yes, it may be crazy, but I saw Toni and saw a reprieve in a face identical to mine. You know I haven't had a panic attack since moving into her loft?"

"You get panic attacks?"

"Since my dad died. I'm under an immense amount of pressure. Sometimes it gets to me." I didn't usually tell people that—actually, I did my best to keep it secret for fear of seeming like a weak, emotional woman in a male-dominated business world.

We sat in silence for a few moments. He must've come to some sort of conclusion, because his next question shifted the conversation to a lighter topic.

"OK, so what's the plan? What do you want to do with the rest of your freedom?" He gave me a brilliant smile.

"I don't know." I laughed. "Exploring New Orleans and having a break from being me is more than enough. Toni keeps telling me I should 'fuck' someone." I put air quotes around the curse word.

He barked out a laugh. "Yeah, that sounds like Toni." Then after a pause, "Maybe you should."

"Should what? Sleep with someone?"

He shrugged. "Why not? I mean, you want a break from your life and want to live Toni's for a while. Let loose. It's what she'd do. It's what she does most nights."

I rolled my eyes but indulged him. "Who would I even . . ." I didn't want to say it again.

"Fuck?" He raised his brows, clearly amused at my discomfort with the word.

I squared my shoulders and sat up straight. This was ridiculous. I was a grown-ass woman. "Yes. I don't even know who I'd fuck."

Andre leaned forward on the table and fixed me with a perplexing look, something between mischievous and suggestive, skirting the edge of intense. "Who do you want to fuck?"

I swallowed, unable to look away from his mesmerizing eyes, and rubbed my thighs together to ease the sudden pressure between my legs.

After another excruciating moment, he flashed me a grin and changed the topic, putting me out of my misery. It made me wonder if he knew the effect he was having on me, if he was maybe even doing it on purpose.

The next day I didn't see Andre until the bar was already open and getting busy. He showed up just as the band arrived, and flashed me a wide grin.

I waved before I had to take another drink order, then turned around just in time to see Ren—one of the casuals had mentioned the asshole's name, solving that mystery—saunter in from the back entrance. The rest of the band followed closely behind, carrying their instruments. Andre and Ren embraced. Andre said a warm hello to the entire band, but his hug with Ren lingered just that little bit longer. There was definitely a story there.

Ren's gaze met mine, and his eyes narrowed into a look of disdain. There was another story I wanted to get to the bottom of. Why did he hate Toni so much?

The night picked up, and the drink orders kept coming in as more people poured into the bar, ready to hear the Thousand Lies play. It didn't take the band very long to set up and do a quick sound check, and then they went straight into the first set. Ren looked like he owned that stage. He looked like sin, bad decisions and eyeliner. He was everything I could never have. That kind of man would never be acceptable for me to be seen with. Maybe that was why I was so inexplicably attracted to him. He was the incarnation of everything my life couldn't be.

But I wasn't living my life. I was living Toni's, so I wasn't going to deny myself the pleasure of watching him play, watching him move across that stage, listening to his velvet voice as it hypnotized everyone in the audience. I let his music move through me as I worked.

The bar was so busy I hardly got a chance to go to the bathroom. Right around the time the band finished their last set, the other bar chick waved me off. "Go have a quick break before it gets nuts again."

I made my way to the back corridor and through the first door, aiming for the storage room. But I accidentally barged into the men's bathroom instead.

My first hint should've been the urinals lining the opposite wall, but that wasn't the first thing I saw. As the door swung closed, my attention went straight to the erect penis pointed at me.

Leaning on the vanity with one hand, his other wrapped around his appendage, was Ren. He was sweaty from his last set, the hair at his temples sticking to his skin, and he was breathing hard.

My mind screamed at me to leave, *go*, but I couldn't seem to make my feet move.

After a beat, Ren cocked his head and looked at me curiously. His hand stilled, but he made no move to cover himself.

For a few tense seconds, we remained in this bizarre standoff, staring at each other. Then my eyes started to move down.

What the hell are you doing? Get out of here! Do not *look at the penis!* My mind tried to talk sense, but I couldn't stop my eyes. They traveled down over the scruff of his chin, past the silver pendants on black leather hanging from his neck, over the graphic print on his too-big tank top and zeroed in on the engorged flesh in his hand. It was maybe a little bigger than average and curved just slightly to the left. A metal piercing shone at the tip.

Seeing something like that usually would have made me wince and wonder how painful it must've been, but all I felt was curiosity. I wanted to touch it, play with it. What would it feel like sliding into me?

"Are you fucking kidding me?" His eyes narrowed, but his hand stayed clamped around his dick. "I don't know what your damn problem is, but you're in the wrong bathroom. And I'm kind of in the middle of something here."

"Uh . . . yes, I see that." My voice was breathy, surprised but maybe also a little intrigued. "What are you doing?"

"What the fuck does it look like I'm doing?" He punctuated his vicious words by completing one long stroke of his cock, up and back down, his eyebrows raised.

I knew I should leave him to whatever bizarre post-performance ritual I'd walked in on, but my body was frozen despite itself. "Just . . . out in the open like this?" I glanced around the empty bathroom.

"Obviously I didn't realize the lock didn't latch properly," he gritted out, then barked, "Either get the fuck out or join in." He started stroking himself again slowly, his eyes narrowed, his smirk pulling at the little piercing in the middle of his lip. He was goading me, fully expecting me to realize what I was doing and leave, horrified.

But it was only yesterday I'd sat around with Andre eating beignets and talking about why I was doing this whole thing in the first place. I'd decided to embrace every impulse, every desire, anything that made my heart race and made me feel free. In this moment, I didn't have to be me. Alexandria would've already run out of the bathroom, but Toni would probably be on her knees with his cock in her mouth.

I wasn't going to leave.

I reached out, flicked the lock on the door, and leaned back against it, meeting the challenge in his gaze with one of my own. His green eyes widened in surprise for only a fraction of a second. I let my eyes roam his body—the sweat around his hairline, the piercings in his face, his eyes hooded with desire—as I reached for the button on my shorts.

I splayed my left hand on the door behind me while my right undid the zip.

Ren's eyes fixed on my right hand as I pushed the fabric down my hips a little.

I didn't let myself think about it. I just slowly pushed my fingers under my underwear. I didn't tease myself with soft strokes—I found my clit and rubbed, my lips parting on a gasp as my eyes half closed.

Ren groaned and licked his lips, his hand moving a little faster.

"I want to see," he ground out, his eyes flashing up to mine. When I paused, they narrowed. "I'm showing you mine, aren't I?"

He jutted his hips forward as if to illustrate his point, making my gaze fall to his dick once again. Precum leaked out of the top, coating half the piercing. I wanted to lick it.

I pushed the shorts and underwear down to my knees, exposing my lower half to a man I didn't know.

Widening my stance as much as the shorts would allow, I put my hand back between my legs. His eyes stayed glued to my hand as I bypassed my clit and spread my folds, moisture saturating my fingers. I stroked myself, teasing my entrance, then inserted two fingers, moaning at the sensation.

Ren groaned. "Fuck." He tightened his grip on the edge of the counter and bent over a little more, the muscles in his arms dancing under all that ink as he pumped himself faster.

I matched his pace with my fingers. I was so wet it was starting to get on my thighs, my fingers sliding in and out effortlessly.

I pulled my fingers out and changed it up, focusing on my clit, rubbing it with firm pressure—the kind of movement only I knew how to get right.

"Show me your tits," Ren demanded, his voice gravelly.

I lifted my top and bra, letting my full breasts out. My nipples were hard. I caressed one breast, pinching the nipple, while I kept my pace up between my legs.

Ren panted as his ravenous eyes took in what my hands were doing. His tongue kept darting out between his parted lips, poking at the piercing every so often. I wanted to bite down on it, take the little piece of metal between my teeth and give it a tug.

Instead, I bit my own bottom lip and banged my head against the door behind me, resting it there and watching him with narrowed eyes.

He was close. His balls were tight, the muscles in his shoulders and arms corded from tension as he jerked his hand faster.

I alternated rubbing my clit with pumping my fingers in and out of my dripping core.

The pressure built from deep inside me, traveling up my chest and down my limbs as I started to moan and writhe against my own touch. My hips gyrated against my hand as I got completely lost in the way Ren was watching me. His gaze was possessive, greedy, his own movements becoming more desperate.

I cried out as my climax washed over me, but I made myself keep my eyes open, watching him. He moaned and grunted, coming mere seconds after me. He threw his head back and cursed, the muscles and tendons in his neck stretching taut as his cum dripped down his hand. Some of it landed on the edge of the counter.

I removed my hand from between my legs and held it out at my side—it was messier than his.

"Beat you to it." I don't know what made me say it, but the words came tumbling out of my mouth on a dark chuckle.

He fixed me with a half-amused, half-frustrated look and shook his head. "You're a twisted bitch."

I wasn't, not really. I was just giving in to every crazy impulse I had. Or maybe I *was* twisted, deep down inside. Who the hell knew anymore?

Ren turned the tap on, washing the cum off his fingers and wiping the rest of the mess up with a paper towel. I took another few moments to catch my breath before pulling my bra and shirt down with my clean hand and shuffling over to the sink next to him.

"Do you do this every time? After playing, I mean," I asked as I pulled my shorts back up.

"This specifically?" He laughed. "No, this is . . . new." Looking me up and down, he dried his hands and threw the wadded-up paper towel into a trashcan. Then he pulled his pants up and leaned back on the wall, running a hand through his messy, sweaty hair. His face was still flushed. "Performing is . . . like no other high in the world. Music is magic, and sometimes, when you get a really good crowd, and you hit every note just right, and everyone in the band just plays together fucking *seamlessly*—it feels really damn good. So no, I don't do this after every gig, but sometimes, after a really good one . . ." He shrugged and pulled a packet of cigarettes out of his pocket.

"You can't smoke in here." I pointed to the cigarette already hanging loosely between his lips.

He took it back out slowly and smirked, his eyes narrowing. "And she's back."

He walked behind me and unlatched the door. "I don't know what the fuck that was"—he gestured in the general direction of the filthy bathroom—"but if *that* Toni ever wants to come out and play again, I'm down." With one more unashamed look up and down my body, he disappeared.

We hadn't even touched, we'd barely spoken, and that very well may have been the dirtiest, most erotic sexual experience of my life.

A: Hey, why does this Ren guy hate you so much?

T: Ugh! Because he's an ass.

A: That's not an answer. What happened between you two?

T: Literally nothing. He just showed up, decided he hates me, and the rest is history.

A: That doesn't sound like the whole story.

T: *shrugs That's how it went down. Doesn't matter anyway. Just steer clear of him. It's what I do. He won't even notice anything is different through his hate haze.

A: Right! Yes! OK! Good plan!

T: ??? Are you having a seizure? What's with all the exclamation points?

A: Nothing. I have to go!

T: WAIT! I need help.

A: What did you do?

T: Why do you immediately assume I did something?

A: TONI!

T: Look, your pooh bear is insisting on taking me out to dinner. Asshole wants to get to know his future wife or some shit. *eyeroll

A: Crap. Don't go. Make an excuse.

T: Can't. He's a persistent fucker. Better get it over with. Just tell me what to say, what not to say, how to behave, and what to do, and I'll be fine.

A: There isn't enough time in the world . . .

T: Oh, ouch! Bitch . . .

A: Hahaha!

T: LOL!

A: Just avoid wine—I know too much about it for you to fake it. Steer clear of politics and religion, and try to keep the focus on him. You'll be fine.

T: Will I though? *squinty eyes

Chapter 9

TONI

The pile of clothes on the bed was growing in direct proportion to my frustration. I groaned and whipped yet another dress off over my head.

Turning to face the mirror, I gave my reflection a disparaging look. "This should not be this fucking difficult," I grumbled. "It's just dinner. With a guy you don't even *like.*"

My hair and makeup were done—not as flawlessly as Alex would've done them, but I'd washed and straightened my hair and applied about half the eye makeup I usually did, and I thought it looked pretty good. I tilted my head, studying my reflection. I really looked like her. Or she looked like me.

I rolled my eyes and turned to the wardrobe—*again*. I didn't have time for another existential crisis. I had to pick a damn dress.

A knock sounded at the door.

"Who is it?" I put on my most polite voice.

"It's George, miss," he answered, just as polite and professional.

I pulled a robe out from the bottom of the clothes pile, sending half the garments tumbling to the floor. The robe was silk with motherfucking lace trim and made me roll my eyes every time I put it on.

I opened the door and pulled George inside. "I need help!"

"Why aren't you dressed?" He propped his hands on his hips. "You're supposed to be leaving for dinner in fifteen minutes."

"What the fuck do you think I need help with?"

He eyed the mess on the bed, then my panicked expression, and snorted, failing miserably to hold back laughter as his eyes crinkled at the corners and his shoulders shook.

"It's not funny, asshole!" I whisper-yelled, and he lost it, letting a peal of laughter loose. I crossed my arms and tapped my bare foot on the timber floor, one eyebrow raised. After a few moments, he calmed himself with a sigh.

"All right, let's see." He rummaged through the pile and then straightened, holding a red piece of fabric. "This one."

I took it and held it out in front of me. It was a knee-length, form-fitting sheath dress with a high neckline.

I gave George a skeptical look. "No. I already tried this one. It seems too plain for dinner. I've tried them all on. *Nothing* is right. How can a person have this many dresses and not a single one of them is right?"

"Put the damn dress on." He wagged a finger at me and exaggeratedly checked his watch. "Ten minutes."

I gritted my teeth. "Fine." I stomped into the wardrobe and pulled the dress on. When I came back out, he was at the dresser, a pair of gold heels in one hand while the other rummaged through the jewelry.

He turned in my direction as I stepped in front of the mirror. It was a nice dress—a deep, rich red and made of a thick silky material. When George pulled the zip up all the way, I saw how well it hugged my curves. But it was still too plain. It looked like something you'd wear with sensible shoes and a tight bun to an office job.

"Put these on." George dropped the flashy shoes in front of me, and I stepped into them. He lowered a long necklace over my head, the gold almost a perfect match for the shoes, and handed me matching earrings. With warm hands on my bare shoulders, he turned me to the mirror once more.

I frowned. "How'd you do that?"

It was the same dress, but with the jewelry and shoes it looked . . . fancier.

He shrugged. "Alexandria wears this one a lot. So don't expect this kind of help again. I can think of maybe three outfits I see her wear that I might be able to pull together." He threw his hands up and backed away.

I smiled at him in the mirror. "Thank you."

George checked his watch again. "Out of time. Go."

A silent, straight-backed chauffer drove Oren and me into the city. We sat in the back, staring out our windows. I spent most of the trip resisting the urge to fidget and wishing for a damn cigarette to take the edge off.

We were dropped off in front of a restaurant I'd walked past a handful of times but never even considered going into. I couldn't afford anything on the menu. Intricate wrought-iron detail decorated the glass door, and lush plants lined the edge of the building outside. It was on a side street, away from the busier bars and restaurants around the corner but close enough to be part of the action. Aloof and intimidating as the customers it served.

Oren guided me through the door with a gentle touch to my lower back, and we were shown to a table. The waiter even pushed my chair in for me. I made sure to keep my knees together under the crisp tablecloth.

We both hid behind the obnoxiously large leather menus. I skimmed the items but gave up trying to guess what they were. With words like *deconstructed*, *reduction*, and *artisanal*, I had no idea what I was going to order . . . or how I was going to eat it. There was more cutlery on the table than I had in my drawer at home.

I peeked at Oren over the top of my menu. We hadn't spoken since before getting into the car, and it was starting to get awkward.

Just as I started running through potential ways to get out of this nightmare, his eyes flicked up and met mine. He held my gaze for a moment and lowered his menu. I followed suit.

He opened his mouth to say something, but before he could get a word out, the waiter appeared. "Can I get you anything to drink?"

Oren turned to me. "Do you mind if I order for us?"

I smiled, making sure it looked polite and not relieved. "Please."

"Can we get a bottle of the Clos Mogador Priorat, please? The 2015."

"Certainly, sir." The waiter bowed and walked away.

"Fantastic choice," I said. I had no idea what the fuck he'd just ordered.

"Thank you. I've been brushing up on my wine knowledge." He looked so proud of himself. My stiff smile relaxed. He was making an effort for his fake fiancée. *Aww!*

"Have you been here before?" I asked.

"Once or twice. I don't spend a lot of time in New Orleans, but with the current expansion of the business, I've found myself here three times in the past year. I have to admit"—he leaned in as if he was sharing a secret—"I didn't like it at first. I thought it was loud and obnoxious, full of bachelor parties and cheap ghost tours. But the more time I spend here, the more it grows on me. It's got a certain vibe that's hard to describe."

Now, this I could talk about for days. "I love the history of it. The fusion of European, Creole, and so many more cultures. It makes for a unique atmosphere."

"I see you've done your research too." He flashed me a smile. There was no suspicion in it, but it reminded me that Alex had never been to New Orleans. I needed to be careful how I talked about it.

Thankfully, our wine arrived—it was a red—and the waiter asked for our orders. Oren rattled off what he wanted, confident in his pronunciation of the complicated foreign words. Then the expectant look was turned on me.

"Uh . . ." I looked at the menu again. "What do you recommend?"

The waiter was more than happy to list some dishes.

"That sounds fantastic." I smiled and held my menu out. He nodded, collected the menus, and disappeared.

"Shall we discuss the terms of our arrangement?" Oren sipped his wine.

"Sure." I took a sip myself, avoiding his gaze. It really was damn good wine. I'd never been a wine person, but maybe I'd just never had any good stuff.

"I think some casual touching in public will be necessary— to keep up the appearance of intimacy. But I want to make sure you're comfortable. Our situation is not ideal, Alexandria, but I do want you to feel safe in it."

I stared at him for a moment. This guy was annoyingly proper, but he also had something I'd never come across in any dickhead I'd let into my bed—integrity.

When I didn't say anything, he kept speaking. "For example, was that all right when we walked in just now?" He nodded to the door, clearly referring to the chivalrous touch to my lower back.

"Oh! Yes, that's perfectly fine. Anything above the hip area is fine." I took another sip and rushed to add, "Except . . . well, the obvious exception . . ." I gestured vaguely to my boobs. Which really did look spectacular in the form-fitting dress, despite not even an inch of cleavage being on display.

He threw his head back and laughed. "Naturally. What about

hand holding?"

I tapped my chin and scrunched my eyes, making a show of considering it seriously. "I'll allow it."

"Your negotiation skills are as astute as I'd been told," he teased, and we both chuckled.

I fixed him with a more serious look. "I'm happy to hold your hand, Oren." It was such an innocent thing, and I doubted we would be in public together much anyway before Alex and I swapped back.

Without thinking about it, I lowered my hand, palm up, to the table. He flicked his eyes to it, then back up to my face, before slowly reaching out. His big, soft hand wrapped around mine and gently flipped it, caressing my knuckles with his thumb. I suddenly found it difficult to look away from his hazel eyes.

The waiter delivered our first course, breaking the moment. I frowned. *What the hell was that?* I decided to put it down to the fact that I hadn't gotten laid in over a week now. My body was reacting to every damn touch as if it were between my legs.

I frowned even deeper once I registered what was on my plate. It looked like a thimble-sized pile of tiny salad leaves.

I took another sip of wine to buy some time and glanced at Oren. He picked up the smallest knife and fork at the very edge of the pile of cutlery, and I followed his lead.

My dish turned out to be tuna and watercress, and it fucking melted on my tongue.

After several moments of silence, Oren asked me how my ride had been the previous day. I avoided saying anything whatsoever about Jack and focused on what I saw on his property, how it felt to be on a horse, the parts I enjoyed.

We spent five mind-blowing courses talking about his properties (the family had about a dozen, and he owned three personally); his business; the struggles of trying to balance doing what his father expected, honoring his legacy, and really stepping into the leadership role himself. It didn't help that daddy dearest was having trouble letting go of the control. At least that answered where Oren's own control issues came from.

I answered his questions as best I could before steering the conversation back to him. By the time they were clearing the table after the dessert course, I knew quite a bit about Oren Charles Winthrop.

I didn't necessarily *want* to know so much about him, but it was the only foolproof tactic I had to keep him from prying too much into me. Bartending had taught me two invaluable things. The first was that if you keep asking questions, people will keep talking about themselves—and will probably like you a whole lot because they *love* to talk about themselves. The second was that most people see what they want to see.

Oren didn't suspect a thing. He saw Alexandria Maria Zamorano sitting across the table—his future wife and guaranteed ticket to his inheritance.

The only parts of me he saw were the ones I couldn't hold back, like my love of animals and riding, or the times I genuinely had no idea how Alex would react, so I had to fill in the blanks.

By the time he flashed his platinum card and we made our

way outside, my core muscles were so tight from the tension of keeping up the deception you could probably have bounced a quarter off my stomach. I took a deep breath of the sweet night air. We'd finished off the bottle of wine, and I was craving something harder, desperate to loosen up a bit. Maybe I could somehow ditch rich boy and go get myself a drink.

I looked up to the sky as a cloud passed over the bottom half of the bright moon, just visible over the top of the buildings.

Oren stepped up next to me. "Oh, damn. I forgot to call the driver before we left." He reached for his inside jacket pocket.

"Wait." I spun to face him and grabbed his wrist. "We don't need to head back yet, do we?" Even if I could lose him, I had no way to get back to his stupidly remote property. I couldn't afford the taxi. But I didn't want to go back yet either. "Let's go get a drink."

His brows pulled down in uncertainty. "I don't know . . . I have an early meeting tomorrow."

I couldn't hold back the eye roll. "Oh, come on. Loosen up a bit. Unless . . . I mean, *I'm* having a good time."

I tilted my chin down, peering up at him through my lashes. I knew he wanted to make an effort, and I was hoping to make him feel guilty. It was a low blow, but I really needed that damn drink.

He sighed, but his lips turned up in a small smile. "I wouldn't even know where to take you."

"That's OK." I grinned, grabbing his hand and pulling him toward the end of the street. "Let's go. I know—" I cut myself off. I was about to say I knew a good little bar just up the street. It wasn't as posh as most of the other establishments in the area, but it had great cocktails. "Uh . . . I know you've been working really hard lately, and I just think you deserve to let loose a little. I'm sure there are plenty of places around here." I flashed him a grin and gave his hand a squeeze as I rounded the corner.

He threaded his fingers through mine and increased his pace to keep from being dragged along. "All right."

Suddenly, I questioned my readiness to agree to the hand holding—this felt too intimate. But before I could think about it too much, Black Lantern came into view. I wove past the people on the much busier street. Unlike the young, messy crowd usually found on Bourbon Street, these people were a little older and cleaner, though still looking for a good time.

"How about here?" I stopped in front of Black Lantern and headed inside without even waiting for an answer.

Oren laughed but came willingly. His hand once again went to my lower back as I led the way through the dark interior to the bar. A band was playing a seamless fusion of modern sound and big-brass-band energy, and the sizable crowd was clearly loving it.

I ordered a whiskey sour.

"I'll have the same," Oren shouted and handed over his card.

"Thank you." I used his shoulder to balance as I leaned up to speak into his ear. Fuck, he smelled good. "You don't have to pay for everything, you know."

I hoped my gaze conveyed how much I appreciated it. There was no way I could've paid for the dinner. That was one thing Alex and I really did have in common, but Oren handled it like the gentleman he was.

"I invited you out. I insist." He gave me a warm smile and accepted our drinks, handing me mine.

I took a sip of the strong cocktail, the whiskey burning my throat a little but the tang pleasant on my tongue and the smoky flavor decadent in my nose. It was an exceptional whiskey sour.

We sipped our drinks and listened to the band. I could feel the bass reverberating through my feet, almost making me forget how fucking uncomfortable those heels were.

I was surprised when Oren ordered another round. I was downright *floored* when he led me onto the dance floor once the drinks were empty.

Looked like rich boy only needed a gentle nudge into spontaneity; he seemed more than happy to roll with it now. We danced close—it was impossible not to in such a dense crowd—but he kept his hands above the hips, as per the terms.

Between the wine and the whiskey, not to mention the intoxicating sound of the band, I felt relaxed. And having Oren's hands on my waist didn't bother me anywhere near as much as I thought it would.

I hadn't even drooled over the sexy lead singer or the bartender with the beard and the tattoo sleeve. In fact, I'd barely noticed any of the men. But I didn't have time to linger on that fact, because Oren surprised me yet again by taking advantage of a gap in the crowd and spinning me in a complicated maneuver. His dexterous hands moved my body perfectly until I was back in his arms, his hands landing on my hips but the respectable distance maintained.

I could've stopped, could've used my grip on his shoulders to steady myself, but instead I leaned into the momentum until my front was flush with his. We stopped dancing, just standing in the middle of the writhing dance floor and staring at each other. His wavy, usually perfectly styled hair was falling over his forehead. His eyes looked dark and inviting in the dim light.

I dragged my hands over his shoulders and wrapped them around his neck. He mirrored the movement; one arm banded around my lower back, drawing me tighter against him, as the other splayed over my upper back, the tips of his fingers brushing the small amount of skin exposed at the top of the dress.

I didn't think, didn't worry about the consequences, didn't consider what it all meant. I just leaned up and pressed my lips to his.

He returned the kiss eagerly, sighing. His lips were so fucking soft, and he tasted like whiskey and something sweet. It started out slow, tentative, but built in intensity as fast as the band whipped the crowd into a frenzy. His tongue licked at my lips, and I opened for him, and then the kiss was desperate, *needy*. Definitely not appropriate for a public place. But I wasn't in the bar anymore—I couldn't hear the loud band or see all the people. There was only Oren, his tongue exploring my mouth, his strong arms holding me, his growing arousal pressing into my belly as I struggled to breathe through my nose.

I'd never been this turned on from a single kiss before. My body was responding to his like a ship in a stormy night weaving around the beam of a lighthouse, and the pressure between my legs was almost unbearable.

A drunk chick lost her balance and bumped into us, and our surroundings crashed back into my consciousness. Oren and I pulled apart, panting.

We stayed for another few minutes, dancing slowly to a fast beat, and then he called the driver to pick us up.

Like on the way to dinner, we didn't speak the whole way back to the house. But when he extended his hand, placing it palm up on the leather between us, I took it. We held hands all the way back as reality crashed into me, every mile bringing the clusterfuck I'd just created into clearer focus.

In the stark lighting of the foyer, I told him I'd had an amazing time and meant it. Then I went to my own room and closed the door firmly.

T: Hey, why are you really doing this sham marriage thing? I know you're in debt and all that, but is it really worth it?

A: Short answer? Yes.

T: Long answer?

A: LOL. Can't really fit it into a txt.

T: Fair enough.

A: It's like . . .

A: What's really important to you? Like, the one thing that drives you?

T: Honestly? I don't know. Nothing?

T: I used to have goals. But then my parents died and everything kinda fell apart. I haven't thought about what's really important to me in a long time.

A: I can understand that.

T: Shit! I can't believe I told you that. I haven't talked to anyone about that

A: Who am I gonna tell? I've told you things I haven't admitted to anyone else too. I think there's something comforting about knowing that the person you're telling secrets to isn't invested in the effects.

T: Yeah, I guess.

A: Anyway, my point is—the thing that drives me is my dad. The most important thing to me is making sure I keep our family legacy alive. A lot of people are relying on me, and I need to prove to them and myself that I can do this.

T: You and Oren have more in common than you know. He's driven like that too. In a good way.

A: Oh ok. That's good :)

T: Alex, I think your dad would be proud of you. I mean, I didn't know him, but how could he not?

A: Wow . . .

A: That's really sweet, Toni. Thank you.

T: xo

Chapter 10

ALEX

After a bumpy first few nights, I started to make decent tips. I knew that money was still Toni's, but I was working my ass off and gathered the courage to ask if I could use some of it to buy food and bus fares so I could get around. She told me I was a weirdo and could use the money for whatever I wanted, then reminded me she would be getting a massive payout when this was all over.

With my conscience clear, I set out on an overcast day to explore more of the city. It was still warm, even with the fat clouds overhead threatening to burst. A perfect day for visiting a cemetery.

I didn't go to the most famous one, opting for one closer to the neighborhood that wouldn't cost as much to get to. A few people were wandering around on the sidewalk outside, but as I passed under the arched wrought-iron gate, no one was in sight. I wandered up and down the rows, reading the ancient headstones, then hovered at the edges of the tail end of a tour and listened in.

I managed to hear a bit about the fascinating history of burials in this part of the world, how the city is around one to two feet below sea level, and every time it flooded, dead bodies would come floating up. Eventually, they decided to start laying their dead to rest *above* ground.

The tour moved off, and I turned in the opposite direction and started making my way back to the gates, taking a different path. As I rounded the corner of a mausoleum that boasted dates from several hundred years ago but looked pristine, I jerked to a stop.

The gates were only a few rows away, but what arrested me was Ren. He was sitting cross-legged and leaning back against a raised grave, notebook and pen in hand, his focus on the page.

"What are you doing here?" I demanded. For some reason, I immediately wondered if he'd followed me.

His head snapped up, brow creasing in confusion before his expression turned to pure annoyance. "It's a public fucking place," he grumbled. "What are *you* doing here?"

I crossed my arms but let some of the suspicion go. He seemed genuinely surprised to see me. "I'm exploring."

"Playing tourist in your own city?"

"Something like that." More like being an *actual* tourist in a place that was new to me, but whatever.

I had my answer. He had his. Logically, it was time for me to leave, but I couldn't seem to make my feet move—couldn't seem to stop staring at his piercings or trying to get a better look at the tattoos peeking out from under his gray T-shirt.

He uncrossed his legs and lifted his knees, resting his arms on them as he cocked his head.

The silence between us was beginning to get awkward, so I filled it, my years of practice making small talk in polite society kicking in. "It's a beautiful place." I cast my eyes over the cemetery. "So full of history."

"Yeah. People get creeped out by cemeteries, but death is just a part of life." He shrugged, his gaze wandering over the rows of dead. "There are so many stories here. It's inspiring."

All my polite small talk skills went out the window, and I blurted, "You come to the cemetery to write lyrics? I didn't think you were that cliché." I didn't mean for it to sound so condescending, so judgmental. I was actually trying to work my way up to telling him his music was unique and mesmerizing.

His gaze flicked back to me, his lips pressing together as he stood to his full height. He stuffed his notebook and pen into the back pocket of his ripped jeans and stepped into my space, looming over me.

I looked up at him and tried to explain. "I'm just—"

"I come here," he said, cutting me off, "because I run tours like the one you sneakily listened in on. Playing gigs doesn't quite cover the bills, so I supplement my income by doing this. Just in case I wasn't enough of a struggling artist cliché for you. And yes,

I write lyrics between tours because I need every spare minute I can find to work on my music."

Before I had a chance to respond, he turned on his heel and stalked away, walking straight to the gates and up to a group of people. As he led them past, starting the tour, he didn't even spare me a glance.

I sighed, my shoulders sagging in defeat. I'd managed to say all the wrong things while trying to say the right ones, and I felt like shit.

As I walked to the bus station, I found myself thinking less about the antagonistic way he always spoke to me and more about how he said he'd seen me listening in on the tour. Had he been watching me the whole time?

I also couldn't stop thinking about how good his butt looked in those jeans and how good it felt to have his gaze on my body as I touched myself. I wriggled in my seat on the bus and tried to think about something else as fat drops of rain started to hit the window. I hoped Ren had an umbrella with him.

Later that afternoon, Dennis and I carried case after case of beer up to restock the fridges while Loretta prepared the grill. We finished mopping the floors just as she finished making us all juicy cheeseburgers.

As we lined up on stools at the bar to eat, I thought about how to bring up the situation with Ren. I couldn't exactly say, "Hey, do you guys know why we hate each other?" So I decided to keep it simple and hope the conversation naturally flowed in that direction.

"Who's playing tonight?" I asked before taking a big bite.

"Isn't it Thousand Lies?" Dennis mumbled around a mouthful of chips. I knew full well it was them.

"You better behave, sugar." Loretta raised her gaudily made-up eyebrows at me and wagged a skinny finger. "Andre doesn't need any more drama from you two."

I threw my hands up in surrender but didn't say anything. When Loretta narrowed her eyes at me, I rolled mine, channeling Toni.

"What is it with you two?" Dennis asked, and I remembered he'd only been working there for a few months.

"Ask him," I grumbled, hoping my answer was cryptic enough to imply I knew the reason but wasn't willing to talk about it.

"All that tension, I'm surprised you two haven't fucked yet." Dennis laughed, and I choked on my burger, spluttering and having to wash it down with soda.

Loretta swatted the young man on the back of the head but laughed at the same time, the sound something between a cough and a cackle. It was infectious, and we all had a laugh.

But apparently Dennis was not done stirring shit. "Never mind what's between you and Ren—you'll either fuck each other or kill each other. I wanna know what's going on between Ren and *Andre*."

"What do you mean?" These weren't exactly the answers I was hoping for, but I'd take any insight I could get into the asshole who'd watched me masturbate in a dirty men's room and the sweet man who sometimes looked at me as if he wanted to say more, see more, *do* more.

"You can't tell me you haven't noticed how close they are, or that you don't know shit about it." He turned an incredulous look to me. "You've been working here for years. You *live* here!"

Loretta saved me from having to stumble through that answer. "Haven't you learned by now that Toni keeps to herself? She doesn't know shit."

"But you do." It wasn't a question. Dennis's focus was now on the older woman, his face full of expectation.

"I know everything about everything, sugar. But I ain't no gossip!"

Dennis and I both laughed. I'd only been around for a few short weeks, and it was plain to see Loretta was as big a gossip as you could get.

She cackled again, and Dennis asked, "So are they together or what? Just keeping it on the DL to be professional and shit?"

"Andre and Ren ain't *together* together," Loretta said when she was done coughing. "They get together, but I don't see them moving in together anytime soon."

"So it's just a casual sex thing?" I blurted.

"Hell no. Those boys take care of each other like family. And before you ask, no, I don't know what the deal is any more than that," she said, sounding a little put out by the fact that she couldn't tell us more.

"So they're gay?" Dennis asked, gathering our empty plates and depositing them on the servery window. "I swear I've seen Ren leave with chicks, and Andre has that nudie calendar in his office."

"Look at him." Loretta crossed her bony arms and leaned her elbows on the bar. "Thinkin' he's some kinda sleuth."

Dennis rolled his eyes but smiled at her. "So maybe they're both bi then?"

"Who gives a shit?" Loretta got down off her stool with a groan, and I resisted the urge to offer her a helping hand. I had a feeling she'd bite it off. "It don't matter what's between your legs." She waved a hand in front of her crotch, then pressed it to her chest. "All that matters is what's in your soul. You don't fall in love with a penis or a vagina. You fall in love with a *person*. And one of the people we're talking about is your boss, so you better get that tight ass of yours back to work. You too." She pointed at me and disappeared into the kitchen.

Dennis watched her go, then turned to me. "I don't know. I can think of a penis or two I could fall in love with."

We cracked up laughing, and I nearly fell off my stool.

I didn't know, or care, any more than Loretta which way Andre or Ren swung, but I found myself hoping they'd both swing in *my* direction.

I got up, pulled Toni's ridiculously tight shorts out of my crotch, and got back to work. But as the night wore on, I couldn't get that wayward thought out of my mind.

Hoping they'd both swing in my direction had turned to fantasizing about it. I wondered what that piercing through the head of Ren's cock would feel like against my tongue. I wondered what Andre's big hands would feel like gripping my thighs as he pushed them open. I wondered what it would feel like to be sandwiched between them.

Sometime around three in the morning, I pushed up the bolt on the front door to the bar and sighed. Usually Andre did the final close, but he'd been distracted all night. Once the other staff had headed home, he'd emptied the till and disappeared, yelling over his shoulder, "You good to lock up?" He hadn't even given me the chance to answer before I heard the thud of his boots on the stairs.

I turned out the lights and dragged my tired ass up a mere minute or two behind him. But as I neared the top, I froze. My hand tightened on the timber railing as my eyes greedily drank in the sight before me.

Andre and Ren were kissing—passionate, hands-all-over-each-other, pushed-up-against-the-wall kissing.

All the things I'd been fantasizing about all night slammed into me, and heat pooled between my legs as my mouth dropped open.

Before I could register I was being a creep just standing there and watching them make out, Andre got the door to his apartment open and dragged Ren away from the wall with a firm grip on his belt. They didn't break the kiss as Andre shoved him inside.

Just before they disappeared into the apartment, Ren opened his eyes. His gaze held mine for one charged moment, and then they were gone, the door slamming shut with a rattle.

The noise finally pushed me out of my daze, and I rushed up the last few stairs to my door, let myself in, and leaned back against it.

He would've seen the pure lust in my eyes. After that incident in the bathroom, he would've known *exactly* what my horny face looked like. I resisted the urge to creep across the hall and press my ear to Andre's door. But there was no need anyway. As I stood there in the dark, moans reached my ears. Deep, guttural, manly sounds that traveled through my body and shot straight to the spot between my thighs.

I bit my lower lip and freed myself from the ridiculous shorts. I didn't think about how wrong it was to listen in on such an intimate moment, how creepy it was to touch myself while thinking about what they were doing across the hall, imagining myself joining in.

I just trailed my hand down, past the hem of my panties, and embraced the moment.

A: Theoretically speaking, how do you just . . . like . . . sleep with someone.

T: What the fuck are you talking about?

A: I'm just curious about your life. And you've suggested that you sleep with a lot of people.

T: Yeah? So?

A: I'm not judging.

T: Feels pretty judgy . . .

A: No! I promise! I just want to know what it's like to have t hat kind of freedom. I've never slept with someone I wasn't in a relationship with.

T: Haha! OK. Well, it's not like there's a trick to it or anything. If you find someone attractive, just go for it.

A: I can't believe I just told you all that! Sorry. Overshare.

T: It wasn't. If you can't talk to your body double about sex positivity, are you even doppelgangers?

A: Hahahaha! I'm still a bit embarrassed.

T: OK, fine. I'll share too. I've never slept with someone while in a relationship. Except for my first boyfriend, who I lost my V-card to in high school.

A: What was his name?

T: Brian. Stop deflecting. You wanna bang someone?

A: Maybe . . .

T: Girl, isn't this the point of this whole exercise? Go have some fun. Sow your oats before you get hitched.

A: Women don't really have oats to sow.

T: Whatever! Go get laid!

A: Yes, ma'am!

Chapter 11

TONI

'd never felt bad about sex, never resisted my attraction to someone or felt dirty after a one-night stand. But then I'd never had anyone else's feelings to consider. Ugh! *Feelings*. This was why I kept my shit to myself.

I rolled toward the window as the first violet light of dawn started to filter through. I hadn't slept a wink, rolling around in expensive sheets and replaying the evening in my mind.

If this was any other situation, I'd be waking up next to Oren, both of us naked, probably ready to go again. Or I never would've gone for him in the first place. But this was Alexandria's life, and she had to step back into it in a few weeks. I couldn't believe I'd complicated shit this badly for her. For *me*. I still had two weeks of navigating this clusterfuck, and I wasn't entirely sure how I would pull it off.

Because the other thing I couldn't stop thinking about was how fucking soft rich boy's lips had felt against mine, how confidently he'd held me, how damn *good* my hand had felt in his as we walked up the street. If I could just jump in the sack with him, these ridiculous thoughts would go away. I just needed to fuck him out of my system—just like I did with every other guy. But I couldn't do that in this situation. I was pretty sure fiancé was catching feelings, and I couldn't let Alex come back into a situation where sex was the status quo.

With no better idea on how to handle the mess I'd made, I went with a classic Toni move—avoidance.

Oren was nothing if not predictable. I'd figured out his OCD routine within a few days, so I knew I had a good thirty minutes before the old pipes creaked with his morning shower.

I brushed my teeth, got dressed, and tiptoed downstairs. I grabbed an apple and a granola bar from the dark kitchen and let myself out the back door before anyone else was awake.

The door to the stables was closed but not locked. It was dark in there, but light was beginning to stream in through the windows high up on the walls.

"Hey, girl." No one was around, but whispering still felt right as I moved toward Honeymustard's stall.

She popped her head over the gate and shook it from side to side, making her mane ruffle. As I gently patted her on the nose, she took my half-eaten apple right out of my hand.

"Hey!" I chastised her with a chuckle but wished I had another apple to give her. I pulled out the granola bar, avoiding Honeymustard's sneaky attempts to snatch that too, and started craving coffee.

Being in the stables made me feel better. It smelled like straw and horseshit, but I didn't mind. I just enjoyed the feeling of Honeymustard's soft hair under my palm as the details of the space came into focus, more light filtering in with the new day. The other horses started to stir, snorting and shuffling about.

The big door slid open to reveal a bright morning, sun shining on the grass beyond, and Jack strolled inside. "Morning! Ready for breakfast?"

His voice was croaky, his hair mussed, his jeans sitting low on his hips. The horses all shifted, heads popping out over stall doors down the line.

Jack spotted me halfway into the cavernous space. He paused and gave me a wide smile before coming to stand next to me. "And good morning to you. You're up early."

"Morning." I yawned.

Jack chuckled, petting the other side of Honeymustard's neck. "Have you been here all night? You know the horses are fine on their own."

I swatted his arm and smiled, grateful for the distraction. "Yes, smart ass, I know. I just couldn't sleep, so I came down to hang out with Honeymustard. Being around animals calms me."

"Me too." Jack's hand paused mid-pat, his eyes fixed on mine.

Chatter and boots crunching on straw announced the

stablehands' arrival. They greeted me politely and got on with their work. Jack set about his duties too, giving them directions as they fed the horses, mucked out the stalls, and brushed the beautiful animals down. Halfway through the morning routine, Jack came out of his office with a steaming mug in each hand. He wordlessly handed me one, and I moaned in thanks as I brought the coffee up to my mouth and settled in on a stepping stool, my back propped up against the wall.

I watched them work and made small talk with Jack and the stablehands as I drank my coffee. As the others moved off to do other things, Jack led a saddled Honeymustard out of her stall.

"I don't know what you're hiding from"—he gave me a knowing look, his voice conspiratorial and low—"but a ride always makes me feel better."

"I'd love to go for a ride." I got to my feet and gave him a smile, choosing not to address his correct assumption that I was avoiding like a pro.

He mounted Benson after helping me up onto Honeymustard, and we took off for the back end of the property.

We visited the spot by the river again, but Jack didn't strip down and jump into the water this time, and he didn't mention it either, saving us both the embarrassment. Instead we let the horses drink and rest while we sat in the shade of a tree and chatted.

Actually, Jack did most of the talking, with me humming nonspecific replies. When he finally led me back to the horses, I had no idea what we'd even discussed.

I was so distracted by what had happened the night before

that I couldn't seem to think about anything else. If I wasn't worrying about how colossally I'd fucked up by kissing Oren, I was obsessively thinking about kissing Oren.

I put my foot into the stirrup, and Jack pushed me up with a firm grip on my hips. He held on to my ankle until I was steady in the saddle.

"Good?" He looked up at me, shielding his eyes from the sun with his free hand.

"All good." I smiled down at him. "Thank you."

His hand on my ankle loosened, and he dragged his fingers up my shin. All distracting thoughts were pushed from my mind by that touch. My heart started to thud against my chest, and when thoughts of Oren's firm grip around my middle as we'd kissed started to invade my mind, I made myself focus on the warmth of Jack's hand through my jeans.

His eyes bored into mine. When his hand reached my knee, he stepped away and mounted his horse with smooth, practiced movements, the corded muscles in his forearms bunching as he pulled himself up.

I cleared my throat and shifted in the saddle.

We rode back in silence.

Every time my mind threw Oren at me, I focused on Jack.

As images of Oren's hazel eyes looking at me as he leaned in for a kiss popped up, I watched Jack roll his hips with the movement of his horse, his broad back swaying.

As the distinct smell of Oren's expensive cologne came to my mind, I breathed in the smell of horses and fresh air.

As my chest swelled at how warm and safe my hand had felt nestled in Oren's, I deliberately took note of how Jack's jeans stretched over his thighs.

We emerged from the trees and gave the horses free rein to meander over the grass back to the stables. Benson pulled up next to Honeymustard, the two animals walking almost in step.

I glanced over to find Jack already watching me, his eyes shaded by his cowboy hat.

A shout from one of the stablehands drew our attention back to what was in front of us.

"We're heading to lunch, boss." One of the young guys waved and walked off, the other three following close behind.

Jack waved them off and jumped off his horse.

He led both Benson and Honeymustard into the stables. A mounting block was just a few feet away, but Jack took his hat off, hung it on a hook nearby, and reached up to help me.

After a moment's hesitation, I leaned forward to swing my leg over the horse's back, then slid down, my front scraping against the saddle. Jack was right there to steady me, his strong hands on my waist guiding my body safely to the ground. He left one hand on my waist as I turned to him, the other going to loosely grip the saddle.

He licked his lips, then looked up and fixed me with an intense stare. "Look, Alexandria, I don't know what's got you so spooked today, but I just want you to know if there's anything I can do to take your mind off it or help in any way, I'm right here."

He punctuated his last statement with a firm squeeze at my waist, and I didn't miss the way his eyes unashamedly drank in my body, the hint of cleavage peeking out of my shirt, the curve of my hip. I was under no illusions when it came to *how* Jack wanted to take my mind off my troubles.

A memory flashed in my mind for the millionth time—Oren swaying with me in a crowd of hot bodies, his arms holding me tightly, his lips so soft.

Instinctually I leaned forward just a fraction, my lips parting as my heart battered against my ribcage.

Jack mirrored my movement. His hand slid down to my hip as his chest brushed against mine. Reflexively, I raised my hand to grip his shoulder.

My eyes focused, slamming me back into the present. It was hay and horses I was smelling, not the sweat and perfume of a party crowd. It was Jack's blue eyes flicking down to my lips as he leaned in, not Oren's hazel ones.

For a split second, I thought about kissing him. His lips were so close already, his masculine, earthy smell assaulting my senses, his chest bumping against my tits with every increasingly labored breath he took.

If I hooked up with Jack, maybe my Oren problem would go away. If I couldn't fuck Oren to get Oren out of my system, maybe Jack would do. Maybe I just needed to get some. I'd found Jack more attractive than Oren when I first arrived anyway. Maybe my brain was just messing with me, making me lust after the one man who was even more off-limits than the first one I wanted to tackle into the hay.

Jack's lips were a hairbreadth away from mine. All I had to do was pucker and we'd be kissing.

Footsteps on timber invaded the tense silence.

My eyes widened and I pushed Jack away.

"There you are, darling." Oren's voice was an octave higher than his usually calm, measured tone. "I've been looking for you all morning."

I stepped back, hoping my movements didn't look as jerky and guilt-ridden as they felt. Jack's movements were much slower and more controlled as he dropped his hand from my hip and turned his back to Oren, reaching for Honeymustard's neck to give her a slow pat.

I cleared my throat and turned to Oren. "I went for a ride. It was such a beautiful day." I smiled, trying to keep the shakiness out of my voice. Had he seen? We'd been so close to kissing it would've looked as if we already were.

"Ah!" Oren stopped halfway to us and propped his hands on his hips. He smiled, but it didn't reach his eyes—his eyes that watched Jack's back as the other man fiddled with the horse's saddle and led her away. "Well, I'm glad I found you. There's something I wanted to show you."

He held his hand out. The tight smile stayed plastered to his face, but his nostrils flared.

He'd seen.

My heart sank.

I made my feet move forward, resisting the urge to hunch my shoulders and drop my head.

When I placed my hand in his, all the memories I'd been

trying to distract myself from flooded my mind. My hand felt right in his warm one, even as he gripped it tightly and pulled me along behind him, his pace steady, his shoulders tight under his tailored shirt.

Once we were away from the stables, he picked up his pace, his grip on my hand tightening. I thought about pulling my hand out of his but found I didn't want to.

He wasn't looking at me; he was storming away even as he dragged me along. I was dreading what he'd say, but I still didn't want to be away from him.

Instead of letting myself get dragged along like a wayward child, I took a few jogging steps until I caught up, then matched his pace. Now we looked like we were rushing toward the main house together, not like he was hauling me.

He wrenched the back door open and hurried through the massive kitchen. We were in and out before any of the staff could so much as greet us.

Down the hallway, and we were in his office. He closed the door firmly and let my hand go, keeping his back to me. His still-tense shoulders rose and fell with rapid breaths.

I was breathing hard too, winded from our powerwalk.

"Oren?" I reached for his shoulder, but he turned to face me before I could grip it, and I whipped my hand back.

In the stables he'd radiated restraint, appeared and sounded calm to anyone not looking too closely. But behind the closed door, he let me see the rage in his wide eyes, the frustration in his thin lips.

"What do you want from me?" he ground out.

I blinked and took an involuntary step back. "What do you mean?" The question cut to the core of why I'd been obsessively avoiding the issue all day, but I wasn't ready to face it.

"We set up this deal, this marriage of convenience"—he lowered his voice to a near whisper, even behind the heavy timber door—"a situation that was mutually beneficial. You wanted to keep it professional, negotiate terms, and I agreed. I don't need complications in my life any more than you. But then last night you kissed me." He hissed the word out, as if he were accusing me of slapping him and not kissing him.

I gritted my teeth. I felt like shit, but I still didn't like being told off.

"I thought maybe . . . last night . . . I hoped that . . ." He was losing his train of thought—a train of thought I didn't want him to finish. It was too much, too soon, too real. "But then you shut down on me, and this morning you disappear. If it wasn't for George telling me you were out for a ride, I would have been ready to report you as a missing person. *Fine*, I thought, *maybe she just needs time to clear her head*. It was a lot. I was confused too, so I get it. But then I find you in the arms of my stable master." He took a deep breath, closing his eyes and pushing the air out of his nose before fixing me with a narrow-eyed stare. "So what fucking game are you playing, Alexandria? What do you want from me? Is it more money?"

I reeled back, stunned, and let every ounce of the hurt and outrage I was feeling enter my features. That gave him pause.

Some of the anger leaked out of his gaze, replaced by confusion.

"How dare you?" I stood to my full height and rolled my shoulders back. "You think I'm some kind of money-grabbing whore?"

Alexandria wasn't like that. All she cared about was saving her family's legacy, doing the right thing for all the people who relied on her. I felt protective of her and her motivations, but I'd be lying if I said Oren's question didn't hit a nerve with me too. I'd never had money, had to work hard for every single thing I had in life, but I earned it fair and square. *On my own*. My life may have been a boozy, sexed-up mess, but I'd never done anything dishonest to get ahead, and I didn't rely on anyone to get what I needed. I certainly didn't spread my legs for cash.

Asshole.

I stepped forward, regaining the footing I'd lost, and got in his face. "I don't give a shit about your money," I hissed. We were both keeping our voices down, having the quietest screaming match in the history of fights. "I don't want a penny more than what's needed to save my family's legacy. I'll live on goddamn spaghetti on toast if that's what it takes to protect what's mine."

"Then what the fuck was that about?" He pointed at the door.

I threw my hands up and huffed. "I don't know, OK? Like you said, this was supposed to be a business arrangement. Last night . . ." I had no idea what last night was. I'd spent so much time trying not to think about it that I had no words to articulate it.

"You're freaked out." The anger and suspicion drained out of him. He sighed and dragged his hands down his face. When they came away, his features were set in a hard, emotionless mask. "I understand. This is a difficult situation and the lines were blurred. We both have a lot at stake. If you'd prefer to stick to the original arrangement, that's fine. But I will not have you sleeping around with my staff. Keeping up appearances was part of our deal—this relationship has to look real to everyone else. I'll not be made to look like a fool. Keep your hands off my stable master, and anyone else for that matter. That's not negotiable."

I crossed my arms over my chest. "I wasn't trying to make you look like a fool."

"Just trying to make me *feel* like one?"

I sighed. "Look, I—"

A knock sounded at the door. I had no idea what I wanted to say anyway. Apologize? Tell him to go fuck himself? Tell him I wasn't even Alexandria? Who knows what would've come out of my mouth had his mother not let herself into the room.

"Oh good, Alexandria, you're here." She beamed at me, then looked at her son. "I'm sorry, did I interrupt something?"

"Not at all, Mother." Oren leaned against the back of a wingback chair, his smile tight.

Caroline turned to me and slightly raised her eyebrows. She was his mother—of course she saw through his shit.

I uncrossed my arms and threaded my fingers loosely in front of myself, hoping the smile on my face was less strained than his. "We were just discussing the wedding." It wasn't a total lie.

"Ah, yes." She nodded and glanced toward the open door. "Well, if you're not too busy with wedding planning, I was wondering if you'd join us for lunch tomorrow?"

Oren flicked his eyes up to his mother, clearly not happy. "I'm sure Alexandria has a lot to do tomorrow. She's a very busy woman."

"Nothing I can't move around." I gave him a wide smile. Who did he think he was to speak for me? Even if we were married, that shit wouldn't fly. I contradicted him on principle alone. "I'd love to join you for lunch."

Oren gave me an incredulous, annoyed look, and Caroline beamed at me.

"Excellent." She took a step toward me, her perfume wafting in my direction as her delicate heels clicked on the timber. "If you don't have a busy day, then you can join us for the morning also. Oren's been working very hard and hasn't had hardly any time to spend with you, but we're going to the site of the new store to check on progress, and I'm sure he'd love to show you around."

Oren opened his mouth, no doubt to try and dissuade me from going, but I spoke up before he could. "I'd love to! Thank you for your kind invitation." I gave Caroline's hand a squeeze, and she responded with a genuinely warm smile.

"We'll leave around eight." She waltzed back out, her skirt swishing around her knees, and left the door wide open.

It wasn't until Oren stormed out without another word, leaving me in his office alone, that I remembered I was supposed to be avoiding these people, giving them as few opportunities as possible to discover who I really was . . . or wasn't.

T: Do you believe in God?

A: Random.

T: ???

A: OK. Uh, yes? I mean, I'm not particularly religious, but I think there is a higher power. You?

T: Nah. Much as I'd like to think my parents are in some paradise that's making up for all the shit they had to go through while alive, I don't buy it. Life's a bitch and then you die.

A: Cynical much?

T: Yep! But unfortunately I do still believe it's wrong to kill people. Ugh!

A: And why are we contemplating murder today?

T: Your boo was a total dick. Basically accused me of trying to scam more money from him.

A: WHAT?

A: That son of a bitch! You OK? Do we need to swap back? I can handle arrogant guys like him.

T: Whoa! Chill. I'm just venting. Everything's fine. Just pissed me off.

T: He's not really that bad, if I'm being honest. I think he was just hurt.

A: Who hurt him?

T: Some inconsiderate bitch. But no worries. We're keeping shit strictly profesh.

A: OK . . .

Chapter 12

ALEX

I groaned and mushed my face into the pillow, trying to avoid the incessant buzzing and the light now trying to creep past my eyelids.

After a few moments the buzzing finally stopped, but the light refused to go away, invading my unconsciousness and making me huff as I rolled onto my back to concede defeat. I yawned and stretched, my right arm shoving up under the pillow and bumping my phone. Ah, the buzzing culprit.

I hadn't had anywhere near enough sleep—it was before midday—but the really worrying thing was the number of missed calls from my mother.

Before I had a chance to call her back, the screen lit up again. I sighed, cleared my throat so I wouldn't sound as if I'd just woken up, and answered it. "Hi, Mom."

"Alexandria?!" She was beside herself. "Are you all right? You didn't answer. I've been calling for ten minutes."

"I was in the shower. Sorry."

"The shower? At this time?"

Shit. I scrambled for an excuse and remembered the photo Toni sent me the other day of her legs on a lounger, sun glistening off the water. "Yes, Oren and I took a dip in the pool."

"Oh, OK then." She sounded calmer already. "Well, then I'm glad you two are getting along."

I hummed in agreement and dragged myself out of bed as she prattled on about her recent lunch with the ladies at the club. With the phone wedged between my ear and shoulder, I put the kettle on for a cup of tea, then moved to the windows to air out the stuffy room.

". . . but you know that man has been having affairs for the entirety of their twenty-two years of marriage. She was the only one at the table oblivious to it."

"Mmhm." I threw back the curtains and flicked the latch on the balcony door.

"Oh! I also ran into your cousin Preston. He was very interested in why you're away from the vineyard for this long, even after I explained you were engaged. He kept hinting at wanting to step in and help if he could. I swear, that man has no concept of subtlety. Not that his father did either. I don't know why they think they can be involved in running such a complex business simply because we share an ancestor that happened to start it."

"Well, it's not like I'm doing a great job at it. Maybe we should let them have a go."

"Oh, Alexandria, honey, you are doing the absolute best—"

I cut her off with a yelp, my heart flying into my throat as I jumped back from the glass. On the other side, perched on the little table on the balcony, was Kennedy. The damn raven just stood there, staring at me with beady eyes.

"Alexandria!" My mother's voice turned shrill.

"Sorry, sorry," I rushed out through panting breaths. I pressed a hand to my chest while keeping the big black bird firmly in my sights. "I'm all right."

"What happened? You gave me a heart attack!"

"There was a bird. A big black one. Landed right on the other side of the window." The feathered fiend cocked its head, as if he knew I was talking about him.

"My goodness! You and birds. It's not even in the same room as you."

"Mom, I need to go." I was busting for the toilet, and my tea was getting cold. With a promise to check in again tomorrow, I hung up.

I narrowed my eyes at the raven. He cocked his head to the other side, then slowly shuffled on the spot, turning away from me while keeping his eye glued to mine. If he were human, I was almost certain he'd be glaring and whispering, "I'm watching you."

I took a deep breath and reached for the handle. "It's just a bird," I whispered to myself. "A bird that Toni trained. It won't hurt me. Come on, Alexandria, you need to get over this."

Kennedy squawked and flapped his wings, making me snap my hand back again.

"Nope! I'll start with a parakeet or something." I stuck my tongue out at him before abandoning my attempts to get over my fears and heading for the bathroom.

When I finished showering, Kennedy was still there, barring my access to fresh air and a breeze with his shiny black feathers and creepy eyes. I sighed and crossed my arms. "I'm telling Toni you're bullying me," I said, my voice raised so he could hear me through the glass. He just flapped his wings once and turned away. Cheeky bastard was calling my bluff.

I put on some shorts and a tank top and decided to head out. The fridge was looking a bit empty, and I only had a few hours before my shift started.

I pulled the door closed behind me just as Andre came up the stairs, panting.

He was in shorts and running shoes but nothing else, breathing hard. His pectorals bulged, every defined abdominal popping, his toned arms flexing as he pulled himself up the last steps using the railing. His entire body glistened with sweat, like some kind of sportswear ad.

I didn't realize I was staring at him with my mouth open, frozen to the spot, until he walked right up to me, his long legs closing the distance in only a few strides. His chest was just inches from my face; I got the urge to put my hand over the spattering of curly black hair, but I closed my hands into fists and craned my neck to look into his face.

Once my eyes met his, he grinned. With a single finger under my chin, he pushed my mouth closed and leaned in.

"You're drooling." His deep voice, pitched low and sexy, reverberated through me and went straight to my core.

My eyes widened and I gasped. "Oh my god," I breathed and ducked to the side, a blush heating my cheeks. I rushed down the stairs, nearly tripping and breaking my neck on the last step.

Once I reached the street, I marched away from the Cottonmouth, berating myself.

I found Andre attractive, but I'd found plenty of men attractive in the past and never lost my damn senses like that. There was nothing wrong with looking, but I couldn't believe I'd done it so blatantly and with so little composure.

Maybe it was the lack of sleep, or the fact that he took me by surprise. Maybe it was because he'd waltzed in half-naked and sweaty, but I didn't want to victim blame. My behavior was on me and me alone. He'd cracked a joke about it, but was he just covering up? Had I made him feel uncomfortable?

I ran my hands through my hair and groaned, hoping my inability to resist checking out a sinfully sexy man hadn't ruined my plan.

As I walked into the grocery store, the air-conditioned air calmed me a little, and I focused on shopping to take my mind off my embarrassment. By the time I was ready to head back, I'd decided to tackle the situation head on, swallow my pride, and apologize.

But when I knocked on Andre's door, there was no answer.

I didn't see him again until that evening. He showed up as the bar was starting to get crowded and the Thousand Lies arrived to set up.

I served drinks and kept an eye on him surreptitiously. At one point I caught him and Ren, heads bent, talking close. Then they burst into laughter, the sound carrying even over the boisterous crowd.

About halfway through the Thousand Lies' first set, I found myself alone with Andre behind the bar during a rare lull in drink orders. I tapped him on the shoulder.

He turned to me and smiled. "What's up?"

I leaned in, keeping my voice down despite the level of noise. He had to bend down so he could hear me. "I just wanted to apologize about earlier today."

He straightened up and chuckled, waving me off. "Don't worry about it."

Someone came up to the bar, and Andre served them a couple of beers. I waited and leaned in again,

"I'm serious. It was inappropriate, and I'm sorry if I made you feel uncomfortable. It won't happen again." I gave him a firm nod.

He smiled and placed his big hands on my shoulders. "Relax. I wasn't uncomfortable." His thumbs rubbed the tense muscles at the base of my neck, and then his hands dragged down my arms as he leaned in, his mouth near my ear. "And I wouldn't be opposed to it happening again."

He stepped back, gave me a wink, and turned to take another order. Dennis came rushing out of the crowd and joined us behind the bar, bumping me back into motion as the bar got busy again.

I was beyond relieved Andre wasn't upset with me, wasn't about to call my plan off and send me packing, but I couldn't quite figure out if he was teasing me or flirting with me.

When I turned back to the bar to take an order, my gaze immediately flew to Ren's. He was crooning a particularly intense note into the microphone, but his eyes were boring into mine. He looked between me and Andre, practically ignoring the audience for the rest of the song. Was he jealous? Loretta said they weren't together exclusively, but they were still sleeping together, and Ren and I had done . . . things in that bathroom. We may not have touched, but it had been intimate and erotic all the same.

And just like that, I was back to fantasizing about dirty men's room sex.

Between these two vastly different but incredibly attractive men, I was in a near constant state of arousal.

I refused to allow social conditioning to make me believe I was wrong or dirty just because I wanted and liked sex, but I'd never lusted after two men at once before. I'd always been a one-man kind of woman. Now here I was—getting myself off in front of Ren while he did the same, thoroughly enjoying seeing him and Andre kiss in the hallway, and getting worked up at the mere suggestion of something more between Andre and me. It was all new and a little surprising.

But wasn't that the whole point of my crazy plan to switch lives with Toni? To give myself the freedom to be a little crazy and surprising for a while?

Between sets, Ren sat at the end of the bar, sipping on bourbon and watching me with an unfathomable expression on his face. If it had been anyone else staring at me like that, so unashamedly and without reservations, I would've felt uncomfortable, asked them to leave. But his gaze made my skin tingle. I wondered if he was thinking about that night as much as I was.

When some patron asked to buy me a drink, I said yes and got myself a glass of the same bourbon Ren had just finished. Ren slammed his empty glass on the bar and disappeared into the crowd. A few minutes later, the band kicked up their last set.

They played upbeat, high-energy crowd favorites and a couple of their originals. The drummer's arms bulged with his effort; the guitarist and bass player swayed along, thrashing about the stage; and Ren made love to the audience.

Where during the first set, he couldn't keep his eyes off me and Andre, during this last one, he didn't glance in the direction of the bar *once*. He ran his hand down the microphone stand, leaned out over the crowd, reached out to high-five them. They were calling out and jumping around as if it were a stadium concert and not a gig in a dingy back-alley bar.

The band was so good I couldn't believe they weren't already doing international tours.

When they finished, Ren didn't come to the bar for one last drink like he usually did, and I found myself craning my neck to try and spot him through the crowd. The rest of the band was leaving through the back entrance, but he wasn't with them. I frowned and wiped down the bar. Maybe he'd snuck off to Andre's room already.

As if I'd summoned him, Andre's big, warm chest appeared at my back. I stiffened, mostly from surprise, but then melted into him, leaning back a little. He gripped my hip with one hand but didn't say anything. With his other hand, he pointed toward the back corridor, where I saw Ren turning the corner.

I looked at Andre over my shoulder and frowned. Was I being that obvious?

He just smirked and nudged me in that same direction, shaking his head in amusement.

I pushed down all the uncertainties, all the reasons I shouldn't follow him. Andre had given me a nudge, and I was going to lean into this moment.

Resisting the urge to smooth down my hair, I marched toward the back corridor. I rounded the corner just in time to see Ren go through the storage room door, and I navigated around drunk girls spilling out of the ladies' room and followed.

"Hoping to catch me with my pants down again?" There wasn't even a hint of surprise in his voice—he was waiting for me. With the door shut, the only light in the room came from a narrow window near the ceiling. The glow of a streetlamp shone like a spotlight over Ren's shoulders, casting the front of his face in shadow. I couldn't tell if he was smiling, scowling, or undressing me with his eyes, but I could feel his gaze on me.

I decided to be bold. "Actually, yes."

"Well, shit, I wasn't expecting you to admit it." He chuckled, the sound low and gritty, the way he'd sung on stage. He leaned back against a rickety spare table under the window, between shelves of supplies and boxes of liquor.

"Yeah, I'm full of surprises." I mimicked his posture and leaned against the door.

"I'm starting to see that. So, what? You want another show?" He gripped the bottom of his gray T-shirt and dragged it up so a sliver of hair and hipbones became visible. The black and silver bracelets on his wrist caught on the fabric of his jeans as he reached for his zipper.

A thrill shot up my spine, making me stand up straight and push away from the door. I loved a challenge, and Ren was the most tattooed, sinfully sexy, complicated one I'd ever come across. "Actually, I was thinking I could be part of the performance this time."

He didn't speak or move a muscle as I crossed the room and stopped directly before him.

I stood between his wide knees, my black boots hemmed in by his much bigger chucks. My eyes were adjusting to the dark, and from this close, his features came into focus—the piercing through his bottom lip, the way his eyes raked over my face, searching.

I kept my poker face on. I'd crossed the distance. He had to make the last move.

After a moment of heavy stillness, his hand shot out and grabbed a fistful of my shirt, pulling me to him. His other hand went to the back of my neck, and we crashed. We didn't start slow. We went from zero to a hundred in one second flat.

No sooner had our lips connected than our tongues did too, our mouths devouring. The feeling of his piercing against my lip drove me wild. When I realized he had one in his tongue too, the warm metal scraping against my own tongue, I moaned into his mouth.

He released his grip on my shirt and grabbed my ass, rolling his hips forward to grind his erection against my front.

We tugged and shoved, our movements against each other desperate and frenzied.

I pulled back only long enough to pull his T-shirt off and drop it into the dark abyss behind us. Nothing existed past the beam of light streaming in through the window.

The black leather necklaces bounced on his chest as the shirt came away, drawing my attention to the ink there. It was too dark to make out any detail, but tattoos covered his chest and right shoulder and flowed down his arm. I ran my hands over the colorful ink as I rested one knee on the desk next to his hip.

As both his hands went to my ass, I leaned forward and took that little round piece of metal at his bottom lip between my teeth. I trapped it there and explored it with my tongue.

He let me. He just watched me, panting into my mouth as our hips started to grind together in rhythmic, fast movements that contrasted with my slow, sensual exploration of his mouth.

His fingers dug into my ass as he gyrated his hips under me, his hardness creating the most delicious friction between my legs.

His right hand raked down my thigh until he had a grip on the back of my knee. He pulled, and I held on to his shoulders for balance as I lifted my knee to straddle him fully. I rubbed up on him, chasing that heady feeling that was building and building, heat radiating from between my legs all the way up to my chest.

He sucked on my top lip, assaulting my mouth with his until I had to release the piercing and kiss him back.

He pulled the front of my shirt and bra down until my breasts popped out, the straps of the bra digging in painfully. But the pain was forgotten when he wrapped one hand around my right breast and banded the other around my back, drawing me up and closer so he could take my hard nipple into his mouth.

I groaned—partly from the pleasure his mouth was bringing and partly from the loss of friction between my legs.

I ran my hands through his sweat-dampened hair and fiddled with the piercings in his ear, touched him everywhere I could reach from the position he had me pinned in.

"Ren." His name came out on a groan, half exclamation of pleasure, half plea for more.

He grunted and bit down on my nipple, making me gasp and roll my hips, desperately seeking friction that wasn't there.

He removed his mouth from my breast and stood, holding me to him with a firm grip on my ass. My heart flew into my throat; I scrambled to clutch his shoulders so I wouldn't fall, but he moved quickly, turning on the spot and dropping me unceremoniously onto the table.

I molded my lips to his once more, and he shoved the straps of my bra down so he could have better access as he kissed me. With one hand gripping the back of his neck, I reached between us with the other, rubbing him over his jeans. He jerked his hips into my touch, then pulled back.

As I worked on his zipper, he undid my shorts, our hands clumsy, our arms knocking in our rush. He got there first, his dexterous fingers working efficiently, and I lifted my hips so he could slide my shorts and panties off in one go. My bare ass met the rough surface of the table.

Ren took a tiny step back, just enough to look at me properly. One hand still gripped my knee; the other finished what I'd started and undid his pants as his eyes raked up and down my body.

I felt dirty and exposed, my shorts hanging off my leg, the shirt shoved below my boobs restricting how much I could move my arms. He was breathing hard and looking at me as if he wanted to lick every filthy inch of my body. It made another rush of arousal pool at my core.

I bit my lip and widened my legs just a fraction—a wordless invitation. If he took another step back, changed his mind and walked out, I wasn't sure I could handle it.

He leaned back in. His forehead dropped to my bare shoulder as his hand trailed up my thigh, straight to the spot between my legs. He groaned as he spread my wetness with his fingers, brushing over my clit and making me buck every time.

"Fuck. You're soaked." His hot breath fanned over my flushed skin.

I gripped the back of his neck tighter and licked beneath his ear. He tasted salty, but the smell of his cologne was mixing with his musky male scent.

"I want you inside me," I growled against his skin and bit his neck, sucking on it as I reached into his open pants and wrapped my hand around his hardness.

I remembered how he'd stroked himself in the bathroom, the erotic image mixing with everything else assaulting my senses. He was rock hard and so smooth. I pumped my hand with confident strokes, spreading the precum, feeling the warm metal of the piercing under my thumb. He moaned and pushed two fingers inside me, making me cry out.

We touched each other, mirroring the way we'd watched each other masturbate.

He removed his hand and pulled back a fraction, extracting a condom from his pocket and tearing it open while I pushed his jeans and underwear down past his hips.

He put the condom on and stepped closer. I widened my legs and leaned back on the table, keeping one hand on his hip.

He pushed all the way into me in one smooth, confident stroke, filling me up completely. My eyes rolled back in my head as I arched my neck.

Ren leaned over me, planting his palms on either side of my waist. He ground against me and I rolled my hips, pressing my breasts against his slick chest.

He licked the column of my neck and bit me just below the jaw, then started to pump his hips. He fucked me mercilessly, the table banging against the wall with our movements.

We kissed, licked, bit, grabbed, and pulled as he pumped in and out of me, hitting against my clit with every stroke.

I was consumed. His musky smell, the corded muscles of his toned body against mine, the way his messy hair fell over his face, the piercing pulling at his bottom lip as he bared his teeth in a grunt, his hands all over me, his moans in my ear.

I saw, heard, smelled and felt only Ren. It was his name on my lips as I came.

I moaned into his mouth, drawing his name out as I shattered. Pleasure pulsated from my core and spread like a volcanic eruption, burning me up from the inside.

I shuddered through the release, but he wasn't slowing down. He kept one hand on the table for balance, but the other banded around my back, holding me against him as he pumped his hips faster.

His moan was deep and guttural against my neck as he found his own release. He swelled inside me, his body leaning farther over mine, the force of his hips making us slide farther back on the little table.

My back connected with the concrete wall, and he lowered his cheek against my breasts, breathing hard, his hand gripping and then releasing my hip. He stayed buried inside me as his mouth nuzzled the top of my breast, as we took a few moments to catch our breath.

Eventually he leaned up and pressed his lips to mine once more. He straightened and lifted me with him as his lips devoured mine. The frenzied intensity was gone, but he still kissed me with long, sensuous strokes of his tongue.

And I was ready to go again. By the time he'd sat me upright, my hips were grinding against his of their own volition.

He broke the kiss to look at me, flashing a surprised grin. His lips were swollen, his cheeks flushed, and there was a hickey on his neck. I ran my thumb over it, getting a kind of sick satisfaction from the fact that I'd marked him.

"You gonna come again?" he whispered and palmed my breast.

"Shit. Maybe," I hissed, my hips moving a little faster, chasing the high.

"Yes." He licked my parted lips, pressing his forehead to mine, jerking his hips to meet mine. "Use me. Come on my cock again, you dirty whore. I want you dripping all over me. Yes, you're so fucking wet. I want to watch you come. Come for me."

He kept whispering dirty, depraved things against my lips, goading me with his words and his body, and like a tidal wave, another orgasm washed over me. I bucked against him as I moaned and watched him watch me. His eyes greedily drank in every detail.

When it was over, I sighed, and he slowly pulled out.

We fixed our clothing without speaking, and he walked to the door. He paused with his hand on the handle and turned to face me. "That was fucking hot, Toni. I'm up for more anytime."

Then he winked, flashed me a grin, and disappeared.

I stood in the dark for a moment. I was up for more of that too, but I wasn't Toni.

Chapter 13

TONI

George wasn't kidding when he said he'd be no more help in the outfit department. He really was a one-trick, red-dress pony. Once again, the bed was covered in clothing as I stood in front of the mirror, scowling at the black pencil skirt and pink silk shirt I had on.

"I don't know about this," I whined.

"You've said that about the last seven outfits." George sat in the chair by the window, on his phone and hardly paying attention. I'd dragged him into my room once I started to get ready for my day with the Winthrops and realized I was in deep shit. I had no idea what one was supposed to wear to tour the new shop of a multibillion-dollar business, followed by lunch, *darling*.

Mr. Winthrop clearly didn't like me, not that he'd even tried. Mrs. Winthrop was either the nicest rich person on the planet or was overcompensating for her husband's disdain by being very interested in me and asking dangerous questions. And Oren . . . Oren was another mess I was trying to avoid thinking about. I couldn't get the feel of his soft lips out of my mind, or the way they'd curled in a scowl when he chastised me. Most of all, I was trying to avoid admitting to myself that I cared. I didn't like that I'd upset him.

"I think it's too . . . what's that word? Corporate!" I snapped my fingers and turned to George. He just grunted.

"Hey, asshole!" I waved my arms like a drowning person until he looked up and sighed. "You're supposed to be helping me."

"I am helping you. I've gotten you out of more than one sticky situation. But clothes are not my department. You're a chick. Shouldn't this be in your handbook or whatever?"

"A vagina does not automatically give you fashion sense."

George groaned, slowly pulled himself to his feet, and approached the pile on the bed. He rummaged around and then threw two items at me. I caught them midair and frowned.

"Alexandria says this will be appropriate. You have ten minutes to get your delinquent ass downstairs." He wagged a finger in my face and walked out without another word.

I should've thought of that! Who better to advise me on what Alex would wear than Alex?

I quickly changed into the simple knee-length navy-blue skirt and floral-patterned shirt and slipped my feet into flats. I looked relaxed but presentable. I looked like Alex.

For the entire ride to the shop, Oren ignored me by burying his head in his phone. His parents were being driven in a separate car, because heaven forbid we had to sit so close that our knees touched.

We pulled up on a trendy stretch of road in the Garden District. I knew New Orleans pretty damn well, but I didn't spend much time in this particular part of it. The streets were tree-lined, the eclectic mix of up-market boutiques and quirky shops interspersed with cafés and restaurants.

"You just beat us here." Caroline rushed up to join us as Oren senior lagged behind. "Shall we head in?"

She looped her arm through mine and led the way toward the front door. A large sign in distinctive cursive text read "Winthrop" above the door, but the windows were covered up with black paper.

Oren rushed ahead to hold the door open for us.

"Thank you." I gave him a smile.

He nodded once, curtly, as his lips thinned. He was *really* pissed at me. He also smelled *really* fucking good.

I took a deep breath and forced myself to focus on something else.

After our fight in Oren's office, I felt bad for jeopardizing Alex's plans and, if I was being honest, for upsetting Oren too. He didn't know I wasn't Alex, and he was just trying to do the right thing by his family, like she was. I had a family once upon a time. I could understand that. I'd give anything, marry anyone, to have them back.

Unable to get my mind off my guilt, I'd spent the previous evening researching.

I wanted to know more about Alexandria, so I looked up Zamorano Wines. I'd seen the wine bottles on the shelves plenty of times—before picking up something I could afford off the lower shelf. The company was over two hundred years old and had been owned by the same family, run from the same winery in California, the whole time. They were one of the best producers of Merlot and Verdejo in the country and constantly won fancy-pants wine awards.

Nothing on the Internet even hinted about how deeply in financial shit they were—Alex was doing a stellar job of keeping a lid on that—but there were several articles about the accident that killed her father. The yacht capsized off the coast of the Bahamas when they were on a family holiday. Alexandria and her mother were the only survivors. I found YouTube clips of a cousin Preston—a tall, lanky man—making statements to the effect of "we are all deeply saddened and shocked," "the family appreciates their privacy during this difficult time," and so on.

As we entered the store, a worker carrying a ladder nudged me, apologized profusely, and went on his way toward the back. The place was very nearly ready, the display cabinets installed and shiny white and navy-blue surfaces everywhere. The only thing missing was the jewelry.

Oren and his father walked off, deep in conversation with another man in a shirt and tie, while Caroline struck up a conversation with a woman about my age. She had dark hair and was supermodel thin, a good foot taller than Oren's plump mother. I stood around awkwardly and tried not to get in the way, completely out of my depth and ready to stab a bitch for one puff of a cigarette.

"Alexandria!" Caroline waved me over. I smiled politely and went to her side. "This is Vanessa, head of marketing. Vanessa, this is Oren's fiancée, Alexandria." Caroline wrapped an arm around my waist and smiled. It didn't even feel fake, and I got another pang of guilt for lying to her.

I extended my hand to the supermodel, doing my best to copy how Alex introduced herself. "It's a pleasure to make your acquaintance."

Vanessa placed her bony hand in mine and gave it one quick shake, but her eyes zeroed in on the ring on my other hand. "Lovely to meet you."

I scrambled for something to say. "The store is looking great."

"Yes, the contractors have done a fantastic job. Other than the painters." She rolled her eyes and didn't even try to drop her voice as a man in overalls came past with a can of paint. "This is the third time we've had to repaint because they can't seem to get the color right."

I looked around. The paint was white. How could you get white wrong?

"Oh. That's . . . uh . . . how frustrating."

But her focus was no longer on me. "Oren." She beamed as he joined us. I felt him come up behind me before I saw him, but he didn't touch me. He stepped around me and went straight to her.

"Hello, Vanessa." They kissed on the cheek as she dug her French-manicured nails into his biceps. I dug my teeth into the inside of my cheek.

"Everything going to plan?" he asked as he backed away.

Her hand stayed on his arm for just a little too long before she finally dropped it. "Other than the painting, yes. The stock arrived yesterday. We have a photographer taking some promo shots out back as we speak."

"Oh, it's here?" Oren's mom sounded excited.

"Yes, it's here, Mother." Oren gave her a warm smile. Then his eyes landed on mine, and his smile fell just a little. My heart clenched, but I kept a neutral expression on my face.

"Oh, Oren, your tie is wonky." Without waiting for permission, Vanessa leaned forward and straightened his already perfect tie, her hands lingering on his chest.

"Alexandria, we had a special piece flown in to put on display for the opening. I was hoping to show it to you." Caroline gestured in the direction of the back room as Vanessa gestured to the front.

"Oren, I need your opinion on something," she said.

I took a step to the side and wrapped my arm around his. He stiffened a little but paused.

"Oren." I ignored the bitch with thinly veiled sights on an engaged man (while artfully ignoring it wasn't me he was engaged to) and looked up at him. His sharp jaw ticked, and then he looked down at me. I injected as much sincerity into my gaze as I could. "Would you show me the piece your mom is talking about? I'd love to learn more about what you do."

There was a pause. Some of the tension around his eyes eased. He looked from me to Vanessa and back again, then bent his arm so my hand was in the crook of his elbow.

"I'll be with you in a moment, Vanessa," he dismissed her before leading me to the back of the store, his mom following. I leaned into him just a little, letting his warmth comfort me in a situation that was making me feel all kinds of awkward.

In a back room that was more like a vault, a photographer was taking photos of shiny expensive things against a backdrop. A man and woman in matching navy suits and white gloves assisted and handled the jewelry.

Caroline greeted them warmly and spoke with them for a few moments as Oren shook hands with the photographer and inspected some of the pictures on her camera.

The two assistants brought out a large leather box and set it on the table. From inside, they pulled out one of those neck display things you see necklaces hanging off of in stores.

Sitting on it was probably the most expensive thing I'd been in the same room with.

"Come, have a closer look." Caroline grabbed me by the wrist and pulled me to her side with a wide, excited grin. Oren stepped up on my other side.

"This is the Adelia. It was made by Charles Fitzwilliam Winthrop in 1803, two years after he opened his first store, as a wedding gift for his wife and was named after her. It's stayed in the family all these years."

"It's very beautiful." I didn't know fashion or fancy rich people shit, but even I could appreciate this. Dozens of the most brilliant clear stones made up the sides, disappearing around the back of the stand, and a massive deep green gem took pride of place in the middle, with three smaller green gems on either side. I kept my hands firmly at my sides; my fingers itched to touch it, to feel the cool stones, but knowing my luck, I'd somehow manage to break it.

"Eighty-six three-carat, VVS1-clarity diamonds; six four-carat emeralds; and the nineteen-carat Adelia emerald," Oren piped in. "It's been worn by Grace Kelly, Sharon Stone, and Angelina Jolie, just to name a few, and has been loaned out to museums on several occasions."

"It has its own guard." Caroline giggled, as if the thought of protecting something literally priceless was just too funny. "When it's on display, it has one of those serious, frowning men with sunglasses next to it at all times."

Her amusement was infectious, and I found myself laughing, partly because her description reminded me of my own serious, frowning friend.

"I bet George knows him." I nudged her with my elbow, and she laughed out loud, startling the photographer.

"Yes, he has that frowning thing down pat, but he's a good man. Good at his job."

"Yes, he's the best," I readily agreed.

"Anyway, I also had it brought down because I wanted your opinion on it."

"Mine?" My eyebrows shot up while Oren's head whipped

around to frown at his mother.

"Yes. I was hoping you'd consider wearing it. For the wedding."

I shook my head and opened and closed my mouth like a fish, no idea what to say, but she waved me down and kept speaking.

"I know you'll want to pick out your gown, and this may not match, or maybe you have a family heirloom you'd rather wear, or maybe you just think it's gaudy. So if you don't want to, that's completely fine. But every Winthrop bride since old Charles Fitzwilliam's wedding has worn a Winthrop piece on her wedding day, and I'd love it if you'd consider continuing the tradition. If you don't like this one, we can have something else brought out of the vaults."

I stood there, stunned, for way longer than what was acceptable or comfortable. Caroline just watched me with a kind look on her face and waited patiently.

I couldn't help liking this woman. She knew very well this was a marriage of convenience, yet here she was, doing her darnedest to make me feel like a real part of the family.

Oren cleared his throat and said in a low voice, "Mother, considering the circumstances of the marri—"

I cut him off with a firm touch to his forearm. "I would be honored to wear it, Caroline. It's beautiful, and I don't think I'll do it justice, but I'd be delighted to keep your family tradition going."

She gave me a bright smile, patted me on the hand, and nodded once, as if it was decided.

When I looked up at Oren, he was watching me with a perplexing look on his face. It wasn't the anger and derision, the barely contained disgust, I'd endured from him for the past twenty-four hours, but it wasn't anything I could place my finger on either.

He didn't say anything as we made our way outside, but as we passed through the front doors, he placed his hand at my lower back. I'd never admit how fucking happy that simple touch made me.

It wasn't until we were strolling up the picturesque street on the way to lunch that I wondered if Alex would be OK with the decision I'd made for her. After all, it would be her wearing the necklace on the day. *Their* wedding day.

The restaurant was nearby, so I didn't have much time to examine the hollow feeling that had appeared in the pit of my stomach.

We were seated in the shade in the alfresco area. With crisp white tablecloths and lush verdant plants all over the place, it felt expensive. I kept expecting someone to strut up and ask if anyone was interested in a game of croquet.

Oren and his father chatted about the new store as we were handed menus. *Great.* Another menu where I barely understood half the words. I recognized one—*tart*—and decided it was the safest option before setting the menu down and reaching for a glass of water.

People walked past on the street, dressed much better than I ever was. Except today, of course. Today I was dressed like Alex, pretending to be Alex, falling for Alex's fiancé.

Fuck! I was falling for Oren Winthrop. I chugged my water, my mouth suddenly parched.

"Cousin Alexandria!"

A loud man's voice startled me and made me splutter my drink. I coughed, dabbing at my chin with my napkin and using the distraction to buy myself some time. Caroline patted me on the back gently.

The man standing on the other side of the restaurant's low fence smiled brightly right at me. He looked in his late forties or early fifties, had a receding hairline, and was wearing a linen suit with a light pink shirt. He was tall—almost as tall as Oren—and on the skinny side.

"Cousin Preston," I finally said, smiling politely. I only recognized him from the videos and photos of him speaking to the press after Alex's father died. Alex had never mentioned him during our cram session the night before we swapped. Were they close? Was I supposed to get up and give him a hug? Did he even know about the arrangement—the one that was making my stomach feel both hollow and in knots at the same time?

"Your mother mentioned you were in New Orleans. What a pleasant surprise!" He beamed at me, but his almost too wide eyes kept darting about the table.

"Yes." I coughed again, not that I really needed to. "I'm here visiting with my . . . Oren's . . . my fiancé's . . ." I was really fucking this up.

Caroline saved me, taking over like the class act she was. "Alexandria is spending some time with us to finalize the wedding arrangements. I'm Oren's mother, and this is my husband, Oren senior."

"It's a pleasure to meet you, ma'am, sir."

There was a beat of awkward silence. "Would you like to join us for lunch?" Caroline asked, and I clenched my teeth.

"Oh, I wouldn't want to impose." Preston pressed a hand to his chest.

"It's not an imposition." Oren smiled politely. "I'd love to meet a member of Alex's family."

"If you insist," Preston agreed.

He didn't waste a single second before flashing a wide smile and making his way toward the front door. He would need to go through the restaurant to come to the alfresco area.

I had a minute, tops, before he was here. There was no time to message Alex for information. What the fuck was I supposed to do?

"Sweetheart, are you OK?" Caroline placed a gentle hand on my arm, her eyes full of concern.

I must've looked downright panicked. It was certainly how I felt—my chest tightening, my breath coming in pants. I cast my wide eyes about the table.

Mr. Winthrop was perusing the menu, looking as if he hardly heard anything being said, let alone gave a shit about it. Oren was looking at me, his brow furrowed.

"I don't know . . ." *Fuck!* I couldn't exactly tell them I didn't know him. He was supposed to be my cousin. "He doesn't know," I blurted instead. If I could convince them to keep the lunch brief and not talk about the wedding, I might just be OK. "About our arrangement. Only my mother knows. I can't . . . can we just . . ."

Oren's hand landed on my knee under the table.

I turned to face him, and suddenly there was only his hazel eyes, only the heat of his hand, only his soft, low voice saying: "It's OK, Alex. I've got you."

My breathing slowed. The tension in my shoulders eased.

When Cousin Preston walked up to the table, the smile pulling at my lips was actually genuine, but it was all for Oren.

Preston shook hands with everyone, complimenting Caroline. Mr. Winthrop put on the charm, engaging in the conversation now that there was someone to put on a show for.

"So what brings you to New Orleans, Preston?" he asked as the waiters brought out our starters.

"I have a friendly business acquaintance who lives here. I'm looking to invest in a new venture of his. Entrepreneurship runs in the family. How is Zamorano Wines tracking this quarter, Alexandria? I can't seem to get onto George for an update."

"Fine." I smiled brightly. "It's going great. George is here with me, so he's been busy."

Oren leaned back, the picture of calm, and rested his arm on the back of my chair. "I've kept Alex busy with the wedding coming up."

"Alex?" Preston's eyes narrowed in suspicion. "You've been insisting on 'Alexandria' since you were old enough to say it without fumbling the vowels."

I laughed, hoping it sounded as carefree as Oren looked and not as panicked as I felt. "I am marrying the man. He can call me whatever he wants."

Oh, how I wished names didn't matter, that it wouldn't be a big deal I wasn't Alex, or even Alexandria.

Oren planted a gentle kiss on my cheek, really selling the happy engaged couple routine. I couldn't help it—I melted into it and sighed. He paused just before pulling away, and our eyes met. For a split second, we shared a moment of absolute honesty. I let him see how strong my feelings were, even if they were confusing. He let me see how vulnerable he felt in this situation.

Thankfully, the rest of the table just saw a tender moment.

"Ah, young love." Preston beamed at us. Was I imagining the hint of mocking in his smile, overly sensitive to being caught out in another lie?

Oren's mother was smiling warmly at us, her chubby hands clasped over her chest. His father watched us too, his expression neutral, but his eyes considered me with a new kind of curiosity.

"So where are you staying, Preston?" Mr. Winthrop asked, diverting the attention from us.

"At the Lafayette. I only booked for a week, and I actually need to stay longer to finish off my business here, but they're booked solid." He sighed dramatically. "I was just on my way to get some lunch before making calls to other hotels in the area, but I fear I may not be able to find anything suitable at such short notice."

"Oh, well, then you must stay with us!" Caroline piped up, her perfect southern manners kicking in before she realized what she was doing.

I gritted my teeth. Oren's arm at the back of my chair stiffened. We both managed to keep the trepidation off our faces, but we didn't reinforce the invitation.

Not that it took much to convince him. He said he couldn't impose; she insisted it would be their pleasure, and they had more than enough room—he was family after all. And it was settled.

Fuck my life. It was hard enough pretending I was a rich, well-educated, properly behaved chick to a bunch of other rich people. How in the devil's asshole was I supposed to convince someone who had known Alex since birth?

We finished our meals, Mr. Winthrop arranged to have a car pick Cousin Preston up the following day, and it was done.

He walked off down the street, and we waited for our drivers to pull up.

As soon as Preston was around the corner, Mr. Winthrop turned to his wife with a scowl. "What were you thinking, Caroline? Jesus Christ, woman."

"I know." She closed her eyes and sighed. "I kicked myself as soon as the words were out of my mouth. Oh, Alexandria, darling, I'm so sorry."

"It's OK. You didn't do it on purpose." I squeezed her shoulder as anxiety squeezed my lungs that little bit tighter. I just couldn't be mad at her.

Oren's strong fingers wrapped around mine, and he tugged. "It's going to be OK." He smiled at me, only me. "I'll make sure he doesn't suspect a thing. You're safe."

I held on to his hand until the cars pulled up. Despite myself, I believed him.

T: Why do women try to tear each other down instead of propping each other up, do you think?

A: I don't know. We're socially conditioned to see each other as competition?

T: Hmm. Maybe. Still, Oren's work buddy is a fucking bitch. She was all over him right in front of me!

A: I mean, it's pretty tacky, but who cares. Not like it's a real marriage.

T: Oh, hey! Also! Your cousin Preston showed up out of nowhere, and now he's staying with the Winthrops, so that's fun! :D

A: WHAT?!

A: You didn't think to lead with that?

T: It's done. But I could use some intel.

A: Can you talk? I can call now.

T: Gmme 5.

Chapter 14

ALEX

The Cottonmouth Inn was closed on Mondays, and I was going to use the time to see as much of New Orleans as I possibly could before we had to switch back. *Which may happen sooner rather than later if Preston becomes a problem.*

I couldn't believe he'd just shown up out of the blue like that. He was so persistent in trying to get a foothold in the family business it was like I'd been swatting at a fly since my father died. At the beginning, it was helpful to have him manage the press and help with the staff while Mom and I grieved. But when he started to make decisions that overstepped, I had to take over. It caused a rift between the two sides of the family, and we didn't speak for months, but by the time Christmas came around, we'd all been able to laugh about it over bottles of Verdejo from our personal collection at the vineyard.

Preston was a chronic entrepreneur. I knew his interest and persistence was just enthusiasm for business, but I'd taken it more personally than I maybe should've, weighed down by the pressure to step into my father's shoes and prove myself.

All those anxieties had flooded back when I got the text from Toni, but we'd had a good talk about it, and as I made my way down the stairs, I decided to put it out of my mind.

It was usually rather difficult for me to put anything out of my mind. I was more the "overthink it until it turns into a panic attack" kind of gal. But something about living Toni's life made it easier. If Preston became a problem, we'd switch back early. Until then, I'd rock the red shorts and one of Toni's less offensive T-shirts and have another carefree day.

At the bottom of the stairs, I paused. The door to the bar was open, and the soft sound of acoustic guitar drifted through the crack.

I glanced at the external door. I'd planned on joining the cheesiest ghost tour I could find and using my tips to play tourist, but the melancholy notes being coaxed from the guitar strings called to me too. I was almost certain it was Ren's dexterous fingers plucking the soulful music from the instrument, but I'd never seen him here during the day.

My curiosity got the better of me, and I pushed the door open.

Most of the chairs and stools were upside down on the tables, and all the lights were off, the only illumination coming through the grimy colored-glass windows. In the middle of the bar, Andre, Ren, and Loretta sat around one of the little worn tables, a full bottle of whiskey and a single glass sitting in the middle.

I frowned, suddenly unsure.

The music cut off abruptly, and my attention swung from the bottle to Ren. He was sitting with the guitar in his lap, one tattooed arm slung carelessly over the instrument, his eyes fixed firmly on me.

"This is a private party." His voice lacked the venom he usually directed at me, but his eyes held plenty of challenge. It made me bristle, even as my thighs clenched, but I pushed the inappropriate feelings aside.

At the sound of Ren's voice, Loretta looked up and gave me a weak, if surprised, smile. Then Andre tore his eyes from the bottle on the table. It was *his* gaze that rooted me to the spot, as if my feet were fused with the decades-old timber floor.

He watched me for a long moment, his expression giving nothing away, before he finally spoke. "She can stay."

His strong, clear words reverberated through those timber boards and into my chest, and they were final. I was staying.

Ren flashed him a confused look, then turned back to me.

I had no idea what the hell I'd walked in on, but Andre's intensity was as compelling as my desire to defy Ren. I walked forward, grabbed a chair from the next table, and sat across from him, completing their weird little circle.

Ren sighed, shook his head, and started playing again. It wasn't a song or even a specific piece of music—it was more like he was just jamming, letting his fingers dance across the strings and seeing what came out.

It would've been mesmerizing if I hadn't been so curious about why Andre was staring at the bottle on the table as if it held the answers to all the world's problems.

I glanced at Loretta. She was reclined in her chair, her bony arms crossed loosely as she stared into space.

I wasn't used to not knowing things. I sat down at tables much bigger and much nicer than this one holding all the cards. In any other situation, I would've already demanded to know what was going on about three times. But now that I was part of this weird little sit-in, it just didn't seem right to speak.

I felt like we were all waiting on something, and I didn't want to rush it.

I leaned back and lost myself in Ren's music. The notes carried me away, driving out all other thoughts.

It wasn't until Andre shifted in his seat that I realized I'd closed my eyes. I opened them to find Ren's stare on my face, his fingers continuing to pluck at the strings. Our eyes locked for a second, and then we both turned to Andre.

Andre propped one elbow on the table and reached for the bottle with his other hand. The cap was already off, resting on the table beside the glass. He poured a standard drink into the tumbler before setting the bottle down with precision.

Ren stopped playing, his lithe body draped over the guitar.

Loretta cleared her throat, and for once, it didn't turn into a coughing fit. She leaned both arms on the table and watched Andre.

We all watched Andre.

He sighed, his big chest expanding with a breath that looked heavy with pain I wasn't privy to. Then he grasped the tumbler and lifted it before his face.

"Happy birthday, Dad," he murmured to the amber liquid before knocking it back.

It was the first time I'd seen him drink alcohol.

I swallowed around the lump in my throat. I simultaneously wanted to know the story behind this odd ritual and hoped I wouldn't get to hear it. I wasn't sure I could handle the pain.

Andre dropped the glass back down to the table and screwed the lid back onto the bottle, his hand lingering on the neck.

Ren started playing again.

Loretta reached across the table and gripped Andre's hand, his big fingers swallowing her bony ones. She patted their clasped hands. "You're doing just fine, sugar."

"Thank you for being here, Loretta."

She nodded and got to her feet, patting him on the shoulder on her way out.

Andre stood too. He placed the bottle back in its spot behind the bar and deposited the dirty glass in the sink.

With the weird little bubble of silence broken, I finally felt like I could speak. "I'm so sorry for intruding."

"I told you to stay." Andre gripped my shoulder before returning to his seat. "You're not intruding."

I still felt uneasy about it. I was just about to apologize again and make my excuses, but Andre started talking before I could make a move.

"It's my father's birthday today." He watched the top of the table intently as he spoke. Ren kept his focus on his guitar. "He died twelve years ago."

"I'm so sorry. I lost my father too."

"My momma died when I was ten years old. My daddy was so heartbroken he just about forgot he had a son, someone else who loved and needed him. He lost himself in the grief and tried to drown it in whiskey. If it wasn't for Mama's friend Delphine, I don't know if I would've had food to eat every day. I definitely wouldn't have finished high school."

I remembered the woman from the restaurant, and a piece of the puzzle fell into place. No wonder they were so close—she practically raised him.

"My parents bought this place before I was born, but by the time my father died, he'd run it into the ground. Hell, he'd drunk half his stock away. If it wasn't for Loretta, this place would've gone under a long time ago, and we would've ended up homeless."

Another puzzle piece—that's why Loretta seemed to know everything about this place. She'd been around from the beginning.

"My father died alone after drinking himself unconscious like he did most nights. I hadn't spoken to him in about a year at that stage. I was living with a girlfriend, being a complete bum and well on my way to following in my father's alcoholic footsteps.

"The day I found out he was dead, I went off the rails. My parents' apartment and the bar were mine. I was finally rid of a parent who had been more of a burden than anything.

"I called all my so-called friends, everyone I knew, and had a massive bender right here. I didn't give a shit about anything. It was a total free-for-all, people helping themselves to whatever they wanted behind the bar, the music way too loud for regulations, people dancing on the tables and fucking in the corners. I got blind drunk—the worst I'd ever been. I passed out right there."

He pointed at a spot halfway between the table and the bar.

"I woke up alone. Yeah, everyone had bailed and I was the only one in the bar, but I mean in the *cosmic* sense. I realized I was alone. Those people weren't my friends. My parents were dead. I had dozens of messages from the girlfriend, the last ones telling me it was over and my shit was on her front lawn. I was alone and I felt like shit. Worst hangover of my life. When I realized I was exactly the same as my dad, letting myself get lost in the bottle to dull the pain of life, I bawled my eyes out. I cried like a little baby, sitting in a puddle of something sticky, in the remnants of my father's failed life.

"Eventually, the tears dried up, and I made a decision—I would not be like him. I would not piss away my life. I picked myself up and started cleaning. I scrubbed my soul clean while I scrubbed this damn bar from top to bottom. I wanted to quit so damn bad, but I kept going."

"You puked every hour." Ren chuckled, shaking his head. "Almost like clockwork."

"That's the day Ren and I met." Andre leaned back in his chair, the invisible weight on his shoulders appearing a little lighter. "He walked in off the street and asked what the fuck happened. I couldn't even pretend to care what other people thought of me in that moment. I told him the whole sad story. Most people would've left, but when I got back from the bathroom after puking again, he was sweeping. Loretta showed up in the afternoon, and the three of us cleaned the place up. I didn't even ask him why he'd walked in until after it was all done and Loretta made us burgers for dinner. He was looking for venues where his band could perform. I gave him a spot without even listening to them play."

They exchanged a look full of shared memories. Not for the first time, I wondered how I fit in with them. The sex with Ren was mind-blowing, the flirting with Andre undeniable, yet there was definitely something between *them*. My logical, organized nature wanted to categorize it, label it so I could understand. But human nature was rarely that simple.

"So you don't drink anymore?" I asked.

"Haven't touched the stuff since that night, except once a year on my father's birthday. The anniversaries are hard."

I nodded. Every time my father's birthday or the anniversary of his death came around, I wondered if I was doing his memory justice, if he'd be proud of me, if I was letting him down.

"I have one drink—just one—on his birthday. To prove to him and to myself that I can have *just one*. That I'm stronger than the bottle and stronger than he was."

I reached out and grabbed his forearm. "You're the strongest person I know. Thank you for telling me your story."

"You're welcome. I think it's important to talk about the difficult things. Telling our stories helps not just others but ourselves know who we truly are. It's important to be honest about who you are."

His dark eyes stared into mine, the weight of the secret he was keeping for me as arresting as the intensity of his gaze. I didn't feel like he was calling me out, subtly taking a dig at me for wanting to live someone else's life. He was just telling me, in his own way, that it was OK to be myself.

Ren was plucking the strings lazily, but his gaze drifted between Andre and me. I had no idea how he'd take it, and I didn't think I could handle him calling me a bitch—not today. So I deflected.

"Well, since you're in a sharing mood, what's the story between you two?"

They both chuckled. Ren darted his tongue out and licked the piercing in his bottom lip, smirking. "I don't like labels."

Andre nodded. "Neither do I."

"We were friends. Then we were more. We're family. Andre lost his parents, and mine are . . ." For the first time that day, a discordant note rang from the guitar. Ren clenched his teeth before setting it aside and leaning forward. "We're just each other's family now. Are we in a committed monogamous relationship? No. Do we fuck from time to time? Yes. Does it have to be weird? Fuck no. Toni, I gotta ask, after years of this silent lone wolf bullshit, why the sudden interest?"

They were both looking at me with amusement in their eyes. I chose to ignore Ren's last question. "So you don't care that Ren and I . . ."

"Fucked?" Andre flashed a wide grin, his eyes sparkling. "No. Actually, since you brought it up . . ."

He leaned forward and I didn't lean back. Not one bit of me wanted to. But whatever he was about to say, wherever this charged moment was heading, was interrupted by a loud banging on the front door.

Andre frowned and growled. "We're closed," he shouted over his shoulder.

But whoever was on the other side was determined. The knocking became louder.

"I refuse to leave until you open this door," said a distinctly feminine voice, the pronunciation indicating a good education, privilege.

My heartbeat kicked up a notch. Had someone found me out? But I didn't recognize the voice. Ren frowned too, cocking his head to listen better.

"Do you hear me? I demand to speak with someone. This is the last . . ." The woman continued to ramble as Andre huffed and stormed to the door.

Just as Andre started to unlatch the deadbolt, Ren's eyes widened. He shot to his feet, one hand extended as if he could reach all the way across the room and pull the bigger man back.

The deadbolt clicked; the door swung open.

I knew the intimidating scowl Andre must be wearing—I'd been on the receiving end of it—but the people on the other side of the door weren't perturbed at all. A woman and a man pushed past him and straight into the bar as if they owned the place.

"Excuse me," said Andre. "Who the hell do you think you are? This is private property, and I'm going to—"

"This doesn't concern you, sir," the man snapped. "We're simply looking for—"

But he was interrupted too. The woman was on a mission. "Renshaw Bradley Lewis Pratt. This is how you treat your mother?"

I'd had an odd pang of recognition as soon as they'd walked in, but the way the woman addressed Ren cemented who she was. She was a head shorter than him but had the same brown hair and intense eyes. Take away the tattoos and add a good twenty-five years, and the man was a carbon copy of Ren.

"Well, Mother, you cut me off, so I cut you off." Ren crossed his arms and stared down at the short woman, who wasn't even remotely backing down from his attitude.

Andre and I shared a look of shock, both of us stunned into silence.

"Oh, for goodness' sake. Don't you two start this nonsense again." Ren's dad pinched the bridge of his nose, coming to stand by his family.

His mother started to go red in the face. "He's been ignoring our calls for three days, knowing full well we were in town specifically to see him."

"Yes, well, dear, let's keep in mind why we're here, shall we?" The dad was the only one who seemed to be keeping his cool.

"What the fuck are you doing here?" Ren sneered at his parents with more disdain than I'd ever seen in anyone's eyes.

"Watch your language, young man." She actually wagged her

finger at him as if he were ten years old, and I couldn't hold in the snort of laughter.

All eyes turned to me as though everyone in the room had just realized I was there. For some reason I found that even more amusing, and a full laugh burst out of me before I could stop it. Out of the corner of my eye, I could see Andre's big shoulders shaking too. That only made me lose it more, and I doubled over, holding on to the back of a chair for balance while I let the laughter loose. Eventually, I got myself under control and wiped the tears under my eyes.

"Who is this . . . *woman*?" The mom gestured in my direction, looking me up and down as though I were a stray dog. "What is this place? Is this what you're doing with your life? This is what you have chosen over your own family?"

"Seriously?" Ren uncrossed his arms, his hands balled into fists. "You came here to shit on my life again? We've been here, we've done this. I'm not interested. That's why you cut me off from my trust fund. That's why I cut *you* off from any and all communication. I'm not *doing* this again, Mother. Just leave."

Mom's finger went up, ready to wag again. She opened her mouth, but Dad came up behind her and placed his hands on her shoulders. Her words died in her throat, her hand and her eyes dropping in defeat.

"Son, we just want to see you." Dad seemed to be the voice of reason in this family. "All we want is to have lunch. Please. We just want to talk."

"No. Get out." Ren pointed at the open door, where Andre

still stood with his arms over his chest, watching everything play out with narrowed eyes.

"Renshaw." Mom's voice was calmer, but barely restrained frustration quivered beneath it. "We came all this way to see you. The least you can do is let us take you out to lunch."

There was a moment of tense silence. They stared at each other, no one backing down.

Andre shifted by the door, his boots squeaking.

"Fine." Ren drew the word out as his lips curved into a slow smile—the kind that usually made me wonder what kind of vicious words would come next. "But I'd like to bring a date."

"Oh." Mom flinched as if he'd sprayed her in the face like a misbehaving cat. "You're seeing someone?"

The jealousy that bubbled up inside was as surprising as it was unwelcome. Then I realized he was probably talking about Andre, and it melted away altogether.

"Nope." He kept that smile plastered to his face. "I wanna bring her."

One tatted hand pointed right at my chest. My eyebrows flew up.

Mom didn't hesitate. "No."

"She comes or I don't."

No one was even looking in my direction. Was anyone actually going to invite me? Did I have a choice here?

"Excuse me." I put on my best boardroom voice—calm and demanding. Four sets of eyes flew to me, but before I could object, Dad piped in.

"Yes. Fine. Bring her. One o'clock tomorrow at Le Clocher. Don't be late."

He didn't give anyone a chance to argue or back out. He just took his wife's hand and pulled her out onto the street.

Andre slammed the door behind them and leaned back against it.

"What the fuck?" I demanded, channeling Toni in all her outraged glory.

Ren had the decency to look bashful, rubbing the back of his neck as he eyed me. "Look, it kills me to ask literally anything from you, but please come? I hate my parents. The only reason I'm going is to get them off my back, but the only way I can get through this disaster is if I can fuck with them while I'm at it. And they *really* seem to dislike you." He chuckled, losing some of that apologetic, groveling vibe. "Like, *instant* disdain."

I gaped at him, then turned to Andre for assistance, bugging my eyes out.

The asshole just shrugged. "Could be fun."

Those words and his smirk reminded me of the conversation we'd had over beignets. I couldn't count the number of times I'd fantasized about saying and doing improper things in a high-class establishment, seeing the outrage on stuck-up, filthy-rich faces. And here was my chance to do just that.

"Fine. Whatever. It's a free meal." I picked at my fingernails to really sell the nonchalant, aloof vibe.

A: Hey, did you know that Ren's full name is Renshaw?

T: LOL! No! But thank you—I'm gonna give him endless hell for it. Maybe I'll make up a rhyme . . .

A: Also, did you know his parents are some rich jerks?

T: Didn't even know he had parents. I just assumed he hatched out of a giant egg, a fully formed asshole, and immediately set to finding me so he could fulfill his species' natural instinct to be a douche.

A: Well, they came to the bar today. They're really awful. I actually kind of felt bad for him.

T: Don't. He wouldn't piss on you if you were on fire. Trust me, don't waste any kind of feelings on Renshaw (LOL!).

A: Toni, I really think if you got to know him a little, you might actually get along.

A: Also, he's ridiculously talented! I can't believe his band isn't already famous.

T: OMFG! You fucked him!

A: What?

A: No. How did you . . .

A: I mean . . .

A: Maybe . . .

T: Fuuuuuuuuck!

T: When I said to get laid, I meant literally anyone BUT him.

A: I'm sorry! I didn't mean to. It was just a bit of fun, OK? It's not like he's expecting a relationship.

T: FML!

A: Now that it's out in the open, can I just say that it was the best sex of my life?

T: Eew! NO!

A: It was so hot! And he has his dick pierced!

T: Gag! Stop!

Chapter 15

TONI

We were silent on the way home from lunch. George walked up just as we entered the house, took one look at my panicked face, and followed the four of us into Oren's study.

Oren senior turned, about to say something, but clamped his mouth shut when he saw George closing the door behind us.

"George knows," I said hurriedly. "He and my mother are the only ones across the whole situation."

"What happened?" George asked, looking between us.

"My wife happened," the older man grumbled, then rehashed the disastrous lunch.

George ran a hand through his sandy hair, propping his

other on his hip. My lungs constricted, as if Cousin Preston were gripping them and squeezing the air right out.

George spoke directly to the Winthrops as if I already knew everything. "Preston thinks of himself as an entrepreneur, but most of his business ideas are . . . for lack of a better word, crap. He's greedy and persistent, though, and has been trying to get a foothold in Zamorano Wines since I can remember. If he found out the winery was in financial trouble, he might just leak the information to hurt the business out of pure spite. I never liked the man and I don't trust him, but as long as he's kept in the dark, he's harmless."

"Oh, I really messed up, didn't I?" Caroline wrung her hands, her big eyes starting to water.

Her husband ignored her. "How long could he possibly stay? We just keep him occupied, keep his focus away from the business, and you two"—he pointed between me and Oren—"better put on a damn good show."

He stomped to the door, wrenched it open, and walked out, grumbling under his breath.

"Naturally he's going to blame *me* for this." Oren sighed, moved to a bar cart in the corner, and poured himself a large whiskey.

Caroline rubbed his shoulder. "Oh, darling, but it was my running mouth that got us into this mess."

"Yeah, but I'm the one who couldn't find a wife like a real Winthrop man," he mumbled into his glass before taking a large sip.

To stop my eyebrows from rising in surprise, I walked over and poured myself a drink too. Oren was tall, handsome, and rich—I found it hard to believe he couldn't find a willing participant. But I couldn't exactly ask him why he'd agreed to this in the first place. For all I knew, he'd already had that conversation with the real Alex.

When I straightened and took a sip of my drink, I found his eyes on me. The alcohol burned a smooth path down my throat as Oren's intense gaze burned a hole in my soul. I couldn't look away. I wanted to tell him everything and be done with it.

But he spoke first. "I didn't want to marry someone just because I had to. I didn't want some poor woman to end up wrapped up in this mess without knowing the details. I didn't want a loveless marriage. At least this way, we both know what we're getting into."

I nodded, and we both took another sip, breaking our stare-off.

"The fact that this had to be organized for me makes me a failure in my father's eyes. He'd rather I just picked some unsuspecting socialite and made do. This puts our family at higher risk of being caught out and shamed. But he's got no choice if he wants the business to stay in the family."

"I'll go talk to him." Caroline was no longer cowering and apologetic. The look on her face was determined; I almost felt bad for Oren senior and what he had coming. "I love you and I am proud of you, sweetheart." She kissed her son on the cheek and marched out of the room, head held high.

"Look, nothing needs to change," George reasoned. "You've had to keep up appearances for the staff anyway. You just have to be a little more careful now."

"Right." Oren nodded and threw back the rest of the amber liquid in his glass. "We just keep pretending. How hard could it be?"

His hazel eyes bored into mine again, rendering me speechless. With George in the room, I couldn't wrap my arms around him like I so badly wanted to. And I couldn't agree with him either. Because I wasn't so sure we were pretending anymore.

Oren placed the empty glass on his table, then walked out without another word.

Once we were alone in the room, George turned to me and slowly held his arms out at his sides.

I narrowed my eyes at him and finished my drink, depositing the glass next to Oren's.

He tilted his head and waved his hands, beckoning me into a hug.

"Eew. No. I'm not a hugger," I said, even as I hugged my own damn self around the middle.

"Stop being a damn brat and come here. We can pretend it never happened."

I sighed and rolled my eyes but leaned into him. His long arms wrapped around my back, and he held me firmly for a long moment. George had strong shoulders, but he was a little soft around the middle.

I couldn't remember the last time someone hugged me for a nonsexual reason. There was no way I'd ever admit it to George, but it was kind of nice.

Eventually I pulled away. "Should we just swap back? This is too dangerous, right?"

He shrugged. "Up to you. I've been telling you from the start you can bail out whenever you want. Alex will understand."

I chewed on my bottom lip. I wasn't a quitter. I needed that money. But mostly, I wasn't ready to leave and never see Oren again. I needed to figure out what the fuck my cold, dead heart was playing at when it came to life around him. "How bad is this really? I mean, he's family."

George bounced his head from side to side as he considered my question. "Yeah, but they were never exactly close. They see each other once, maybe twice a year. If he didn't already realize you're not her, I don't think he's going to."

"Fuck." I sighed. "OK, let me sleep on it."

George nodded. "Whatever you decide, I'm ready."

"Thank you, George," I told him and meant it.

I headed upstairs, locked myself in my room, and spent the remainder of the afternoon trying to hold back a panic attack. The shortness of breath, the increased heart rate, the thoughts of all the many and varied things that could go wrong in this scenario just kept bubbling up like a volcano ready to burst. Somehow, eventually, I managed to get it under control.

I was determined to see this through. Not just for the money, not just to prove to myself that I could, but because of *him*. I couldn't deny it anymore. Oren Charles Winthrop had somehow managed to crawl his privileged, coiffed way under my skin.

It was never, *ever* going to happen. We were from two completely different worlds, and we had no future. I needed to use the time I had left to figure this out and nip it in the bud before we parted ways. Because in another month, he would be marrying Alexandria, and I would be going back to my dingy life above a bar. Nothing was going to change that, and I needed to get over it.

After a long bath and a steak dinner I had the chef bring to my room, I got into some comfy pajamas and flopped back onto the ridiculously soft bed, staring at the tall ceiling. I was tired, emotionally spent, but my mind still wasn't ready to switch off, my body not quite ready for sleep.

It was getting late and the house was quiet. Maybe a movie would help me wind down. I peeked my head into the entertainment room Oren had pointed out. It was empty. I made my way downstairs in bare feet, hunted down a giant bag of cheddar cheese–flavored popcorn, grabbed a soda out of the fridge, and made my way back upstairs.

As I rounded the corner, I paused. The TV was on, and Oren was just lowering himself onto the couch. I was about to back out of the room quietly, but his head whipped around, and once again I found myself frozen to the spot by his stare.

"You beat me to it." I held up the popcorn and gave him a wry smile. "I'll just read in my room or something." I turned to leave, but he reached a hand out and spoke over me.

"No. Don't go. I only just sat down. I haven't even picked a movie."

I bit my lip and regarded the single couch. I was supposed to be figuring out how to get him out of my system, not spending movie night with him.

"Come on." He waved me over with a smile. "I'll let you pick the movie. I'll let you spread out on the couch. I'll even share my candy with you." He held up a bag of peanut butter M&M's and shook it.

I padded over to the couch and lowered myself into the opposite corner, crossing my legs under me. "I guess I could share my popcorn with you as well."

He grinned, leaned back, and threw the remote in my direction. "What are we watching?"

"I don't know. What do you like?"

"Honestly? I can't remember the last time I watched a movie. I'm usually too busy. I used to watch a lot of fantasy and sci-fi when I was a kid."

"You're a nerd? I never would've picked it under those perfectly tailored shirts and that smoldering stare."

"My stare is smoldering? What does that even mean?" He chuckled, but then he gave me the *exact* smoldering stare.

"Please. Like you don't know the effect you have on women." I wriggled in my spot and pulled a blanket over my lap.

He didn't respond, but I didn't miss his smug smile before I focused on flicking through the available films. I settled on some action movie with a ridiculous premise and mediocre acting.

Oren turned the single lamp off, and the only illumination came from the large-screen TV—the explosions and car chases throwing shadows over his face.

Slowly, as the movie played, we inched closer together.

He leaned over to reach into the popcorn. I scooted across to take the last of the candy. I offered him some of my soda; he mixed it with his scotch, but there was only one glass. We ended up shoulder to shoulder, passing the drink between us.

He was slouched, his head leaning back into the soft cushions, one foot propped up on the coffee table. His warm shoulder pressed against mine, seared me. That one little spot of heat spread from my shoulder throughout my body until I felt like I was burning up from the inside, and I had to throw the blanket off.

But then it was obvious how heavily I was breathing, my breasts rising and falling with every breath.

I took a big gulp of the scotch and Coke, finishing the last of it. Oren reached for the glass without looking. His fingers brushed mine, sending more heat shooting up my arm. He brought the glass to his full lips and tipped it, then chuckled when he realized there wasn't any left.

He leaned forward and placed the glass on the table. The corded muscle in his back danced under the cotton.

When he flopped back next to me, suddenly his whole arm was pressed against mine, his head so close that if I tipped mine just a fraction of an inch, I'd be leaning into him.

Before I could give in to the instinct, he turned his head and gave me a lazy smile. "You want another drink? If you pause it, I'll run to my office and grab the bottle."

I held his stare for a moment. His usually bright eyes looked really dark in the dim light.

I *needed* another drink. But I didn't want him to leave.

I shook my head.

His easy smile fell, replaced by something more serious,

something heavier.

His gaze dropped to my lips, mere inches from his, then darted back up to my eyes.

It took every drop of control I had to keep my gaze fixed on his as I swallowed, as my breathing got shallower, as my heartbeat kicked up.

I managed to control my eyes, but my body took on a mind of its own. I shifted my arm against his. The movement was tiny, but we were so still the brush of my finger against the back of his hand may as well have been a scream in a library.

His sharp intake of breath would've been subtle in any other situation, but I was so focused on him, my body so aware of his, there was no missing it. His lips parted, and I lost the battle to keep my eyes off them. They were so full, so soft and inviting.

As though my light touch had spurred him into action, he made the next move—a much more bold, intentional one.

His free hand landed on my knee as he angled his torso in my direction. But he kept his head still, resting on the cushions in the same spot, those lips begging me to lift my head and claim them.

I gave up trying to pretend this wasn't affecting me, and my own lips parted with my labored pants. We breathed each other in as he started to caress my knee, every pass of his fingers inching higher up my leg.

The T-shirt felt almost painfully tight against my straining nipples. I'd never been so turned on in my life, never been so wet before I'd even been kissed. I felt like I was in high school again. Hormones flying, the lust almost impossible to resist, the allure of what might happen next as exciting as his hand—on my thigh now, halfway to where I wanted it most.

I lifted the arm that was flush with his and caressed his cheek with the back of my hand. His stubble was coarse, electric against my skin.

He sighed and closed his eyes as the grip on my thigh tightened. His fingers dug into my flesh, and moisture pooled at my core. I had to bite my lip to stop myself from moaning. How embarrassing—he wasn't even touching me, not really.

Oren kept his eyes closed as his hand resumed its agonizingly slow path up my leg. He licked his lips, and I nearly moaned again at the sight.

The tips of his fingers reached the spot where my leg met my pussy, and I couldn't take this torture any longer.

I leaned forward and mashed my lips to his. They were so wonderfully soft and responded to mine immediately.

Our lips moved in perfect synchronicity, our tongues tangling, our teeth bumping in our desperate need to get closer.

I stopped thinking, forgot who I was and where I was. There was only Oren. I was consumed by him, his smell, his touch, his very soul crawling its way into my chest.

The hand at my thigh went to the back of my head, his fingers tangling in my hair.

Finally, I let myself moan into his mouth.

He leaned farther into me, and I leaned right back.

I pushed away from the back of the couch. Keeping my mouth against his, I swung a leg over his hips and straddled him.

The hand in my hair tightened, pulling lightly at the strands, as his other arm banded around my back and drew me against his chest.

I spread my knees wide and rolled my hips, no longer able to hold back my moans. He was rock hard, almost painfully solid against my aching flesh. His hips moved with mine as we found a grinding rhythm.

He nudged me back just enough to shove a hand between us and grab my breast, kneading it lightly. He growled into my mouth and broke the kiss, only to kiss, lick, nip, *devour* his way down my neck. Pulling the wide collar of my T-shirt down, he ducked his head until his hot mouth wrapped around the nipple. I increased my pace, grinding my hips harder, faster, chasing that heady feeling. But it wasn't enough.

I wanted to crawl inside of him, be completely consumed, but feeling his skin against mine would have to do.

I leaned back and tugged at the hem of his T-shirt until he sat up so I could remove it. His hands dragged up my sides, taking fabric with them, and my T-shirt was gone too.

Every dip and bump of smooth muscle on his lean body begged me to lick it. His auburn hair looked almost black in the dim light, and his broad shoulders glowed in the illumination of another explosion on the TV behind me.

He pulled me against him, bare chest to bare chest, and kissed me once more, his hands running all over me, his lips begging.

I broke the kiss again and scooted back to tug at the waistband of his pajama bottoms. He helped me drag them to his ankles as I backed up and got to my feet, then his hands were at my hips, tugging my shorts and underwear down in one go.

"Fuck." The curse didn't fall from his lips as an awed utterance; it tumbled out dripping with frustration as he ran a hand through his hair.

I leaned back, already preparing myself for rejection even as my heart started to constrict.

Oren looked up into my face with eyes full of lust, his hands gripping my bare hips, not letting me run away. "I don't have any condoms in here."

Relief washed through me so fast it almost knocked me over. I'd never wanted anything as badly as I wanted him inside me in that moment.

"I have the implant." I gestured to the inside of my arm. "I'm pretty sure I'm clean."

"I am too." His smile was brilliant, almost giddy, as he drew me back into his lap.

The smart thing would've been to put our clothes back on, go to one of our rooms, get the rubber, not take the chance. The smart thing would've been to remember who I was, who *he* was, why this couldn't happen.

But I wasn't thinking about all that. I only saw him, felt him as he pulled me in for another searing kiss, his tongue doing incredible things to my lips and mouth.

I rubbed myself on him, sliding my dripping lips up and down his length, and he moaned into my mouth before pulling away to stare into his lap.

"Fuck." That time it came out on a lust-filled whisper. "You're so wet."

In answer, I shifted myself up slightly. He gripped his cock at the base, giving it one quick stroke before I lined myself up and sank down onto him. I slid all the way down until he was buried to the hilt, our hips flush, and we both moaned at the sensation.

I started to grind on him as that consuming fire inside me intensified, making sweat bead at my brow. We kissed, we caressed, we gripped and tugged and writhed against one another as I rode him deep.

His cock filled me up so perfectly, every roll of my hips creating delicious friction against my clit. Coupled with Oren's strong yet gentle hands on my body, it had me making incoherent sounds in minutes.

With one hand on the back of the couch for balance and the other holding on to the back of his neck, I chased my orgasm. It wasn't hard to catch. Pleasure exploded, the burning heat spreading from my core, through my chest, and down my limbs, leaving nothing but ash in its wake.

He captured my moans with his mouth as I rode it out, his kiss messy, desperate.

As my orgasm faded, I found my balance on shaky knees and lifted up just a fraction before slamming back down onto him.

He grunted and bit my bottom lip gently. With both hands on my hips, he set the pace, meeting me thrust for thrust as his hands shoved me down onto his cock over and over again.

His back stiffened and arched off the couch as he pushed me onto him one last time and ground his hips into me, moaning through his release.

He dropped his forehead onto my shoulder and panted against my flushed skin. I rested my cheek against his hair, running a hand through the soft strands as we came down off the high.

After a few minutes, he held me to his chest and stood up. He lifted me until his cock slid out, then set me on my feet. Immediately, his warm, sticky cum started to trickle down my thigh.

"Shit." I looked around for a tissue, but Oren was already wrapping a blanket around my shoulders and sweeping me into his arms.

My eyes widened. "Oren, you're going to get jizz all over this blanket. Let me go clean up."

"Shh." He kissed my cheek. "Let me take care of you."

I melted at his words, relaxing against his chest as he carried me to his room. I kept my eyes trained on his strong jaw as we passed the door to my room, deliberately avoiding thinking about why I had a separate room in this house, why I was even here.

It had happened. There was nothing I could do to change that, so there was no harm in indulging in the fantasy for another few hours.

Chapter 16

ALEX

A knock rattled the glass in the door to the studio apartment, making me rush from the bathroom to answer it.

"Hey!" I opened the door, glimpsed Ren leaning in the doorway, and rushed back to the bathroom. "I'm nearly ready."

His laughter carried through the small apartment as he followed me to the bathroom. "Take your damn time. The later we are, the more pissed off my parents will be. Is that what you're wearing?"

I lowered the mascara and turned to glare at him. "Hey. I'm doing you a favor here. This is the best I could do."

I gestured to the simple black dress with spaghetti straps and buttons all the way down the front. It was one of the few items of clothing Toni owned that wasn't intentionally ripped and didn't have an offensive picture on it.

I pointedly looked at Ren's outfit, properly taking him in for the first time. He looked like sin in black leather pants, a red vest over a sheer tank top, and his leather necklaces hanging down the front. Black bracelets, several rings, and all his piercings completed the rebellious look. He'd even put on a little bit of black eyeliner.

"Are you trying to look like a spoiled rich bitch?" He raised his brows and smirked.

I took a breath and pushed the hair out of my face. "Again. I'm doing *you* a favor. I'm trying."

"Yeah, that's the problem. I don't want them to think we're making an effort. People have been bending over backward to accommodate those two assholes my whole life. I'm trying to make a point here."

I leaned back against the sink. "So what you're saying is, I look too nice?"

"Yes. Put something trashy on and let's go."

I rolled my eyes and turned back to the mirror to finish my makeup, making it Toni's standard of heavy instead of the light look I'd originally planned.

I didn't know the full story, but Renshaw clearly had some serious friction with his parents. If he wanted to piss them off by bringing an "unsavory woman" to lunch, then I figured it was time to really embrace my Toni persona. I smiled to myself as I pulled the dress over my head and opened the wardrobe. I was actually a little excited at the prospect.

I'd heard of the restaurant we were going to. It was fine dining at its most pretentious, but they had an extensive and excellent wine list. Several Zamorano varieties were on the menu.

I'd spent so much time in these stuffy places I was getting a thrill at the prospect of being that person all the rich, stuck-up people stared at with shock.

"Screw lunch." Ren appeared behind me, his necklaces tickling my bare back as he ground his erection into my ass. "Let's just blow it off and fuck instead."

His dirty words sparked another, naughtier kind of excitement in my chest. It was tempting, but after arching my ass against his boner, I pushed him away. "No. I was promised a five-star meal. I'm hungry."

He groaned but backed away enough for me to change into the denim skirt and low-cut neon green top. I pulled on Toni's combat boots and held my arms out at my sides, silently asking if I looked trashy enough.

He grinned and licked his lips. "Perfect."

We showed up to lunch nearly half an hour late. I cracked a joke about sweaty balls and Ren's leather pants in this heat, and we pushed through the heavy doors of the restaurant, laughing boisterously. Several wide eyes turned in our direction.

Ren's parents greeted us with pursed lips.

"Would it have killed you to put on a tie?" his father grumbled as we took our seats.

"If I hung myself with it, it just may have." Ren flicked his napkin with a flourish and a wide grin before the waiter could get to it.

"Isn't it a beautiful day?" I smiled politely at Sarah. Ren had filled me in on their names on the way—they didn't bother to ask mine.

She looked at me and blinked, as if surprised I was speaking to her. "It's much too hot. I abhor the south and this god-awful humidity. I much prefer the breeze coming off the water in the Hamptons."

"Oh, that sounds refreshing." I smiled. The ruder and more negative they were, the more it made me want to be over-the-top chipper. "Is that where you're from?"

"No. We have a residence in Manhattan. We like to spend time at our property in the Hamptons in summer. Renshaw used to love going there as a boy."

She looked lovingly across the table at her son. The pain in her expression was wiped away quickly, and I almost felt sorry for her.

William and Sarah Pratt had looked vaguely familiar when they barged into the Cottonmouth and accosted their son, but I just put that down to their looking like Renshaw. When he'd told me their names, I got another pang of recognition, but it wasn't until Sarah talked about where they lived that it all clicked. The Pratts owned Pratt Hotel Group and had hotels up and down the East Coast. I'd bumped into them at any number of stuffy charity galas and exclusive social events. Not that we'd ever really talked, which explained why they didn't recognize me.

The waiter handed out menus and gave William the wine list.

I picked the bronzed redfish with mirliton slaw and lemon beurre blanc, and an heirloom tomato salad for my starter. William handed the wine list to his wife, but no one offered it to me before the waiter appeared.

William ordered steak and a glass of Pinot Grigio—a horrible combination, as the white varietal didn't contain the level of tannins ideal for balancing the rich texture of the steak.

Sarah opted for a pasta dish and a martini.

The waiter turned to Ren.

"I'll have an Old Forester 1920, double." He smiled.

"And to eat, sir?"

"Nothing. Thank you. I plan on getting tanked on an empty stomach so I can pretend I'm not actually here."

"Oh, for god's sake, Renshaw." His mother huffed.

I clenched my teeth to hold back a laugh as the waiter, not knowing what else to do, turned to me.

I gave him my food order first.

"And to drink?"

"Well, I haven't had a chance to look at the wine list, but—"

"I'm sure they can get you whatever beer you want, but the wine selection here is a little more complex than red or white." Sarah sneered at me. The expression on her face was hateful, full of derision as she took in my clothing and heavy makeup, deciding I was trash based on nothing more than her own prejudice.

I'd gone into this wanting to have a little fun, but as I sat across the table from everything I hated about high society, anger bubbled up inside me.

Ren wanted to play into his parents' prejudice, goad them and try to get a rise out of them by being exactly what they thought we were.

I decided to take a different approach.

I slouched a bit farther in the chair and turned back to the waiter, who looked as if he was considering forgoing the excellent tips and just going home early.

"I'll have a glass of the Bass Phillip 'Premium' Pinot Noir—2016 vintage—with my starter and the Villa Raiano Ventidue Fiano with my main. I find the high aromatics in the Fiano pair well with the medium texture of the redfish. And please bring my boyfriend a bowl of the rosemary chat potatoes. He says he's not hungry, but he's only going to end up picking food off my plate." I chuckled lightly and handed my menu to the stunned young man. He rushed off, and I turned to face three sets of wide eyes and gaping mouths.

I smiled politely and took a massive gulp of my water, letting it trickle down my chin. I wiped my mouth with the back of my hand and slammed the glass down. "It is a beautiful day, but you're right, Sarah—it's humid as the devil's armpit. I was fucking parched."

Everyone continued to watch me with shocked expressions. Then Ren threw his head back and laughed. It was a loud, carefree sound with a tinge of relief to it, and it drew the attention of multiple people. His parents squirmed in their seats.

Sarah cleared her throat. "You're trained as a sommelier?

Then why on earth are you wasting your time and skills working at that dreadful bar?"

"Nope. I'm not a sommelier." I smiled courteously at her and ignored the rest of the rude, passive-aggressive question. What she really wanted to ask was "Why does someone like *you* know so much about wine?" I wasn't going to make it easy on her.

Our meals and drinks were delivered, and we suffered through a mostly silent lunch, with Ren's parents making the occasional derisive comment about his clothes, his choice of profession, his friends, and pretty much everything in his life. By the end of it I was seething. They hadn't said a single positive or encouraging thing to their insanely talented son.

"While we're in town, we thought we might see the exhibition of Cindy Sherman's photography at the gallery downtown," William mentioned as he finished his meal.

"Yes, your father wants to go." Sarah all but rolled her eyes. "But I don't know if I want to. Her work is basically a bunch of selfies. It's dull and derivative."

"Derivative? What exactly do you think it's derivative *of?*" I may have studied business at university, but like any good little rich girl, I knew my art history. "I find Sherman's self-portraits to be particularly relevant today. Her work is a critique of gender and identity, an exploration of selfhood and how it aligns with physical appearance."

Again, everyone stared at me open-mouthed, as if they couldn't quite believe something so intelligent had come out of the mouth of someone wearing scuffed combat boots and a bra visible under her skimpy top.

I really loved it when people underestimated me. Usually it was a man in a high-powered meeting, but this was even better. Ren's parents had underestimated me in every way possible, and I was determined to flip their narrow-minded, small, whitewashed world upside down.

Instead of taking the bait, because she clearly knew nothing about art, Sarah decided to change the subject. "Anyway, we are running out of time, and we should probably discuss the reason we're here." She gave her husband a pointed look.

William looked like the last thing he wanted to do was raise this topic of conversation, but he sighed and did anyway. "Son, we want to know when you're coming home."

"I am home." Ren crossed his arms over his chest and scowled at his father.

"Renshaw, enough is enough." She may have demanded her husband start the conversation, but Sarah was the one who actually had the most to say. "You've had your fun playing your little instrument, getting drunk, sleeping around." She raised an eyebrow in my direction and pursed her lips. "You're an adult, and it's time to act like it. You have responsibilities, and your father is running out of time to properly train you in the business."

"You can't *possibly* be fucking serious." Renshaw kept his voice dangerously low, but every inch of him was so tense he looked like a wild animal ready to pounce. "I don't know how many damn times I have to say it. This isn't a phase. This isn't some rebellious bullshit. This is my *life*. I don't care about your money. I don't care about your business. I don't care about what *you* want. I spent my entire childhood trying to live up to your impossible expectations, trying to be what you wanted me to be. And I ended up in the damn hospital with several stitches in each wrist." He held his arms up, wrists out, to illustrate the point. I half expected to see black stitches and blood running down his forearms, but there was nothing but a faint pinkish scar that wasn't even discernible under the black bracelets until he pointed it out. "When are you going to get it through your thick skulls? This is my life. You don't get to dictate how I live it anymore."

Sarah's eyes were getting misty, but she kept her back ramrod straight, her shoulders pulled back. It wouldn't be appropriate to show emotion in a public place.

"Ren, you know how much it hurt us both to see you in such a dark place." William leaned forward on his elbows, his hands clasped in front of him. He looked tired. "We just want what's best for you, son. We hate to see you throwing your life away."

Ren threw his arms into the air and let them flop back into his lap. He opened his mouth several times as if to say something, then shook his head incredulously.

Anger continued to churn inside me. I couldn't believe how dismissive Ren's parents were of their own son's wishes. I couldn't believe how blind they were to how much this stubbornness was driving a wedge between them and their son—their only son. I couldn't believe how much their pride and arrogance were preventing them from having him in the family.

I'd had enough.

I stood, my chair screeching loudly on the polished floors of one of the most exclusive restaurants in New Orleans, and threw my napkin down on the table for good measure. Once I was sure I had their attention, and probably the attention of half the restaurant, I spoke.

"Have either of you ever even listened to him play? Have you ever even come to a gig? Your son has a talent that is a gift from God. People come to the bar just to see him perform. His voice is ethereal, his fingers like magic as they pluck the strings of a guitar. He has an *incredible* talent. Can't you see that all he wants is to be happy? And how the hell can anyone truly be happy if they're pretending to be someone they're not? You're asking your own son to be someone he's not just so he fits in with your fucked-up idea of how the world works. Just because he doesn't want to spend the rest of his life in a goddamn suit, pandering to the misogynistic boys' club that is corporate America and marrying some stick-figure, uptight socialite who's probably never even done anal, does not mean what he's doing with his life is not worthy or not important."

I turned to Ren and held my hand out, effectively dismissing the two assholes who called themselves his parents. "I know that was probably out of line, but hey, you wanted me to stir some shit, so here I am—stirring some shit. Now how about we get the fuck out of here and go do something fun?"

Ren didn't even hesitate. The shock was washed from his face by a wide, surprised grin as he pushed himself to his feet and slapped his hand into mine.

"Fuck, but you know how to cause a scene." He laughed and pulled me to his side, wrapping his free arm around my back and drawing me against his chest. Not to be outdone, the cocky bastard tipped his head and kissed me—an open-mouthed, messy, writhing, passionate kiss. Right there in the middle of the restaurant.

We pulled apart and marched out without a second glance at his outraged parents or anyone else. I didn't care to look at anyone but him, mostly because he was so beautiful and I couldn't tear my gaze away, but also because I just didn't give a shit what anyone thought.

I'd told the truth, and maybe I'd done it in a somewhat abrasive way, but anyone who was offended or irritated that we'd interrupted their lunch was exactly part of the problem.

It was not lost on me that some of my outburst wasn't specific to Ren's situation—that I'd let out some of my own deep-seated frustrations and worries about my own sheltered, privileged life. But in that moment, I was a loud-mouthed, inappropriately dressed chick making a scene at a fancy restaurant as I walked out hand in hand with a tattooed bad boy. I was going to enjoy every damn second of it.

A: Causing a scene is fun!

T: Did you dance topless on the bar?

T: Woohoo!

A: What? No!

A: I went to a fancy AF restaurant and acted inappropriately.

T: Hahaha! Good for you.

A: Wait. You danced on the bar topless?

T: I mean . . . I didn't NOT dance on the bar topless.

A: LOL! You really don't give a shit what anyone thinks, do you?

T: Nope!

A: I wish I had that kind of freedom.

T: Why don't you? I mean, you're literally the only person who controls your thoughts. Just decide not to care.

A: You know, you're wiser than you look.

T: Fuck off.

A: xoxoxoxoxox

T: xo

Chapter 17

TONI

Cutlery clinked against plates, mingling with the soft music in the Winthrops' formal dining room. The sounds would've been deafening in their muted restraint if it weren't for Caroline Winthrop.

She felt awful for inviting Preston to stay with us, but you'd never know a single thing was wrong from her wide smile and relaxed manner. She'd invited a few people over for dinner, kept the conversation going like a pro, and had Preston distracted better than a magician practicing sleight of hand.

"This venison positively melts in your mouth." Preston took another bite of his entrée and made a sound of appreciation.

"Yes, our stable master is quite the outdoorsman. He likes to hunt—caught it fresh yesterday." Caroline smiled widely from the other end of the table.

One of the other guests cracked a joke, and half the room laughed. Grateful they were distracted, I took a moment to wipe the look of disgust off my face. Thankfully, I was already nearly done with my plate—there was no way I could finish it now that I had images of Jack shooting some poor Bambi down in my head.

A warm hand landed on my knee under the table, and Oren leaned in. "Are you OK?"

I gave him a smile and nodded. Just feeling his firm touch made me instantly feel better.

"Is this one of ours, Alexandria?" Preston held up his glass, red liquid swishing around inside it. "It tastes like it might be a Zamorano Merlot, but I can't be sure. Was this the best pairing? You're the expert."

He turned his wide smile to me, and he'd spoken loudly enough to draw the attention of some of the others.

"Oh, I do love a good glass of wine." A woman about Caroline's age with strawberry-blonde hair in a complicated up-do called down the table. It was pretty clear she loved a good glass of wine—she was on her third, and we hadn't even had the main meal. "But I must confess, other than my favorites, I really don't know much about it. What is this we're drinking?"

Several sets of eyes turned to me.

Panic seized my lungs. I'd just decided the best course of action was to say I was violently ill and excuse myself for the rest of the night—I was pretty sure I wouldn't even be lying about the vomiting.

But then George strode into the room and stopped at my side.

"My apologies for the intrusion," he said, addressing the whole table, then turned to me, "but you wanted to know as soon as I had an update. The 2004 Pinot Noir was delayed in Houston due to a connecting flight issue. I hope the 2014 has been all right in its place."

"Thank you, George." I smiled at him, beyond grateful.

He gave me a curt nod and left the room.

Preston whistled under his breath and leaned back in his chair. "I wouldn't want to lose a case of that in Houston, or anywhere else." He chuckled. "What's a bottle worth these days? Six hundred dollars?"

The wine lover at the other end gasped. "Oh my goodness!"

"Which is why I wanted to know as soon as possible where it had got to. Sorry again about the intrusion." I borrowed George's words and hoped I was convincing enough picking up his lead.

Thankfully, Oren senior started a conversation with his dull old white man friends about the stock market or some other rich guy bullshit, and Preston inserted himself. The next course was served, and everyone forgot about the wine except to drink it.

I wanted to get wasted so badly. Just let the ridiculously expensive grape juice wash away any fucks I had left to give. But I needed to be on alert. One slipup and we were done. No money, no college . . . no more Oren.

Preston had arrived at Hazelgreen Manor that afternoon with more luggage than Alex had. The staff had taken his things to a guest room—on the opposite side of the giant house to where I was staying—while Oren and I gave him a tour.

It was a much shorter version of the one he'd given me when I first got there, but I got a disturbing amount of pleasure from holding his hand the entire time. It almost took the edge off constantly worrying I was about to get caught.

When Preston spotted Alex's expensive suitcase in my room—not Oren's bedroom—he narrowed suspicious eyes on me, but Oren cracked a joke about closet space in these old houses, and I seamlessly picked up the line, remarking that I loved the view from this room and used it to work and read. The book on the nightstand supported my lie.

Oren expertly breezed through every potentially dangerous topic or question, and George was like a fucking ninja. On several occasions, he'd appeared out of thin air and interjected a comment or question that saved my ass.

Oren was helping me keep a secret from Preston, but George was helping me keep the other, related secret from *everyone*. So many damn secrets! I felt like I was on a soap opera. I was half expecting a heavily made-up woman to come around a corner and slap me dramatically.

"So you're in the wine business too, Preston?" the husband of the strawberry blonde asked.

"I am a Zamorano." He smiled, a little stiffly this time. "But I have no stake in the winery."

"Oh? I thought it was a family business." The man picked up his glass, curiosity dancing in his eyes.

"It is. Zamorano Wines has stayed in the family since it was established in 1788. But we have a large family and . . ." He turned to me and smiled. "Would you like to tell the history of our family legacy, cousin?"

I smiled just as politely and dug my fork into the fondant that had been delivered to the table a few minutes earlier. The candlelight glinted off the ridiculously shiny dessert fork. *Why the fuck do I know what a dessert fork is?*

"I'm enjoying dessert too much. You tell it." I shoved an unladylike portion into my mouth to punctuate my refusal, but Preston was the kind of guy who loved the sound of his voice. It didn't take much to get him to do the talking.

"Alexandria and I have a common great-great—et cetera—grandparent, Emilio Zamorano. He's seven generations back. In 1788, he came to America with his wife and cuttings of Merlot and Verdejo from his father's vineyard in Spain. He purchased land in California, planted the grapes, established Zamorano Wines, and had a son."

The other conversations at the table ceased. He had everyone's attention and was lapping it up, gesturing with his hands as he told the story.

"When Emilio died, the vineyard was passed down to his son, and then the next son and so on for four generations. Luckily, there was only one male child in each generation until Alberto Zamorano had two sons. He left the winery to Alexandria's great-great-grandfather. My great-great-grandfather, the younger son, was more interested in gold mining, looking for a quick buck."

Everyone laughed lightly along with Preston. I had another bite of fondant.

"Skip forward to the next generation, and Zamorano Wines is prospering. We've purchased more land. We're starting to get a reputation, exporting to other regions of the continent, then even to Europe. Meanwhile, *my* great-grandfather has found himself in a spot of trouble. A series of unfortunate events leads to his bankruptcy, and he goes to his cousin for help. He's given a job on the winery, meets a good woman, and gets married, eventually negotiates for his half of the Zamorano family to buy into the business.

"The business continues to prosper, but my grandfather and Alexandria's have a falling out, and my grandfather is purchased out of the business. He never spoke about the incident, and my father didn't seem to know a single thing about it. He was the kind of man who wanted to know everything, rest his soul, but that's one secret he never got to the bottom of. You don't know what caused the fight, do you, cousin?"

All eyes turned to me. I paused with my last forkful of fondant halfway to my lips. "No clue." I bugged my eyes out and smiled.

"If you ask me, it was probably over a woman." Preston slapped the table, and everyone burst into laughter.

Oren's warmth pressed into my side as his arm rested on the back of my chair. "You doing OK?" he whispered into my ear, his fingers caressing my bare shoulder.

I swallowed the rich chocolate and licked my lips. When I turned to face him, I found him staring at my mouth. I immediately wanted to lean forward, close the distance, and lick his lips, but I just nodded and placed a hand on his thigh, melting into his casual embrace.

Preston was finishing his story. "Alexandria's side of the family has kept Zamorano Wines in the family generation after generation. A knack for business runs in our blood though. My father owned several restaurants up and down the West Coast, and I've followed in his footsteps. So I don't officially have a stake in Zamorano Wines, but my ancestor established it, and our families have remained close, so I do feel connected to it."

"What a rich and fascinating family history," Caroline remarked, and her friend piped in excitedly.

"Oh, yes! I was riveted. Someone should make it into a movie."

Everyone laughed again and started speculating about which Hollywood actors would play whom. It seemed everyone had had a little too much to drink. Even Oren's father, usually surly and scowling at everything, was smiling widely and talking animatedly.

"I just have to say"—Caroline raised her voice, drawing everyone's attention—"it is *so nice* to see such a strong sense of family. I mean, the two of you are what? Fourth, fifth cousins? And yet here you are, still in each other's lives. Family's so important."

She fiddled with the pearls at her neck and turned her misty eyes to Oren, her gaze lingering on his arm around my shoulders.

"And that's enough of *that*." Oren senior pulled Caroline's wine glass away exaggeratedly and cracked up laughing, setting the entire table off again. She slapped him lightly on the shoulder, but she was giggling too.

"Well, we have a rich history, and we make an effort to honor it." Preston reached over and covered my hand with his, giving me a warm smile. "Isn't that right, Alexandria?"

"Wouldn't have it any other way." I smiled back at him.

I endured about another hour of having to pretend and lie about more things than I could keep straight in my head. Then the guests left, and everyone headed up to bed. Oren and I were the last ones to climb the big staircase, hand in hand.

As we reached the top, he pulled me to a stop and backed me up against the ornate timber railing.

"I was thinking," he leaned in and whispered against my cheek, his breath sending tingles down my spine, "it may be better if you stayed in my room for the next few nights. Just so we don't raise any suspicions with your cousin."

"Right, just to make sure we don't raise any suspicions." I smiled against his cheek and gave him a kiss. He gripped my hips and pressed his lips against mine, bending me backward over the railing a little bit.

"Let's get to bed then, wife-to-be." He took my hand and headed for his bedroom, so he didn't see when my face fell. I was really starting to hate being reminded of all the things I was lying about.

I pulled my hand out of his. "All my things are in the other room . . ."

"OK. Do what you've got to do, and I'll meet you in my room." He gave me a quick kiss on the forehead and turned away, not even realizing that was my lame-ass attempt to get out of staying in his room. If I was being honest with myself, I hadn't really tried all that hard.

I went to my room and smoked a cigarette. The intense day had made me feel like I was on a knife's edge the entire time. I hadn't even been able to drink to deal with it. As the smoke filled my lungs and melted some of the tension from my shoulders, I contemplated chain-smoking another two cigarettes, then realized I had only three left in the pack.

I knew Oren would come looking for me eventually, and he'd be able to smell the smoke on me, so I showered, brushed my teeth, and put on a pair of Alex's silk pajamas. Then I took a deep breath and headed to his room.

Just as I reached his door, footsteps sounded on the stairs, and I turned to find George climbing up. He spotted me before I reached the door.

"I was just coming to check on you." He narrowed his eyes, taking in the skimpy sleep shorts and tank top and my position next to Oren's door.

"I'm doing fine, all things considered. Thank you so much. You saved my ass on more than one occasion today." We were both keeping our voices low. Oren was just on the other side of the door, and you never knew when someone was lurking around a corner.

"Don't mention it." He sighed and propped his hands on his hips. "Are you sure this is a good idea?" He raised his eyebrows and tipped his head toward the door.

"No. I'm pretty sure this is a terrible, awful, *disastrous* idea.

But I'm also pretty sure I won't be able to stop myself from going in there." That was the closest I'd ever come to admitting I felt more for Oren than just sexual attraction. The heaviness of the confession hung in the quiet hallway between us.

George looked genuinely worried. "Shit. Toni . . ." He shook his head at the ground before looking up at me with pity in his eyes.

I fucking hated it when people looked at me with pity. There was nothing he could say I hadn't already said to myself. No argument he could make I hadn't already tried to batter into my own stupid head. "I know, George. I just . . . I can't."

I let myself into Oren's room and closed the door, closed off my conversation with George.

Oren was already in bed, shirtless, the covers pooling around his hips. A single bedside lamp illuminated the room in a warm glow. He looked like he was already asleep, his face mushed into a pillow.

George was right. *I* was right. This was dangerous, bad, and I was only making it worse by being here. The best thing to do would be to turn around and go back to my room.

He opened his eyes and smiled, those soft, full lips curving around his perfect teeth. He flipped the edge of the covers back and patted the empty side of the bed. Any resolve I had, any common sense that had been making so many good points a moment earlier, disappeared, chased away by his brilliant smile.

I went to him, my feet carrying me across the floor of their own volition, and crawled into the bed. He traced my cheek with his fingertips, his touch feather soft as he brushed some hair off my face. He leaned in and gave me a gentle kiss, full of emotion and tenderness.

Leaning back, he flicked the light off, plunging us into darkness, but in the next instant his strong hand was on my hip as he scooted closer to me. Our feet tangled, and I found myself tucked into his chest, breathing him in as he ran his hands through my hair.

It felt so natural, as though we'd been sleeping next to each other our whole lives.

We fit.

T: Hey, do you think I could even fit into your world?

A: What do you mean? No one suspects a thing.

T: No. Not as you. Not pretend. Like, as me—just more polite and better dressed and whatever. But still me.

T: Do you think people would accept me?

A: What is this about? I thought you didn't give a shit what people thought.

T: You're right. I don't.

T: Never mind.

A: Toni? What's going on?

T: Nothing. It was stupid.

A: You can tell me.

A: Toni?

A: Hello?

Chapter 18

ALEX

The tires of Andre's truck crunched on the gravel as he pulled into a spot and killed the engine. I looked around, desperately seeking any clues.

"Did you bring me out here to kill me?" I backed myself against the door and widened my eyes. We'd driven about half an hour out of the city and into a more remote area. Other than the parking lot with about a dozen other cars and a path leading around a bend, the only visible things were bushes and trees, especially those drooping, furry ones common in Louisiana.

"No." Andre chuckled, then deadpanned, "This is nowhere near remote enough to dump a body."

We both burst out laughing, but I slapped him on the

shoulder—it felt like hitting stone. "Tell me what we're doing."

My tone was whiny, but I really hated surprises. Andre had knocked on my door early that morning and asked if I had any plans. All I planned to do was keep exploring New Orleans, maybe do some washing. When he offered to show me another experience, I didn't hesitate, but then he refused to tell me exactly what we were doing. I'd spent most of the ride trying to coax, beg, and threaten the information out of him.

"You really have to know everything, don't you?" he teased.

I shrugged. "I run a business. It's my job to know everything."

"It's OK to relax sometimes, Alex, to let someone else make the decisions."

I liked that he called me Alex when no one else was around. At the bar, I was Toni, but out here, wherever *here* was, I could have the best of both worlds. I could take a break from my real life and still be me. Stressful as it had been at the time, I was really glad Andre had figured me out.

I chose to ignore his sage advice. "So are we going to sit in the car all day?"

"No. We're going in a much louder, much more exciting vehicle." He grinned, his dark eyes sparkling.

I frowned, but he was out of the car before I could ask. I jumped out and hurried after him down the path. "What kind of vehicle might that be?"

"An airboat."

"A what?" The path was shorter than it looked. A low building came into view, water visible beyond it.

"It's like a little boat with a giant propeller at the back. It's the best way to explore the bayou."

"The bayou?" I glimpsed the boats he'd described lined up on a small wooden dock.

"You can't say you've seen New Orleans if you haven't seen the bayou." He paused near the bottom of some stairs leading up to a narrow porch and turned to face me. "My buddy owns a few airboats. Takes people out fishing and shit from time to time. I called in a favor."

Excitement bubbled up, making me want to jump up and down on the spot like a toddler, but I just grinned and gripped Andre's forearm. "Really?"

He nodded. "Really, really."

I couldn't wait!

"My god, this thing is like a marble pillar." Momentarily distracted, I lifted his forearm between us, digging my fingers into the muscle.

Andre chuckled and curled his fingers into a fist. The muscle and sinew under my hands rippled and then solidified. I ran my hand down his arm to his wrist and took a step closer.

The screen door banged against the side of the house, and we stepped away from each other to look at the man striding out.

"Andre! Long time no see, man." He was shirtless and tanned, his messy hair poking out from under a trucker's hat.

"Hey, Dale. How you doin'?" Andre met him at the bottom of the stairs, and they shook hands.

"This your little lady?" Dale flashed me a genuine, crooked-toothed grin.

"Who you calling little?" I channeled Toni's attitude and propped my hands on my hips but let the amusement show in my face.

Dale held his belly as he laughed. "I like her."

"Me too." Andre gave me a warm look, and I felt myself begin to blush.

Dale threw some keys, which Andre caught effortlessly, and shouted for us to have fun as he headed back inside.

Andre led me to the nearest airboat and helped me inside. It felt like standing on a tin can. The bottom was completely flat, but the bench seat was padded. The giant fan thing at the back looked like it might suck me in once it got going.

Andre handed me earmuffs as we sat down. "These things are ridiculously loud, so don't take these off. Make sure you keep your butt planted to the seat, and hold on to the rail."

Those were all the instructions I got before he settled his own earmuffs over his ears and turned to face the front. I hurried to protect my ears as the engine came to life with a deafening roar.

I made an embarrassing squealing sound in surprise, but thankfully it wasn't audible over the noise.

Andre gave me a questioning look, I nodded, and we were off. The noise intensified as he pulled away from the dock and took off like a bat out of hell.

Air whipped at me, the breeze cooling me down as trees and murky water blurred past. I held on to the metal bar in front of me for dear life, but I couldn't seem to wipe the smile off my face. It was downright beautiful out there. The bayou was a maze of wide and narrow channels, some ending in dead ends, some interconnected. Every once in a while, we passed another airboat. A few were smaller, carrying just the driver, while others were three times the size of ours, a dozen tourists packed onto rows of seats.

After zipping around some of the open areas, making my heart repeatedly jump into my throat with sharp turns and complicated maneuvers, Andre steered the airboat into a narrow tunnel and slowed right down. The noise from the engine dulled, as did the light. Only a few beams of sunlight shot down through the thick foliage. Trees on either side joined above our heads, occasionally making us duck to avoid low-hanging, mossy vines. I craned my neck to gawk at the scenery.

Andre killed the engine, and the boat bobbed to a stop. He whipped his earmuffs off, and I followed suit. Angling his body toward mine, he gripped the back of my seat and pointed. "Gators."

I whipped my head around, my eyes going wide. "What? Where? Should we go?"

He lowered his pointing hand to my shoulder, giving it a comforting squeeze. "Calm down. They can't get in, and these things are near impossible to capsize. They're only babies anyway."

The panic subsided, and I peered into the murk, trying to spot the scaly bastards. "I can't see them."

Andre pointed to a patch of dirt between gnarled tree roots. One of the alligators moved, and suddenly I could see all three. They were just sitting there, chilling. One of them had its mouth open. They looked about two feet long.

"These look like they're about two or three years old. The males can grow to about fifteen feet. The biggest one I saw was way out in the bayou a few years back. Dale and I went fishing, and we spotted this huge bitch. Must've been twelve feet. We just dropped our rods and got the hell out of there." He whistled. "Now, *that* one may've been able to capsize us."

"Uh . . ." I turned my worried gaze in his direction.

"We don't see any that big around here." He waved me off before I could voice the concern. "Honestly, around here, I'd be more worried about spiders and snakes falling from the trees." I followed his gaze upward, the anxiety returning. The foliage was so thick anything could be up there. And now that he mentioned it, I could see cobwebs *everywhere*, stretching between branches and glistening in the sun.

"I remember this one time—"

I clamped a hand over Andre's mouth before he could say more. "Stop. You're freaking me out."

He gently tugged my hand away and dropped the teasing smirk. "Alex, you're safe. Yeah, there are dangerous things out here, but I know what I'm doing. I wouldn't put you in danger."

I nodded and took a deep breath, turning back to the baby gators.

"How was your lunch with the Pratts?" he asked after a beat of silence.

I laughed. "About as scandalous as Ren hoped it would be, I think. Did you know his parents are loaded? They own a hotel chain."

"Yeah, I know. He doesn't keep it a secret or anything."

"God, he and Toni are so similar." I rolled my eyes.

"Don't let either of them hear you say that." He chuckled. "I gotta ask, Alex. Are you two getting in too deep?"

I turned away from the gators to look at him. The airboat swayed gently, but Andre's gaze was unwavering. Was it me he was worried about? Or Ren?

"It's just a bit of fun." I shrugged. "I'm marrying another man in a month. Even if I did like . . . someone more than just for fun, what's the point in entertaining the thought?"

"So you're just sowing your royal oats before you settle down?" He flashed a grin. I wasn't sure I'd convinced him, or myself for that matter. Thinking about going back to my heavy responsibilities always made my heart clench, but thinking about never feeling the kind of passion I did with Ren, never feeling as seen or accepted as I did with Andre—it added another layer of dread that was almost too much to bear.

"Something like that." Why was I suddenly whispering?

"Then why aren't you screwing around? Plenty of guys would jump at the chance to have you take them upstairs."

"I don't know. There's just something magnetic about Ren, you know?"

He nodded slowly, bringing his head closer to mine. "Don't I ever."

"Not that I'd be opposed to hooking up with someone else . . ." I deliberately glanced at his lips. We were inches apart. I could smell that intoxicating manly scent of his.

"Alex?"

"Yeah?"

The roar of another airboat broke the charged moment, and we pulled apart. Andre gestured to the earmuffs, and I focused on making sure they were right over my ears, trying to ignore how I could feel my pulse in my groin, the tight shorts only making it worse.

Andre started up the engine and pulled our airboat to the side as another one came into view.

It was carrying six tourists and a driver. As they approached, my gaze snagged on a woman in the front row. She looked familiar—dark hair pulled back, heart-shaped face, full breasts covered by one of my favorite silk shirts.

Shit!

Our eyes finally connected, and both hers and mine widened at the same time. Their boat was barely ten feet away now. Oren looked different from the pictures I'd seen online. He was dressed casually in khakis and a short-sleeved shirt, his auburn hair messy under the earmuffs, his smile relaxed as he looked in the opposite direction.

As he started to turn his head, Toni glanced between us in a panic. At the last second, I leaned forward and ducked behind Andre's knee.

The other engine roared past, and I sat up as they sped out of sight. I took a deep breath while Andre pulled the boat to a stop near the entrance to the narrow channel.

I gave him a wide-eyed look, but he was chuckling as he took off his earmuffs. I removed mine and whacked him on the shoulder.

"Hey! What was that for?" he asked, even as he kept laughing.

"It's not funny!"

"It's a little funny. I mean, of all the places for you two to bump into each other, you end up face-to-face in the damn bayou?" He burst out laughing again, and this time, I couldn't resist his infectious mirth. I laughed too.

Once we calmed down, I wiped the tears from under my eyes. "We should probably head off so we don't accidentally cross paths again."

He nodded. "Or . . . we could have some fun."

I narrowed my eyes but couldn't help returning his mischievous grin.

The next thing I knew, we were zipping around the waterways, darting past their boat every chance we got. We were going way too fast for anyone else to notice our resemblance, but Toni's face got more and more furious every time we came into view. I could've sworn I saw them holding hands once, but we were moving so fast I was sure I was mistaken.

Andre and I roared with laughter after every pass, getting way too much enjoyment out of torturing Toni. It was a little reckless, but the wind whipping through my hair felt incredible, the sun glinting off the murky water was beautiful, and Andre's shoulder shaking in laughter against mine was electrifying.

Our good mood lasted well into the night. It was midweek; the live act at the Cottonmouth was a solo performer on an acoustic guitar, and the crowd was mellow. The last patrons left before one, and I locked the doors as Andre started tidying up.

I cleared the last few abandoned glasses and bottles on my way back to the bar. We didn't usually do a full clean at the end of the night, preferring to do the hard scrubbing and restocking the next day when all the staff weren't tired after a long shift. But Andre started to stack the glasses into the dishwasher, and I grabbed a clean cloth to wipe down the tables.

We worked at a leisurely pace, chatting and laughing about our adventure on the airboat that morning.

When all the tables were clean, the bar gleaming, the dishwasher on its third load, I removed my apron. I was getting tired, but I didn't want to go upstairs, so I hoisted myself onto the bar and had a big glass of water.

Andre glared at me. "I'm gonna have to wash that again."

"Just do it in the morning." I chuckled as he squatted down next to me, peering into the beer fridge. "You're not going to restock now, are you? It's nearly two."

Instead of answering, he closed that fridge and scooted in front of me, nudging my boot so he could open the other one. I moved out of his way and ended up with my feet spread wide on either side of the fridge.

"Andre." I pushed the fridge closed with my foot. "What's gotten into you? Aren't you tired?"

He stood up and rubbed the back of his neck with one hand, propping the other on his hip. "I dunno." He sighed. "Just don't feel like going to bed."

He was so close I could feel the heat of his body at my knees. His eyes were level with mine, thanks to my perch on the bar, and we stared at each other for a charged moment. He'd been flirting with me for weeks, and I was pretty sure he was delaying going upstairs just like I was, but that little voice of insecurity still wondered, still made me fear rejection . . .

But I was here for a reason, risking so much for a month of freedom. I had to seize every opportunity.

"I don't feel like going to bed either." I grabbed a handful of his red T-shirt and spread my knees as I tugged. He was easily twice my weight, but his boots shuffled forward, and he leaned into my space willingly.

"So what should we do instead?" He gripped the bar on either side of my hips but didn't touch me. His naturally deep voice had dropped to a lusty growl; it traveled straight through me, spurring my own lust and settling between my legs.

"For starters, a little less talking." I placed my hands on his neck and did something I'd been fantasizing about since I met him. Taking my time, I ran my hands down his front, over his defined chest, down the hard bumps of his abs, all the way to the waistband of his low-slung jeans. I wriggled my fingers under the cotton of his shirt and rubbed my palms up his sides. Every part of him was hard and smooth like marble. He sighed into the touch, and his eyes lowered. When I got to his chest, I could feel his breaths coming shallower and faster, his chest rising and falling under my hands as my fingers brushed over the wiry hair, then trailed back down.

Bit by bit, he leaned farther into me but still didn't put his big hands on my body. With deliberate movements, giving him plenty of time to step away, I unbuttoned his jeans and slid the zipper down.

He was commando, nothing between me and the warm, hard flesh just beyond the zipper. My lips parted on a sigh as heat and moisture pooled at my core.

Being with Ren was dirty and exciting. This? This was erotic and sensual in a whole other way.

I wrapped my fingers around the base of his dick. He pressed his forehead to mine.

I stroked him up and down slowly, taking in every inch of his hardness and committing to memory what it felt like in my palm. He was about the same length as Ren, but thicker. Why did I keep comparing them?

I pushed his pants down his hips a little so I could have better range of motion. I stared at what I was doing—at the precum leaking out of the tip, at the contrast of my lighter complexion against his dark skin—mesmerized by the way his hips started to rock back and forth in time with my hand.

"I know you said less talking, but I have to ask." His breath washed over me, his lips inches from mine.

I moaned something that could pass for a sign to keep talking.

"Can I kiss you?" He leaned away and gave me a clear-eyed look even as his hips kept rocking slightly.

I slowed, then stopped, my hand halfway down his length. I

frowned and shook my head slightly. "Can you . . . I have my hand wrapped around your cock, and you're asking if you can kiss me?"

"Consent is very important to me." He wasn't teasing or cracking a joke; there was no mischief in his gaze. He still hadn't touched me.

"Oh . . . shit, I . . ." I'd basically molested him. He was respectfully checking if I was comfortable with his advances, and I'd just shoved my hand into his pants. I loosened my grip and almost pulled away, but he wrapped a hand around my wrist gently but firmly.

"I would've told you if I wanted you to stop." He smiled, wiping away my anxiety.

I bit my bottom lip and gave him one more deliberate stroke. "Yes, please kiss me. *Fuck me*, Andre."

"Yes, ma'am." That growl was back, making me clench my thighs.

He released my wrist and palmed the back of my head, his other hand gripping my waist as he leaned in. There was no hesitation, no restraint, when Andre finally kissed me. His lips were firm and demanding, his tongue sure and confident in its caresses. The hand at the back of my head held me in place as his mouth devoured mine. I kept stroking him, but my movements became jerky and uneven. I was too distracted by the all-consuming kiss.

He was dominating without being aggressive, bold but not cocky with every movement, every stroke of his tongue, every pass of his hand up and down my side until it gripped my ass and held on. He was everywhere, his fresh apple smell mingling with a hint of sweat from a night working behind the bar.

Now that I'd given him the green light, Andre was taking charge, full speed ahead like a racecar.

He broke the kiss but trailed his lips and teeth down my neck as I tried in vain to catch my breath. He deftly unbuttoned my shorts and leaned away, making me lose my grip on his impossibly hard length. I lifted my hips, and he removed my shorts and underwear in one go. He had to pull off one boot to get them over my foot but abandoned the other, leaving the scraps of fabric hanging off my ankle. The smooth metal of the bench was warm under my ass.

I yanked on his T-shirt again, and he pulled it over his head in that effortless way men had—gripping the fabric at the back of his neck and pulling it off in one smooth movement.

He managed to grab his wallet out of the back pocket before I shoved the jeans down to his knees, and he extracted a condom and slid it on. The muscles in my vagina contracted and relaxed almost involuntarily. I could hardly wait to feel him slide inside.

"I want you inside me." I voiced my desire, and he flashed me that grin I'd grown to love as he stepped between my knees again.

"So fucking impatient," he growled. With a big hand on each knee, he pushed my legs open as wide as they'd go. I leaned back, my shoulder blades connecting with the high part of the bar, and wrapped my hands around his wrists.

He dragged his hands from my knees to my hips, his thumbs caressing the inside of my thighs. One hand kept going, shoving up under my tank top to palm my breast. I sat up long enough to unhook my bra and remove the last pieces of my clothing, then returned my hands to his wrists. I loved how the muscle and sinew danced under my palms as he touched me.

The hand at my breast kneaded with firm pressure while the one at my hip cupped my pussy. His hand was hot against me, but he didn't torture me long. He dragged his palm up, gave my clit a firm rub, then moved his fingers over my folds until they found my dripping entrance. We both moaned as he spread the moisture.

I released my grip on his wrists, one hand going to my free breast to play with my nipple, the other caressing Andre's arm all the way up to his shoulder and back down, feeling the smooth muscle. He pushed two thick fingers inside me and rubbed my clit with his thumb.

"Oh god." I jerked my hips against his hand.

He worked me until I was panting, right on the edge of an orgasm, my pussy squeezing his fingers, and then he removed his hand. Before I could protest, he gripped his cock and rubbed the head of it against me, coating himself in my arousal.

I pulled him against me so I could kiss him. As our lips met, tongues tangling, he pushed his hips forward and slid inside me effortlessly. Our hips flush, completely connected, deliciously stretched—it was so satisfying yet nowhere near enough.

I rolled my hips, begging him to move, grind, thrust, *something*. The man had steely self-control.

Both hands gripped my hips, but his mouth kept devouring mine as he pulled out and slammed back into me. I moaned and closed my eyes. He pulled out and shoved in again, a little faster this time. I gripped his strong shoulders for balance.

Andre pulled out and, again, rammed his hips forward, faster and harder. With the next thrust, he pulled my hips against him, raising the intensity once more.

Our kisses got more and more sloppy—teeth biting lips, tongues licking, hot breath mingling in between.

The fervor of Andre's thrusts increased until he was fucking me hard and fast, my breasts bouncing as I moaned into his mouth unabashedly.

I gave up trying to hold on with my hands or knees, giving up to him completely, letting him move my body against his and trusting his strength would keep me from falling.

Every thrust ground against my clit, sending a jolt of pleasure through each and every nerve ending until I was an incoherent, writhing mess. Heat spread from my core through my entire body, and I had to pull away from Andre's devouring lips to throw my head back. I rested it on the bar, jutting out my chest as I cried out. The timber ceiling went out of focus as my orgasm washed over me in waves, each one more intense than the last.

He rammed into me one last time, his chest pressing against mine as he roared through his own climax.

His arms wrapped around my middle as I caressed the short hair on top of his head. We held each other close as we came down, our breathing slowly returning to normal.

After a few moments, he pulled away and kissed me on the lips tenderly. I closed my eyes and sighed.

He pulled his jeans up, not bothering to fasten the zipper. I managed to push into a sitting position, but my legs felt like jelly—hell, my whole body felt like jelly. I wasn't sure how I was going to make it up the stairs, but Andre gathered our discarded clothes, dropped them into my lap, and picked me up bridal style.

He carried me all the way up and into his apartment. We didn't speak while we showered together, but we didn't shy away from touching each other, caressing and kissing.

After we dried off, he took my hand and guided me through the dark space to his bed. I fell asleep almost immediately.

I wasn't sure how long I'd slept before I woke up to Andre's mouth between my legs, his tongue drawing me into wakefulness in the best possible way, but it was still dark outside. After two orgasms, he cleaned me up and insisted we go back to sleep. It was well past midday when we finally woke up again, tangled up in the sheets and in each other.

T: You are such a bitch!

A: I'm sorry! It was Andre's idea.

T: Whatever. I saw you laughing. You gave me a fucking heart attack!

A: I feel awful. I really didn't mean to. It was just a bit of fun. We made sure to go too fast for him to see me properly.

T: It was still risky, Alex!

A: You're right. I'm sorry.

T: OMFG! When did I become the one telling you off? Who even am I anymore?

A: Hahaha!

T: It's not funny! This whole thing was your idea! And I'm the one having damn heart attacks on an airboat!!!

A: It won't happen again. I promise. We switch back in a few days anyway. Am I forgiven?

T: Yes. Fine. Whatever. I can't stay mad at someone with such a pretty face.

A: Did you just compliment yourself?

T: And you.

A: Fair enough. We do have a pretty face . . . and a bangin' body.

T: Bangin'? When did you start saying bangin'?

A: What were you guys doing out there anyway? Oren doesn't strike me as the airboat type.

T: He's not. You should've seen how hard I had to work to convince him. But I needed to get away from the house and your nosy cousin.

A: Good thinking!

Chapter 19

TONI

The smaller airboat zoomed past for the third fucking time. I wanted to launch myself into their boat and throttle them both. They were grinning like idiots, having way too much fun at my expense while I had a damn heart attack every time they whizzed past.

What if Oren noticed? I was the one who'd have to explain why there was another woman with my face flying around the bayou like a maniac.

As they disappeared around a bend, I let my shoulders relax and made sure to keep a smile on my face. We were supposed to be having fun—hiding and having fun.

Oren gripped my knee and grinned at me. His sunglasses

reflected my face as his auburn waves flew about in the wind. I couldn't help smiling back, and this one was genuine. Now that he'd relaxed into it, he seemed to be having a great time.

I'd practically had to drag him out there that morning.

The sun hadn't fully risen when he'd stirred in the bed next to me, but it was definitely lighter than when I usually heard him start the shower.

"You slept in," I murmured against his back, my voice husky from sleep.

"Mmhmm." His wordless agreement reverberated through his back. I pressed my cheek to the warm skin between his shoulder blades and held him.

The sun kept rising, its light drawing me further from sleep and into the stark reality of what I'd done.

I shouldn't have slept with him.

My heart rate sped up, and I released him, rolling onto my back.

He rolled over too, turning to face me, and placed a hand on my belly. "You made me miss my workout." I could hear the lazy smile in his voice, but I was doing all I could not to look at him. If I caught sight of those warm hazel eyes, I'd forget why I was supposed to resist him. "But I need a shower before I get to work."

He yawned into the pillow and nuzzled my cheek with his nose. As he sat up, I reacted without thinking.

"No." My hands shot out and tugged his arm until he fell back down beside me, chuckling.

I looked into his eyes. I wasn't ready to push him away. Not yet.

"Let's do something." I smiled.

"What did you have in mind?" His voice dropped into a suggestive tone as he lifted himself onto an elbow and wedged his knee between my legs.

"Not that." I slapped him on the chest—but dragged the hand up over his neck and into the soft locks at the back of his head. My hips rocked against his of their own volition, his morning wood digging into my hip. "OK, maybe that."

He groaned and dropped his head to my shoulder. "Damn you, woman. We can't start this now. I really need to get moving."

"No. Please." I hooked my free leg around his hip and wrapped my arms around his neck, holding him against me. "Don't leave . . ." I stopped just before I said *me*.

He frowned, his gaze searching, the playfulness gone. "Alex? What's going on?"

He caressed my cheek as I swallowed around the lump in my throat. "I just . . . there's so much pressure . . . I hate the lying. I'm so stressed out about my cousin being here, and the wedding is so close, and I've barely left this property since I got here. I just want to be with you. Alone. Without any pressure. Let's just go out and have some fun and ignore our responsibilities."

"I know." He sighed. "But I have meetings . . ."

He chewed his delectable lip. He wanted to be with me. I could tell that much. But anyone who spent even an hour with Oren Winthrop the third could tell he was the kind of guy who had to line his pencils up on the desk before he could concentrate. Changing plans at the last minute would not be easy for him.

"Please, Oren." I let the desperation show in my gaze.

He regarded me for a long moment, his eyes tightening with worry. "All right. I'll get my assistant to move my appointments."

I pulled him down into a tight hug, and he laughed softly against my neck. "But we'd better hurry," he added. "If we bump into anyone, our getaway plans will be foiled. Our best bet is to get out before they're up."

"I can be ready in five." I shoved him back and kicked the covers off like a toddler refusing to go to bed. I was down the hall before he could blink.

We rushed through getting ready, narrowly avoided bumping into George in the kitchen, and snuck out a side door, then flew out of the gate like a couple of teenagers who'd stolen their parents' car, laughing hysterically. At the end of the road, Oren slowed his BMW down and indicated as if to head into the city, but I made him turn in the opposite direction.

Getting him to the touristy airboat place out in the sticks was no easy feat. I was trying to be spontaneous, but the less he knew, the more he got worked up. He kept trying to plan the day out, asking me where I wanted to have lunch, offering to make a reservation, all between demanding to know where we were going.

When I finally caved and told him what I had in mind, he had a million and one questions.

"Where is this place? Is there anywhere to eat nearby? What if they're booked out? Maybe we should call ahead? Maybe we should just do this another day? What if we're not dressed appropriately?"

"Would you fucking relax?" I chuckled to take the sting off the harsh words and hoped he didn't notice my casual use of the curse word. It was too easy to forget I was pretending to be someone else when it was just me and him. "If they're booked out, we'll go do something else. The point isn't to do this particular thing. The point is to just be spontaneous."

"I don't know if you've noticed, but I don't do spontaneous. My life is scheduled and planned out almost to the minute for the next six months. How do you even know where this place is?"

I was starting to realize what a miracle it was I'd convinced him to ditch all his responsibilities and hang out with me. We'd even left our cell phones behind, after Oren called his assistant.

I couldn't avoid his question, so I said something about having researched things to do in the New Orleans area and seeing it on the Internet.

We pulled into the parking area behind a bus full of Japanese tourists and managed to snag a spot on one of the smaller boats, which were more expensive. But hey, I was with a billionaire, and it was like spare change to him. I had no qualms about letting him pay and jumping into the airboat as though the giant propeller could whisk me away from all my problems.

Oren had been tense and unsure for the first ten minutes, grumbling about having to wear earmuffs, questioning the safety, and even trying to convince me to cancel and go do something else. But after a while, a grin pulled at his lips, and his shoulders relaxed. The first half of the tour was fun and carefree as the guide told us about the native wildlife in the bayou, stopping here and there to speak to us and answer questions.

And now I was hardly paying attention to anything, constantly on the lookout for my infuriating body double and my boss/ landlord/supposed friend, who were whizzing around on their own damn airboat and making my life a living nightmare.

Just my fucking luck—I'd managed to run away from one problem only to go hurtling, propelled by a giant fan, straight into another.

Thankfully, they disappeared before it was time for us to head back, and I didn't catch sight of them again.

After the airboat tour, we drove to a nearby dive bar and had greasy burgers for lunch, then chased them down with beer and played several games of pool. Other than a handful of haggard-looking drunks and the bar staff, we were the only ones in there, laughing and carrying on like teenagers while I kicked his ass and he shook his head in disbelief. He kept asking where I'd learned to play so well, and I kept dodging his questions by being coy. I just couldn't find it in me to think up another lie when what I really wanted to do was tell him I'd learned to play pool working in bars because that's what my life was, and that I wasn't *her*.

But I just as badly wanted to enjoy this moment, this perfect day with him. So I shoved that urge to be honest deep down and committed his easy smile, his ruffled hair, his lean build to memory—searing them into my brain so I would never forget this moment as he leaned on the pool cue and grinned at me, his eyes wide with wonder as I sunk another ball into the corner pocket.

We got home just before dinner, only to find that Preston had gone out for a business meeting and Oren's parents were on their way out to attend a charity dinner.

Before rushing out the door, Oren senior took a moment to scold his son for being so irresponsible for an entire day.

His mother just looked between us and gave us a broad smile. "I'm glad you two had some fun. You both deserve it." She rushed off after her husband, closing the door behind her.

Oren wrapped his arms around my waist and pulled me close. I fiddled with the hair at the nape of his neck.

"I really did have fun today. Thank you for convincing me. But I *do* need to do just a little bit of work. Maybe we could watch a movie or something after?" His cheeky grin and the way his eyes darted to my lips told me he was thinking about the last time we watched a movie together. I remembered too, my body already responding to his, pressing against him, leaning up to kiss him.

He returned the kiss, taking his time as his lips explored mine. Eventually he pulled away, gave me a kiss on the forehead, and went into his study.

After a quick shower and a sandwich for dinner, I pulled out one of my two remaining cigarettes. I hadn't had one all day, but with the lighter halfway to the smoke, I paused and lifted my thumb, letting the flame die. I kind of wanted it, but I also kind of didn't. Every second I'd spent here, the need to light up had been in the back of my mind, the stress and worry only making the craving worse. But as I sat at the open window, an unlit cigarette hanging from my lips, I realized I hadn't thought about it *once* all day.

I pulled the cigarette out of my mouth and put it away.

Instead, I made myself comfortable on the bed and cracked open my book, but before I knew it, a knock at my door startled me midchapter. I grinned and dropped the book on the pillow before bouncing to the door and pulling it open.

My smile fell.

It wasn't Oren on the other side; it was George, one eyebrow cocked.

"Don't start with me, George." I crossed my arms and mirrored his disapproving gaze.

"Toni, what are you doing?" He kept his voice low, and even though it was reproachful, it was also tinged with worry.

"Look, I'm not going to destroy Alex's one chance to save her family legacy, OK?" I dropped my arms, my shoulders slouching in defeat. "I just . . . I don't know. I thought he was an arrogant, spoiled rich boy. But then I started to get to know him . . . He's just a really decent fucking guy, you know? I don't meet a lot of those. I'm not used to it, and he defends me and protects me and . . . I don't *know*, man." I ran my hands through my hair in exasperation, the weight of the situation yet again tumbling over me with the force of a waterfall. "This is just a really weird situation, OK? I spend a lot of time with him, and now I'm pretty sure I'm gonna fucking miss him when this is over. I don't know what to do with that." Even I heard the hint of hysteria in my voice.

George sighed and stepped into the room, pulling me into another one of his hugs. It was brief but comforting, the simple gesture convincing me it wasn't just Alex's interests and well-being he was worried about.

"Toni, are you in love with him?" George fixed me with a stare. It wasn't judgmental or accusatory—it wasn't really anything other than questioning.

I opened my mouth to answer, no idea what the fuck would come tumbling out and hoping beyond hope George would actually know how to fix it. But before I could say anything, another knock sounded at the door.

Oren didn't wait to be let in—he simply opened the door. "Hey, Alex . . . Oh, hey, George. You guys catching up too? I guess you would've missed a full day's work as well." He rubbed the back of his neck.

"Nothing that couldn't wait." The easy smile on George's face didn't give anything away. "Sounds like the two of you had a fun day."

George and Oren spent five minutes chatting about our excursion and joking around. It was just enough time for me to pull myself together, beat back the tears stinging the backs of my eyes.

Oren invited George to join us for a drink, treating him like a friend and not a member of staff—the same way Alex treated him.

George declined, cracking a joke about how hard he'd had to work in our absence, and excused himself to his own room.

"He's a good man." Oren wrapped his arms around my waist. "I really like him. But I'm kind of glad he said no to that drink. I want you all to myself." He punctuated his statement by pressing a gentle kiss to the side of my neck.

The next thing I knew, we were in his room, peeling each

other's clothes off and stepping into the steamy shower. We lathered each other's bodies, exploring every bump and crevice in a slow, sensual way. Oren's strong arms held me up as the water sluiced over our bodies, and we made love in the shower. Then we dried off and made love again in his bed.

For the second night in a row, I fell asleep in the arms of another woman's fiancé, and I wondered when in the hell I'd started referring to sex as "making love" and not "fucking."

Chapter 20

ALEX

'd never seen the Cottonmouth Inn this busy. It was a Saturday night, and the Thousand Lies were playing, Ren rocking the stage as if it were Madison Square Garden and not a tiny stage in a dingy bar.

The place was at capacity; the bouncers were turning people away at the door. Four of us worked the bar while Dennis ran around like crazy collecting dirties, and no one had more than a five-minute break to go to the toilet.

"Behind you!" Dennis yelled as he shuffled past me, a tray of clean glasses in his arms. They were gone within ten minutes.

Andre had closed the kitchen at eleven and called last orders, but Loretta was only just pulling the servery window down at a quarter past midnight. She gave us a wave as she disappeared out the back door.

"Runnin' out back to get more beer. Fuck me, those college kids can drink." Andre rushed off without waiting for an answer.

"What can I get ya?" I pointed to the nearest customer, a guy in a red trucker hat, as a trickle of sweat ran down my spine.

"Four Budweisers."

I popped the tops on the beers with speed and precision I didn't have just two weeks ago, took his money, and turned to the next customer.

The rowdy group with trucker hats were celebrating some sports win—baseball? NASCAR? I really had no idea—while the college crowd was celebrating the end of finals. They only added to the bigger crowd Ren and his band drew every time they played.

It had also been a stinking hot day, the temperature hovering around a hundred, and people were thirsty. Instead of hydrating with water like they should, they were downing cold beers and frozen margaritas.

My back ached. My romper was sticking to my sweaty skin. My feet burned in the boots. But I retied my hair and turned to take the next order, pointing at a blonde.

She smiled and her lips moved, but the song reached a crescendo, and I didn't catch what she wanted. I frowned and leaned forward.

She leaned in too and opened her mouth to shout her order again.

Fast movement to my left caught my attention, and I whipped

my head around.

There was a commotion at the entrance, several drunk men trying to muscle their way past the bouncer. A second security man shouldered through the crowd to help, leaving only one bouncer at the other side of the room to keep an eye on the dance floor.

"Hey!" A scowling man slapped the bar in front of me. "My woman's trying to order."

"Sorry," I shouted over the noise. "I couldn't hear you. What can I get you?"

The blonde pushed her ass into the guy's groin as she leaned over the bar with a smug look. "Can I get a pitcher of—"

Shattering glass drew my attention to the right, just in time to see a fist flying near the door to the back corridor. I wasn't sure what had smashed, but judging by Andre's empty arms, I had a feeling it was the case of beer he'd been bringing out.

A fight broke out right in front of him, some of the college guys throwing sloppy punches at each other. Andre got between them, trying to break it up, but there were already several people involved.

Dread made the bottom of my stomach feel hollow, but I had to trust that Andre and the bouncers knew what they were doing.

I glanced at the stage and met Ren's worried gaze. The band continued playing, like pros, but the lead singer kept darting his eyes between the mess Andre was trying to stop and me.

A large, sweaty palm wrapped around my wrist and yanked me forward; my hips hit the edge of the bar with a painful crunch.

"How many fuckin' times we gotta order?" The blonde's

boyfriend looked ready to climb over the bar and strangle me. Judging by how hard he was gripping my wrist, I had no doubt he could. "Get our damn drinks, bitch!"

My heart hammered in my chest as my eyes went wide with panic. "Let go of me, asshole!" I screamed, getting the attention of the other bar staff as I tried to twist out of his grip.

I glanced at the other side of the room, but the last bouncer was gone. Was he on his way to help Andre with the college guys? Or to me?

My wrist burned; my hips and back ached from the awkward position. The man's breath reeked of alcohol, and his eyes were filled with rage, his pupils huge. Spittle flew from his mouth and landed on my cheek as he screamed something else into my face.

The words didn't register. I frantically batted my free hand around on the bar, looking for something, *anything*, I could use to defend myself. Sticky surface, bottle opener, wet rag . . . My fingers brushed the automatic water-soda dispenser. I grabbed the little contraption and raised it like a gun to his face, pressing the button.

Brown liquid spurted out of the nozzle and straight into his eyes—I guess I'd pressed the button for Coke. How ironic.

He spluttered and stumbled back, but his girlfriend sneered and lunged forward. Before she could get to me, a beefy arm wrapped around her waist, and she was yanked off her feet by the bouncer. He grabbed the guy by the collar and hauled them both toward the front door. The crowd parted to let them through.

"Toni? Toni!" I startled and batted an unfamiliar hand away, only to realize it was one of the casual bar girls who had been trying to pull me back from the bar. She must've reached my side just as the bouncer did—it all happened so fast.

"You all right? That was fucked. What an asshole." She smoothed her hands down my shoulders, concern in her eyes.

I rubbed my sore wrist and nodded. "Yeah, I'm OK."

"Go have a break. God dammit, where's Andre?" She turned away, rushing to take orders. Once the crazy people were removed from the crowd, people didn't give a shit anymore—they just wanted their drinks.

In a daze, I backed up until I hit the counter with all the liquor bottles, then looked to the front door. The commotion there was gone—just a single bouncer standing in his spot. I turned my head in the opposite direction, toward the back corridor. The other two bouncers were escorting several stumbling drunks toward the exit, a few of whom had blood running down their faces. That fight was over too, but I couldn't see Andre.

I also couldn't seem to move. I just wanted to get out of this room, get away from all this noise so I could convince my body it was no longer in danger. But it was so damn loud, and the lights were flashing, and there were people *everywhere*.

I looked up to the stage. It was empty, the abandoned drum set only just visible over the crowd. When had they finished their set? Everything had happened at the same time, and now I'd lost them both, and I was alone with no idea how to make my feet move through the crowd of strangers.

My breaths became ragged, and I closed my eyes, trying to focus on slowing my hammering heartbeat. I gripped the edge of the counter and started to slide down. My knees didn't feel like they could hold me up any longer.

Warm hands wrapped around my arms, halting my descent, and my eyes flew open.

Ren's wide green eyes stared back at me. I could see the questions in his concerned gaze. He turned me, pressed his chest to my back, and shuffled me through the crowd to the back corridor.

As the door swung closed behind us, Ren spun me around to face him. But before he could speak, the door flew open again. Andre's big arm flattened it against the wall, his frame filling the opening.

In the next instant, Andre had the door firmly closed, and the two of them were boxing me in.

"Did he hurt you?" Ren demanded.

"Are you all right?" Andre ran gentle fingers down my arm, ghosting over the wrist and lifting my hand between us to inspect it. "I couldn't get to you in time. I'm so sorry."

"I finished the song just as that asshole lunged for you, but I couldn't get from the stage to the bar fast enough either." Ren gritted his teeth and shook his head. "What the fuck happened? I've seen you take out bigger and meaner dudes than that asshole a hundred times."

He brushed the hair off my forehead. The touch was so tender, not at all like the possessive, rough way he touched me when we had sex.

"Uh . . . I, umm . . . I'm not . . . I couldn't . . ." It took my brain a beat to catch up—to realize he was actually talking about Toni. I had no doubt in my mind she knew exactly how to handle rowdy, threatening men with no problem. How common was this shit?

I'd been underestimated in business meetings, talked down to in boardrooms, propositioned in offices. I could handle a misogynistic asshole businessman, or even a tradesman on the vineyard. *That* I was used to. *That* I could handle. *This*? I'd never had someone grab me, invade my personal space, and physically threaten me. It made my skin crawl all over again just thinking about it.

"It was fucking pandemonium out there." Andre saved me from having to fumble through an answer. "We just realized some asshole's been selling molly all night. Looks like it was laced with something bad. The bouncers had to call an ambulance for a few of those frat boys. I've got 'em bootin' anyone who even *looks* at someone wrong."

"Fuck. Do you know who it was?" Ren ran his hands through his messy hair. I wanted to do the same—feel the strands under my fingers, maybe give them a tug. I needed something to tether me to the present moment.

I hissed when Andre touched a tender spot on my wrist.

"Motherfucker," he muttered. "That's gonna bruise, but it's not broken. Let's get some ice on it."

"Did he hurt you anywhere else?" Ren raked his eyes up and down my body.

I cleared my throat. "My hips hit the bar pretty hard," I said, trying to make the words sound less vulnerable than I felt

They both reached for my waist at the same time, then

realized I was wearing a romper.

"What the fuck is this thing?" Andre grumbled as he tugged at the fabric, and Ren scratched his head.

Laughter bubbled up in my throat—my body's response to a highly stressful situation. But the sight of these two dominant, manly, abrasive men being foiled by an item of clothing was suddenly hilarious.

I burst out laughing, leaning my head back against the wall and letting all the tension out. I even snorted at the end before wiping tears from the corners of my eyes. They were both smiling now, their eyes crinkled in amusement.

"I'll get some ice. You get her upstairs," Andre ordered and turned for the door.

Ren turned his back to me and crouched down, flapping his hands behind himself. Despite the situation, I smiled. I couldn't remember the last time I'd had a piggy-back.

I wanted to jump up, but my legs were still shaky, so I lifted first one knee, then the other slowly. He straightened and adjusted his grip. Pain shot through my hips, making me hiss again, and his whole back tensed under me.

"I got you. Here we go." He climbed the stairs slowly, his movements careful. By the time he lowered me gingerly to the ground at the top of the stairs, Andre was back with a bag of ice. He moved past us and unlocked his studio door, and Ren took my hand in his and pulled me inside.

Andre turned on the overhead lamp; the harsh light made me squint after the dimness of the bar.

Ren lowered my zipper, his fingers trailing down my sweaty back, while Andre gently took my wrist and covered it with the ice.

"Uh, I can just go take a look at my hips in the mirror," I offered, suddenly realizing I was about to be semi-naked in front of them both.

"Why?" Andre frowned.

"Yeah, we've both already seen you naked." Ren pushed the fabric over my shoulders.

"Good point, I guess." I frowned. Had they discussed me? Swapped notes? Neither one was acting jealous, but then, it wasn't as if I'd made promises or commitments to either of them. I burned to know what they'd told each other.

Andre removed the ice so Ren could slide the romper down my arms and over my hips. The fabric pooled at my ankles, leaving me in a plain black bra and neon-yellow boy shorts.

Andre returned the ice to my wrist even as he bent down to inspect my hips. Ren stayed at my back, his hands loosely on my waist, and leaned around my side to get a good look.

They both stared for a really long time, poked the hipbones and the soft flesh around them. Their prodding didn't hurt. I didn't think I was bruised or injured. I was pretty sure I was just sore from the sudden impact and the way all my muscles had tensed at once.

Their touch became less exploration and more caress.

I rolled my eyes. "Guys, I'm fine. Pretty sure it's just tight muscles."

They murmured their agreement.

Andre placed a gentle kiss to my bellybutton before straightening. Ren waited until he was upright before kissing my shoulder, his lip piercing digging into my skin in a way that made me shiver.

One of his hands moved to my belly, fingers splayed, as Andre rested my injured wrist against his chest and held it there with the bag of ice. He stepped closer until Ren's hand was squished between our bodies, then draped an arm over both our shoulders.

For a few moments, they just held me. I breathed in their scent, felt their heat pressing into me from all sides, and slowly, my muscles relaxed.

Andre was the first to pull away. "We're a bar chick down, so I gotta go make sure everything's OK downstairs. Keep icing this, OK?" He gave me a pointed look. "Have a shower and get into bed. I'll close up and be back as soon as I can."

Ren released me too. "I'll just help the band load the gear into the van, and I'll hang around to help." He didn't say he'd be coming back upstairs, but he didn't say he was leaving either.

Which would I prefer? Logically it would be a bad idea to jump into bed with both of them—it would only complicate things more. But my body practically hummed at the very idea of it.

They shuffled out the door, and I found myself standing there with my romper around my ankles, holding the ice to my own wrist.

What happened at the bar had really shaken me. But within minutes, those two had gotten me out of there, checked me for

JUST BE HER

injuries, made me feel safe, and even unwittingly made me laugh. They'd even managed to hold off a panic attack that had been moments away.

I toed out of my shoes and used Andre's shower. By the time I'd dried off, I felt like myself again.

I was glad Andre and Ren had been there for me, but I also had to give myself credit. I'd faced a dangerous, unfamiliar situation and managed to defend myself. I wasn't sure how many gallons of Andre's Coke I'd wasted, but it had worked to get that whacko off me.

I was a capable, confident woman who didn't take shit from anyone—in the boardroom or in a rough bar. And I wasn't going to hide upstairs while everyone else dealt with the mess. If I cowered now, I'd never get behind that bar without it causing me anxiety again.

A little voice in the back of my mind reminded me that, come next week, I wouldn't ever need to. But I ignored it and dashed across the hall buck naked to pull on a fresh pair of shorts and a tank top.

I made my way downstairs before I could change my mind, the thumping music getting louder with every step.

Chapter 21

TONI

The light was hazy with the purple tinge of dawn when I woke up, but Oren wasn't in the bed next to me this time. The shower was running, the old pipes making that loud whining noise I'd gotten used to.

I stayed perfectly still, staring at the rapidly brightening sky through the open window. Maybe if my body remained still, so would my mind, keeping me from thinking about the clusterfuck I'd created.

A cloud shifted, the first rays of sun glinting against the diamond on my left hand.

This wasn't my ring.

This wasn't my life.

This wasn't even my name. I was such a fucking idiot.

I'd spent years—*years*—keeping people at arm's length to avoid this exact situation. Three weeks with Oren, and he'd batted my outstretched arms out of the way to wrap himself around my soul. I just wasn't sure why I'd let him.

Without him in the bed next to me—his mesmerizing eyes distracting me, his intoxicating scent enveloping me—I could actually think clearly. I'd told myself I needed to get him out of my system before I left, but all I'd ended up doing was letting him burrow his way further in. Now when I went home and had to pretend we'd never even met, I'd miss him. It would hurt as badly as the loss of my parents. He wasn't dying, but he may as well have been—I was never going to see him again. Now I'd have three gaping holes in my chest.

I needed a cigarette so badly I'd cut a bitch to get to a discarded butt in a gutter. I wanted a stiff drink too, or maybe ten. I wondered if my dealer had changed her number again—I hadn't been in touch with her for months, but I had a feeling I needed something stronger than booze to numb *this* pain.

I rolled onto my back, hoping to ease the pressure in my chest, but it just felt like the elephant's ass found a more comfortable spot on my clavicle.

The shower shut off. My heart started hammering.

I flung the sheets back and was halfway across the room when the bathroom door opened. A plume of steam preceded Oren stepping out, a towel slung low on his hips.

"Hey, you're up." He beamed at me, rubbing the top of his

hair with another towel. Then his smile fell. "What's wrong?"

He took a step forward. I took two back and grabbed the door handle. Why couldn't I make myself turn it?

"This was a mistake." I shook my head, and his frown deepened. "I can't . . . I'm not who you think I am."

"What? Alex, we're still getting to know each other. Neither one of us is who the other thinks."

I chuckled darkly. He wasn't getting it. But then, I wasn't exactly spelling it out for him either.

"This is too much. I can't handle this." Why had I stayed with him that first night? Why had I come back for more? What the fuck did I think would happen? There was no universe in which the billionaire with a heart of gold ended up with the foul-mouthed, uneducated orphan white trash. Oren senior would probably dig his own grave just so he could climb down and turn over in it. Caroline would clutch her pearls and do her best to get rid of me quietly to avoid a scandal.

"You can't handle what? What's changed overnight?" His voice was going hard, angry, but I could hear the pain lacing it. His lips pressed into a firm line, but his eyes were pleading, hurt—just like they were when his father made him feel like a disappointment.

My heart squeezed in my chest. I'd put that look on his face.

I was so damn angry—mostly at myself for letting this happen. But there was no one else around to let it out on. "You don't know me," I snapped. "Not really. What did you think would happen? You stick it inside me a few times, and I swoon, learn to speak when I'm spoken to as we ride off into the sunset? That's not me, Oren."

"No shit. It's not me either. Look, I know we made this agreement as more of a business deal, but we're still getting *married*. Would it be so fucking bad if we happened to also like each other, maybe even fell in lo—"

"No! You don't know what you're saying. I can't do this."

"Can't do what?" he barked. As I wrenched the door open and fled, he raised his voice for the first time. "Alexandria! Can't do *what?*"

He was worried about his precious inheritance. It would always come back to that. How could I compete? I didn't belong here.

Oren's door slammed. I slammed mine too, just for good measure. The door slamming and yelling was not a good idea. Someone would notice; it would raise eyebrows. Not that it mattered anymore.

Fuck the money. Fuck proving to anyone I could do this. Fuck the fact that I only had to stick it out for another few days. I was *done*. I wanted my own life back.

Except this wasn't just about me.

I growled and pulled my hair as I paced the room. It was all well and good for me to quit, but I couldn't ruin Alex's life in the process. She still had to come here and live it.

I didn't know what to do, couldn't think straight. The walls of the airy room felt like they were closing in, suffocating me in a bedroom bigger than my entire apartment.

I went to the toilet, brushed my teeth, and put on a white T-shirt and the only pair of jeans Alex had packed. Pulling my hair up into a ponytail, I grabbed my cigarettes and rushed down the stairs.

At the bottom I came face-to-face with George.

"Whoa. What's the rush?" He had a smile on his face, but it fell as soon as he saw me.

"Not now, George," I snapped at him and kept walking. I heard him coming after me, but Preston appeared at the other end of the hallway, hands in his pockets, and George made himself scarce.

"Alexandria." Preston grinned and sped up to catch me. "I've got most of the day free. I was wondering if you wanted to catch up." He nearly reached me, but I kept going, heading for the kitchen at the back of the house.

"I can't. I'm sorry."

"Are you OK?"

"I'm fine." I hoped I didn't sound terse, but I wasn't slowing down either. "Just need some fresh air."

He frowned as I passed him, but his steps faltered, and he didn't follow me into the kitchen.

Caroline stood next to the island, her worried gaze fixed on me.

"Alex? What's going on, dear?" She must've heard me brush Preston off.

"I just . . . I *can't* . . ." Why was I even attempting to explain anything to her? How could she possibly understand? There was just something inherently friendly and warm about Caroline that made me want to sit down with a cup of tea and pour my heart out. But that was never going to happen. "I just need some space.

I need to be alone."

I didn't wait for a response before I shoved the back door open and rushed across the porch and down the back steps.

I power-walked across the neatly trimmed grass, the bright morning sun making me squint as I cast several looks behind me to make sure no one was following. At the edge of the trees, I slowed down. I walked the narrow paths for a while aimlessly, not really able to put my thoughts into any kind of coherent order. By the time I realized my feet had carried me to the stables, I still hadn't figured out what I was going to do.

I leaned on the wall next to the wide back entrance and pulled out my cigarettes, lighting one up and taking a long drag. The smoke burned my lungs, but it gave me something other than my fractured feelings and thoughts to focus on.

One of the stablehands came around the corner carrying a bucket and stopped dead in his tracks. His wide eyes zeroed in on my cigarette.

"Not a fucking word to anyone." I pointed at him with the fingers holding the cigarette and gave him the "don't fuck with me" look I used on rowdy drunks.

The young man nodded rapidly before rushing inside.

I finished my cigarette and lit my last one. I'd cut down so much in the past few weeks that the two smokes were making me a little dizzy. I welcomed the feeling—another thing to focus on other than my rising panic and this churning in the pit of my stomach.

"God dammit. I thought I told you assholes you couldn't smoke back here." A deep angry voice made me push off the wall.

Jack came marching out of the stables, then froze when he saw me. "Oh, it's you. Sorry. Didn't mean to yell." He pulled his cowboy hat off and scratched his head, giving me a wide smile.

"That's OK. I didn't realize I wasn't supposed to smoke here. Sorry." That explained the hint of fear in the young man's eyes.

"It's all right." He shrugged, shoving his hands in the front pockets of his jeans. "You didn't know. This is a popular spot for the guys to take their breaks. Gets shade in the afternoon. But I had to ban them from smoking. It's just too dangerous this close to all that hay."

I finished my cigarette and nodded as I blew out the last of the smoke, making sure to put the butt out properly.

"So you just come down here to smoke?"

"No. I don't know. I've been trying to quit." I wandered into the stables, and Jack fell into step beside me. He kept eyeing me as if he wanted to ask questions, but something in my eyes must've told him I didn't want to talk.

I went over to Honeymustard and gave her a pat. The palomino Morab leaned into my touch, the affectionate gesture taking some of the weight off my chest.

Jack floated between paperwork in the back office and more practical things in the stables while ordering the other staff around. He showed me how to brush the horse, and I busied myself with the task as he chatted about mundane things.

As I finished with the brushing, the horse's coat glistened, resembling spun gold even more now that she was free of dust.

I looked around and realized it was just Jack and me in the

stables.

Dropping the brush, I dusted my hands off and leaned against the stall door, watching Jack put away a saddle and tidy up some of the items on the wall next to it.

He turned to face me and glanced around, noticing the same thing I had. "Guess it's just you and me." He gave me the same crooked grin that, when I first got here, made me wish we'd met under different circumstances.

I was glad for the distraction of the past few hours, but I realized I didn't want to talk to Jack. I didn't want to be around him; I didn't think I wanted to be around anyone. The walk had helped get some of my nervous energy out, the cigarettes had made me feel like myself again, and focusing on the task of brushing Honeymustard had given me space to think.

I needed to get back to the house, call Alex, and tell her we needed to swap back. It was less than a week before the agreed-upon time; maybe she would be generous and agree to still give me part of the money. I just hoped I could get out before seeing Oren again. I seriously doubted I'd be able to walk away from him if I had to look into his tortured eyes one more time.

"I know why you came out here." Jack swaggered over and came to a stop right in front of me.

"You do?" I folded my hands behind my back and leaned on them, hoping to look casual. But he looked so confident, his smile kind of teasing, that alarm bells started to go off in the back of my head. Had he figured out my secrets? Did I let something slip in my emotional state? Was I busted just as I'd decided to pull the plug?

"Yeah." He propped one hand on the wall next to my head. "I know we shouldn't . . . Look, I can't keep denying this thing between us either."

"What?" I frowned. Relief flooded through me—I hadn't fucked up and accidentally given away the secret. But the relief was quickly chased away by dread. The intense look in his eyes clearly indicated he thought I was more into him than I actually was.

"I see the way you look at me." His other hand went to my hip. "I can't keep my eyes off you either. The way you ride a horse, I can't help imagining what you'll look like buck naked ridin' me."

His eyes raked up and down my body as he leaned in, as if he was trying to decide which piece of clothing to remove first.

I finally broke out of my shock and placed my hands firmly on his chest. "Jack, no."

I pushed, but he didn't budge. Instead he pressed his hips forward and jammed his knee between my legs. His erection dug into my belly. "I know you feel like you got to say that. Because of your fiancé." His voice was low, gravelly with lust—something that usually turned me on like crazy—but I just didn't want to hear it. Not from him. He just wasn't getting the message. "But it's OK. I know you want me. I want you. I don't know what's going on between the two of you, but I know something ain't right. You look worried and on edge half the time. He doesn't have to know. I'll make you feel better. Today and any day you want."

"Jack, I said no. Back the fuck off." I bucked my hips while shoving against his chest. He had a hundred pounds on me, strong muscles toughened by daily physical work, but my sudden jerking movement took him by surprise, and he stumbled back a step.

"Come on." This time his growl had a bite of anger to it, his hands curling into fists. "You can't spend weeks fucking teasing me like that and then not follow through. I *know* you want me. What's the goddamn problem?"

I glanced to either side of me and grabbed the first thing my eyes landed on—some kind of heavy, long metal thing. I had no idea what it was, but its weight felt good in the palm of my hand. "I said no, motherfucker. I don't care how much you think I flirted with you. That doesn't give you the right to just take something that's not yours. Come at me again. I fucking dare you."

I gave him a wide grin, letting a crazy glint into my eyes. I'd never let any asshole take advantage of me, and there were plenty of them at the Cottonmouth. I'd knock his teeth out before he had a chance to lay another hand on me.

Jack narrowed his eyes but smiled, the look pure menace. He started unbuckling his belt and took a step forward. I tightened my grip on my weapon.

"You fucking spoiled rich bitch. I'm gonna get what—"

Oren appeared out of nowhere, landing a right hook to Jack's jaw. His punch had momentum behind it, and the stable master ended up on his ass.

Jack recovered fairly quickly and lifted himself onto his elbows to stare at us, more than a little fear in his wide eyes.

"You have twenty minutes to pack your personal belongings and get off my property. Your services are no longer required." Oren's voice was menacingly low, but it didn't waver. His back looked rock hard with tension as he put himself between me and my would-be attacker, towering over the other man.

Jack didn't utter another word. He scrambled backward, got to his feet, and rushed away, giving us another sneer only when he was a safe distance away.

I lowered the weapon to my side as Oren turned to face me.

"Are you all right?" He shook his hand out and took a step toward me, his gaze searching my body for injuries.

"I was handling that asshole. You didn't need to swoop in and . . ." I gestured at the spot where Jack had fallen.

"I know." Oren sighed. "You can take care of yourself in every single way. I wasn't trying to patronize you. I was just trying to be there for you. I saw a man attacking my fiancée, and I defended her. Fucking sue me." His hands flopped to his sides. A bit of exasperation had leaked into his voice, but his gaze was still full of concern.

I released my grip on my makeshift weapon, and it clattered to the ground. I closed the distance between us and wrapped my arms around Oren's waist. He didn't hesitate for a second. Even after the way I'd pushed him away, he immediately folded his arms around me and held me to his chest, one hand at the back of my head.

Oren Charles Winthrop was a good man, and I didn't deserve him.

"I know you're independent." His words reverberated through his chest, and I felt them on my cheek as I pressed closer and breathed him in. "I know you don't need me to take care of you. We're the same in that regard. But is it so wrong to want to be there for each other? That's all I want, Alex. I just want to give us a chance. I know we're getting married because we need to, but why can't we explore an actual relationship because we *want* to? I haven't felt like this about someone in a long time. Call me crazy, but I think that's a good thing in our situation."

I didn't know what to say, couldn't get any words past the lump in my throat anyway. I could take care of myself, but the thought of having someone who *wanted* to be there for me was really damn nice.

This was exactly why I'd wanted to get out before I saw him again. He made me want to hold on and never let go.

Rushed footsteps came from the doorway, and then one of the staff from the house rounded the corner, looking harried.

"Oh, I'm so sorry to interrupt." The young woman took a small step back but didn't leave. "It's just that you're both needed up at the house. Mrs. Caroline sent me to find you."

"Jessie, what's happened?" Oren kept one arm around my shoulders as we separated and faced the woman.

"Oh no, it's nothing bad," she rushed to explain. "It's just that there's a visitor. And it was supposed to be a surprise. But she's here, and you weren't at the house. I'm sorry, I'm not supposed to say anything—just get you to come back." She gave us an apologetic look and rushed off, probably to avoid further questions.

We exchanged a confused glance and started back up to the house.

Chapter 22

ALEX

I winced as I unloaded the last of the glasses from the dishwasher tray. My back was still stiff from the incident the night before.

Andre looked up and frowned before plopping the mop back into the bucket and marching over to me.

"I'm fine. Just a little sore," I insisted. He'd left the floors half-done.

"Whatever," he grumbled as he faced me toward the bar with an insistent grip on my shoulders. "Maybe if you'd rested like I told you to, you wouldn't be wincing in pain, and I wouldn't be forced to listen to this crap."

I sighed as his strong hands kneaded some of the tension from my shoulders while the Backstreet Boys crooned about the shape of their heart.

The bouncers had booted about a quarter of the patrons by the time we'd made it back downstairs the night before. With the extra help from Ren, who wasn't precious about bussing tables like I thought he would be, we'd closed up within an hour.

The police showed up just as I was insisting I was fine and that Andre and Ren didn't need to babysit me for the night. Andre answered their questions about the drugs he suspected were being dealt in his bar as I slipped upstairs.

After another shower, I peeked out the open balcony doors. The police were gone, and the street was empty. There was no missing the two men locked in an embrace in the halo of a streetlight.

Andre and Ren held each other close as they kissed, and I couldn't seem to look away. I was as mesmerized as I'd been that first time I saw them. There was something irresistible about the intimacy, the heat, the two sets of strong muscles moving against one another.

They pulled apart and spoke for a few moments, and then Ren walked away. I turned out my light and, a few minutes later, heard Andre come past my door.

That morning I'd come down to the bar to help him clean up. He'd refused at first, threatening to carry me upstairs, but I'd fiddled with the fancy sound system until I managed to put my boy bands playlist on and started wiping down the bar, ignoring him completely.

"What the actual fuck are you two listening to?" A bright ray of afternoon sun beamed across the bar when Ren opened the door and let himself in.

"Nineties classics." I grinned, then moaned when Andre hit a tight knot in my shoulder.

Ren looked at me incredulously and then turned wide eyes to Andre. I felt him shrug behind me.

"Fucking whipped," Ren muttered under his breath. He was in ripped jeans and a light gray T-shirt with a deep V that allowed his ink to peek out, his brown hair messy on top of his head. "You still sore from last night?" He made himself comfortable on a stool across from us.

"Yeah, but it's loosening up." I rolled my head to give Andre better access.

Ren tipped his in the same direction and smirked. "Know what else helps you loosen up?" He lifted a little ziplock bag containing several wads of dark green stuff.

"Is that marijuana?" I bugged my eyes out, and he cracked up laughing.

The door opened again, and Loretta walked in, coughing up a lung. We all cringed at the mucousy sound.

"Take that shit upstairs." She waved us off, heading straight for the kitchen. "The staff will be here soon."

"You are staff," Ren called after her, and Andre leaned across the bar to smack him on the shoulder.

"She's family." He wagged a finger in Ren's face. "And she's right. Let's go upstairs."

Tonight wasn't expected to be as busy, so neither Andre nor I was working. Ren took the lead up the stairs, and Andre took my hand and tugged me along behind him.

"Set up on the balcony." Andre waved Ren on ahead. "I'll make us some iced tea."

He waited until Ren was outside before turning to me and lowering his voice. "You can bail if you want. Just because Toni's done every drug under the sun doesn't mean you have to."

I rolled my eyes. "It's just a bit of weed. I went to college. I've been high before."

He smirked and nodded but didn't say anything else as he moved away.

I'd tried weed a handful of times, though certainly not in the past decade. But what was the worst that could happen? I was supposed to be embracing fun experiences.

By the time Andre brought out a tall pitcher of iced tea, Ren already had two joints rolled and was working on the third, his dexterous fingers tucking the finely chopped stuff into the delicate paper.

Ren lit the tip of the first joint, inhaled deeply, and passed it to Andre, who did the same and then passed it to me. The pungent aroma surrounded me, the smoke momentarily obscuring the rich colors of the sunset.

I brought the joint to my lips and puffed, like Chad, my college boyfriend, had shown me. The smoke burned my lungs. I only managed to hold it for a few seconds, but I also managed to hold back the cough threatening to burst through.

Andre poured the tea. It was sweet and refreshing. We sat

around and smoked as the sun set and the ornate streetlights flicked on below. The music from the bar drifted up faintly, and we chatted about nothing, lapsing into silence now and then.

Bit by bit, my muscles did relax, and I melted into the chair, slouching. The thought of how my mother would look if she saw how I was sitting, my T-shirt dress riding up dangerously close to my crotch, made me giggle.

"Shit. She's a giggler?" Ren took another puff. "I would've thought she was the paranoid type, for sure."

"That's a funny word. Giggler." Andre's voice was even huskier than usual, his stare fixed on the twinkling lights of the city.

"How do you do it?" I rolled my head to stare at Ren. There was just enough light from a lamp inside to see by.

He gave me a questioning frown.

"How do you live the life you live, considering where you come from?" I tried to explain, but my brain was a little slow, the filter between it and my mouth apparently a little thin. I made a mental note to say no to the next joint. I couldn't afford to accidentally let something slip.

"How's the rich boy surviving slumming it with the commoners, you mean?" He had that look on his face, the one he wore when he antagonized me and called me a bitch.

"No, that's not what I meant. I saw what your parents are like . . ."

"Ah. You mean how do I defy them and everything that was expected of me growing up?" He relaxed again.

"Exactly."

He shrugged. "I stopped giving a shit. It wasn't easy, but eventually I realized it doesn't matter what anyone thinks. If I couldn't live my life how I wanted to, it wasn't worth living. If I can't be what I was born to be, what's the fucking point of it all?"

"A musician." I nodded.

"You think I was born to be a musician? You think I'm that good?" There was a hint of surprise in his voice.

I rolled my eyes. "Anyone with half a brain cell knows as soon as they hear you play that you were born for it."

"Man, you know you're good. Quit fishin'," Andre piped in, and my brain jumped to another question my filter failed to hold back.

"Why aren't you two together? Like, a couple?"

They both laughed.

"When Renshaw walked into my bar, I was in no state to start a relationship," Andre said. "I was a fucking mess, and I'd just decided to get my life together after my dad died."

"And I'd only just given my parents the middle finger and started a new life. I was still making peace with myself. And I still wasn't completely accepting of my sexuality," Ren added.

"And now?" I pushed.

"Now . . ." Andre cocked his head at me and blinked slowly. "Look, we've been hooking up for years, but we're there for each other above all else. Now we know who we are enough to not give a shit about what people think."

"Now I'm grown up enough to know that just because he fucks someone else doesn't mean he wants to stop fucking me." Ren shrugged, and Andre pointed at him and nodded in agreement.

A moment of silence fell between us, and then my stupid filter failed me once again. "You two look good together."

Two slow, questioning grins made me feel hot under the collar of the T-shirt dress. Or maybe it was the warm Louisiana night.

"I saw you kissing in the hallway recently." I cleared my throat. "And again last night, on the street."

They kept watching me, not saying anything.

"I liked it." Wow. Zero filter. *None.*

"Pervert," Ren whispered, but instead of throwing me out, he turned Andre's head toward himself with a gentle nudge on the bigger man's jaw and leaned in to kiss him. He kept his eyes on me the entire time.

Their kiss was slow but intense, Ren's hand caressing Andre's chest, Andre gripping Ren's knee. Ren's eyes never once closed, never stopped pinning me with their stare, making me feel like I was the one kissing him—or both of them.

When they pulled apart, Andre turned his head in my direction. "You wanna watch? Or join in?"

"Join in," I breathed, not even a second of hesitation. I'd wondered how I would fit in with them. It seemed now I was about to find out.

Andre twisted to face me and leaned over the chair arms. I met him halfway. He grabbed my waist and pulled me closer as he kissed me. His mouth was warm and slick. I knew I was imagining it, but it felt like I could taste Ren.

I placed my hand on Andre's thick thigh, the denim soft under my touch. Another hand covered mine. Ren kneeled in front of

Andre, one hand on his knee, the other covering my hand. His eyes were hooded as they met mine, his lips parted. He darted his tongue out and licked his piercing, and I moaned into Andre's mouth.

Ren nudged my hand, and together we caressed Andre's thigh until we reached the hard bulge between his legs. Now it was Andre's turn to moan into my mouth.

We stroked him together, his erection like a steel rod through the fabric. Then Ren tugged my hand away. With one last lick against his full lips, I pulled away from Andre and let Ren help me to my feet.

With a confident grip on my hips, he maneuvered me until I was facing Andre, my legs spread wide on either side of his thighs, but when I tried to lower myself, he kept me upright.

After a moment his hands released me, and he knelt to undo Andre's jeans and pull them down his hips. His thick erection sprang free. Did he never wear underwear?

I held on to Andre's shoulders for balance and watched between my legs as Ren wrapped his lips around Andre's cock, his messy brown hair falling forward and mingling with the wiry black hair.

Andre moaned and threw his head back, his gaze fixed on mine. He palmed my breasts and kneaded them, rubbing his thumbs over my nipples. I arched into the touch.

I was beyond turned on, completely lost in the lust and sensuality of the moment. I was so wet, and no one had even touched me between my legs yet.

As if he'd read my mind, Andre dragged both hands down my

sides and hiked my dress up around my waist before grabbing my ass. His hands slid up and down, gripping firmly and making me lean forward until my cleavage was in his face.

Andre dropped one hand to the back of Ren's head as he moved the other to my front and rubbed me over my underwear. He moved his hand in rhythm with Ren's head, and I started rocking my hips involuntarily.

"Fuck." Andre groaned. "She's soaked through her panties already."

Ren pulled back, letting Andre's gleaming cock rest on his belly.

One firm hand pushed between my shoulder blades, making me press my chest flush with Andre's and stick my ass out. The other hand joined Andre's between my legs.

While Andre rubbed my clit in circles, Ren nudged the soaking fabric aside and spread the moisture, teasing my entrance with his fingers pressed flat.

The friction was wonderful, but I wanted more. "I need something inside me now. Please." My words were breathy, desperate.

"Yes, ma'am." Andre banded one strong arm around my back, gripping my ass with the other as he stood. Ren helped him step out of his pants, and he carried me inside and dropped me on the bed.

I bounced on the dark sheets and laughed, the shot of adrenaline only adding to the desire already coursing through my veins.

For a charged moment, they both just stood there, looming over me and watching me with their hungry eyes.

I sat up and removed my dress. They both took my lead and whipped their shirts off. I unclasped my bra and removed it slowly as I took them in—one chest broad and dark with black hair, one lean and pale, decorated with ink.

Andre palmed his dick and gave it a stroke as he stepped closer. He was the only one completely nude.

I pulled my panties off and spread my legs. If they were going to watch me so lasciviously, I was going to give them something to look at.

Two sets of eyes—one dark brown, one vibrant green—immediately dropped to my lap. Their gazes felt like a caress, so heady I could almost feel it on my skin.

Ren still had his pants on, so I reached out and pulled him toward me by the waistband. Andre's hands snaked around from behind him and undid Ren's pants for me. I pushed them down, and he stepped out of them.

I gripped him by the base and did something I'd been fantasizing about since I'd first walked in on him in the men's room. I darted my tongue out and flicked the piercing.

He heaved a shuddering sigh.

"Give it a little tug with your teeth. He loves that." Andre sat on the bed next to me, his low instructions sending a shiver down my spine.

I did as he said, gripping the smooth metal between my teeth and giving it a little tug. Ren moaned. Andre started kissing my neck, his hand dragging up the inside of my thigh.

As I took Ren into my mouth and sucked, Andre pushed a

finger into me. He worked me while I worked Ren, but after a few moments, Ren took a step away.

He pushed on my shoulders until I was flat on my back, one hot, hard male body on either side. They pulled my legs apart, trapping them between their thighs, and then Ren kissed me. He devoured my mouth as Andre's closed over my nipple and sucked.

Andre added a second finger and started pumping them into me at a steady pace. I moaned into Ren's mouth, and he bit my bottom lip before releasing it so I could breathe and pant and writhe under them.

Ren's hand joined Andre's between my legs and rubbed the most sensitive spot in rhythm with Andre's thrusts. The combined sensations pushed me over the edge. I came hard, calling out as my abdominal muscles clenched and pleasure crashed through me.

As my vision began to clear, they removed their hands. Ren grabbed Andre by the wrist and licked his fingers clean. Then they were kissing, locked in a passionate embrace inches from my face, their bodies writhing against mine.

It was the single most erotic thing I'd ever seen.

Seeing them kiss those few times had been intriguing and exciting, but seeing it up close, threading my fingers into their hair, caressing their shoulders as I unashamedly watched every second of it—that was on a whole other level.

I wedged my arms between hard chests and tight abs and wrapped my fingers around two rigid, twitching cocks.

They both groaned and pulled apart, turning to look at me.

My core clenched, already ready for round two. As I stroked

them slowly, reveling in the sensation of the smooth skin in my palms, I rocked my hips, desperate for someone to touch me too.

Andre pulled away while Ren leaned down to kiss me, caressing my body, palming my breasts, gripping my hip, but stopping just short of touching me where I wanted him most.

Then he pulled away too.

A bottle of lube landed on the bed next to me, and they both made quick work of sliding on condoms.

I wondered how this was going to work but bit my lip to stop myself from asking. I'd never been with two men before, but I had an imagination, and scenario after erotic scenario flashed through my head. But instead of demanding to know everything, like I usually did in every aspect of my life, I relaxed into the bed and let the moment go where it would.

Andre leaned over me, wrapping a strong arm around my back so he could lift me farther up the bed and rest my head on a pillow. It smelled like him, and I sighed. My taut nipples pressed against his chest, and I leaned up to kiss him.

He brushed my hair out of my face with both hands as he kissed me back. His tongue stroked mine, his mouth stealing my breath as he lined his hips up and started to push into me.

I felt Ren's hands push my knees wider, and I opened my eyes. He was watching us with a smirk, his gaze meeting mine, then trailing down our bodies as Andre filled me up inch by slow inch.

When his hips were flush with mine, his hard cock deep inside me, he sighed and broke the kiss to look over his shoulder.

Ren grabbed the lube and positioned himself behind Andre.

I couldn't see past his waist, but I had a pretty good idea what he was doing.

Ren's lips parted, his eyes drooping—Andre's expression mirrored his. The pressure on my hips increased just a fraction as Ren leaned forward a bit.

Slowly, they started to move, Ren thrusting in and out of Andre as Andre thrust in and out of me in shallow, intense strokes. I rolled my hips to meet his on every stroke.

Eventually, we found a good rhythm, all of us moving and moaning and reveling in this incredible feeling together.

Ren held himself up with his hands on either side of my shoulders, the muscles in his arms taut and popping. I ran my fingers up one of his arms, raking my nails over his shoulder. With my other hand, I gripped the back of Andre's neck. I needed to touch them both, hold on to them both.

Ren was holding his weight off us, but it still didn't leave Andre's bulk a lot of room. He was pressed against my chest, the weight of his muscular body only adding to the incredible feeling of fullness between my legs.

He started to groan, burying his face in my neck. He licked and kissed the spot between incoherent sounds of pleasure.

Our moans and grunts and skin slapping against skin mingled with the thump of music from the bar below.

Andre lifted his head and cried out, the deep sound reverberating through his chest. The muscles in his neck stretched as he climaxed, his hips grinding into mine.

His release set Ren off.

"Come with me," he demanded through clenched teeth, his intense gaze fixed on mine. He pounded his hips, the motion helping Andre grind into me harder.

Ren's eyes rolled into the back of his head, and he moaned through his release, rocking back and forth.

We were like a chain reaction, and I went next. With both of their gazes on me, I shattered. I completely let go and became a ball of sensation, pleasure shooting through my entire being in waves.

We detangled our bodies, and they collapsed on either side of me, all of us breathing hard.

I looked at one man, then the other, then up to the ceiling and smiled.

I didn't let myself think it, but somewhere in the back of my mind, I wondered how the hell I was supposed to walk away from this.

Chapter 23

TONI

Everyone was in the grand foyer at the front of the house when Oren and I came in through the kitchen.

"Ah! Here they are." Caroline spotted us first, motioning us closer as Preston stepped aside to reveal the woman by the front door.

She was a little shorter than me, her dark hair pulled up in a neat bun and her plump figure draped in a conservative blue dress, shapely legs under the pencil skirt. She had a heart-shaped face and a thin nose. Her eyes were hazel, but she looked enough like an older version of me that I knew immediately this was Alex's mother.

Shitcuntshit!

My heart dropped into my stomach, my brain scrambling for

ways to duck out of the way before she saw me, but it was too late. We were already standing before the group.

Caroline placed a gentle hand on Oren's arm. "Annabelle, meet my son, Oren." Caroline beamed at her boy, but Annabelle's eyes were glued to my face. Confusion and then shock flicked across her features. I shook my head, a tiny movement that, coupled with the plea in my eyes, I hoped would be enough to keep her from exposing us all.

She smiled widely, as if nothing were amiss, and peered up at Oren. "What a handsome young man. You should both be very proud. Hello, Alexandria, darling." She reached a hand out, and I took it. Her fingers gripped mine tightly. I didn't dare shake her off, even though all I wanted to do was run like hell straight out the front door.

"It's such a pleasure to meet you, ma'am." Oren shook her other hand.

"What a surprise." I laughed, hoping it didn't sound as hysterical as I felt.

"I hope you don't mind." Caroline giggled like a schoolgirl. "It was a little secret between your mama and me. We wanted to surprise you with a visit. She was missing you like crazy."

"And I know how you like to know absolutely everything, so I didn't tell a soul I was on my way." Annabelle kept my hand in her iron grip.

Preston laughed. "Look at her. She can hardly believe it. No one can keep anything from my cousin."

Everyone laughed.

The sudden squeak of a shoe on polished floor made us all turn. George was standing near the hallway, his eyes wide.

"You've even managed to surprise George, Mrs. Zamorano," Oren said.

"It would seem so." Annabelle smiled, but it didn't reach her eyes. The hand still clasping mine started to shake.

George visibly gathered his wits and smiled. "What a wonderful surprise."

"I'd like to catch up with you both." Annabelle gave him a meaningful look, then turned to the group. "Winery business. I hope I'm not being terribly rude if I excuse myself for the moment? Traveling takes it out of me, and I think this southern heat is not helping. I'm suddenly a little light-headed."

"Of course." Caroline's gaze held nothing but concern. "Let me get someone to show you to your room."

"That's OK," I interjected. "I'll take her up to mine for now."

Annabelle didn't wait for anyone to respond, heading in the direction of the stairs. She kept her grip on mine all the way up and into my room. It was only when I closed the door that she finally released me.

"This isn't what it looks like, I swear," I told the door, then slowly turned to face her. "Alex knows I'm here. In fact, it was her idea to—"

My words died in my throat. Her hands were covering her mouth, her eyes watering. So many deep emotions ran through her gaze I had no chance at guessing what any of them were.

"Antoinette." My name on her lips was something between a

plea and a prayer.

"How the hell do you know my name?"

"They kept your name. My baby. My sweet, precious child." Tears ran down her cheeks, her shoulders shaking, as she reached her arms out and stepped toward me.

With the door at my back, I had nowhere to run, but the intensity of her reaction kept me rooted to the spot anyway. She wrapped her arms around my shoulders and held me as she cried. Reflexively I hugged her back, holding her around the waist.

After a few moments, I realized how bizarre this whole situation was, and I dropped my arms. She held on for a little bit longer, sniffling as she tried to get her crying under control. When she finally released me, she kept her hands on my shoulders and stared into my face, as if she couldn't quite believe what she was seeing.

"What exactly is happening? Who do you think I am?" I frowned and stepped out of her reach. I didn't like this stranger's hands on me, her tears soaking my shoulder, her grief squeezing my heart.

"I just can't believe it's really you. After all this time." Her words were shaky with emotion. She visibly tried to calm herself, smoothing down the front of her dress and reaching for some tissues on the desk nearby.

A quick rap sounded at the door, and George let himself in, closing it firmly behind him.

"Why did you keep this from me?" Annabelle demanded.

"I had no idea what it was I was keeping from you." George

held his hands up in surrender. "I swear. We ran into her by chance, and honestly, I just thought it was a fluke. They say that, statistically speaking, there are at least two or three people walking around with looks identical to each other."

"You still should have told me. I'm her mother. I need to know what's happening in her life."

"With all due respect, she's a grown woman, and I was simply following her instructions."

"Excuse me." I raised my voice, interrupting before they could keep arguing. My bubbling frustration was making the turbulent, emotional day I'd already had even worse. I had no idea what the hell was going on. "Can someone please explain?"

"It's been so long." Annabelle looked weary, the kind of tired that comes with carrying a burden your entire life. "I don't even know where to begin."

I turned to George and raised my eyebrows. He reached into his back pocket and pulled out a manila envelope that had been folded lengthways to fit.

"May as well start with the facts." He sighed. "The lab results came in this morning. I was on my way to find you. I've tried calling Alexandria several times, but she's not answering. According to this"—he waved the envelope in front of me—"you and Alexandria are sisters. Twins."

The room tilted, and I reached for the desk chair just in time to sink down into it. "How is this possible?" I'd had parents. They died. I mourned them. Was my whole life a lie? "Let me see that."

I yanked the envelope out of George's grip and flipped

through the pages inside with shaky fingers. I skimmed the text I couldn't understand, then made myself read the first page more carefully. It outlined the results in simple English—twins.

"There has to be a mistake. Maybe they accidentally tested Alex's DNA against her own instead of against mine. We'll get another test." I shoved the papers back into George's chest. Annabelle wrung her hands, tears streaming silently down her cheeks. There was just no way I was adopted. It didn't make any sense.

George calmly tucked the papers back into the envelope. "The results wouldn't say twins. This is a secure, discreet lab. There is no way anything was tampered with. Toni, Alexandria *is* your twin."

"Don't lose that, George." Annabelle lowered herself onto the bed across from me. "Alexandria will need to see it with her own eyes. But I don't need any tests to be sure this is my child I'm looking at. My baby I never thought I'd see again." Her voice wavered once more.

I had a million questions but no idea which one to ask first. I just stared at the distinguished woman across from me, hoping she would start filling in some of the blanks.

"Your father was on a business trip the night you went missing," Annabelle began. "We were vacationing at our property in the woods, and he had to fly back to the city for some kind of emergency meeting. I didn't mind. You girls were five months, three days, and about eighteen hours old the last time I saw you. Twins can be a handful, but I was getting the hang of it, and a live-in nanny was sleeping in the next room—or rather, she was drugged, but we didn't realize that until later. If I hadn't gotten up in the middle of the night to use the toilet, I may not have even realized you were gone until the morning. I may have lost you both. I went in to check on you. Alexandria was on her back, asleep, her soft little bunny clutched in her fat little hand. But your crib was empty, *your* little bunny abandoned on the ground." She paused, sobs racking her body as she bent over and clutched her chest.

Tears stung my own eyes. My heart went out to her, the pain and loss evident in every word she uttered. I was speechless, just trying to absorb the unbelievable story.

George sat next to her and wrapped a comforting arm around her shoulders. She leaned into his touch and pulled herself together enough to keep speaking.

"I turned on all the lights, tried to wake the nanny, frantically started searching for you. I called the police while I clutched Alexandria. Whoever had taken you had either not realized there were two babies, only wanted one, or only managed to get one of you before I spooked them. It took the police half an hour to reach us. The cabin was somewhat remote. They interviewed us, went through the whole house, spent days searching the surrounding woods, weeks questioning anyone in the area, trying to get any kind of lead. But you'd disappeared without a trace."

"How did Alex not immediately suspect I was . . . that it was me? That I was that baby that went missing?" I finally managed to get words past my lips.

"She doesn't know," George answered, lifting the envelope again before dropping it onto the bed. "She would've discussed the possibility with me. She wouldn't have bothered to even order these tests."

Annabelle nodded in agreement. "We never told her. There wasn't a single lead, not even a tiny trace for the police to follow. Your father and I were devastated. We didn't let Alexandria out of our sight, struggled even to let her go to school when the time came. One of us was always with her, holding her close, terrified we'd lose both our baby girls. I know it turned me into an overcautious, overbearing, clingy parent. But I couldn't bear the thought that something might happen to her if I looked away for even a second.

"But we didn't know how to move on, how to be the parents our remaining child deserved, while constantly on the verge of tears. Every mention of you, every time someone asked if there were any leads, every time we wondered what the hell had happened that night, we cried. I cried a river of tears for you. Not a day goes by that I don't think about you, to this day. But we just couldn't bear to talk about it. We couldn't bear to have Alexandria grow up under a shroud of grief. So we decided to focus on the positives and the happiness we still had in our lives. It was the only way we could move forward."

"I don't even know what to say." This was insane, completely ridiculous. This shit would've been laughed out of the writing room of a soap opera. But apparently it was *my life*. I wished I hadn't smoked both my cigarettes that morning.

After several long moments of silence, all of us reeling from the shock, Annabelle spoke again. "Do you know anything about your name? We named you Antoinette. Do you know how it came to be that you kept it?"

I shrugged. "No idea. My parents never really said anything about it. But I did have this baby blanket with my name embroidered on it. They were very insistent about keeping it—I thought they were just being nostalgic. I think I still have it somewhere."

"Crochet, yellow-and-white wool, with your name in pale pink?"
I nodded.

"You were wrapped in it the night you were taken from me." Annabelle swallowed and squared her shoulders. "I'm almost too scared to ask, but I need to know. Did you have a good childhood? Were you happy? Were you OK?"

"I had no idea I was adopted until today. We didn't have much, but my parents loved me. I was their whole world, and they were mine." *I missed them so fucking much.*

It was my turn to break down crying. I dropped my face into my hands and sobbed. I hadn't cried like that since my father's funeral, since I'd realized I was truly alone in the world. Now here was this woman, telling me I wasn't. I didn't know what to do with that. I didn't know how to handle this many fucking emotions elbowing each other out of the way inside me. Not to mention I hated, *absolutely despised*, crying in front of other people. And regardless of what that lab report said, regardless of this woman's story, at the end of the day these people were still strangers. I didn't really know them.

I growled and wiped under my eyes, taking deep breaths as George rubbed my shoulder. When I looked up, Annabelle was standing close by, looking awkward and unsure.

I stood up. "We need to tell Alexandria. Where's my phone?" I needed something else to focus on, someone else to help me navigate this shit. Alexandria would know what to do. She was organized, logical, and practical. Not to mention, she *deserved* to know.

"I've tried to call her several times." George propped his hands on his hips and frowned.

"Then we need to go find her." I needed to be doing something. "We need to go to the bar and talk to her."

"What bar? Where exactly is Alexandria?" Annabelle finally moved through the shock of realizing who I was and woke up to the other weirdness of the situation—the fact that one of her daughters was pretending to be the other one. It felt weird to think of myself as this woman's daughter. But now wasn't the time to dwell on that.

"Come on, I'll explain in the car." I headed for the door, but George stopped me with a hand on my shoulder.

"I'll go bring the car around and let the Winthrops know the two of you are going out for some mother-daughter time. But you should both take a minute to freshen up. In case you bump into anyone on the way."

He was right. Regardless of this situation that had me reeling, we still needed to be careful about what we revealed to the Winthrops. I was so sick of secrets.

Chapter 24

ALEX

Renshaw looked so peaceful in his sleep. He was on his side, facing me, his lips slightly parted and his lashes resting on his cheeks. Andre was at my back, one arm slung over my waist.

I blinked, struggling to get my eyes open again. I was in that haze between sleep and wakefulness where you're not quite sure what's real. The more that consciousness invaded, the more certain I became about one thing.

I had to tell Ren.

Logically, I knew it was insane to feel this strongly for not one but two men after such a short period of time, but after last night, there was no denying the connection we had. The thought of walking away from that and marrying another man made me feel sick.

I had no idea what I would do about Zamorano Wines, or about the money I'd promised Toni, but I'd figure it out. For now, I just needed to speak my truth to the two sleeping, nude men beside me.

Something buzzed—again—reminding me what had woken me up in the first place; my phone kept going off. I rolled over, careful not to disturb either of them.

Andre sighed and settled onto his back. His mouth fell open, and he started to snore lightly. I stifled a laugh as I lifted onto my elbows and squinted against the sunlight streaming in through the half-closed curtains.

The buzzing was coming from somewhere on the ground next to the bed. I leaned over Andre and felt around for my phone.

"I could get used to waking up like this." His voice was even deeper, even more gravelly than usual as he grabbed a handful of my ass.

I deliberately dragged my breasts across his belly as I straightened back up, phone in hand. "Me too," I whispered and shared a giddy smile with him.

I unlocked my phone and frowned. I had dozens of missed calls and messages from my mother, Toni, and George. I wasn't surprised about the ones from my mom, but the others had me worried. I sat up a little straighter.

"Come here," Andre whispered, dragging a hand up to my bare breasts and trying to pull me back down to the bed. "It's time for round three."

"Crap." I batted his hand away and skimmed some of the messages. They'd started about an hour earlier. "Shit." I dropped the phone and ran my hands through my messy hair.

"What's wrong?" Andre sat up to look over my shoulder.

"Oh no, no, no, no, no." Panic pumped adrenaline through my system, and I was fully awake now, scrambling to get out of bed.

Ren grumbled, my manic movements finally rousing him.

"They're coming here." I bugged my eyes out at Andre, stumbling over him to search the floor for my clothes.

"Who?" He looked so damn confused.

"What the fuck is going on?" Ren rubbed his eyes and yawned.

"Everyone," I hissed. "Where the fuck is my dress?"

A loud knock rattled the glass in the door. I grabbed the first piece of fabric I saw as Toni burst into the room.

"Andre!" she yelled as the door sprung open. "I need to find Alex. It's an emer—*whoa*! OK! I did *not* need to see that." She stopped dead in her tracks and looked up to the ceiling as I slipped a giant red T-shirt over my head. It smelled like Andre. "Well, I'm at least glad to see you took my advice and got laid," she grumbled.

"Who the fuck is this?" We all turned wide eyes to Ren, propped up on his elbows and looking between me and Toni as if he were trying to do a complex mathematical equation without a calculator. "Did we take something stronger last night? Did I forget that part? I thought we just smoked some pot."

"Ugh! Him again?" Toni pointed at Ren and gave me a disgusted look. "Fucking gross."

I widened my eyes at her, my heart thudding in panic even as it sank into the pit of my stomach in despair.

"What are you doing?" I demanded through gritted teeth. From the messages I skimmed, I got that my mother had shown up unexpectedly and known immediately Toni wasn't me, and they were coming to find me, but I hadn't picked up *why*.

She didn't get a chance to answer.

"Holy shit. *Toni?*" Ren looked between me and Toni, wide-eyed. "Then who the fuck is this?" He pointed at me.

"I can explain." Hand held out in front of me, I took a step toward the bed. He backed away, pressing his back against the wall. My heart cracked in the pit of my stomach, where it had taken up permanent residency.

Andre got out of bed just as more footsteps sounded outside the door.

"Alexandria." My mother appeared in the doorway, George right behind her. Her gaze flicked to the scene behind me. "Thank goodness we found yo—oh! My . . . big . . . penis . . ."

Eyes wide, she started to go pink, turning to the side to avoid looking at Andre's, admittedly, big penis.

George cleared his throat and took her by the shoulders. "We'll wait downstairs while you get dressed."

Mom nodded and let him guide her away.

"Hi, Mom," I grumbled at her retreating back. Could this mess get any worse?

As Andre pulled on his jeans, Ren got out of bed. Shoulders tense, teeth gritted, he started gathering his clothes.

"Oh god!" Toni shielded her eyes dramatically. "I've seen way too many cocks I have no interest in seeing *ever* again. As if this day wasn't traumatic enough."

"I should've known the second you stopped being a bitch"— he pointed an accusing finger at me, his T-shirt gripped tightly in his hand—"that you weren't *her*." He pointed the same finger at Toni but didn't look at her. "I'm such a fucking idiot." All that rage and disdain that had disappeared as we'd gotten to know each other was back in his beautiful eyes. And I'd put it there.

"Ren, I'm sorry. Please, just let me explain," I pleaded, moving toward him.

He stepped away. "No. I don't even know who the fuck you are. Get away from me. Can you believe this shit?"

He turned his incredulous gaze to Andre. Andre sighed and rubbed the back of his neck. He didn't speak, but the resigned, regretful look on his face said it all.

Ren took another involuntary step back, as if Andre had shoved him in the chest with his betrayal. "Un-fucking-believable."

Incredulity turned to rage in Ren's eyes as he shoved his feet into his boots and pushed past Toni through the door.

"Ren! Wait!" Andre finally found his booming voice and rushed after his lover.

I was hot on his heels, Toni following close behind. We made a procession of hurt, confusion, and anger down the narrow stairs, all talking over one another.

Ren attacked the back door leading to the alleyway, only to find it locked. He changed directions and smacked the side door leading into the bar. It banged against the wall, and Ren stormed across the room, pulling his shirt over his head. George and my mother stared at him. So did Dennis and Loretta from behind the bar. They were setting up to open.

"God dammit, Renshaw, stop runnin' away from me!" Andre brought his fist down on the bar, making Dennis jump. The young man turned wide eyes to me, then Toni, then me again.

Ren spun to face him. "Oh, so I can't run from you, but you can lie to me?" He scoffed.

"It wasn't my secret to tell," Andre explained.

"Bullshit! The second the three of us got into bed together, you should've told me."

"Oh my . . ." I was pretty sure my mother was clutching her pearls, but I was making a point of not looking at her.

"You're right. But none of us exactly planned last night. She and Toni—the real Toni—were supposed to switch back this week. It was supposed to be a bit of harmless fun. She just wanted to screw around. No one was supposed to get hurt. By the time I suspected it might be more . . ."

"You should've told me from the start, asshole! Instead of letting me stick my dick in someone whose name I don't know."

"Dude, you stick your dick in nameless people all the damn time."

"Fuck you!"

"It's not his fault. This is on me. Be mad at *me*." I couldn't believe how much damage I'd caused. Maybe if I'd had a chance to sit him down and tell him myself, explain the situation, he wouldn't have been so hurt. But he'd found out in the worst possible way, and now I was driving a wedge between them. I felt like the worst, most selfish piece of scum on the planet.

"Is this some kind of sick practical joke? Who the fuck even are you?" Ren looked me up and down with a sneer.

"My name is Alexandria Zamorano," I rushed to explain while he was still listening, still here. "I met Toni by chance and convinced her to switch places with me for a little while. I know it sounds insane, but the reasons why are complicated. I can explain everything. Let's just go—"

"I'm not going anywhere with you," he interrupted me. "Fuck this shit."

He turned around and stormed out. Andre followed without hesitation—barefoot and shirtless, he ran out into the bright afternoon sun to try to fix my mistake.

It wasn't until the heavy timber door swung closed that I realized two more men were standing inside.

One of them I'd known my entire life, even if we didn't see each other often. The other looked exactly like his photos on the Internet, except for the angry expression. In all the commotion, no one had noticed Preston and Oren.

I'd ruined *everything*.

Chapter 25

TONI

As Oren and I stared at each other across the room, I felt the color drain from my face.

How long had they been standing there? Judging by their expressions, long enough.

The look on Preston's face was pure shock.

Oren looked angry, his lips pressed together, his brow furrowed. But I knew this man now. I could see the hurt and the disappointment underneath.

This was not how I wanted him to find out. What was he even doing here?

"Was that the Pratt's boy? Renshaw?" Alex's mother broke the silence. "My, he got a lot of tattoos since I saw him last. What is he doing here? Alexandria? I am so confused."

"Mother." Alex shook her head, a warning in her gaze.

Annabelle finally turned to look at what had everyone else's attention. She gasped. "Oh, Oren."

Oh, Oren, indeed. I was speechless. I had no idea if I should try to explain, get on my knees and beg for forgiveness, or run away and pretend none of this had happened. So I found myself rooted to the spot, wearing another woman's clothes, dread settling over me as the first person I'd allowed myself to care about in years stepped forward.

"Preston and I drove here together when we realized we had meetings around the corner from each other—just a block away." He stuffed his hands into his pockets, his voice low, flat, every word measured. "We saw you three duck in here and decided to join you for a drink instead. I wanted to get to know my future mother-in-law."

Oren took slow steps until he stood directly before me. His voice carried so everyone could hear, but his hard stare was reserved for me alone. I resisted the urge to drop my gaze. He deserved to have me look him in the eye as the truth came out. I couldn't be a coward now, not anymore.

"I was engaged, and I was falling for a woman. Imagine my shock when I realized the two were not the same woman. What a fool I've been." He seethed, then turned to Alex. "Alexandria." It wasn't a question. Alex met his gaze with as much dignity as possible while wearing nothing but a man's shirt, and she nodded.

Oren turned back to me and raised an eyebrow.

I swallowed around the lump in my throat. "My name is Antoinette. Toni."

He nodded, pressing his lips together. "That must be the first true thing you've told me since we met."

"No. Oren, *no. Please . . .*"

I had no idea what I was pleading for. I reached out to touch him, only to pull my hand back at the last second. I wasn't sure how he'd react to my touch, even though all I wanted was to feel his arms around me, feel the steadying beat of his heart under my cheek.

He took my hand in both of his, and my heart soared. If he felt even half as strongly for me as I felt for him, maybe there was hope. Maybe he wouldn't be able to walk away from me any more than I could walk away from him.

I covered his hands with my free one, but he shook it off. Just as fast as it had soared, my heart plummeted.

He lifted my hand between us and held it in place.

It was never mine to begin with, but as he carefully tugged his mother's ring off my finger, it felt like he was ripping my heart out—tearing it right out of my chest and stuffing it into his pocket along with the diamond. He didn't look at me again, didn't utter a single word as he turned and walked away. He didn't rush out, angry and emotional, like Ren had. No, Oren's steps were steady and measured, the hard set of his shoulders saying more than words ever could.

He pulled the timber door open and stepped outside into the blinding afternoon light, leaving me standing in the middle of a dingy bar with a gaping hole in my chest, blood and despair dripping all over the dirty floor.

I stared at the closed door, just trying to breathe as bile rose in the back of my throat and my eyes began to sting.

"Shit." George sighed. "I'll head back and try to do some damage control." He gave my shoulder a squeeze as he passed.

"Thank you, George." Annabelle's voice was low, cautious.

"I'll give you a ride back, Preston." It wasn't a suggestion. George opened the door and waited. Preston still looked shocked, but there was a hint of amusement on the asshole's face. Why did he have to be here? Why did Loretta and Dennis and *anyone* else have to witness my destruction?

As the door closed behind them, I turned and walked on numb feet behind the bar. Dennis stepped out of my way, eyes wide, his hands gripping a tea towel. I grabbed a bottle off the top shelf and poured the amber liquid into a shot glass.

"Ah, shit," Loretta croaked but managed to avoid another coughing fit. "At least it's all out in the open now."

"You knew?" Alex's surprised voice asked from right next to me.

"Child, nothin' happens in this bar without me knowing."

It didn't matter anymore who knew. *Oren* knew, and everything was fucked.

Silent tears poured down my cheeks. I gripped the edge of the bar for something to hold on to, something to keep me from plummeting completely into despair. Or maybe I was already there and just didn't realize it.

"Antoinette?" Annabelle's gentle voice came from directly

opposite me, on the other side of the bar.

I lifted the shot glass and realized I'd poured a shot of the same whiskey we'd been drinking that night we'd pretended to watch a movie. I slammed it back down on the bar, the alcohol splashing over my hand. My tears mingled with the whiskey as my shoulders quivered.

"Toni." Alex placed a hand between my shoulder blades. "What happened?"

"I . . ." I croaked. "I fell in love."

With the whole, heavy truth finally out, sobs racked my body. Alex wrapped her arms around me, but my knees buckled, and I collapsed to the ground, ugly crying. Snot poured down my face, my shoulders shook violently, and the sounds coming out of my mouth were pure, unadulterated anguish.

Alex kneeled with me and pulled me against her, holding on tightly as I fell apart.

I clung to her, this woman who was a stranger and also apparently my sister. Except she wasn't a stranger, not really. She'd shared her life with me, both by letting me live it and by talking to me every damn day. Hadn't I done the same? Without even meaning to, I'd let Alex in, allowed her to know me, *see* me.

I was at my lowest point since the day I'd wandered into the Cottonmouth Inn, on my last penny and on the verge of homelessness. As the sobs subsided, I was glad she was there, happy she was the one trying to hold me together. Alex was the smartest and most confident, capable, determined woman I knew. Having her at my side made me feel stronger. Strong enough to take the tea towel from Dennis's outstretched hand and wipe my face. Strong enough to look into her eyes—eyes identical to mine—and say my truth again.

"I fell in love, Alex."

She was crying too, her eyes red-rimmed and puffy. "Me too," she whispered. She wiped her cheek, but another tear tracked a wet path down her face immediately.

"Fuck." I handed her the tea towel, not entirely sure I wouldn't need it again. "Which one?"

She sighed and wiped at her face again. "Both."

"Oh my god." I pulled her in for a hug. Now it was *me* trying to comfort *her* broken heart.

"I don't think I even realized it fully until they both walked out that door." She clung to me and cried.

"I hate that fucking door," I growled. As if it were the door's fault the men we'd fallen for had walked through it, taking our hearts with them.

She cried into my shoulder for a few minutes, and then we pulled apart and just stared at each other.

"Only you would set out to have a month of freedom and fun and end up falling in love with two guys," I deadpanned.

"Only you would set out to take advantage of the lap of luxury for a month, only to cause chaos for one of the richest men in the country," she shot back.

We laughed darkly, even as tears kept trickling down our cheeks.

I shook my head. "We really fucked up, didn't we?"

"Yeah, but it was my stupid idea to begin with. This is all my fault."

"Shut up. I agreed to it, didn't I?"

She sighed. "Why did you all march down here anyway? Why didn't you wait for me to return your call?"

"What difference would it have made? Would you really have been able to walk away from them and switch? Because I was fully intending to come clean with Oren after speaking to you." It hurt to say his name. "There was no way I could just leave him. Not that it matters—he's walked away from me."

"No. I was never going to be able to just leave them. I couldn't marry Oren. Not after all this."

"What a mess. He was engaged to one sister and sleeping with another. Sounds like a soap opera."

Alex's eyes went wide, and she shook her head. "Sister?"

"Oh, fuck. Yeah. That's why we rushed here to find you. Your mom showed up at the same time as the DNA test results. Turns out we're twins."

After all the drama of the past hour, that bombshell didn't even seem that crazy to me anymore, but Alex was hearing it for the first time.

She craned her neck to look up at her mother, and I followed her gaze.

The older woman sat on a bar stool, her head in her hands. After a beat of silence, she sighed and lifted her head. Her eyes were glassy, her makeup streaked down her face. I guess it was an emotional day for everyone.

"Mom. How is this possible?" Alex got to her feet, flashing me her bare ass under Andre's T-shirt.

I leaned away and averted my gaze. "Maybe put some underwear on first?"

She yanked the hem of the shirt down and gave me an embarrassed look.

"I'll get some food on while you gals talk." Loretta disappeared into the kitchen.

We all turned to look at Dennis. Poor kid was still standing near us, a dumbfounded look on his face. He snapped out of it, turning first in one direction, then the other. "I'll just . . . uh . . . go clean . . . something." He rushed out from behind the bar and started wiping down already clean tables.

"Right." Alex took small steps toward the back stairs, trying to preserve her modesty. "I'll go get dressed, and then you need to explain, Mother."

"Of course." Annabelle looked tired but resigned. "I'll answer all your questions."

"Good. Don't even think about going anywhere." With a firm look in her mom's direction, Alex disappeared out the back.

"Wouldn't dream of it." A small smile pulled at the older woman's face. "I'm never letting either of you out of my sight again."

Chapter 26

ALEX

"You snore." I took a sip of my green tea as Toni narrowed her eyes. "You really should get serious about quitting."

She stared me down and took a slow, deliberate drag of her cigarette, exhaled the smoke, and chased it down with a sip of black coffee. Neither of us could eat breakfast first thing in the morning, but where I had to have my tea, she was addicted to coffee.

"Fuck off," she finally responded, flicking the ash off her cigarette and lifting her feet onto the balcony railing. It was overcast but still warm. "You're lucky I didn't kick your ass out of the bed. You twitch. You smacked me several times."

I chuckled and smacked my hand over her face lightly. "Like

this?"

She leaned away, unable to defend herself with her hands full. "Seriously?"

"Sorry," I said, completely without remorse, and propped my own feet up to mirror her pose. "Just trying to teach my little sister who's boss."

"I told you, I'm the oldest," she argued.

"Can't wait until Mom gets here and proves you wrong."

The previous afternoon, after everyone was dressed and had stopped crying, Mother had filled me in on the story of what happened to Toni. I couldn't believe I had a sister. A *twin*! I'd wanted a sibling my whole childhood, had always been jealous of the special bond my friends shared with their brothers and sisters— even when they were fighting. We'd certainly found each other in the strangest possible way, but at least we'd found each other.

By the time Mom had given me the gist of the story, it was time for the bar to open.

"I messaged Andre and told him we've got the bar covered for the night." Loretta propped her hands on her hips. "Now you two better get some aprons on and get ready to work. Way I see it, you started this mess. Least you can do is keep the man's bar staffed for a night."

She didn't wait for a response, disappearing back into the kitchen as the happy hour crowd in suits and heels started to trickle in.

She was right. I'd been waiting for him to come back through that door all afternoon, even as I listened to my mother's outrageous story. The knot in my stomach would not ease until I could find out how pissed off he was with me, find out how Ren was doing. I hated myself for putting them in this situation, but I was glad they had each other.

Toni and I stepped behind the bar and got to work. When they walked in and saw two Tonis, the other staff gave us wide-eyed looks and asked all kinds of questions.

"We're twins. Didn't know the other existed until recently. It's a long-ass story. Now go take that frat boy's order." Toni didn't pull any punches. We hadn't sat down and decided anything, but we were both done hiding, pretending, and lying.

Toni was fantastic at her job. The staff listened to her, and she ran that bar as if it were hers, directing everyone, keeping an eye on the stock levels, making sure no one got rowdy, and buzzing around the place like a worker bee on crack.

My mom sat at the bar, nursing a gin and tonic and watching us work for hours. She even broke her clean-eating diet and had one of Loretta's burgers.

Around eleven, George joined her and tried to convince her to get some rest. Both she and Preston had been asked to leave the manor, our whole family evicted from the Winthrops' lives, but Preston had rented an apartment nearby, as he still had business in New Orleans to attend to. He'd graciously invited us to stay.

It was too busy to get much more detail from George, but I wasn't sure I wanted to know how badly I'd messed everything up anyway.

"George, I'm not leaving until these two do," Mom insisted.

"We're going to be here until well past midnight, Mom," I argued while pouring a beer. "We need to close the bar. Just go with George. Get some sleep."

"What if something happens? I can't leave my girls again." She started to cry; she'd been doing it on and off all night.

Toni appeared next to me. "Look, it's gonna be really late when we finish. Alex can crash here with me, and we'll see you tomorrow. We'll take care of each other, OK?"

I gave her hand a squeeze under the bar, and she returned it. We'd been taking care of each other for the past month.

With the three of us convincing her, Mom finally let George lead her away. The rest of the night wound down without incident—and without Andre's return. The other staff left, and we closed up and headed upstairs.

We'd shared a bed, as most sisters would've done countless times growing up, and woken up midmorning to a million messages from Mom. I'd spoken to her on the phone and convinced her we were both fine while Toni made me a green tea and herself a coffee.

"How long until your mom and George get here?" Toni asked, setting her empty mug down on the little round table between us.

"She was on her way when we hung up, so not long." I drank more tea and studied her profile.

"I know she's technically my mother too, but it doesn't feel natural saying 'our mom.'" She frowned.

"Of course not. You only just met her. You and I only met a month ago."

"You jumped into bed with me after only knowing me a month." Toni gasped dramatically and smiled. She was deflecting, trying to lighten the mood, but I wasn't going to let her.

"Toni, I'm serious. This is a crazy, messed-up situation, but I want you to know no one expects you to just start calling her Mom or me Sis or whatever. But I do want to be in your life. I want to know you."

"I know. Me too." She gave me a sad smile. "I want this more than you know. To have family, people. I don't even think I realized how much I craved it. It just feels like a betrayal on some level."

"Toni, your parents would want you to be happy."

"I know. It just feels like I'm letting them go, moving on." Her voice cracked, and I set my tea down to grip her hand. She held on tightly but kept her gaze on the thick clouds above the buildings.

"Moving on is a good thing. But it doesn't mean you have to forget them or pretend they never existed."

She nodded. The silence settled between us for a few moments before she let my hand go.

"I'm sorry about the money," I said.

"What?"

"The money I promised you in exchange for switching."

"Oh, right. Yeah. That's the last thing on my mind. Honestly, I'm glad the marriage isn't going ahead."

"Me too. Despite what it means for my finances."

"Shit. That's not what I meant. I'm sorry you won't be able to save your family business. I just don't think I could've handled Oren marrying another woman."

"I know. I get it."

"And now he'll never speak to either of us again, and he'll probably end up marrying some socialite who gives really bad head."

I threw my head back and laughed. The situation was beyond messy, but Toni's dry wit never failed to make me feel a little bit lighter. Especially when it wasn't used against me.

I wiped the tears from under my eyes. "I can't believe you fell in love with my fiancé."

She snorted. "Same. Didn't think I was capable of love, to be honest."

The thud of heavy boots in the hall carried all the way through the small apartment and past the open windows, making me lose track of whatever consoling thing I was about to say.

My heart jumped into my throat, and I leaned forward and gripped the armrests, ready to chase after him. But what if he didn't want to speak to me? What if he hated me for how much I'd hurt Ren? What if I'd hurt him more than I realized?

"Dude." Toni's firm voice snapped me out of my crippling self-doubt spiral. *"Go."*

She bugged her eyes out at me and pointed to the door.

I sprang out of the chair and dashed across the studio on bare feet, wearing nothing more than underwear and a Jack Daniel's tank top.

I wrenched the door open and nearly copped a fist in the face.

Andre dropped his arm, abandoning his knock. He was in jeans and boots, a white T-shirt stretched over his defined chest. He looked tired, his eyes bloodshot and his big shoulders hunched.

"I didn't realize you were still here." God, I'd missed that gravelly voice.

I clasped my hands in front of me to keep from reaching for him. He didn't want to see me. He was looking for Toni, knocking on her door.

"I'll get Toni for you." I hated how defeated my voice sounded as I stared at his tan boots. They looked massive next to my bare feet.

"I can talk to her later. I was coming to see if she knew where you were."

When I looked up into his dark gaze, he was smiling faintly. Hope welled in my chest, just a tiny spark spreading from deep in the center.

I wrung my hands. "I don't even know where to start, Andre. I'm so sorry for this whole mess. How's Ren?"

"Are you going to go through with it?" He dragged his hands over his head and down his face. When they came away, I was struck by how nervous he looked, how unsure. "I need to know if you're going to marry that guy."

"No. Even if I still wanted to, he's made it clear the deal is off. His family want nothing to do with us. Can't say I blame them. I'm pretty sure I've lost my family business, but all I can think about right now is you and Ren."

"Even if you still wanted to?" He raised his eyebrows.

"I can't . . . I don't want to be away from you. I know it sounds crazy. We only just met."

"Fuck, I kept telling myself it was all just a bit of harmless fun. Even as I started falling for you, I kept reminding myself that you were planning to leave, go back to your real life, that I—we—were just a blip on your radar. I kept trying to convince myself that whatever time we had would have to be enough. I'd show you a good time, and you'd leave, and I'd have to get over it. I was such a damn idiot . . ." He shook his head.

My heart hammered in my chest. I couldn't stand this. Did he hate me? "And now?"

"Alexandria, I know we've only known each other a month, but I love you."

Tears pricked at my eyes. I wanted to throw myself at him like I did that first day, but the tortured look in his eyes kept me in my spot. "But?"

"But I love him too."

I squeezed my eyes shut, tears trailing down my cheeks. Of course he'd choose Ren. They had history. They were in each other's lives, already connected. "I understand."

"Woman, you don't understand shit."

My eyes snapped open just as he grabbed my wrist and pulled me against his chest. I wrapped my arms around his middle and gripped the fabric of his T-shirt, as though if I could just hold it tightly enough, he wouldn't leave me. He smelled so damn good. I committed every last detail to memory. If this was the last time he'd ever hold me in his strong embrace, I didn't want to forget any little bit of it.

"I spent all night talking to Ren. We had a lot of shit to work through, shit that doesn't even have anything to do with you. It wasn't until I had to face the idea of you leaving that I realized I needed you both in my life. I want to be with you, but I want to be with him too."

I frowned. "What are you saying?"

"I'm saying, I'm not gonna choose sides. I want you both, dammit, and I'm done letting my life pass me by. I'm getting what I damn well want. But Ren needs time. We need to give him time and put the brakes on this."

I craned my neck to meet his gaze. "So . . . there's hope?"

He smiled, that big grin of his lighting up his dark eyes. "Yeah. Everything's just fucked at the moment. So you focus on sorting out your business. Ren will come around eventually, and I'll be right here, waiting for you both to get your shit together."

I lifted onto my toes and pressed my lips to his, reveling in the feeling of being held by a man who loved me. The relief flooding my body was palpable. He was right—everything was fucked—but maybe, *just maybe*, it could get better eventually.

Andre broke the kiss. "Much as I love it when you throw yourself at me in your underwear"—we chuckled at the shared memory—"we should cool it. We all need time, and I don't want Ren to feel like we're doing shit behind his back."

"Right. Of course." I nodded but couldn't seem to get my hands to stop white-knuckling his T-shirt. "How bad is it? Does he hate me?"

Andre sighed and pressed his forehead against mine, not making a move to release me any more than I was. "You gotta understand, he's had people manipulating him his whole life, trying to get him to be something he's not, pretending to be something they're not. It's hit a pretty raw nerve. Plus, he's so damn stubborn."

"Should I talk to him? Explain?"

"I don't think that's a good idea. I told him the whole story. I think you should give him space. Let him cool down."

"OK." I so badly wanted to hunt him down and make him listen to me, but Andre knew him better, and I needed to respect what they wanted.

Now that the dust was starting to settle, I was beginning to see things a little more clearly. It was time for me to put my big-girl pants on and pull my head out of my ass. I'd been desperate to switch with Toni because I was overwhelmed. I'd put myself in an impossible situation and convinced myself there was no other way out. But there was *always* another way.

Sometimes everything had to fall apart to put things in perspective. Andre had my back, and all I could do was hope Ren would come around. In the meantime, I had a sister I never knew about, and I was excited to have her in my life. It was time to focus on the positives. People were relying on me—and while that didn't feel so heavy and oppressive as it did one month ago, I still needed to figure out how to save their jobs.

It was time to change out of the ripped jeans and tank tops and put my pencil skirt back on. It was time to get back to work.

A: Fave color?

T: Black

A: Green

T: Fave movie?

A: The Parent Trap. LOL!

T: hahahaha! Really?

A: Nah. I don't know. You?

T: Probably Thelma and Louise

A: Fave food?

T: Loretta's burgers.

A: Beignets

T: If you could have a superpower, what would it be?

A: Mind reading.

T: Shapeshifting. Always wondered what it's like to have a dick.

A: OMG! Hahaha!

A: What's your earliest memory?

T: Holding my parents' hands as they swung me between them. Don't remember where we were or anything. Just remember the sun shining in my eyes and this feeling of exhilaration.

A: Coffee. My dad let me stick my nose in a bag of ground coffee. I don't drink it, but I've always loved the smell.

Chapter 27

TONI

I tucked the phone under my chin and tried to light my cigarette as quietly as possible.

"Toni!" Of course Alex heard and interrupted herself halfway through her own damn sentence to chastise me. "I thought you were quitting."

I took a drag and leaned on the wall near the back door. The little covered area at the top of the stairs was the only place in the alleyway safe from the softly falling rain.

"No, you told me I had to quit while I was pretending to be you. I'm dealing with a lot of shit. Leave me alone." It hadn't even been a week since we realized we were sisters, and she was bossing me around—although she'd been bossing me around since we met if I really thought about it. No surprise she was the eldest—by a whole four minutes. "Now, what were you saying about the winery?"

"I know you're deflecting, but I don't care. I need to talk about this. So Preston has offered to bail us out."

"What? That's excellent." A genuine smile crossed my face. I wasn't smiling much these days. I was doing my best to move on, not think about him, focus on the fact that I had a fucking family I never knew anything about. But it still felt like he was haunting me, squeezing my heart as I went about my day, wringing tears from my eyes every damn night as I tried to go to sleep.

"Yeah, the business will be saved, and no one will lose their jobs, but . . ."

"What? I only have another ten minutes of my break. Spit it out." The Thousand Lies were halfway through their first set, and I'd ducked out to have a break. I wasn't drinking like I used to, and I certainly hadn't taken any losers to bed since I got back, but I couldn't seem to let go of the smokes. It was like they were my last bit of rebelliousness, some semblance of the old Toni I wasn't quite ready to let go. Plus, it was stressful as fuck having people in my life I actually gave a shit about.

"I'll give you the Cliffs Notes version." She sighed. "So Preston was in New Orleans to meet with a bunch of businessmen. He was liquidating assets—some holdings his family had and a few of the restaurants. He was planning to use all the money for some big deal, a new opportunity. He didn't give me details. Anyway, when everything came out about the winery being in trouble, he apparently decided to put that money to another use. He's offering to bail us out, basically—all the debts will be repaid, we can get back in the green with our suppliers, and we can even invest. But he wants fifty-five percent of the business. It would technically remain in the family—we *are* cousins, however distant, and he *is* a Zamorano—but he'll have the majority share. I'd lose control of my own business. He'd have final say on all decisions."

"Shit. There's no other way?"

"The only other option is to look for other investors or take the company public. But with this much debt, the stock wouldn't be worth much, and who in their right mind would invest in a crippled business? I'd probably have to give up an even bigger share."

"Then I guess this is the best option." I took another drag. I felt bad for her. She'd been working her ass off all week, trying to find a solution. Now here was one that sounded about as good as it could get, but it didn't *feel* right.

"Yeah, you're right. I just feel like I failed him." All she'd ever wanted to do was make her dad proud.

"Alex, you are many things, but a failure is not one of them. Get your shit together."

"I know. It's just hard. You sure you don't want in on this mess?" She laughed, and I snorted. Technically, half the business was mine. Alex and Annabelle had been very transparent about that. They'd brought over reports and statements and paperwork to officially make me part owner. But I said no. No one in their right mind would give me a student loan if I was part owner in a multimillion-dollar company that was up to its eyeballs in debt.

They understood but said it was mine as soon as I changed my mind. I didn't see that happening anytime soon. I may not have been getting any of the money Alex had promised, but the whole experience had made me realize I really did want to go to college. I wanted to work with animals, and I was going to make that happen. Andre had even agreed to let me pull back my hours.

"Positive." I nodded.

"Have you sent those applications in yet?"

"I'm doing it after work tonight." Summer was coming to an end, so I wasn't sure when I'd be able to start classes, if it was too late to apply, but I was going to try. "How's Annabelle doing?"

"She's driving me nuts." I could practically hear her grinding her teeth on the other end. "George left this morning to head back to California. We really need someone to explain the situation to the staff, and I need him there to help manage this mess. But now my buffer is gone. I spend half my time convincing her she can't just sit at the bar day and night watching you work."

I laughed and extinguished my cigarette, blowing the last of the smoke out. My birth mother was sweet but neurotic. Considering what she'd been through, I guess it made sense. She was an emotional mess, but she was so determined to be in my life, to explain things, to know me.

Now that we had more information, George's people were able to fill in some of the gaps. Whoever had taken me had managed to get over the state line before the police could reach the remote cabin where Annabelle was. By the time an amber alert was issued, I was long gone. According to records from the adoption agency, I was dumped at a small church in Wisconsin before dawn three days later. By the time the pastor discovered me, whoever had dropped me there was probably hours away. It was assumed I was the result of an unwanted pregnancy, and I was soon adopted by my parents. The reason my birth certificate had a different birthday from Alex's was because I was issued a new one, and they had to guess the date.

"Just send her my way if you need a break. Maybe I'll hold off sending the applications until tomorrow. She can do it with me." My offer was met with silence.

"Alex?"

"Yeah, I'm here. I'm just stunned. I don't think you know what you're getting yourself into."

"Yeah, I do. She's been here every damn day anyway." I laughed to show I really didn't mind that much. Annabelle had agreed to Alex's "one check-in text per day" rule for both of us, but she still showed up every day. Even when I was working, she'd just sit at the bar and nurse her gin and tonic, waiting for the lulls in the crowd. Then she'd tell me some silly little story from Alex's childhood, or she'd ask about my parents. She was avoiding the heavy topics, but she was there.

"Hey, wouldn't it be better if you or your mom went to speak with the staff?" I asked. "George is great and all, but he doesn't own the business."

"We don't want to leave yet."

"Why?"

"Because of you."

"Oh." My chest swelled and contracted at the same time—the anguish of losing Oren making room for another strong feeling. I didn't know what to say. I hadn't had anyone consistently show up and give a shit about me since my parents died. But maybe that was because I'd never given them a chance.

Then Alex had demanded her way into my life, and next thing I knew I had a sister and I was calling her on my breaks because I actually wanted to.

The door creaked open, and Ren let himself out into the narrow covered area, cigarette already hanging from his lips. As the door swung closed with a thud, he spotted me and sneered.

"Fucking fantastic. Can't even have a goddamn cigarette without stepping in crap these days," he grumbled.

I narrowed my eyes.

"Is that Ren?" I could practically see Alex sitting up to attention at the sound of his voice. She'd taken Andre's advice and given them space, but unable to stand it anymore, she'd tried calling Ren the previous day. He wasn't taking her calls or replying to messages.

"Yeah. I gotta go."

"Toni! Be nice, please," she rushed out. "He's hurting because of me."

"I'm hurting too. But I'm not taking it out on anyone. I'll speak to you later." I hung up before she could say anything else and tucked my phone into my back pocket.

The rain continued to fall softly but steadily. There was a slight chill on the breeze, but I was still comfortable in my ripped jeans and loose V-neck T-shirt. My rage was keeping me warm.

"Did I just hear you say you're hurting?" He chuckled around his cigarette, holding the lighter up to it and flicking it repeatedly— it wasn't catching. "Didn't know you were capable of emotions, you cold-hearted bitch."

I gritted my teeth. Ren had always been a dick to me, and I'd always given as good as I got, but this past week had been next level. He was taking *everything* out on me. Andre was moping around and in a surly mood, and Alex was staying away. None of them needed fucking space. They needed to get over themselves and get their shit together. If I couldn't be happy, they should at least try. I just didn't know how to get through to someone who genuinely seemed to hate me.

"God fucking dammit!" Ren gave up on the lighter and threw the faulty bit of plastic into the alleyway. He plucked the cigarette out of his mouth, slid down the wall until he was sitting, and leaned his head back. "Toni, can you please just leave?" He kept his gaze on the trickle of water falling from the corner of the roof. There was plenty of hostility in his voice, but I heard the pain too.

For the first time since we'd met, I found common ground with Renshaw Pratt. We were both pining for people we loved. But at least he could do something about it.

I glanced at the heavy door, then back down to his slumped form. I really didn't want to do this, but I had a feeling I needed to. There was no chance he'd just open up to me or listen to anything I had to say. I had to give him something first—I had to show him my own gaping wound.

I sighed and crouched down. He rolled his eyes and groaned.

I pulled my lighter out of my cleavage, flicked it on, and held it out to him. He frowned at me and flicked his eyes down to my boobs.

"Gross." He sneered, but he brought the cigarette up to his lips and lit it.

I took a deep breath. "I fell in love."

He looked at me as if I'd lost my mind. Maybe I had. "So?"

It hurt to say it, to think about it. "I fell in love with the man Alexandria was supposed to marry. A privileged, entitled, spoiled rich boy. Can you believe it? Me? Falling for someone like that? Except I got to know him, and he's none of those things—except rich. But that's not important. My point is, I may not have told him my real name, but I let him see the real me. I didn't even realize I was doing it, but I bared my fucking soul to this man. For the first time in years, I gave a shit about someone. And then the truth came out."

"What the f . . . I don't give a shit. Why are you telling me this?" I didn't know it was possible for someone to smoke angrily, but he was doing it like a pro.

"I'm telling you because I'm trying to show you that I get it. You're hurt. I am too."

"Fuck you, Toni." He finally looked me dead in the eye. "You're not the one who was lied to. The two of you did the lying."

I laughed darkly. "I've been lied to my whole damn life by my parents. They're both dead, so I can't even rage at them, demand answers, ask why they never told me. My whole life's been turned upside down. I'm thinking maybe you know a bit about that too."

"Lying piece-of-shit parents? Yeah."

I kept my mouth shut. I loved my parents and didn't like him lumping them in with his, but I knew this wasn't about them.

Silence settled between us, the rain and the muffled thumping of the music from inside keeping us company.

"Why do you hate me?" I finally asked.

He gave me a disparaging look, and I waved him away. "I know why you're pissed about what's gone down recently. I'm talking about all the shit before that. You've been a dick to me from day one, and I have no idea why."

He finished his cigarette and flicked it into the rain. "Honestly? I was in love with Andre. I was struggling to figure out what to do without my trust fund. Then you show up, and that same day he gives you a job and clears out his dad's old office for you to live in. I thought you were taking him away from me. Turns out that fell to another bitch who looks just like you."

I pushed myself to my feet and looked down on him, letting the frustration show in my face. "That's my sister you're talking about, asshole. Yeah, she fucked up. We both did. But can you really say you're perfect? She woke up that morning ready to walk away from it all for you. She was going to lose her family business, give up on a goal she's had her whole damn life, because she realized she needed you and Andre more. She loves you, and you wouldn't be this cut up if you didn't love her too. So get over yourself. In twenty years' time is any of this shit gonna matter?"

I pulled the door open and got back to work. The bar was

slammed with orders, and it was a busy night, but Ren stayed out of my way.

The next day, I went to Preston's apartment. Annabelle and Alex helped me submit the college applications, and then we had lunch. I couldn't believe how easy it was to let them into my life, how open I was to getting to know them better, letting them know me.

My walk home took me past the same park George had stalked me to so Alex could convince me to switch lives with her. I was in no rush, so I sat down on a bench under a big tree. I watched a little girl playing with a beagle in the distance and smiled. Hopefully one day I'd have a house big enough to get a few animals. Ones that stayed permanently instead of coming and going like Kennedy did.

The sound of heels clicking on the paved path drew my attention.

Caroline Winthrop smoothed her cream A-line dress and perched on the bench next to me, following my gaze to the little girl with the beagle.

She didn't say anything at first. My heart hammered, and I sat up a little straighter. Should I run away? Was she here to give me a piece of her mind? Could I really blame her?

After a few moments she turned to face me with a sad smile on her face.

"Hey, Mrs. Winthrop." I watched her, wide-eyed, not really sure what I should say.

"Didn't I tell you to call me Caroline?" Her smile widened.

"Now, it's Antoinette, isn't it?"

"Uhh . . . yeah . . . yes. Most people just call me Toni."

"Toni." She nodded definitively and folded her hands in her lap. "I thought it was about time you and I talked."

"OK. Sure, let me have it." It was the least I could do. God help whoever crossed a southern woman. I'm sure whatever she had to say to me, she would be giving Alex a serve too. We deserved it.

"Oh, sweetheart." One of her perfectly manicured hands covered mine, and I looked up into her face, surprised. "You misunderstand."

I frowned. I had no idea what the hell was happening, but she wasn't ripping me a new one.

"I'd like to give you the money necessary to save your family legacy, and a little bit extra for college." She waved her hand around as if she were talking about spare change in her pocket, not millions.

"Give me . . ." My eyes narrowed, and I pulled my hand out from under hers. "You want to pay me off? No. I'm not gonna tell anyone about what happened. I don't want your money."

She chuckled. "I do so admire your integrity. I'm not looking to buy your silence. I simply want to do the right thing. Just like you."

"I don't understand."

"My husband is prideful and he's angry. My son is stubborn and he's hurt. But men are idiots, and now that I know the full story, I'd like to help. I know what kind of financial difficulty Zamorano Wines is in. I know all about how you were taken from your mama as a baby. I know about you and Alexandria bumping into each other and deciding to switch. I know you're planning to go to college. I have the means to help, and I've decided I'm going to."

She rolled her shoulders back and nodded with a satisfied smile. She'd just *decided*. Never mind what anyone else wanted. Rich people, man . . .

"I just want one thing in return," she announced.

My eyebrows went up so high I was worried they'd merge with my hairline. There it was. "And what might that be?" I'd already decided to tell her to shove it. I wasn't going to put myself at the mercy of a rich, powerful woman. I'd rather be poor and free.

"I want you to fight for my son." Any hint of levity left her expression. She looked at me with so much intensity it felt like a punch to the guts.

"What?" I gripped the edge of the bench, digging my nails into the dirty wood.

"What you and your sister did was . . . somewhat foolish. But I'm damn glad you did it."

"You are?"

"Yes. You see, when Annabelle and I arranged this deal, I simply hoped it would give my son the freedom to run the business as he saw fit, that having his father out of the way would allow him to relax a little bit more. I never expected to see him come alive the way he has in the past few weeks. That's because of you, Toni."

I shook my head, hating that tears welled up at the mere mention of him. "He hates me. He made it perfectly clear. I fucked it up. Shit! Sorry about the language." I lifted my wide, watery eyes to her, and she smiled warmly.

"I don't give a flying fuck what words you use, sweetheart. Just use them to talk to Oren. He's miserable. He never expected to find something real in a sham marriage, and now that you're gone, he's even worse than before. He's thrown himself into his work. He won't speak to anyone. He's short with the staff. Please." She took my hand again. The richest person I knew was pleading with me to do something I ached to do anyway. But was there any hope?

"I don't know if there's any point. I've hurt him too much."

"You have to try. My husband is already talking about who else might make a suitable marriage partner so Oren can get his inheritance. Vanessa is all over him at work, even if he doesn't see it. I don't want that fake, social-climbing Barbie as a daughter-in-law. I want you."

"You do?" What in the actual fuck was happening? Was she about to pull out her magic wand, conjure an elaborate gown, and turn a pumpkin into a carriage to take me to the love of my life?

"Oren will do what he thinks is right—the practical thing. He needs you to make the first move. You have to bring that chaos back into his life. Bring that light back into his eyes."

"I don't know." We were too different; I wasn't good enough for him. I wasn't sure I could handle the humiliation of having him say it to my face.

Caroline reached into her purse and handed me a card. "This has my number and the number of my lawyer. The money is already on its way to you—just call him to arrange the details. It's yours regardless of what you decide, but I certainly hope you'll decide to try one last time."

She stood, smoothed her dress, and walked away, her heels clicking on the concrete.

Chapter 28

ALEX

"Oh my god." I burst into tears, the relief rushing through my body so intense my knees went weak. I lowered myself into a chair at the dining table and sobbed into my hand, my other shaking hand holding the phone up to my ear. "Are you sure?" This was too good to be true.

"I'm sure, Alex." Toni sounded choked up on the other end, but I was so overwhelmed I didn't even tease her about it.

"Absolutely positive?"

"I just got off the phone with Caroline's lawyer. He ran me through the whole thing, and when I looked at my bank account, the number of zeroes made me hyperventilate." She laughed, the sound a little manic. "I've never seen that much money, man!"

"And you're sure what you want to do with it is bail me out?"

"Dude, accept the good news. Fuck!"

This time I laughed with her, even as the tears continued to stream down my cheeks. "Oh my god, Toni, thank you so much. You have no idea what this means."

"I think I have a pretty good idea."

"I can't believe this." I took a deep cleansing breath. "Dad would be so proud. Of both of us."

Toni cleared her throat. She was embracing getting to know us way more than I ever could've hoped for, but she still got a bit weird when I referred to Mom and Dad as *our* parents, which I could understand. She had a mom and a dad, and she'd lost them.

"The only thing I don't understand is how she knew all those details. Do all rich people have PIs on call?"

"Oh, that may be my fault. I sent her a letter and an email a couple days ago, explaining the situation and apologizing for how spectacularly it went wrong. I'd made a commitment and reneged on it—I felt like they deserved an explanation. I sent the same note to Oren, but I haven't heard back from him."

"Do you think he could ever . . ."

"What?"

"I don't even know. Forgive me? Get over it? Speak to me even, so I could say my piece? Thing is, when Caroline accosted me in the park, she basically begged me to try to win him back. Or win him. I guess he was never mine to begin with. I don't know. God! This is so confusing."

"He was always yours, Toni." That I was sure of. Oren

Winthrop and I could never have been more than friends—not when my heart belonged to two impossible, incredible men, and had since before I'd even known it.

"I don't know about that," she grumbled.

I was ready to launch into a lengthy argument to try to convince her Caroline was spot on, that she should try to talk to Oren, but the front door opened, and Mom's heels sounded on the tiles.

"Toni, I've got to go catch Mom up on the news. Just promise me you'll think about it. You deserve to be happy."

"OK. I'll talk to you later."

She hung up first, and I sprung out of my chair to meet my mother in the kitchen, bursting with excitement to tell her the amazing news.

I spent the rest of the afternoon on the phone with lawyers, accountants, and my managers, setting the new deal in motion.

With Preston's offer, I'd dragged my feet. Despite it being the best option on paper, it had still felt wrong. With this new development, I couldn't get things happening fast enough. Toni and I would own Zamorano Wines fifty-fifty—equal share, just like it should be. Although I was pretty sure she had no interest in running a multimillion-dollar business with me.

That evening, Toni was working, Preston had been out all day, and Mother was having dinner with some old friends, so I found myself celebrating alone. As midnight approached, I was nearly at the bottom of a bottle of Shiraz and on the third episode of a documentary when Preston got back.

I shot off the couch, eager to tell another person. He wandered into the living room looking tired, his linen shirt crumpled, and dropped his keys on the kitchen bench.

"You're back!" I practically shouted, and he startled.

"Yeah. Dinner and drinks turned into . . . well, more drinks. I was with the friend whose venture I was originally going to invest in. Didn't mean to stay out this late, but I needed to mend that bridge after pulling out at the last second." He ran long fingers through his hair.

"Oh, then I have doubly good news. You can go back to your original plan and invest in your friend's venture. Zamorano Wines is saved! It's a long story, but Toni has come into some money, and she's going to bail us out. And considering the circumstances, half the business is hers anyway."

"What?" Now I had his full attention.

"Thank you so, so much for offering to bail us out. It means more than you know. But I know the deal you had to break was more lucrative. This is perfect. You can go back to that, and Zamorano Wines can get back to business as usual."

Preston's face paled, and he gritted his teeth. "This is unbelievable." He ran his hand through his hair again, this time tugging it in frustration.

"What's wrong? I thought you'd be glad."

"Glad? *Glad?*" He bugged his eyes out at me. "You ungrateful bitch."

I took an involuntary step back. "Whoa. Calm down."

"Don't fucking tell me to calm down, *Alexandria*." He spat my name as if it were a curse word. "The original deal is gone. My friend found another investor."

"Look, I'm sorry about that, but there will be other deals. You have the capital now, and you know all kinds of people. It won't take you—"

"I don't give a shit about other opportunities!" he roared. Spittle flew from his lips, and he curled his hands into fists.

Every muscle in my body tensed. He was losing his shit, and I suddenly didn't feel safe in a house alone with my cousin. I couldn't understand why he was so upset. This was just business—he was a businessman.

"Preston." I worked to keep my voice even, calm, even as my hands started to shake with adrenaline. "Business deals come and go all the time."

"You're such a fucking moron." He took a step toward me. I took one back, but my knee connected with the arm of the couch. "This isn't business for me. It's *personal*. It's as personal as it can get. I've been trying to get what's *mine* my whole entire life, as has my father and his father before him. We're from the same damn bloodline. That vineyard is just as much mine as it is yours. But you just sit around drinking the fruits of our ancestors' labor while driving it into the ground, you whiny little cunt. I shouldn't have to buy something that's rightfully mine."

He growled and stepped forward again. I had nowhere to go. Panic started to settle in, making me tremble as I watched the madness in my cousin's eyes unravel.

"But I figured, at least this way, when I take over, the business will no longer be in debt. I came this fucking close"—he held his thumb and forefinger an inch apart in front of my face, and I flinched back—"to fulfilling my father's dying wish, and now you're telling me *no*?" He laughed, a low menacing sound, his teeth bared. "I don't fucking think so."

I knew deep down there was no point reasoning with him, but cornered and alone, I had no other option. "Preston, I don't know what your father told you, but legally Zamorano Wines is mine, and I'm just doing what I think is best."

"Do you have any idea what it's like to devote your entire life to something and keep failing at it? I was determined to be the generation that got what's rightfully ours back. I don't give a shit how many more people I have to kill."

A cold chill ran down my spine, both at the clear threat and the insinuation.

"What are you saying?" I had to keep him talking.

"You know, if your stupid mother had drunk the spiked tea I'd given her, she would've slept through the night like the nanny did, and all of this could've been avoided. You and Antoinette would've been raised by some pathetic middle-class couple desperate to procreate, and I would've stepped in to take over from your father. But no, that bitch had to wake up before I could get you into the car."

I didn't think my eyes could open any wider from shock. Every nerve in my body was on alert—he was clearly unhinged.

"Why?" I breathed, horrified, as tears started to pool in my eyes.

"*Why?*" He leaned into my personal space and tapped the side of my head. I flinched but kept my arms by my sides. "Fucking pay attention, Alexandria. I had to have Zamorano Wines. I had to succeed where my father had failed. You think I like killing? I don't. It's such an undignified solution, but there's no denying its effectiveness. Once your father was out of the way, I just needed to be there, let you see that you needed me to step in and run the business. But you're so fucking stubborn." He ground his teeth. "It runs in the family, you know."

Tears spilled down my cheeks, but rage filled my chest, burning hot. Preston had killed my father. He was responsible for breaking my heart and turning my world upside down. He was responsible for so many awful things in my life.

"You're a piece of shit." I spat in his face.

His retaliating backhand snapped my head to the side. Pain exploded in my face, and my ears started to ring.

"And you're a dead woman. Toni will be much easier to manipulate." He didn't wait for an answer. My father's murderer lunged for me.

I shoved against his chest, scrambling to get away, but he got a fistful of my hair and yanked my head to the side. I tripped against the couch, and we tumbled into the gap between the couch and the coffee table. My elbow hit the edge, pain shooting up my arm, and I cried out.

Preston landed on top of me and released my hair. I scrambled to get away, but he was taller, stronger. His hands closed around my throat. I kicked out, desperate, but he pinned my legs with his, his weight holding my hips to the floor.

His hands squeezed.

I couldn't breathe. Panic coursed through me, and I scratched at his face, his arms, his hands. He didn't even seem to notice, his lips pulled back in a snarl, his eyes bulging, his face grotesque.

My mouth opened wide, trying in vain to find a breath, as stars started to appear in my vision.

Preston grunted, apparently unsatisfied with how long it was taking to kill me. He tugged me up by the neck, only to slam my head back into the ground. My vision momentarily flickered out as pain exploded at the back of my skull.

I started flailing my arms, my body's last-ditch effort to fight for survival.

My right hand knocked over the half-empty glass of wine on the table, smashing it. Shards of glass fell over my shoulder as my hand connected with the wine bottle next. It toppled onto its side, and I gripped the neck.

With the last bit of strength in my body, I swung.

The bottle connected with Preston's head with a sickening crunch, but it didn't smash.

His grip on my neck loosened as his body tipped to the side.

Air rushed into my lungs, burning everything it touched on its way down. My vision cleared just in time to see Preston shake his head. His eyes narrowed on me again, his expression pure rage.

I swung the bottle again, this time aiming for the corner of the coffee table. The impact reverberated up my arm, but the glass smashed.

Preston's hands closed around my throat again. I gritted my

teeth and slashed at his face. The jagged glass cut two deep gashes in his cheek and jaw, blood dripping from the wounds.

He roared and pushed away from me, then hit me in the face again—this time with his closed fist. More agony. I wasn't sure how much more my head could take before I passed out.

I swung again, catching his throat this time. Warm blood splashed onto my face and chest. Bile rose in my throat, but the wound was enough to make him lose his focus on me.

He reached for his throat, eyes wide with panic. Blood oozed between his fingers, and he swayed. I dropped the bottle and shoved him in the chest, and he fell sideways onto the couch.

I scrambled out from under him and got to my feet.

I didn't look back, didn't stop to check if he was following—I just ran.

Hands slick with blood, it took me a few tries to get a good grip on the door handle as my heart threw itself against my ribcage and adrenaline surged to my limbs, every fiber of my being demanding that I *run*.

Finally I wrenched the door open and sprinted onto the street.

I turned right, toward the only place I knew in the area—the Cottonmouth Inn. It was only two blocks. I knew the way—I'd walked it so many times in the past few days. People on the busy street gasped and jumped out of my way, some of them calling out, but I wasn't listening, wasn't stopping, still wasn't completely sure he wasn't following me.

The sign with the snake above the door swung in the breeze. People milled about outside, their conversations dying midsentence as I barreled through, pumping my legs.

The bouncer at the door—Tim? Tom? I couldn't remember— took a step forward, holding his hand out as if to stop me. But a fight broke out just inside, drawing his attention away as he turned to deal with the bigger threat.

I rushed through the door, past the fight, and finally came to a stop. My chest heaved as my eyes flew frantically about the room. People watched me warily and shifted away, creating a wide uneven circle around me.

I must've looked like something out of a nightmare—my hair a mess, blood coating my face and chest—and as I registered the sticky floors, I realized I'd run there in bare feet.

The music stopped. First the voice, then soon after, the other instruments. I looked up, past the crowd and right into Ren's panicked eyes.

"Alex?" His smooth voice had never sounded so discordant through a microphone.

He jumped off the stage and disappeared from my view as he pushed through the stunned crowd, but it was Andre's voice that reached me next.

"Call an ambulance," he barked. He rounded the bar, heading straight for me. "Someone turn the stereo on. Move, asshole!" He shoved a guy out of the way in his rush, spilling half the man's beer, but Ren reached me first.

Ren gripped my shoulders, his touch tentative, as his wide, horrified gaze flew up and down my body. He was sweaty from performing, his messy hair falling over his forehead. I wanted to reach up and brush it back, but my hands wouldn't release his forearms. It had been over a week since I'd seen him, and despite the crazy, messed-up situation, having him standing before me made me realize just how much I'd missed him.

"Where are you hurt?" He sounded panicked.

The music came on through the speakers as Andre reached us. He stood shoulder to shoulder with Ren, reaching out as if to touch me but then just ghosting his hands uncertainly over my body instead.

"Alex, show me where you're hurt. Where is the blood coming from?" Ren shouted over the music and the crowd. Now that the bar's patrons realized there was no immediate danger, they were getting back to partying.

I opened my mouth and tried to tell him it wasn't my blood, but my throat wouldn't cooperate, so I mouthed the words instead.

I wasn't sure if he understood me, but in the next moment, he was picking me up bridal style and holding me to his chest. Andre cleared a path through the crowd, and we piled into the back corridor.

Ren sat down at the bottom of the stairs, holding me in his lap. I clutched the front of his T-shirt with shaky hands, his leather necklaces tangling in my fingers.

"We need to get her to a doctor. Right now. Fuck, there's so much blood." Andre looked frantic, stepping toward me as if to treat my injuries, then stepping toward the door as if to go get someone better qualified to do so.

I shook my head, but Ren answered for me, proving he had

managed to read my lips earlier. "It's not her blood."

"Holy shit, Alex." Toni's panicked words made me look up; she'd followed us. "What the fuck happened?"

"Who did this to you?" Andre growled.

Both of them looked about as shaken as I felt. The only thing keeping me from losing it completely was the feeling of Ren's chest against my side, his strong hands holding me to him, his steady heartbeat under my fists.

"Pres . . ." I couldn't seem to get my throat to work. I tried a few times to get Preston's name out, but he'd stolen my ability to speak the truth along with all the other things he'd taken from me. Tears of frustration welled in my eyes, but Toni figured it out.

"Preston?"

I nodded, and her eyes widened in surprise.

"Who the fuck is Preston?" Andre couldn't seem to say anything without growling, his hands constantly closing into fists and reopening.

"He's her cousin," Toni explained. "He was going to buy half her business to bail her out of all the debt, until today."

My body was starting to realize it was no longer in danger—the adrenaline draining from my limbs, the oxygen returning to my brain—and my mind started to work properly again.

I gasped.

Releasing Ren's shirt, I tried to scramble to my feet. In my rush to get away from my attacker, I may have allowed my mother to walk right into his clutches. She would be back from dinner with her friends at any moment. I had to get back there.

Ren held me to him, and everyone spoke over each other, urging me to calm down, telling me I was safe, trying to soothe me.

"No!" I managed to get the word out. They paused and watched me with questioning, wary eyes. "Mom . . . he's still . . . there."

"Toni, call the police," Andre ordered, then pressed his forehead to mine for the briefest of seconds. "I'll make sure she's safe. I love you."

I nodded as he rushed out the back door and into the alleyway, Toni shouting the address after him. She pressed her phone to her ear and rushed to the back of the corridor.

Ren just rocked me back and forth.

Toni came back a few moments later and handed him a wet tea towel, keeping another one for herself. With slow, gentle movements, they started to remove the blood from my skin. By the time the previously blue-checked tea towels were completely covered in crimson, the ambulance had arrived.

They checked me over and asked me a bunch of questions, which I did my best to answer despite my throat not cooperating. They insisted on taking me to the hospital, saying there could be permanent damage and that my left cheek would likely need a scan. My whole head felt swollen, sore and throbbing.

"One of you can ride in the ambulance with her," the EMT told Ren and Toni as he packed his bag up.

Ren hadn't released my hand the entire time I was being examined, and he didn't seem likely to relinquish it now as the stretcher was lifted into the back of the ambulance.

Toni shot him an annoyed look but waved us off and said she'd meet us there.

As we took off, Ren sat next to me and held my hand in both of his, his thumbs caressing the back of it as he took in the injuries on my face. His eyes filled with tears, and he dropped his head, breathing hard.

I couldn't say the comforting words I wanted to. I pulled my hand out from between his and cupped his cheek. He looked up at me, and a tear dripped off his chin.

He opened his mouth to say something, but his phone went off in his pocket, and he rushed to answer it. The conversation was brief, a couple of OKs and an update on where they were taking me before he hung up.

"Your mom is safe. She's coming to the hospital with Andre," he told me right away, his hands enclosing mine again.

I breathed a massive sigh, even though it hurt my throat to do it. Tears of relief tracked down the sides of my face and into my hair.

"I can't believe I nearly lost you." Ren's voice was hoarse with emotion. "I've been such a dumbass. I'm so sorry, Alex. I hate that this is what it took to make me realize it, but I don't want to imagine a world without you in it. I don't want to live my life without you in it. I love you."

My heart swelled. I mouthed the words back to him, managing a smile but then wincing when it made my face hurt. The drugs they were pumping into me started to take effect, and I kept my gaze on his beautiful green eyes as I floated away on a cloud.

A: I'm bored. Can you bring me my laptop so I can work?

T: I literally just left!!! Watch some daytime TV like a normal person.

A: BORING!

A: So you gonna speak to Oren?

T: This is your solution to hospital boredom? Harassing me?

A: ???

T: I don't know. I don't think he's interested. It's over.

A: Caroline didn't think so. You two haven't spoken since it all came out. He might be willing to listen.

T: I think you're all seeing something I'm not. He's probably relieved he doesn't have to go through with a sham marriage. Caroline said his dad is already talking about setting him up with other women so he can find a wife "the old-fashioned way." *eyeroll

A: Toni, I think you need to do this. You owe it to yourself to try. You told me you fell in love with this man, and now you're just going to give up on that? That's not the strong, confident, takes-no-shit woman I've gotten to know. If I'm being honest, I think you've been deliberately pushing people away for years.

T: You think I don't know this shit?

A: What do you have to lose? If you try and he says no, you'll be in the exact same position you're in now, but at least you'll know for sure.

T: Shit, Alex. Maybe it's better not knowing. The possibility of a yes not realized is so much less intimidating than the possibility of a definitive no.

T: What if it was all in my head? What if I'm head over heels for him, and he was just having a bit of fun during a business transaction, and now he's pissed because it didn't go to plan. The man is textbook OCD. He can't handle it when shit goes wrong.

A: Remember when we first started this? You were convinced no one in your life knew you, no one cared enough to realize I wasn't you?

T: Yeah?

A: And then Andre picked up on it on day one. And it turned out Loretta knew all along.

T: What's your point?

A: That, sometimes, you underestimate how much people care for you. That it's time to start letting them in. Just like you let me in.

T: Get some rest. xo

Chapter 29

TONI

I stood under the spray for so long, scrubbing the sleepless night and the blood of my sister's attacker off my skin, that the water started to turn cold.

The doctors had insisted on keeping Alex in for another few days as they continued to run a battery of tests. Apparently a victim of strangulation could die days, sometimes even weeks, after the attack if the effects were left untreated. We'd stayed with her all night. When they tried to get us to leave, Ren flat out refused, parking himself in a chair in the corner and glaring at the nurses. The rest of us made peace with the waiting room.

Annabelle was hysterical at first, clearly reliving the trauma of losing a child. She clung to me until the doctors convinced her Alex would be OK. There was bruising and damage to her trachea, and she wouldn't be able to speak for a little while, but they expected her to make a full recovery.

Ren was snoring in his chair in the corner when Andre and I left to get a change of clothes for everyone. Alex had shooed us away silently, and we'd spent the entire drive home texting. It made me feel close to her; it was how we'd gotten to know each other while living each other's lives. There was something comforting about seeing the three little dots appear and then getting her responses—she was still there, still being stubborn and demanding and sticking her nose in my business.

When all traces of heat in the spray disappeared, I shut the water off.

I got dressed in the first things my hands found in the wardrobe—a hot-pink pair of skinny jeans and my favorite T-shirt with the skull hand giving the finger. I piled my still-damp hair into a messy bun, then turned to find Ken had let himself in through the open balcony doors.

"Hey, buddy." I smiled at him and crouched down but didn't approach. Crows were dangerous and stubborn. You had to let them come to you. "Long time no see."

He tipped his head back, watching me intently.

"Yeah, it's me. I promise. Sorry I was away for so long."

He maintained his skeptical pose, still as a statue.

"You're mad. I get it, but I'm back now. And guess what? I went and fell in love with a billionaire pretty boy, like a basic bitch."

After another moment of stillness, he squawked and walked

toward me. He turned his head to the side, and I patted him gently with the back of my pointer finger. His shiny black feathers were impossibly soft under my touch.

"So Alex—the one who looks like me but way less cool—turns out she's my sister. And she thinks I should go try to win Oren back. That's the billionaire pretty boy. I lied to him a lot, and now he hates me, so I don't know."

Kennedy squawked again and flapped his wings.

I pulled my hand back, resting my elbows on my knees, and sighed. "Of course you agree with her. Thing is, she nearly died last night, so I feel like I have to do what she tells me."

Ken cocked his head to the side, and I rolled my eyes.

"OK, fine. Last night may or may not have made me realize life is short and shit and maybe I should try to go after what I want and, like, try to find happiness or whatever."

The more I thought about what happened, and all the points Alex had made, the more an odd feeling grew inside me. It was like a little spark of energy that propelled me to get moving, made me feel invigorated and terrified all at once.

I'd been pushing people away since my parents died, not letting anyone see the real me. I was trying to protect myself from the pain when they inevitably left me, but I'd come to realize I didn't like being alone.

Letting Alex in—and Annabelle and Andre and even Ren to an extent—felt good. It was kind of nice having people who gave a shit about what happened to you. And even though he'd done the thing I was most scared of—left me—I was even glad I'd let

Oren in. Because in the few weeks we'd had together, I'd never felt more alive.

"Shit, I'm gonna do this, aren't I?" I pushed myself to my feet and bugged my eyes out at my raven friend. "Naturally, I decide to go fight for the man I love when he's opening his new fancy-as-fuck jewelry store in front of a crowd of people. Maybe I should wait . . ."

In response Ken flapped his wings and waddled toward me, practically shuffling me out the door.

"OK, I'm going. Jeez!" I laughed as I pulled my boots on and grabbed my keys.

Andre stepped out of his apartment at the same time, freshly showered, a duffel bag slung over his shoulder.

"Ready to head back?" he asked.

"Actually, I gotta go do something. You got this?" I was already walking toward the stairs, bursting to get going, but his large hand wrapped around my elbow. He pulled me to a stop, then yanked me into a bear hug.

I stiffened—old habits die hard—but then hugged him back. Fucker really did give good hugs.

He pulled away and looked me dead in the eye. "Thank you, Toni."

"What for?"

"For bringing her into my life."

"Well, shit. Since we're sharing . . . thank you for having my back since day one, even though I was a total bitch to everyone." It was awkward to say, but I resisted the urge to lower my gaze. I wanted him to know I was sincere.

He shrugged. "It was worth it in the end. Now, what the fuck are you doing standing around talking to me? Go get your man." He turned me toward the exit and gave me a sportsy slap on the butt that somehow managed to be encouraging and not creepy.

I rushed down the stairs and jumped the last three like a maniac. My knee bounced with nervous energy the whole Uber ride there.

The driver dropped me off around the corner, unwilling to brave the crowd of people spilling onto the street. Of course I'd arrived just in time for the opening. I could hear Oren's voice saying something about everyone's hard work, but I couldn't see him over the crowd.

"Excuse me, sorry, coming through," I mumbled under my breath as I shuffled forward. The people present were a mixture of trust-fund types, business types, and regular Joes who'd noticed something going on and stopped to rubberneck.

I was just close enough to see between the gaps in the crowd as Caroline lifted a giant pair of scissors and cut a wide red silk ribbon hanging over the front doors. The onlookers clapped, and then chatter and movement spread throughout. The official part of the opening was done. Now the invited guests would be heading inside for champagne and canapés. I knew this because Oren had asked me for advice on which champagne to serve.

I had to get to him before he disappeared inside.

Squeezing between a guy wearing way too much aftershave and an overweight tourist with a fanny pack, I finally made it to the stretch of sidewalk right outside the front doors . . . just in time to see Oren disappear into the store. A perfectly tailored tan linen suit covered his broad shoulders, and his wavy hair was styled back, but that was all I could see before other nicely dressed people blocked my view.

By the time I reached the door, a security guy in sunglasses was pulling it closed.

"Excuse me." I flashed the muscle a quick smile and tied to rush past him, holding my shoulders back and doing my best to look like I totally belonged there.

"Whoa." His beefy hand went to my abdomen and stopped me in my tracks. "Where do you think you're going?"

"Inside," I said, as if it were obvious.

"Are you on the list? What's your name?" He held up a clipboard with his free hand. *Dammit!* Oren had probably made sure I was not on that list.

"I don't know," I lied. "I know the Winthrops, OK? I just need to speak with Oren."

He looked me up and down and raised an eyebrow. Everyone inside was in clothing that cost my yearly wage, and I stood on the other side of the glass in hot-pink pants and an obnoxious T-shirt. He had a point, but it was still rude.

"I'm gonna have to ask you to step back, ma'am." He put a bit of pressure on my abdomen, where his hand was still holding me at bay.

"Look, dude, I'm trying to do some epic shit here, OK? I just need to *talk* to the guy. So can you just do me a solid and—"

"What's going on here?" A feminine voice drew both our attention. Vanessa stood halfway out the door, one hand on the ornate handle. Her dark hair was pulled back in a sleek style, her tall frame draped in a deep green wrap dress. She looked stunning, even as her eyes took me in from head to toe and she smirked.

"This lady is trying to come inside, but her name's not on the list," Sunglasses tattled on me.

Vanessa's cruel smile widened, and she snickered. "Lady . . ." she muttered under her breath, as if the mere suggestion was hilarious.

I wanted to punch her in her perfectly straight nose, watch the blood stain that green silk. But I swallowed my pride. I had bigger fish to fry. "Vanessa, please."

Before I could get the rest of my groveling out, Caroline appeared at Vanessa's side. She pulled the door open the rest of the way and placed a hand on the security guy's shoulder.

"Now, you don't know who this is, young man," she said sweetly, her perfectly made-up face tilting just slightly, "so I won't have you fired today, but you'd best take your hand off this woman and let her come in."

The beefy hand disappeared immediately, and the security guy stepped out of my way. "My apologies, ma'am."

"That's quite all right." She patted him on the shoulder before nudging Vanessa out of the way to pull me in for a hug. The bitch gave me a disgusted sneer behind Caroline's back and walked off without another word.

"Does this mean what I think it means?" she whispered before pulling away.

I nodded. "I'm going to try. I have to."

She did a little fist pump, her eyes shining with excitement. "You picked a hell of a time." She laughed.

"Yeah. I don't do anything by halves."

"I know. It's why I love you." She stepped to the side so we were shoulder to shoulder and pointed to the middle of the room. Oren stood surrounded by a handful of people, one hand in his pocket, the other holding a glass of champagne. His posture was relaxed, but his wide smile didn't reach his eyes.

My stomach did a summersault. I wanted to run to him, shove bitches out of my way until I was in his arms. I also wanted to get the hell out of there, pack my shit, and pick another city where I could be no one and answer to no one again.

Oren looked up, and his gaze slammed into mine. Whatever he'd been saying died in his throat midsentence, and the people around him glanced in my direction, confused. Despite the shocked, disapproving look in his eyes, my feet only moved faster until I stood before him.

"What are you doing here?" he asked. The tension in the air was drawing attention, people pausing their conversations to stare.

I resisted the urge to wring my hands and kept them in fists by my sides. I'd come all this way, fought to get to him, but I had no idea where to start.

Vanessa appeared at Oren's elbow and leaned in, her small tits pressing against his arm. "Want me to have her removed?"

"I let her in." Caroline appeared at my side, head held high, her voice confident. Vanessa slunk backward like a chastised toddler.

"Caroline." There was a hint of a growl in Oren senior's disapproving voice. "What is this? I do apologize for the interruption, everyone." He smiled at the crowd around us, waving his champagne glass as if this were a silly mistake about the kind of canapés that had been served.

"Well, I don't." Caroline clasped her hands in front of herself and lifted her nose higher into the air. "I think it's about time some things were interrupted."

"What on earth . . ."

"Mother . . ."

"Oren, I can have security here in . . ."

"Excuse me, is there a problem . . ."

Everyone, including the security guys, started to speak over one another, causing a much bigger scene than my mere presence had. Every single person in the room now watched with rapt attention as voices and tempers flared.

I looked around in panic. Caroline and Oren senior were arguing. Oren wasn't even looking at me anymore, his attention split between his parents and an annoyingly persistent Vanessa, who kept gesturing to me.

"Alex nearly died, and I love you!" I shouted over everyone.

The room went silent, all eyes on me now.

"What?" Oren frowned and took a step toward me. "Is Alexandria OK? What do you mean you love me?"

"Shit. I guess we're doing this with an audience." I took a deep breath. "Alex is going to be fine, but she was attacked last night, and she nearly died. It put some things in perspective for me. I know what we did was pretty messed up, and I'm sorry." I looked around before focusing back on Oren. "I'm sorry to everyone who we deceived and hurt. But no one was supposed to even know. No one was supposed to get close enough to realize or care. And then I started to get to know you, and honestly, I didn't even think my cold black heart was capable of it, but I fell in love with you, Oren Winthrop. Head over heels, hook line and sinker, every cheesy rom-com declaration you can think of in love with you. And since I've brought up rom-coms, I may as well go full cheese here—I know I don't fucking deserve it, deserve *you*, but I want the happily ever after."

He stared at me with wide eyes for an uncomfortably long time, the expression on his face indecipherable. People started to shuffle and whisper. My heart started to shrivel up in my chest.

"Wait," he finally said, holding a hand out and shaking his head in confusion. "You love me?"

"Come on, man. I did a whole speech, and you only listened to the first part."

"It's the only part that matters."

Oren handed his champagne glass to Vanessa without even glancing at her. Then he stepped forward, cupped my cheeks, and kissed me.

My heart swelled. My ribcage wasn't strong enough to contain it. Surely it was going to burst right out of my chest.

People clapped and cheered, but my full focus was on the man I loved.

I wrapped my arms around his waist and breathed in his expensive aftershave, reveled in the feeling of his soft lips against mine. He banded an arm around my back and kissed me like no one was watching, his tongue in my mouth, his hard body flush with mine.

After a severe throat clearing from Oren senior, we pulled apart, breaking into goofy grins, but held each other close.

"I thought you didn't care," he whispered against my lips, pain palpable in his words. "I thought it was just a bit of fun, an easy payday, that I was just a joke to you. I thought I'd fallen in love with you and you were laughing about it the whole time."

I kissed his pain away before answering. "I didn't set out to fall in love with you, but I didn't set out to hurt you either. Then I went and did both. I've been a fucking mess this whole time. I've missed you so much."

We rocked from side to side, completely wrapped up in each other, as conversation resumed around us, glasses clinked, music played.

"So it's Antoinette, right?" He chuckled.

"Yes." I grinned. "You can call me Toni."

Chapter 30

ALEX

ONE YEAR LATER

The song Ren was playing on his guitar slowed, coming to an end as people chatted in their seats.

I turned to face my sister. "Ready?"

"Fuck yeah." She grinned.

"You're not nervous at all?" I did one last check of her veil, making sure the ivory tulle fell down the back of the midnight-blue dress in a perfect cascade. The Adelia emerald and matching earrings complemented the dress perfectly.

"Nah." She shrugged. "I think, deep down, I knew I wanted this from the moment I met him. Hey, sorry I stole your wedding and your groom."

We both laughed. "He was never mine."

Someone asked the guests to stand, and Ren began to play an original he'd written just for this occasion.

I started to turn, but Toni clasped my hand. "I love you, Alex."

Not for the first and certainly not for the last time that day, I got teary-eyed. "I love you too, Toni."

We shared a look full of emotion, and then she squeezed my hand and let go. "Go. You're gonna make me late to my own wedding."

I chuckled and started walking down the aisle, my hands clasped around the simple bouquet of white peonies from Mom's garden. My dress was a knee-length white cocktail number with large midnight-blue roses all over it. Toni's was floor-length dark raw silk, almost iridescent in the afternoon sun.

The late-spring weather was perfect for the occasion, the vineyard verdant and vibrant, the rolling hills of our family legacy a perfect backdrop.

I smiled at familiar faces as I passed the standing guests.

Various Zamorano family members and distant cousins were in attendance, but no one from Preston's branch of the family dared show their faces. After trying to kill me, the bastard had managed to survive. His lengthy recovery had been followed by a lengthy trial. He was convicted of my father's murder, Toni's kidnapping, and my attempted murder and was now serving a very long sentence.

On the other side of the aisle were some of the loyal Zamorano Wines staff. With the money Caroline had given Toni, we were able to pay off all the business's debts, hire a good wealth manager, and future-proof the winery with better, smarter investments.

Toni's friends from college looked excited and a little wide-eyed—we hadn't spared any expense for this wedding. Toni was in her first year at USF and planned to major in animal science, then start up an animal rescue nonprofit after she graduated. I already had a patch of property on the winery picked out. It was going to be my birthday present to her next month.

She'd moved to California when classes started, and since the Winthrops had jewelry stores all over the world, it wasn't too much of an effort for Oren to move his base of operations to San Francisco. They were both close enough to drive to the winery for lunch or dinner at least once per week.

Near the front, Loretta and Dennis were clasping hands and crying. Dennis had proven to be a hardworking and very capable young man, and Andre had made him manager of the Cottonmouth Inn—after Loretta turned it down, saying she was "too old for that shit" and declaring she was retiring.

Andre was in the process of preparing the Cottonmouth Inn for sale. We planned to open a restaurant on the winery, and Andre was going to run it.

In the front rows sat Oren's parents and some of Oren's family, as well as George and Andre. My gruff, tall, dark, and handsome man looked good enough to eat in a gray suit and red shirt that popped against his dark skin. He flashed me a brilliant smile, then flicked his eyes down my body and gave a lascivious wink.

My smile widened; I was glad I'd picked a shorter, strapless dress—easy access from the top *and* bottom. I'd been so busy making sure Toni and Oren's day was perfect I'd hardly had time to see my men for the past week. As soon as the formal parts of the evening were done, I planned on sneaking away with them for a bit of three-way action in the cellar.

Ren was seated to the side of the archway, which was decorated in vines and flowers. He wore black pants and a black vest over a simple white shirt. But nothing about Renshaw Pratt was ever simple. An inappropriate number of buttons were left undone at the top, ink and leather necklaces peeking out, and his rolled-up sleeves revealed his lithe forearms as he made love to the acoustic guitar in his lap.

The first time Oren heard Ren's band perform, he got on the phone to some college buddy who had connections in the music world. It came as no surprise to any of us when they got themselves an agent and a recording deal. The Thousand Lies' first world tour would be kicking off in a few months. Andre and I were planning to join him for certain legs of it—sometimes just one of us, sometimes both. All three of us were making compromises to make sure we could be together, but we all supported each other's dreams and goals, so we were making it work. Plus, the sex was phenomenal!

Toni had started her walk down the aisle, everyone oohing and aahing at her ethereal appearance, but Ren had eyes only for me. He'd written the song for the ceremony, but I felt like I was the only one he was playing to.

I had to tear my gaze away from his as I passed Mom. She was standing two-thirds of the way down the aisle, waiting to take Toni the rest of the way.

My sister had wanted to walk herself down the aisle—she was independent in so many ways, and this was no exception—but one week out from the big day, she'd asked Mom to walk with her for the last section. "I was taken from you a long time ago, but maybe on my wedding day you can stand with me as I give myself to the man I love?" Toni had asked. Mom promptly burst into tears and agreed. I had no idea Toni could be that sentimental and cracked a joke about a head injury. I guess we were both rubbing off on each other.

Toni still never referred to Mom as "Mom," and I didn't think she ever would. But their relationship was growing every day. Mom now had two children to obsessively call on a daily basis. One would've thought this would mean the calls would be shorter, but they weren't.

I shared a smile with my mother and finished my slow walk, coming to a stop near the archway.

Oren gave me a quick smile before he looked back at the aisle. Toni looked stunning, but I always loved to watch the groom at weddings as the bride walked up.

He stood with his feet planted, his hands clasped in front of himself, his shoulders relaxed. He was in a cream suit, a single tight peony pinned to his lapel. His handsome face looked calm, but his eyes gave him away. They were full of emotion, full of love for her.

Toni reached my mom, and they took the last few steps together before Mom took her seat and Toni handed her bouquet to me. Dad's favorite pair of cufflinks pinged against Toni's parents' wedding rings where they all hung off the bottom of the flowers—her way of acknowledging those who couldn't be here.

When she took Oren's hands, everyone sat down, and Ren stopped playing.

The ceremony was short and relaxed, nontraditional and full of laughter. Oren even made a joke, pretending to accidentally say my name instead of Toni's.

At the reception, we danced under an open marquee draped in fairy lights and drank some of our best wine. It felt intimate, despite over three hundred people being in attendance.

As the music changed to a mellow song, I snagged Toni's hand before Oren could pull her into another sickeningly sweet slow dance. I placed my hands on her waist and she put hers on my shoulders, and we swayed like a couple of teens at a prom.

"When you first saw me in that disgusting alleyway, could you ever have imagined this is where we'd end up?" I asked.

She grinned. "Not in a million years. But I'm sure as hell glad it played out like it did. Other than the whole attempted murder shit, of course."

I threw my head back and laughed. "Of course. And the whole devastating heartbreak bit when the truth came out."

"Eh." She shrugged. "Pain is a part of life."

"It is, but so is happiness. I'm grateful you made it possible for me to meet the men I love, but most of all I'm glad we found each other."

"When we didn't even know to look." She nodded. "Me too."

THE END

acknowledgements

You may or may not have noticed that there is no 'dedication' page in the front of this book. I felt it was kind of douchey to dedicate a book to myself so I just left it out. Hahaha! Now, let me explain! I thought about dedicating the book to myself because that's who I wrote it for – me. It was a total passion project that just wouldn't leave me alone. Toni kept cursing at me to write her shit while Alex was standing behind her with her arms crossed, nodding and giving me her boss-bitch look. They demanded that I tell their story. I had a lot of fun writing this book and, in some, small, possibly insignificant way, exploring the idea of identity. What makes us who we are? What shapes us? What's really important in life? It's something that I've been thinking about a lot in my personal life over the past few years so it's no wonder that these themes bled into a book about two women pretending to be something they're not!

Anyway! I think I've waffled enough. My point is, I really hope you enjoyed this book and I'd like to thank myself for writing it. Kidding!

I'd like to thank my husband, John, for being an unwavering pillar of support from the very start of this crazy author thing I'm doing.

Thank you to my family and friends for helping to shape me into the person I am today and for always having my back.

Thank you to my writers' group, my beta readers and my ARC readers for your invaluable feedback. My work is always stronger because of you.

Thank you to my PA and friend Sam for being with me through the fun AND not so fun parts of this journey.

Thank you to my editor Kirstin who never fails to elevate my words to a level I could never achieve alone. (Please don't ever leave me!)

Thank you to every member of The Snow Lodge, every reader, every person who's cheered and supported me in any way.

I couldn't be who I was always meant to be without you all.

note from the author

Thank you so much for reading Just Be Her! I really hope you enjoyed it and you'll consider leaving a review. And if you didn't like it, that's OK too – I'm always open to feedback.

about the author

Kaydence Snow has lived all over the world but ended up settled in Melbourne, Australia. She lives near the beach with her husband and a beagle that has about as much attitude as her human.

She draws inspiration from her own overthinking, sometimes frightening imagination, and everything that makes life interesting – complicated relationships, unexpected twists, new experiences and good food and coffee. Life is not worth living without good food and coffee!

She believes sarcasm is the highest form of wit and has the vocabulary of a highly educated, well-read sailor. When she's not writing, thinking about writing, planning when she can write next, or reading other people's writing, she loves to travel and learn new things.

MORE BOOKS BY
KAYDENCE SNOW

Variant Lost

Vital Found

Vivid Avowed

stay updated

To keep up to date with Kaydence's latest news
and releases sign up to her newsletter here:
www.KaydenceSnow.com

Join her reader group here:
www.facebook.com/groups/KaydenceSnowLodge

Or follow her on:
Facebook: facebook.com/KaydenceSnowAuthor
Instagram: instagram.com/kaydencesnowauthor/
Twitter: twitter.com/Kaydence_Snow
Goodreads: goodreads.com/author/show/18388923.Kaydence_Snow
Amazon: amazon.com/author/kaydencesnow
BookBub: bookbub.com/profile/kaydence-snow

Printed in Great Britain
by Amazon